P9-DDI-024

LaGrange Association Library

3 2387 00018 7099

F
HUN   Hunter, Jack D.   3/91
           The Potsdam bluff.

$18.95

DATE	BORROWER'S NAME	

LaGrange Association Library

DISCARDED

© THE BAKER & TAYLOR CO.

THE POTSDAM BLUFF

Tor books by Jack D. Hunter

The Potsdam Bluff
Tailspin

LaGrange Association Library

THE POTSDAM BLUFF

Jack D. Hunter

TOR

A TOM DOHERTY ASSOCIATES BOOK
NEW YORK

This is a work of fiction based on historical incidents. The real people, places, and events portrayed in this book are used fictitiously; other people and events are purely fictitious.

THE POTSDAM BLUFF

Copyright © 1991 by Jack D. Hunter

All rights reserved, including the right to reproduce this book, or portions thereof, in any form.

A Tor Book
Published by Tom Doherty Associates, Inc.
49 West 24th Street
New York, N.Y. 10010

Library of Congress Cataloging-in-Publication Data

Hunter, Jack D.
    The Potsdam bluff / Jack D. Hunter.
        p.   cm.
    "A Tom Doherty Associates book."
    ISBN 0-312-85086-7
    1. Potsdam Conference (1945)—Fiction. I. Title.
PS3558.U48P6 1991
813'.54—dc20   00-48775
                                                              CIP

Printed in the United States of America

First edition: February 1991

0 9 8 7 6 5 4 3 2 1

"The Presidency of the United States carries with it a responsibility so personal as to be without parallel. Very few are ever authorized to speak for the President. No one can make decisions for him. No one can know all the processes and stages of his thinking in making important decisions. Even those closest to him, even members of his immediate family, never know all the reasons why he does certain things and why he comes to certain conclusions."

—Harry S Truman

"Despite the enormous quantities of documentation available to historians of this last World War, the real reasons behind many of our decisions are comparatively obscure. For many of our most important moves were decided upon at informal conferences where no memoranda were kept."

—Omar N. Bradley

"The public weal requires that men should betray, and lie, and massacre."

—Michel de Montaigne, 1595

THE
POTSDAM
BLUFF

THE
ANTE

CHAPTER 1

Near Butova, Russia
2 February 1945

The American news correspondents had been authorized to visit one of the fighter squadrons that were supposed to protect Moscow from Nazi bombers, which, as everybody knew, no longer represented any kind of threat to anybody anywhere, especially here in Russia. Brandt, who, among his cover duties at the embassy, served as assistant press attaché, was included in the party. He stood in the cold morning and watched the hungover fatsos from New York and Detroit and Washington and L.A. ask inane questions of the flat-faced stoics in helmets and goggles and fur boots, who grunted monosyllabic answers which Rimsky, the interpreter, translated into official party-line grandiloquence.

Brandt was bored, and his feet were freezing, and he wished that the fatsos would shut up and climb into the bus and go back to the Metropole and begin work on the thousand gallons of vodka they seemed to consume each day. This was the worst part of his job, this pretending to be something everybody pretended not to know he really wasn't. The Russians, from Stalin to Greta Koogal, the gray and rumpled Spasso House scullery maid, were aware that his primary involvement was the gathering and sifting of intelligence. And yet, in a quaint and inconsistent fealty to the bourgeois etiquettes of international diplomacy, the communists seemed willing to tolerate his presence in their midst precisely so long as he and his fellow Capitalist Swine made no fuss over the bugs and shadows lavished upon them by the NKVD. To complete the charade, they dutifully played to his "press attaché" role by sending him all information releases and press conference invitations, and he was compelled to meet the fiction with suitable journalistic response. Still, for all its annoyances, the charade had worked to everybody's advantage.

Moreover, the Russians were not only socialist, they were sociable, and, since he had considerable capacity for wining, dining and wenching, he had become very popular among the middle-aging swingers in the echelon directly below the Kremlin's topmost graybeards. If a party was under way, Brandt was sure to be there, telling droll stories in his unaccented Russian, playing bawdy American tunes on the piano, and testing his chugalug muscles against those of all comers. In the peculiar logic of the Red hierarchy, he was deemed unable to do any dirty work while being so busy as an entertainer. Official censure therefore rarely fell on those officers who hobnobbed with him at these blowouts, and he rarely embarrassed those who were actually his informants by asking them to pass along intelligence goodies on such occasions. He did his best

4

work in moving elevators or at the Tschaikovsky Concert Hall, where proximities were natural and bugs didn't work. There the passage of information was more like amiable conversation and less like treason, thus easing the morning-after guilts of idealistic Russians who had sold themselves the fiction that the sharing of truths with the United States would eventuate in a better, more peaceful world.

As he watched a flight of *Shturmoviks* that snarled past, bellies nearly brushing the restless snow, he thought of all those idealistic Americans who believed that sharing truths with the Soviet Union would bring a better, more peaceful world. Why not, he wondered irritably, bundle up those Russians and Americans who thought that way and put them in charge? They would quickly lose their idealism in the discovery that the fastest way to start a fight is for one well-intended person to tell another the truth.

The correspondents were inspecting a line of Lend-Lease Douglas C-47s, fresh from America and wearing the red star of the Soviet air force. A Red Army band, peopled mainly by busty women in baggy uniforms, blared and thumped some Sousa, and the newsmen unconsciously stepped along in cadence. It was a noisy morning, what with the music and the blattering planes and the incomprehensible commentary that thundered from a loudspeaker pole down the way, and Brandt, in what seemed to be an irrelevance, remembered the misty silences of his boyhood in the Ukraine, and then he thought of his parents and how their faces glowed when they caught sight of the Statue of Liberty and how—despite the crowd at the railing—the only sounds had been those of the ship's muted throbbings and splashings. Such recollections used to be accompanied by guilt, but he had long since outlived whatever sensibilities he might have had as a youngster. Today he was an unfeeling—what?

There was a touch on his sleeve, and he turned.

5

"Good morning, Mr. Brandt." It was General Chesnikov, one of the diminishing few who began their soldiering under the czar, then survived the First War and the Revolution and its purges and the subsequent ascendancy of the political commissars in the military structure. He had often joked about his ability to survive, citing as his favorite example his execution by a company of rogue cossacks during the uprisings of '17. He'd been shot and buried hastily in a shallow forest grave, from which he had clawed his way the following day, weak and bloody, at the feet of a thunderstruck peasant who had been gathering twigs for firewood.

"Ah. Sweet deliverance," Brandt said. "I've been smothering in self-pity, despairing over the boredom of this place and these people and wondering where all the good fellows have gone. And now here you are, the best of the good ones, come to assure me that some of you are still left."

The general's smile was wry, skeptical. "You are a master of blather, Mr. Brandt. Your reputation as a windy flatterer is well deserved."

"Windy, maybe, but flatterer, no. You are indeed the best of the good ones."

"Good what? Soldier? Russian? Bolshevik?"

"You're all of those, to be sure. But, if I didn't think it would abrade your socialistic sensitivities, I'd describe you with a good old-fashioned Middle-America label: a kindly gentleman."

The general sniffed and made a face. "Not only are you windy, you're sickening."

"How true. But I have other traits I'm not nearly so proud of."

Something was wrong, Brandt realized. Normally the general could be expected to twinkle over such broadstroke schoolboy stuff, but this morning there was a
6

somberness about him, a hint of something dark and hurting behind the clouded eyes. It was oddly disturbing, and Brandt decided that it must be defined. "You seem troubled, my friend. Is it something I might help you with?" he asked, suddenly serious.

General Chesnikov's faded blue eyes followed a plane that twisted and turned and spun, engine moaning, high in the pale sunlight. "Keep smiling, Mr. Brandt. We are probably being watched, and I want to give the impression I am trading small talk with a mildly dotty acquaintance."

"Ah. But what are you really doing?"

"I am about to betray my country."

Brandt worked hard to sustain his grin. "What in hell does that mean, General?"

Chesnikov sighed. "I have reached the point of glut. I have been a soldier for more than thirty years now, and I have seen my homeland devastated three times—twice by foreign invaders. I have seen thousands, literally thousands, of my countrymen shot, blown to bits, disemboweled or hacked down. I have heard men weep, women scream. I have smelled the burning, touched the decay, endured the loneliness and hunger and thirst. And I will not contribute to these things any longer. I simply will not, ever again."

Brandt laughed, as if the general had just passed along a great joke. And perhaps he had. To hear a professional soldier renouncing violence was to hear a farmer refusing further association with soil, a physician repudiating chemicals, a musician forswearing rhythm.

"But my dear General," Brandt said, "you are still in a war. Your countrymen still bleed, your cities still burn. I fail to see—"

Chesnikov stiffened, his eyes narrowing in a study of something in the middle distance. Unable to resist following the general's stare, Brandt spotted three men in long

7

overcoats and wide-brimmed fedoras, moving free of the crowd and making their way toward them along the hangar line.

"I have only a moment, Mr. Brandt."

"What is it? What can I do for you?"

"I can tell you only this: there will soon be a very important defection. One of us will come over to you—"

"Who? When? How?"

The general stepped away, a small shuffling of his glistening boots. "He will bring—"

The men in overcoats were hurrying now.

"What, General? Tell me. Quickly."

A kind of surrender seemed to settle over the big man, a subsiding, a recognition of fulfillment. His eyes, clear and steady, gave Brandt a final, earnest inspection.

The planes returned, low, blattering loudly. The general raised his voice, speaking precisely, deliberately, but his words were muffled by the engine racket.

"There is," Brandt heard him rasp, "a fox among your poplars."

"What? I—"

But the men were running now, and General Chesnikov stepped back a full pace, faced the Soviet flag atop the airfield headquarters shack and, poker-stiff at attention, saluted.

"God save my beloved Russia," he intoned.

Then he drew his service pistol from its holster and fired a shot through his head.

TOP SECRET

TWX 5 FEB 45

TO: AMBASSADOR MOSCOW

FROM: CATHCART, DEPT. OF STATE

UR TWX OF 4 FEB 45 RCD, NOTED. EMBASSY PRESS ATTACHE, C.G. BRANDT, WILL PROCEED VIA EARLIEST PRIORITY AIRCRAFT DIRECT TO THIS LOCATION FOR

8

EXTENDED DUTY. NO DELAY EN ROUTE AUTHORIZED.
ADVISE SOONEST RE DEPARTURE AND ETA.
CLASSIFIED FILE TUJJ/435A
TOP SECRET

CHAPTER 2

Near Holzdorf, Germany
22 April 1945

The twilight was fiery. Its light laid a wash of red on the distant Württemberger rises and made a hellish lace of the winter-stiffened orchard that flanked the road. To the northeast, where the U.S. Seventh pounded at the SS fanatics obstructing its push across the Danube, the guns rumbled and sent fitful flickerings along the darkening horizon. But here there was a peculiar lull, an unreal quiet, a suspension of motion and sound, as if the war itself had paused for breath, wearied by its own excesses.

They had come upon this barricade, a tangle of trees felled across the road's two lanes. It was the first obstacle since their departure from the bridgehead near Ulm. The only

10

surprise was that it had taken so inexplicably long to find any signs of the Wehrmacht—any suggestion of organized resistance.

The Unteroffizier came forward, his features shadowed by his pot helmet, his figure lumpy in the huge field coat. He held his machine pistol at the ready. "Who in hell are you?" he said, his voice soft and suggesting Westphalian origins. "And what are you doing on this road?"

Lukas, indolent in the rear seat of the Mercedes touring car, yawned noisily. "SS Sturmbannführer Lukas." He waved a mittened hand toward the rear. "These are my people and my vehicles. We are on a very important mission to the south of here. Now how do we get past that pile of firewood you have placed in our way?"

"The more important question at the moment, Sturmbannführer, is how you got past the Americans."

"Americans?"

The Unteroffizier shook his head irritably and pointed his weapon vaguely northward. "Up there. The countryside is teeming with them. They are said to be preparing for a drive for Augsburg and Munich, and the rumpus around Regensberg is only a feint, to throw us off guard here."

"Then what are you doing about that, Unteroffizier?" Lukas projected a touch of SS sarcasm. "Shouldn't you and your Wehrmacht comrades be mounting a counterattack, or something, instead of hiding here in the bushes?"

"You saw no Americans, then?"

The man's irritability had become anger, and Lukas, deciding to end the matter, leaned forward so as to allow the dying sunlight to light his face. "I don't like your tone. I suggest you brush up on your military courtesy."

A pause, during which the man obviously remembered that it was hazardous to be snotty to a superior officer. And that it was doubly dangerous if the superior officer was wearing SS trappings and had eyes like ball bearings.

11

"Sorry, sir. No offense intended. We have been manning this godforsaken roadblock since yesterday at noon. My men are tired and hungry and want to know what in hell is going on."

"What is going on right now, Unteroffizier, is my attempt to get some very important American prisoners to Munich, where they will undergo a special High Command interrogation. And if you persist in delaying me I shall have no recourse but to have you summarily shot."

The man was undaunted. "Where are your prisoners, sir?"

Lukas swung out of the car and said, "Come with me."

They went to the canvas-topped truck where, opening the rear flaps, Lukas threw the beam of his flashlight on the pale faces of four American officers—a colonel, a major, and two captains. Each was handcuffed. Each was obviously worried and frightened.

"Satisfied, Unteroffizier?"

The man was about to answer when Lukas barked another question. "Who is in command here? You?"

"For the time being, sir," the noncom answered coolly. "Leutnant Griessmaier left us this morning to look for our company commander, Oberleutnant Kolbert. To see if our orders still held. He hasn't come back."

"And so you are confused and frightened over the sudden and magical appearance of an IPW team—an SS prisoner-of-war interrogation section—under special orders. Right?"

The Unteroffizier was determined to hold his temper, Lukas saw, yet the affront couldn't be tolerated. "Frightened is not the word to use, Sturmbannführer. Confused, perhaps, but frightened, no."

"What's going on here?" A Wehrmacht lieutenant had materialized in the dim light, his manner officious.

The Unteroffizier explained. "This Sturmbannführer and

12

his IPW section came down the road, sir, and, as you have commanded that all movement on the road be investigated, I am in the process of checking these people out."

"You are Griessmaier?" Lukas asked the lieutenant icily.

"Yes, sir," the man said, stiffening like a cadet, suddenly obsequious. "How might I help you?"

"We are en route to Munich from Ulm, where we took custody this evening of the American officers in that truck. American officers taken in the fighting at Aschaffenburg. The bomb damage to the roads is severe, and we made a wrong turning outside of Senden somehow. We've ended up in this miserable stretch of nowhere and I now insist that you let us pass so we may keep our rendezvous."

"Of course, Sturmbannführer, at once. If you'd be so kind as to drive your car to the left"—he pointed in the manner of a traffic policeman—"you and your section will find an open lane which eventually rejoins this road about five hundred meters to the south. I'll pass the word that you are coming through."

The Unteroffizier shifted his weight from one boot to the other and cleared his throat. "Pardon, Herr Leutnant, but aren't you going to ask the Sturmbannführer for his papers and travel orders? Oberleutnant Kolbert was quite emphatic about the need to check everybody's papers. No exceptions, he said."

This, Lukas perceived, was a challenge—a subordinate evoking the name of one superior to put down another. He watched closely, curious as to how Griessmaier would handle it. Predictably, he handled it poorly.

"I remind you, Mueller, that I am in charge here. I see no reason to delay this SS Sturmbannführer and his people. It is inconceivable that such a party would be on this road without a valid reason."

Mueller was not convinced. He shook his head and was about to speak when Lukas decided to end the silly scene.

13

"Here are my papers, Leutnant. As you will see, we are traveling on the highest of priorities established by the highest of authorities."

Leutnant Griessmaier carefully unfolded the documents and held them up to the dying light. After an interval his lips puckered into a low whistle, and Mueller craned to read over his shoulder.

Lukas grated impatiently, "The letterhead is that of the Reichssicherheitshauptamt and the signer is Reichsführer SS Himmler, himself. I suggest that it's very much in your personal interest to assist us on our way with no delay."

"There. You see?" Leutnant Griessmaier smirked. He was enjoying his little triumph.

"We will have to see the Soldbücher and travel-date stamps of the other men in the Sturmbannführer's section, Herr Leutnant." Mueller was gathering self-righteousness about him. "We must follow our orders to the letter."

The Unteroffizier was becoming a real problem.

Lukas lifted his helmet and wiped the sweatband with a Wehrmacht-issue handkerchief. Simultaneously there was a sudden commotion behind them, and the twilight showed them two of the Americans, hands still chained, leaping from the truck and running hard for the orchard.

Lukas glanced at the guards, who had dropped from the truck and looked to him for orders. He resettled the helmet on his head and said, "Shoot them."

The guards raised their Schmeissers and fired three rasping bursts, and the fleeing Americans spun in the air, then rolled into a ditch.

"Who were they, Scharführer?" Lukas asked one of the guards.

"The major and one of the captains, sir. They must have passed a signal between themselves. The first thing I knew was that they had swung over the tailgate. No clues, no warning. Just over they went."

"No matter, I guess. We still have the colonel. He's the
14

important one. You and Stilmann bury those bodies in the orchard. I don't want anybody finding them for a while yet." Regarding the Unteroffizier with stony eyes, Lukas appended, "You will forget what you've just seen here."

The noncom, shaken, said softly, with a new respect, "As you wish, sir."

Leutnant Griessmaier, dealing with his own shock, said, "That shooting might very well attract some attention from the Amis. I think we ought to—"

He was interrupted by an outbreak of furious firing close by, to the north. A flare rose in the gloom at the orchard's far rim, and there was more shooting.

The Unteroffizier took charge, shouting orders to the men he had deployed among the trees. "The Amis have arrived! Gittelmann: Take your MG squad to the east fence line and scissors-fire with Kunkel's section! Braunig: Re-lay your mortars on the red C-stakes and fire at will on the creekbed sector!" He added, snarling to himself, "And hope to hell that we get some goddam tanks."

Lukas pulled Leutnant Griessmaier to one side and shouted over the clamor, "What's the best way to get out of this silly thicket and continue on to Munich? Our mission is of the most extreme urgency, and I don't want to get tied up in any local brawls."

"I can't rightly say, sir. The situation to the east and south is unclear. My company commander sent out a westbound patrol late this afternoon. They got back about a half an hour ago. The patrol leader says he spotted a recon section of a French armored infantry outfit, so it looks as if we're sitting on, or near, the dividing line between the Ami Seventh Army and the French First. It's my guess you'd be best off if you stay on this road until you get to the bypass at Krumbach. You can cut east there to Augsburg. From there it's any man's guess. Under any circumstances, though, I'd stay clear of the Autobahn. It's a mess, and where it isn't holed by bombings it's lousy with check-

15

points. There's an unbelievable lot of air activity along the major highways. The Ami planes shoot at anything that moves. So I suggest that you back-road it as much as you can, wherever you go."

Lukas went to his car and checked his chart, using his penlight. Griessmaier looked over his shoulder.

"Any reports on the Amis, Leutnant? Any actual confrontations in strength?"

"The same bunch says that up near Donaufeld they drew fire, but nothing like our boys on the Regensburg perimeter have been getting today."

"How about our resistance overall?"

"In this area it's pitiful, Sturmbannführer. Some Waffen SS. Nothing really heavy, though. Scattered Wehrmacht units, none larger than company-size, all milling about, apparently waiting for word on how and when to do what. No cohesive defense perimeters, no strongpoints forming up, no significant mine fields or armor concentrations. I hate to say it, sir, but our forces seem to be pretty badly demoralized and confused just about everywhere in this neck of the woods. Ever since the Amis got to the Danube we seem to be running around like ants whose hill's been kicked."

Lukas sniffed. "That's defeatist, Leutnant. Haven't you heard? We have a thousand-year Reich going here."

The man showed no appreciation of the little joke.

"So, then," Lukas said, once again all business. "Have my men returned from their little burial detail?"

The Leutnant peered into the gathering night, which was hazy with flare and grenade smoke. "Yes, sir. Looks as if they have."

"All right, then. We'll be on our way. Much obliged, Leutnant."

"You're welcome, sir."

As Lukas's driver slid the car into gear, a shout sounded,

16

and Lukas saw Unteroffizier Mueller running toward them, machine pistol waving. "Stop those people, Leutnant! Stop them! They are frauds!"

Leutnant Griessmaier was annoyed. "What's the matter with you, anyhow? I—"

"They didn't shoot those Amis." Mueller arrived, panting. "I watched the two men carry those bodies into the orchard. Only they weren't bodies. They stood and ran away to the north, and the two men didn't raise a finger. Just turned around and came back here."

Leutnant Griessmaier's little brown eyes came around to give Lukas puzzled examination. "Sir, I—Well, can you explain this? I mean, it's quite irregular—"

"Of course I can explain," Lukas said. He reached into the map pocket of the car door beside him and withdrew the silencer-fitted Beretta. Resting his forearm on the sill, he squeezed the trigger.

The shots were soundless in the prevailing din. Leutnant Griessmaier went down like a rag doll. Unteroffizier Mueller peered down at his chest for a moment, as if discovering a gravy spot on his Sunday necktie, then turned as if to walk away. He sagged, dropping his pistol with a mild clatter, and, sighing like a man preparing for bed, rolled into the ditch beside the road.

"All right, Otto," Lukas said to his driver, "take us down the lane to the left, as the Leutnant suggested."

"Yes, sir."

The motors rumbled, the gears clacked, and the column ground into motion.

"Leutnant Griessmaier was a stupid ass-kisser, Otto."

"Yes, Sturmbannführer."

"With officers like that, no wonder Germany is losing the war."

"Yes, Sturmbannführer."

17

CHAPTER 3

They made good time, despite the turmoil. Ami aircraft had made a sea of debris, and tank hulls and truck skeletons smoldered beside the highways, where houses sagged in on themselves, broken and forlorn. Everything smelled of burning and rust and spent gunpowder and sweat and the gagging sweetness of undiscovered, decaying flesh. To the north and east, smoke from flaming fields and forests rose to the edge of the cosmos itself, veiling the pale moon with towering cauliflowers, and there was the far-off insect clamor of socially acceptable mass murder.

Besides the Mercedes and the truck containing the Ami prisoners, they had a VW recon car and an

18

ancient Sd. Kfz. 232, an eight-wheel scout car with a small gun turret and a veritable grandma's attic of radio sending and receiving gear. Lukas, in the regal solitude that is the privilege of rank, rode at the head of the column with Otto, the melon-faced Scharführer who served as chief navigator and unofficial worrier. The VW recon carried Ludwig and Dieter. Klaus and Josef, the documents specialist, and Manfred, the radio technician, brought up the rear in the 232, driven by Franz.

They negotiated the smoky clutter of the Krumbach bypass and, after clearing Augsburg, kept to the road that wound east, then south for Mering. Near Kissing, there was a checkpoint; the narrow roadway was choked with trucks and wagons and horse-drawn artillery and refugees, standing silently with IDs in hand. Lukas decided to turn this liability into an asset by taking the column into a woods already crammed with cars and ambulances and courier bikes—presumably the vehicles of a field hospital cadre preparing to set up shop—and instructed his people to park together in the defilade of the highway embankment. A Flakabteilung bivouaced nearby, its radio murmuring the inescapable *Lili Marlene*, its Vierling guns aimed without enthusiasm at a night sky owned by the enemy.

Lukas assembled his group at the rear of the truck and flashed his light through the canvas flaps. The two PWs blinked against the glare.

In English, Lukas said, "Okay, Bill. We're all here."

"All right," the colonel said quietly, "so far, so good. Now I want us all to get something to eat. When we're finished, you German people check your gear. Don't forget to look at the gas and oil in the vehicles. Use dipsticks. I don't trust the gauges on these relics. Franz, when it's convenient, you and Dieter give Lou and me some exercise—march us around a bit so that the people in this park will see you've got prisoners. Then we'll get a bit of rest and be on the road

19

at oh-eight-hundred. But keep loose, folks. We can't count on anything, with the overall fluid military situation that prevails in this area."

Lukas asked, "How are you two doing back here, sir?"

"All right. The cuffs are a pain in the ass, but in general we're okay. Wouldn't you say, Lou?"

The captain sighed. "Frankly, I'd rather be in Philadelphia."

They all chuckled over the tired old joke because, in this context, it bespoke the safe, the familiar.

"I'll have Otto look at the cuffs, sir. Maybe he can make them fit easier."

"No big deal." The colonel asked then, "Did Sam and Harry make it all right?"

"Sure." Lukas strove for the sound of assurance. "Easy as pie. My hat signal, a squirt of Schmeisser blanks, a diversionary attack by the backup patrol as planned, and Sam and Harry were on their way. A couple of Germans had to be canceled when they saw through our little act, but nobody else tumbled, and we got through clean from there on."

"Good." The colonel seemed satisfied.

Lukas rinsed his mess gear at the Lister bag, stretched, then went to the Mercedes. He stood in the shadows, sipping coffee and staring down the valley, where the dawn light softened the harshness of the countryside's scars. Manfred and Dieter were marching the colonel and the captain back and forth in a nearby patch of meadow, counting cadence raucously and occasionally kicking the colonel in the rear to hurry him along. Members of the nearby Flak battery watched all this with undisguised amusement.

Josef materialized in the gloom beside Lukas, pretending interest in the view. But Lukas knew what was really on his mind. He felt a return of his resentment over the willingness of Colonel Jamieson and the headquarters brass to risk Josef's presence on this operation. Surely the hotshots must have known of the man's problem, and their indifference to it when the team's security might lie in the balance was unconscionable. He was a first-class forger of papers, to be sure. But he was also, as Lukas discovered in Dijon by a chance witnessing, a furtive, solitary-drinking, hopeless alcoholic. Josef was a ticking bomb, and if Lukas had been in charge of this little caper he would have sent the man packing.

At once.

Josef nodded toward the antiaircraft gunners. "What do you think about them?" His voice was husky, anxious. "They keep watching us."

"What's to think? They're curious. When a Sturmbannführer and a gaggle of SS lackeys show up in a cow-dung nowhere with some Ami prisoners, it's guaranteed to attract attention."

"They are waiting for something, I think. They know something is going to happen, and they are waiting."

Lukas gave him a look. "Happen?"

"It's just a feeling I have. All's not well."

"I've felt that from the moment I was inducted into the army. So what's new about uneasiness?"

Josef shrugged. "This is something special. Something dreadful is in the air."

Annoyed, Lukas was about to deliver a lecture on the need for self-control. But then he saw the futility of it, and so he climbed into the car's backseat, pulled his helmet low over his eyes, and tried to fall asleep.

But his mind would not shut down.

In slightly over sixteen weeks Lukas had experienced a kind of apotheosis, having been lifted out of one of the most execrable cellars in the military monastery and placed among the archangels in the steeple. At first the disbelief

21

was absolute, causing him to stand entranced as Captain Ballard's sullen voice went on about *effective date* and *per diem payments* and *mileage* and *records jackets*. Later, with the arrival of written orders, stamped top and bottom with the crimson block letters, TOP SECRET, the matter had gathered substance, and he had reverted to the animal wariness that had evolved in his years as an enlisted man. One needs no more than an hour in the rank of private to learn that the military world around him is only marginally interested in the fact of his existence. "Feed the soldier a bit, clothe him basically, and permit him occasional sleep until that time when, in your judgment, he can get his ass shot off to the best possible press." So reads *The Brasshat's Manual for Self-Aggrandizement*, and Lukas had endured —survived—assorted practical applications of this root philosophy since February, 1942. Thus the letter's instructions to report to Special Squad, 33d Military Police, Fort Meade, Maryland, had put his old-campaigner's suspiciousness on red alert. It simply made no sense to transfer a private first class with a documents-translator MOS to an MP outfit. What kind of cops need a man who can read captured German laundry lists and letters to dear little Kurtchen, on tour with the Wehrmacht in France, from Mutti and Vati, at home in Outhaus am Rhein? It was like assigning a librettist to duty with a railroad construction battalion.

Still, one should never be surprised by anything the army did. After all, his MOS had not disqualified him from serving for thirteen sunbaked months as company clerk and gofer for Captain Llewellyn F. Ballard III, executive officer, champion roué and after-hours host of the clandestine poker-and-dice club operated by, and in the interest of, the commissioned faculty of the 21st Basic Training Regiment, Camp Riggles, Alabama—the latest and longest and most stupefying tour in a dreary succession of nowhere places.

22

From the beginning Lukas was, clearly, the nation's most unpromotable soldier, a puzzling embarrassment to all commands, thanks to a German immigrant father who, during the Great Depression, had earned a dollar a day passing out Socialist Party literature on Buffalo, New York, street corners, and to a Russian immigrant mother who, while scrubbing office floors to backstop him on his four-year scholarship to Penn State, had withstood the catcalls and slanders of their Hertel Avenue neighbors. No matter that she was loving and lovable and entirely apolitical; she was a Russian, and therefore, by God, "one a them frigging Bolshevik revolutionaries." His father had taught him German and a respect for composers and artists and scientists—"the dreamers who make the politicians and robber barons endurable." His mother had taught him Russian and a respect for hard work, fidelity, and gratitude. Lukas loved his parents very much, and the abuses they had suffered because of their foreignness sometimes made it hard for him to love his country as intensely as they insisted he should.

Their intellectual and emotional legacies had been of little advantage to him in the army. No Officers Candidate School for Alex Lukas, despite his bachelor's in journalism, his master's in political science, and his aggregate of five years as reporter and editor on *Der Tägliche Berichter*, the flagship German-language newspaper in the Middle Atlantic states. A cloudy political heritage, suggesting dubious loyalties, the army had ruled; limited service as a documents translator, and that only under close supervision.

There had proved to be little demand for a limited service translator of dubious loyalties. His army service had been a series of humiliations leading inexorably to slavery as a clerk-typist in the basic training regiment.

Last May, while he was home on furlough, his mother had cheerily dismissed his complaints about the shoddy treatment he'd been getting at Camp Riggles. "Alex, I have

23

trouble with all this—with all your groanings. For someone like me, even America's bullies are acceptable. Compared to those I've known other places, other times, America's nasty people are mere brats, mean children with runny noses and bad manners. Be thankful that you don't know what really nasty is, my boy."

What do you say to somebody who can look at life like that? Lukas could only stand there, half amused and half incredulous.

He had since learned new lessons.

The Special Squad at Fort Meade was in truth special. It served as a kind of airlock for those benighted souls who—for reasons known mainly to God—passed from the normal atmosphere of the normally crazy outside world into the hyper pressure of the abnormally crazy inside world of the Office of Strategic Services, the arcane bureaucracy that spawned American spies.

A large manor house in Chesapeake Bay country. Rigorous physical training. Days of field craft, demolitions, Morse code, hand-to-hand combat, map reading, weapons, techniques of sabotage, aircraft and vehicle identification; nights of reading, cramming for tests, short periods of exhausted sleep, then more of the same. Eventual service as an audience of one for a sardonic man named Brandt.

"What am I doing here, Brandt?" Glum. Testy.

"We are making you into a specialist in the covert penetration of enemy territory, Mr. Lukas. You will become expert in such activities as vehicular movements and field expedients, small-arms assualt, demolitions, quick identity changes, radio traffic, counterpropaganda and the cultivation of underground support among local populations. We are, in other words, about to make you into a sneaky, fast-moving hell-raiser."

"Why me?"

"Because you are fluent in the German and Russian languages. Because you are intimately familiar with
24

German and Russian folkways, mores. Because of your straight-A performance in all aspects of infantry basic training, including leadership. Because of your college education."

"What's this business about underground support from local populations, or whatever?"

Brandt lit a cigarette and blew a cloud toward the ceiling. "There've been some interesting developments in southern Germany. Restless and disillusioned farmers and religionists there are setting up an underground resistance to Hitler's rule, and we hope to exploit this discontent by sending in teams of MO people who can give the dissidents leadership and the technical means—fake newspapers, leaflets, radio messages and the like—by which to spread word of their resistance among like-minded Germans everywhere. The goal: a general uprising against the Nazi government, first in Bavaria, and then, hopefully, throughout the nation."

"And you want me to get into this kind of thing?"

Brandt shook his head. "We have a specific mission for you. But if you paint yourself into a corner you should know where you might look for some help."

"Seems to me this is pumping air. Germany's finished. Why play around at this late date with pamphleteers and anti-Nazi graffiti writers?"

"Wars don't necessarily end when the shooting stops," Brandt said enigmatically.

"Why Russian? Why do you need a Russian-speaker in southern Germany?"

"Later, my friend. You'll be told this later."

Lukas had asked the obvious question. "Why am I suddenly so trusty? How come I can't be trusted to be an officer, but I can be trusted enough to raise hell in Bavaria?"

"As an army officer, you could, feasibly, expend the lives of your men from a comfortable distance while serving

25

selfish or disloyal ends. As a secret agent, the lives that you spend would almost assuredly include your own. We trust you as an agent, Mr. Lukas, because we trust your animal instinct for self-preservation."

"You're a real sweetheart, Brandt."

"Oh, I can give you loftier reasons, Mr. Lukas. Our background investigations reveal that you are an idealist, a liberal, an outspoken champion of the underdog and all that rigmarole. And, happily, that you are sensible and healthy."

"What's my health got to do with it?"

"A healthy man facing great danger is guaranteed to be, as military people put it so crudely, scared shitless. A sensible, healthy man in that condition becomes inventive, ruthless, and determined to survive. Combined with all your other attributes, your good sense and excellent health should make you a very good secret agent indeed."

Word had spread, apparently, that the special SS unit with VIP prisoners had better not be screwed around with. When they pulled out of the hospital park at 0803, the SS troopers manning the highway checkpoint waved them through without so much as a glance at their papers.

And it was just as well, too, because four P-47s, those USAF fighter planes shaped like milk bottles, tore along the adjacent river in a rumbling shriek, guns racketing. Team Lukas managed to find cover in the treed flank of a low hill, and they watched as the planes expended a hundred thousand dollars' worth of ammunition to smash the windows and knock down the chimney of an out-of-business roadside café at a fork in the lane ahead.

"Idiots," Otto grumped.

Lukas sighed. In English he muttered, "You must show more respect, Otto. That's the American Way of Strife."

Otto smiled. He was a Princeton graduate and therefore was able to recognize puns.

26

Lukas knew very little else about Otto or the other members of the team. Manfred, of course, had a Munich accent. But the others? Enigmas. The mission, and the roles each were to play, had been rehearsed and memorized until they became ineradicable parts of their psyches. Yet just who each was, and why each had been selected for this exercise, was known only to Brandt, their control officer, now at long last due to arrive in Dijon after months in puzzling obscurity in Washington. Cover and its maintenance were consuming preoccupations of OSS. Brandt had allowed Lukas to retain his real name, because it was a common German name and its use would make things simpler. Usually, though, real names and biographical data were never divulged—a truth apparently forgotten for a moment by Otto one evening at mess when, in a light-hearted mood, he told of an amusing incident during his college graduation party. As they followed the twisting highway, Lukas thought about this, and inevitably began to weigh the team's other vulnerabilities.

"Stop the car, Otto. Then go back and tell Josef that I want him to ride with me for a while."

The change was made, and after the drive resumed, he said, "Do you still have that feeling? That something awful is going to happen?"

Josef shrugged, his gaze fixed on the road ahead.

He persisted. "What's bothering you, Josef?"

"Nothing. Everything."

"Give me a specific."

"I can't be specific. There's something fishy about this mission. Something that makes me very damned uneasy. Something Brandt hasn't told us. Something our noble leader, Colonel Jamieson, isn't saying. It just isn't normal, an absentee boss establishing a team in February and then keeping it in Dijon until April, rehearsing a trick nobody can describe that's supposed to be played at a place and on a date nobody knows."

They rode in silence for a time. Eventually Josef gave him a sidelong glance and said, "What's really on your mind, Lukas? Something's been eating at you for weeks."

Lukas's return stare was direct, unblinking. "I am aware of your appetite for the grape, Josef. And I'm putting you on notice that I'll not tolerate behavior that interferes with what we're trying to do—that might get us all killed."

"What the hell do you mean by that?"

"Just keep the cork in the bottle."

Josef's face was red with sudden anger, and his answer was in hushed, heated English. "Who in hell do you think you are, you son of a bitch? Just because you're wearing the Nazi honcho suit, don't try to give me orders. Jamieson is in charge of this little roadshow, buster, and I answer to him, not you."

Lukas sighed and turned his gaze to the evening sky. "I'm going to admit something to you, Josef. It's something quite personal, and so it's not easy to bring out. But I admit to you, here and now, that ever since I got into this OSS thing I've been terrified, absolutely frightened out of my skin. Compounding the problem is the fact that I'm not really a warrior. I'm a very friendly fellow, actually, slow to anger and quick to forgive. Yet here I am, a mild-mannered man who isn't sore at anyone, in the heart of Nazi Germany, surrounded by millions of people who would kill me in an instant. And you know what? I'm so scared I'm just this side of throwing up. Really.

"But there's something else you need to know. Yesterday, at that roadblock, when we got through the line with that phony firefight, I learned something about myself. I had to shoot those German officers. I wasn't the slightest bit angry at those fellows, but they scared me bad, and I killed them the way I'd kill roaches. Bang, bang. Just like that. And you know something else? It was easy. I'd never before—in my whole life—done serious physical harm to anybody. But yesterday, at that roadblock, I discovered

28

how easy it is to kill somebody who frightens me." He sighed again, the sound of deep and abiding unhappiness.

"So what's your point, Lukas?"

"Just this: Your fondness for the jug frightens me. And I'm putting you on formal notice. If you frighten me the least bit more than you frighten me now, I'll shoot you where you stand."

CHAPTER 4

Near Eckerdorf, Bavaria
2321 hours, 23 April 1945

It went better than she expected.

She made a soft landing in a corner of a meadow whose snow cover had all but vanished, thanks to an earlier thaw. The night was clammy and redolent of damp earth and pine, and in the distance, down the shallow valley, the wan moonlight reflected on the roof tiles and gilded church spire of Eckerdorf, a nothing of a village in a Bavarian nowhere. She judged that she could be no more than a hundred yards off her pinpoint, which, if true, amounted to a triumph of precision.

To the south, a distant throbbing in the high mists, the C-47 turned for home. With the sound came the familiar feeling—part loneliness, part vigilance, part panic. It lingered, then, as usual, subsided into a manageable tension.

She collapsed the purple silk of her parachute, dragged it to the tree line, and rolled it into a bundle, which she hid in the rotting hollow of a fallen yew. The cold became a sudden electric shock when she pulled off the coveralls; the cotton underwear, fake silk dress, worn tweed topcoat and galoshes of synthetic rubber were, as she'd suspected they would be, pitiful protection against the Oberbayern night. Still, it could have been worse. It could have been like that jump east of Vienna, when the wind carried her into an icy lake. She'd nearly drowned before cutting herself free of the tangle of silk and harness and clothes. Since her papers had been lost with the rest, she'd been forced to abandon her mission, hide in a corncrib, and wait three days for a Red Army overrun—all the while wearing no more than a raincoat and wooden sandals stolen from some farmer's shed. Worse, she had endured a fourth day in a tarpaper office, naked and blue under the lusting eyes of the division's intelligence officer and his vodka-sodden political commissar, until that idiot Vishinsky had arrived to vouch for her.

Well, she thought now, shivering and dour, war was never meant to be enjoyed.

A check of her watch told her she had fifty-eight-and-a-half minutes to remove the traces of her own landing and to reach and take up watch at the other drop point. It would be close. She had two kilometers of strange country to walk through, and an overcast was moving in, obscuring the sliver of moon and deepening the shadows around her.

She brushed her footprints out of the slush with a branch, then, keeping close to the hedgeline so as to minimize signs of her passing, she made her way to the blacktop highway beyond the rise to the west.

Because she was a professional, the map was in her mind, not her pocket. But maps, especially mental ones, need to

31

be oriented, perceived north to real north, so twice she paused to consult the radium dial of the tiny compass she carried under her topcoat lapel. When she reached the crossroads she would jettison this incriminating device, but for now she must take the risk so as to be certain that she was indeed on mark. Night does strange things to landscape, and the wrong stretch of road, or stand of trees, or clump of houses can take on a deceptive likeness to the correct one.

She was only a hundred meters from the intersection when two men emerged from the forest beside the road. They were dressed in lederhosen and hunting jackets, and they carried fowling pieces. The taller man turned on a flashlight and held the beam on her face. She struggled to control the surprise and alarm.

"What are you doing out here, young woman?"

She took her cue. They were farmers, obviously, out on civil security patrol. To them she was a young woman alone, and, probably, helpless and lost. She sounded a mixture of confusion and fright. "I—I am Gretl Keller, and I live in Kufstein, on the Austrian border. The bus was attacked by Ami planes this afternoon, and I've been walking since. I'm trying to find my way to Murnau. I'm trying to meet my husband, a Landser with the sappers' school there. He has used up his furlough time, so I'm going to visit him."

The shorter man, a shadow against the trees, sniffed. "You're a hell of a way off course, lady. Are you sure you didn't just pop out of that plane we heard?"

"Don't be an idiot, Fritz," the other grumped. "The enemy doesn't use women agents. That's right in our manual."

"The manual says the enemy doesn't often use women as agents, that's what it says."

"Look at her. Does she look like a spy?"

"What kind of spy looks like a spy, for God's sake?"

She decided it had gone far enough. "Please—May I ask

32

who you gentlemen are? I heard that plane. And, well—I mean, you could be spies, too."

The taller one laughed. "Now there's a droll idea. Do we frighten you?"

"You terrify me, sir."

Both men laughed this time. "Sorry to disappoint you, young woman, but Fritz and I are dairymen out of Eckerdorf, heroically serving our country as air wardens. Neither one of us would know a spy if he were to fall in our soup. Even so, may we see your papers? The manual requires us to ask."

She took the Kennkarte and ration book from her sorry little purse and handed them to the taller man.

"What's that?" Fritz asked, holding his flashlight on the paper folded into the purse's side pocket.

"A letter from my husband. Giving me directions to Murnau and his barracks area. Would you like to see that, too?"

"The Kennkarte will do. We are not snoops."

The men studied the papers for a time, seeming to be embarrassed by their intrusion. Bavarians are amiable, polite people, more often than not, and these two were straight from the mold.

"All right, Frau Keller, you may go on your way," the taller one said, returning the papers. "For Murnau, go to that crossroads there, turn left, and follow the gravel road for two kilometers. There will be another paved highway, which, if you turn right, will take you to Fendorf, a village where you can catch a bus to Murnau."

"Thank you, sir. I thank you both. I don't know how I got so terribly off my route."

"It's easy to do in this neck of the woods, Frau Keller. Especially in blackouts."

"Well," she said, sounding grateful relief, "I'll be on my way, then. I appreciate your kindness."

"Good luck, Frau Keller."

33

She walked off, irritated over the incident. The men were from Eckerdorf. They would be around to recognize her. They would have to be dealt with.

But first things first.

She found a waiting place in a copse beside the high meadow and was on watch nine minutes before the appointed time of arrival. She was numb with cold.

The C-47 was three minutes late. It came in low, its engines burbling under reduced throttle, then was gone, a flitting shadow lost among shadows.

The parachute was a shifting blur in the gathering mist.

She waited until it had been gathered, rolled and buried with a trench shovel before she moved to the edge of the patch of trees. Then she stepped into the clear and showed the parachutist the glow of a match held in her cupped hands.

"You are Brunhilde?" the other woman asked, tense.

She drew the knife from her stocking top and said cheerily, "No, I am your assassin."

She stabbed the woman beneath the chin. Then, to avoid staining her own clothes with blood, she stepped back to wait out the final, silent convulsions.

The woman's papers were in a plastic envelope in her musette bag. After folding them into her purse, she dragged the body into the shadows and, with quick swings of the trench shovel, buried it in earth softened by the thaw.

Finished at last, she returned to the road and made for Eckerdorf.

"So then, Gretl," she said aloud, "the job begins."

THE WHITE HOUSE

C. G. Brandt
Special Assistant to the President

* * *

For all the clout that's been handed me, it's taken a seemingly endless time to set up shop. But finally I'm able to say that things are under way. Dingbat has been contacted and I've made the appropriate openers in Moscow and Europe to put a radio tap on the Olga thing. A personalities dossier has been set up, agents' report folders have been prepared, and correspondence files are in place. OSS Communix is establishing a special scrambler phone between here and Dijon, plus a TWX net linking Dijon with Eisenhower's G-2 at SHAEF and a mysterious "Abie" in Honolulu who, I understand, knows everything the Japanese are up to before the emperor himself is told. And now, with all the formalities handled, I'm opening this file, backed up wherever possible by recordings. It's the kind of personal log which, I hope, will cover my ass if the bureaucracy gets bent and somebody looks for a fall guy. I've worked too long in the Sacred Halls of Statecraft to trust in the basic decency of mankind.

The stationery.
I keep looking at the letterhead.
What a couple of weeks it's been.
Events since the president's death on the twelfth have seemed to tumble over each other, a boulder slide triggered by the shock his passing has sent through the world. There remains an unreal quality to much that goes on here in Washington, as if the city is in some weird suspension and the people await a signal to resume their normal idiocies. As many of them do, I feel a specific, intimate loss. And, as many others do, I still think of him as The President, words capitalized, even though Harry Truman has assumed the office.

35

Harry S (the initial doesn't stand for anything) Truman of Independence, Missouri.

The haberdasher. The Prendergast machine political gofer.

Now president of the United States.

And look at me. At my letterhead.

Now who's the gofer, eh?

Extraordinary.

Even for these extraordinary times.

I was never wild about Harry. It's nothing personal, really, since I've never been at ease with any of the professional pols, and Harry, with his Cagneylike strut and his ready grin and his natty double-breasted worsteds, is, to my jaded eye, the archetype. I voted for him for vice president only because he was Roosevelt's running mate, and that's all he's remained in my mind until last week. I suppose that's why I was jolted when the crisp voice on the other end of the line told me that the president wanted to see me at 2200 hours—alone and confidentially—in his Connecticut Avenue apartment. I'm quite used to mixing with the high and mighty, thanks to the job in Moscow and a boss who had me do his VIP briefings because he considered me such a glib, overeducated son of a bitch, as he put it. So it wasn't so much the summons that surprised me, it was the stir of hope—no, the excited premonition— that this particular summoner was about to end my months of dreary limbo.

The conversation was brief.

He apologized for the late hour and the meeting place, pointing out that he and Mrs. Truman will not be occupying the White House until Mrs. Roosevelt has had plenty of time to move out. He said I could make notes if I cared to.

He was appalled, he said, to discover how I'd been victimized by the Cathcart case. Cathcart was a big gear in the Foreign Service who had taken his admiration for the
36

Soviet Union to an extreme that bordered on treason. As a Red sympathizer he had bent rules, warped policy, played favorites, forgiven Soviet trespasses and, in general, made a world-class horse's ass of himself. It turns out I was one of the objects of his disaffections; as soon as I filed on the Chesnikov incident of last February, Cathcart shot off a TWX to the ambassador, ordering my transfer to Washington. To cover himself, I guess, Cathcart told me to "investigate" the Chesnikov thing, and I did—building quite a dossier on the matter and keeping my lines to our Moscow moles open against the time when Chesnikov's prediction of a defection might become a reality. But for all my work and all my tries at definitive action, Cathcart put the entire matter on a siding and me on the raw edge of a squirting fit. I'd sat in my Foggy Bottom office and might as well have done crossword puzzles. But then the Law of Eventual Justice took hold and Cathcart, overstepping himself on a Lend-Lease deal that would have delivered to the Russians forty thousand bazookas free of obligation, got himself reduced in rank and transferred to a regional bureau in Inter-American Affairs. I, personally, thought the son of a bitch should have been thrown out of government altogether, but Roosevelt's people have never been famed for firing the inept or unsavory.

Anyhow, President Truman said he was sorry, and now that he's read my Dingbat File he wants me to pursue it with all possible vigor. I will, he said, be given more details as soon as he's had a chance to settle a bit into his own new job. Meanwhile, I will be placed on the payroll as special assistant to the president, with an office—a "cubbyhole under the stairs"—near the White House map room. Everything about my work—"including," he said, "the very damn phone number"—will be classified Top Secret and I will report to no one but him. I'll be given a White House pass, a government car and parking place, and an unlimited gasoline ration. If anyone asks me what my job is, I say

37

that, as a former State Department security officer responsible for VIP safety at the Moscow embassy, I've been asked to review the executive mansion's overall security system, both manned and electrical. Only the president and the OSS chief, General Donovan, will know what I'm really up to.

"Most respectfully, sir," I remember asking, "do you mind if I know, too?"

His answer, according to my shorthand:

"Hitler's Reich is collapsing. The Nazis are falling back on all fronts. Allied forces hold the entire west bank of the Rhine; have made three major crossings of the river. General Patton is cutting across the German's belly and General Patch is running down his leg. The Soviets are pressing in from the east and are about ready to assault Berlin. In the Pacific, our B-29s range virtually unimpeded over any piece of land or sea the Japanese still hold, and our army and navy are winding up for the knockout. I'm in charge of all that now, Mr. Brandt. But I'm a greenhorn, filling in for a fallen pro. And so I'm going to be very damned busy. Too busy to keep a minute-by-minute watch on what that goddam Stalin is up to. That he's up to no good is clear as hell. I want you to stay on top of it and advise me daily."

My question: "Why the sudden intense interest in Stalin, sir? I mean, there's a lot of buzz about the generalissimo these days, and—"

His answer: "An awful lot of people in our government think he's a peachy kid. FDR himself was convinced he could get along with him through plain old folksy neighborliness. But I, for one, think that's a crock. I don't trust Stalin as far as I can throw this apartment house. And I don't mind telling you that I intend to cut him off from Lend-Lease as fast as I possibly can. He's been living off the American taxpayer too long, and we've loaned him billions of dollars' worth of American treasure, given him uncounted gallons of American blood, and the son of bitch won't even acknowledge that fact. And now we're picking up all this other stuff—the strange radio traffic, the unaccountable shifting of combat divisions, the reassembly of airpower, the very peculiar warning and suicide of General Chesnikov, long known to be one of our best friends in the USSR. I want to know what's going on, Mr. Brandt, and you'd better goddam well tell me what it is."

(He was shaping up as a man who dealt in, and expected, straight talk. I gave him some:) "It's a mistake to put me under the steps at the White House, Mr. President."

His answer: "How so?"

"I'll do better running things from a European base. I can keep you apprised, daily, if need be, via TWX or radio phone and scrambler."

(My note: His eyes are large behind those thick glasses.)

His comment: "All right. Do the job as you see fit. But do the job. There's more afoot than I've told you. So do the damn job yesterday. Yesterday, do you get me?"

"I get you, sir."

"All right, then. Get cracking." (End shorthand.)

I'd come back to my cubbyhole under the stairs and started firing off cables to Dijon, where, I knew, Jamieson and the other mixings for a line-crossing in force were sitting on their collective asses. Now, a week later, I'm sitting on my own in a plane, staring at my new letterhead, which is already out of date, and waiting for whatever lies ahead in France.

God, what a world.

CHAPTER 5

**Eckerdorf, Bavaria
24 April 1945**

The village was a clutch of half-timbered houses that seemed to huddle against the bitter wind—closed, silent, lost in melancholy. A crossroads place, unchanged since the days of Charlemagne. A mean and dreary place, drab, and devoid of cheer.

Lukas examined it through his binoculars. There was a fountain in the central square, bone-dry and chalked by generations of pigeons. The onion-top steeple of a church glowed dully in the afternoon sunlight. A Konditorei, shuttered, appeared to dream of long-gone times. A woman in a faded blue coat pumped water at a community well. Behind her, a newspaper skittered aimlessly across the cobblestones.

40

An oxcart, unattended. A dusty black Opel sedan, parked in front of what seemed to be the town hall.

No troops. No military vehicles.

A town too small, too insignificant, either to be used or to be destroyed.

Brandt was right. It should be just what they needed as a way station.

Colonel Jamieson called from the truck, his voice low. "How does it look, Lukas?"

"Fine, sir. As expected."

"Good. Dieter, are you ready?"

"Yes, Colonel."

"Let me look at you."

Dieter moved to a spot near the tailgate of the truck. He was wearing his cleric's garb: black wool suit, severe and threadbare at the elbows; white collar, not too clean; black shoes, turned at the heels; broad-brimmed black hat.

"Where's your Bible?"

"Here, sir. I have the small one in my coat pocket."

"Ration tickets? ID card? Berufsschein? Pictures of your family, your church? Letter from your bishop?"

"In my wallet, sir. All checked out by Josef."

"All right. Move down the hill, but hold to the woods. We don't want anybody spotting you until you get to the roadside crucifix. Wait there, as if you're meditating, until dark. Then go to the house with the red shutters. That one there, on the side street, down from the square."

"I see it. I knock three times, then once."

"What do you tell the man who opens the door?"

"That I'm Pastor Linck, from Tegernsee, en route to a synodical meeting in Ulm. I bring greetings for Albert Grummel from Karli Boden."

"Then what?"

"If the man says he is Albert Grummel, I'll present him with the note from Boden. If he takes it to the flatiron and

41

heats out the invisible ink, I'll go to the upstairs front window and light a candle. Which will mean I've made contact and will be spending the night. I will learn all I can about the religionists' plans for insurrection and will report to you here in the woods tomorrow at dawn so that Lukas can begin negotiations with Ressel and his people."

"And if the man does not say or do what he's supposed to? If it's not a man at all, but a child, a woman?"

"I simply ask directions to Memmingen, then return here at once."

"If, when you return here, you discover that we have been picked up by a patrol, or otherwise have vanished for whatever reason, what do you do then?"

"I go as directly and quickly as possible to Amtstrasse Fourteen in Memmingen, where I identify myself as Wilhelm Gottschal and hole up until one of the Allied armies overruns the town. I then send the code word 'Bagel' to Brandt via G-2 SHAEF. He will retrieve me for debriefing."

The colonel was satisfied. "Very well. Off you go."

After a supper of Wehrmacht field rations, the team countered the tension of waiting by losing itself in make-work. Guns were cleaned once again, maps were studied for yet another time, the vehicles were examined as if they had never been seen before. Josef put the finishing touches to the ID cards to be carried by the colonel and the captain as deaf-mutes Karl Liess and Hans Wurfl, en route to hospital at Bad Tölz. This was to cover them if they were forced, for any reason, to go deep-dish.

An hour after nightfall, a candle glowed in the upstairs window of the house with red shutters.

The colonel was pleased. Lukas was scheduled to make the team's first German-language Joan-Eleanor contact with Brandt at 2245 hours, and this gave him something

42

positive to report. A successful line-crossing was a rare accomplishment in any event, the colonel said, but it was icing on the cake when a crossing so complex and deep could report good results on schedule.

The Joan-Eleanor was a radio developed especially for communications between secret agents and their control officers. Until its introduction, OSS had been forced to use standard shortwave wireless sets, suitcase-size apparatus requiring external power sources and aerials, which could communicate only via the dots and dashes of Morse, arranged in carefully designed—and breakable—secret codes. The disadvantages were obvious: When an agent transmitted, the whole world could listen to the dit-dah-dits that he sent out in great, spreading circles, and the enemy's direction-finding equipment could backtrack on the signal and pinpoint the agent's location. Worse, the agent needed a friendly support system to get on the air—friendly locals who would provide him with cover and arrange the power connections and aerials his set demanded. All of which amounted to acceptable problems and risks when the agent was operating in Occupied France or the Low Countries, where there had been legions of anti-Nazis, but which promised mostly disaster when the agent tried to send from Germany itself, where every housewife and raggedy-ass kid was a hard-nosed enemy and where the Gestapo kept a continuing check on civilian electric power usage so as to discover in nothing flat where and when an Allied agent tapped into a local circuit.

The J-E was something else, though. It was no larger than a briefcase. It operated on batteries and needed no giveaway aerial. But its main blessing was its conical signal. When it was on the air, its message beamed straight aloft in a narrow cone which could only be received by a similar set carried by an airplane flying a tight circle some

43

thirty thousand feet directly above. And, glory be to the OSS Research and Development people and other gods, the communicants were liberated from the anxious toil that characterized Morse; using mikes, the agent on the ground and his control officer in the plane could chat away like party-line gossips in Gump Stump Junction, I-o-way—without being overheard, or located, by anybody outside the cone. And the plane people recorded the entire exchange, allowing Home Plate to break down and analyze the conversation in case of garblings or trash sounds. The trick was to have the plane in precise conjunction with the agent on the ground. If either was in the wrong place at the agreed-upon time, all bets were off.

At 2246, the connection was made. They spoke German. English, if overheard in German territory, was prima facie treason. Wary, coded German dialogue was nothing unusual. Everybody in the Reich spoke circumspectly these days.

"This is Creampuff, calling the Bakery. Over."

"Hello, Creampuff. Glad to see you made it."

"The crossing went as planned. But the drive to Eckerdorf was a bitch. Did Sam and Harry get back home?"

"Safe and sound. What's with the villagers?"

"There's a light in the window."

"Excellent. You'll call on the folks in the morning?"

"After we get a report from Dieter. The colonel doesn't want to walk in cold."

"Sounds reasonable."

"How about our target, Bakery? Is it still stable?"

"Choo-choo says he's had a watch on the building around the clock. Routine movements only. No signs of Dingbat."

"Well, with luck, if Dingbat's there, we'll get him out."

"It's imperative that you do."

"On tomorrow night's J-E contact, we would like to hear what Choo-choo has to say about the current physical
44

layout at the target site. The colonel has the feeling that the stuff you gave us at Home Plate was pretty dated. He'd hate to have to open an oil drum with a feather duster."

"If the building proves to be too rugged, or if anything else is wrong, you'll just have to go into ad-lib. But whatever you have to do, Dingbat must come out. And he must be returned to Home Plate. At all costs. The requirement is absolute."

"I know. You've told us often enough, God knows."

"Will you be able to keep your timetable?"

"Provided the villagers agree to backstop us. If they poop out, we've got to revise."

"The Ivans will be working the same turf. So you must keep ahead of them, ahead of whatever they come up with."

"You never stop telling us that, either."

"Well, it's the main problem."

"Our main problem here, Mr. Bakeryman, is to keep our asses intact. There's a war on, you know."

"Your cover is working all right?"

"We had a couple of bad moments at two checkpoints— one on the Fellbach bypass north of Stuttgart, the other at Gelslingen. And during the crossing-over, of course. That had a nervous moment or two, sure enough. The others were Gestapo daily blacklist problems. We had the bad luck to have a name turn up on the list that was the same as one of our boys. It was straight coincidence. But a rotten one. Happily, Josef's paperwork is first-class, and it carried the day. After a couple of hours of arguing, we convinced the checkpoint honchos that it was a coincidence, pure and simple."

"You didn't change the name, the papers, after the first coincidence? How come?"

"Josef tried to work while we kept on the road. It was impossible. And then an officer on duty at the Gelslingen checkpoint bummed a ride with us to Ulm. What the hell

45

were we going to do—say, 'You mind waiting an hour or so, Herr Major, while we change the ID papers of this fellow with the embarrassing name?'"

"Any reason for anybody to put a tag on you? Something you did or said—at the checkpoints, or anywhere else?"

"Not that I know of."

"All right. Anything you need you haven't got?"

"Yeah. Assurance that we'll pull off this caper."

"I can give you that. You're going to pull it off. Because if you don't, you'll lose your PX privileges."

To his surprise, Lukas heard himself laughing. "Go on home, Bakeryman. Who needs you?"

"Nighty-night, Creampuff. Out."

Gretl Keller lowered the night glasses and turned from the attic window to activate her radio. She signaled her call letters and sent coded Morse on 2575 kilohertz:

RED GLARE: AGENT USURPED. ON STATION AS PLANNED. SIPHON HAS ARRIVED. EXPECT HIS CONTACT WITH RESSELS MOMENTARILY. WILL KEEP ADVISED. OLGA.

CHAPTER 6

Eckerdorf, Bavaria
25 April 1945

Friedrich Ressel had lost his right arm just below the shoulder. He'd been an infantryman, a participant in the breakthrough in which the Wehrmacht swept all the way to the French coast. And then a British grenade had rolled into a cellar one day, and that was it. His war was over. Now, four years later, he and his wife, Elsbet, impoverished by fate and ignored by the Fatherland, lived in this ancient house, left to Frau Ressel by a barely remembered uncle. The dossiers said the Ressels were Liberal Protestants, constantly invoking God because nobody else would listen.

Lukas sat with them at the worn table under the low, time-stained ceiling beams, watching them as they

47

looked earnest and spoke in soft Bavarian accents of peace, and the brotherhood of man, and the sharing of wealth. Their naïveté was something to behold, and he struggled to conceal his impatience with their smug self-righteousness by asking his questions with careful courtesy. *(Can you tell me, please, Herr Ressel, exactly how many dissidents there are in this area? Will you, perhaps, Herr Ressel, pinpoint on this map the locations of your people? May I ask, Herr Ressel, how you recruit?)*

For all his rustic earnestness, Herr Ressel's German was ornate, larded with glossy constructions that sounded as if they had been memorized:

"We use our churchly dedication as the rationale for our travels hither and thither, for our visitations, for our assemblies in the homes of communicants. Until now, the Gestapo has accepted our little group as a gaggle of nincompoops indulging in voodoo. Once we even had a Gestapo spy in attendance at one of our meetings, and I spoke of possible armed-resistance measures by using Bible verses and ecclesiastical jargon. It all went right over the poor chap's head, of course."

"*Is* there any armed resistance, Herr Ressel?"

"Well, not exactly. We are peace-loving folk, you must remember, and violence is repugnant to us."

Lukas could no longer hide his annoyance. "Then how do you plan to resist the Nazis, Herr Ressel? By sticking out your tongues behind their backs?"

Frau Ressel gave him a severe glance. She had been antagonistic from the first, and Lukas's testiness had obviously increased her own. She snapped, "The American has been asking a lot of questions, Friedrich. I think it's time we ask him precisely what he's doing here and what he wants of us."

Lukas did not return her glare, choosing instead to shrug and say simply, "The war is all but over for Germany as a nation. But there remains a lot of fighting, a lot of suffering.
48

And the Nazis will attempt to keep the coming occupation off balance. That's why we are here: to take a secret canvass. My government would like to identify the elements in Germany that might be counted upon to resist the Nazis, guerrillas to work with us toward a stable peace. Your name was given to us. There are those who say you are brave, peace-loving people, you and Frau Ressel."

Frau Ressel was unconvinced. Stonily she asked, "A peace mission, you say. This is why you have arrived in a convoy of battle vehicles, armed to the teeth, sneaking about like SS troopers?"

"Do you have any better ideas, Frau Ressel? With the Wehrmacht still in control of Bavaria and the Tyrol, you think we might better have strolled in, wearing top hats and cutaways?"

Herr Ressel, having been flattered, assumed a mediator's role. "There is," he crooned, "in the vicinity of Starnberg, I'm given to understand, a communist cell—a small group of Soviet sympathizers who infiltrated the UFA studios in Munich during the late twenties and early thirties and who now, as middle-aging, middle-class movie-production specialists, are employed by the Nazi propaganda film industry. Their leader, who is known along the grapevine as 'Herr Felix,' is said to be looking for ways to set up a resistance organization. I have made overtures via a cutout in Pullach, but I was rejected summarily because of our religious orientation. We've been informed that the communists deem it to be incompatible with their worldview."

The annoyance growing in him, Lukas came to the point. "All right, so we can't count on the communists to help us. How about the members of your church? Where are they in all this?"

"Well, they are, ah, hesitant. They hesitate to go against the existing, duly constituted authority." Ressel paused, staring at the wall as if more eloquent phrasings might be

49

written there. "They prefer to render unto Caesar what is Caesar's."

Lukas shook his head in open dismay. "In other words, resistance to the Nazis, persecutors of the church, is incompatible with your church's worldview."

The sarcasm was lost on Herr Ressel. But his wife gave Lukas another glare.

Herr Ressel sought to explain. "Our church is unhappy with Hitler and the Nazis because they have consistently and calculatedly ignored us as a force for moral and political equilibrium in the German context. We who are the direct representatives of the almighty God in heaven are a force to be reckoned with, but the Nazis have, in effect, sneered at what they see as our vacillation and hypocrisy and have relegated us, individually and corporately, to the parking cellar of the great German national edifice. Such indifference amounts to rejection, and for this reason I and my fellow churchmen are prepared to protest, to take the matter to the highest councils, even to the Führer himself. We shall insist on recognition; we shall demand inclusion in the hierarchy of whatever German national government eventuates after the current hostilities cease. We might even ask the Führer for the privilege of representing the Reich at the peace table."

Lukas, sickened by this grandiloquence, pushed back from the table and stood. "Well," he said, stiff, correct, unsmiling. "I think that does it for now. Thank you, Herr Ressel, for your advice. And thank you, Frau Ressel, for the tea."

Ressel made a gesture that suggested disappointment. "We haven't helped you much, I'm afraid. Is there anything else we can do?"

"You might recommend the best route to Munich."

"Munich? You're going there?" Ressel exchanged glances with his wife.

Frau Ressel shook her head, and told her husband, "I don't think that would be a good idea."

"Why not?" Ressel said expansively. "It would give her a quick, safe trip."

"I simply don't like the idea of her traveling around with Ami spies, or whatever."

"But these Amis are wearing SS uniforms. No one will dare question them."

"The Gestapo dares to question anyone."

"What's all this about?" Lukas asked.

Ressel's smile, always too quick, was now obsequious. "My wife's sister has been visiting us. She's from Kitzbühl, in the Austrian Tyrol. Her husband was a Landser. He fell in Russia two months ago. She has been wanting to return to her home, but her travel papers have expired, and she fears the roadblocks, the security checks, and all of the other rotten things going on. It occurred to me that you might take her along with you. At least as far as Munich."

"We are a military column. It would be difficult to explain the presence of a civilian woman—"

"Nonsense. Anything goes around here these days, my friend. Officers come through here all the time, their big cars loaded with loot and ladies. Besides, she could tell you all the shortcuts, the least damaged roads—that kind of thing. Since she and her husband lived in Munich for years, she knows the city as she knows her own hat."

Lukas considered the idea, and he began to see some advantages. "Where is she?"

"I'm here." The woman stepped out of the shadows in the hallway. "I apologize for eavesdropping. But I'd most certainly like to ride with you as far as Munich."

She was a striking woman of indeterminate age. Youngish, to be sure, but with a knowingness, a worldly savvy.

Ressel beamed fondly. "May I present my sister-in-law, Frau Gretl Keller? She'll be happy to be your tour guide. Provided, of course, you keep her from being arrested."

51

CHAPTER 7

Gretl Keller, concealed in the hallway, had been watching with
great interest. She was particularly
amused by Frau Ressel's discomfort
in the presence of the man called
Lukas. Frau Ressel had a morbid preoccupation with sex—a fact Gretl had
learned from the incident in the sheep-
cote yesterday. She had gone to the
feed bins to check her radio and,
as she worked, Frau Ressel had ambled into view. Gretl had watched un-
seen as the woman, glassy-eyed and
flushed, ogled the mating of a ram
and a ewe. It was no trick to see the
similarity between the expressions
then and now. Lukas was as sexy as
they come, a fact which clearly was
not lost on Frau Ressel, and it was
52

probable that her truculence was a device calculated to dam her own flowing juices. Gretl had also noted the woman's irrational anger when, while Gretl was undressing for a bath, Frau Ressel had come into the room. Gretl knew she had it all: exquisite breasts and a rounded, dimpled bum. And now Frau Ressel knew it, too, and, since Frau Ressel was built like a tuning fork, it was inevitable that her undisguised jealousy would sour their relationship.

Gretl had given much care to evaluating Lukas and his mission. She had scouted his little convoy, parked coyly on the wooded hill, and past experience showed her its inner composition. A line-crossing in force, such as this one, would demand that, in addition to its heavy weapons, the 232 contain a cache of blank documents, printed in London with Continental type on precise duplications of German paper stocks; an assortment of rubber stamps and metal seals, stolen from the Germans by other agents in earlier times; a camera and compact photo-lab for the production of passes, civilian ID cards and military Soldbücher, as needed; ration tickets for food and fuel; a packet of convincing trivia, such as theater stubs, pawn tickets, laundry claim slips, all showing signs of wallet wear; and at least twenty thousand dollars' worth of European currency, to be used for acquisitions, rentals, or bribes, and to be precisely accounted for at mission's end, provided the mission ended right-side-up. The truck's belly, she assumed, carried an ingeniously camouflaged tray of civilian clothing, authentically tailored in authentic cloths and bearing authentic labels, buttons, and laundry marks. It was almost certain that the job of one of the crew was to decide which documents would be needed to go with which wardrobe on which occasion, and it was up to Lukas to specify the occasion at a moment's notice.

Lukas was impressive in his Sturmbannführer's guise, she decided. No doubt about it, the Germans had the best-looking uniforms in this war. The Americans looked like Boy Scouts on a hike, the British like old Errol Flynn movies, the French like railroad conductors, and the Russians like ill-used sandbags. But the Nazis, the world's largest collection of puckered anuses, had uniforms that made them look as if they were in the military business. Lukas, cool and regal in the gray and red and black, the silver piping and the little dingdoolies, could have been the lead in some outlandish operetta. He looked wonderful.

As a graduate political scientist with a minor in the sociology of the Western world, she assumed that Lukas, as an American in his thirties, was tyrannized by the Puritan legacy, which copyrighted the God idea, made proprietary judgments as to who would be granted admission into Paradise, and established the plumbline for sexual morality. She was willing to wager that, for Lukas, orgasms achieved via means that Plymouth Colony had decreed improper remained perversions not to be permitted or enjoyed.

Which was too bad. He was beautiful, and under other circumstances it would be great fun to re-educate him, to free him from the shackles he didn't even know he was wearing.

She wondered now what he was really like beneath all the clench-jawed warrior posturing.

Her hunch said that he was no warrior at all. He sat there in his Nazi trappings, riffling through maps and pointing with pencils and nodding sagely and kissing Ressel's rump in the hopes of making some sense of Ressel's nonsense, as if he'd really rather be planting flowers or doing watercolors. There was nothing basically wrong with a man's setting out petunias or daubing paints. But a Ferdinand the Bull couldn't make an Alexander the Great, and she was sure that Lukas's efforts to deny this truth would—if he were permitted to live long enough—bring on an eventual explosion.

* * *

54

Later, having completed her transmission, she returned the tiny radio to its hiding place in her cardboard suitcase. She rearranged the extra underwear and stockings, acquired via Herr Ressel's influence with the Eckerdorf ration board, and then turned to regard herself in the dresser mirror, suddenly heavy with the memory of a dozen such dreary rooms in a dozen such melancholy intrigues.

The door eased open and Ressel came in from the hall. "I told the American I have to go to the toilet," he said in a low voice. "Is there anything you need?"

"No."

"The Ami seems to be swallowing our line."

"I suppose. It's really not important at this point."

"You called Mischa and his team?"

"They're on their way, disguised as Gestapo people."

"How will we explain things to the villagers?"

"What's to explain? There'll be a shootout between an SS armored column and some Gestapo agents on the ridge outside of town. Do you think for a moment that any villager will run up there and demand to know what's going on?"

Ressel frowned. "Do you think it's wise for you to go to the ridge with Lukas? Mischa might shoot him in all the excitement. And maybe you, too—"

"I want Lukas to see his team wiped out. So that he has no choice but to work with us. He is, after all, a potential gold mine—a direct route into Ami intelligence. We can have Eisenhower eating out of our hands if we play things right with Lukas."

Ressel was unconvinced. "Things go wrong, though. And I don't want to be left in charge. Something gigantic is moving, and I don't think I'm up to taking responsibility."

"Wait until you see what Moscow wants before you get your trousers damp. And never fear: I'll be in charge."

"There's the matter of the Kripo, too. They're sending a detective to look into the deaths of Gormann and Hinsel. He's supposed to arrive this evening, according to Bostik, the postmaster. What do we do about that, eh?"

"We do nothing. They were killed by a hit-and-run car while on night civil patrol. We can't be linked with that."

"I still feel badly about Gormann. He was my friend."

"And he would have reported me to the Gestapo if he'd seen me pretending to be your widowed sister-in-law. When he and Hinsel surprised me on the road the other night I told them I was on my way to Murnau to see my husband. I had to kill them. As I had to kill that Ami parachutist whose orders were to penetrate your little organization here."

"I still don't like it. Everybody in the village is upset. And you dented my Opel."

She snapped, "Then ask Commissar Mikoyan to replace me, goddam it."

After perfunctory good-byes at the Ressels' doorway, she and Lukas made for the VW he had parked in the alley. As they rounded the corner, there was a snorting of motors and a thumping of tires on cobblestones, and a pair of black cars circled the fountain in the square at the end of the street.

"Trouble has arrived," Lukas said.

"It's the Gestapo, is my guess. We'd better get a move on."

Lukas shook his head. "No. We'll wait them out. They'd hear our car and be all over us. The VW's not very noticeable in that alley where I left it. We'll push it into the stable there—that one behind the drygoods store—and cover it with hay."

"People are watching from behind all those shuttered windows. They'll tell where we are."

56

"I'm not so sure. These are farmers. They're not likely to want to take sides in an argument between the SS and the Gestapo. They'll play it safe. They'll stay behind the shutters and say nothing about seeing anybody. Besides, we won't be in the stable."

She gave him a look. "Where will we be?"

"We'll be running up the cow path to the fence line, then to the woods and my people."

"That's a hell of a run."

"You seem to be a healthy girl."

In the woods, Team Lukas was standing in a line beside the vehicles, hands up. Four men in long black overcoats faced them, waving pistols.

Colonel Jamieson was lying at the feet of the Gestapo raid leader, who was a tall man with a hawk nose and jutting chin. The colonel had been shot twice in the face. He was most certainly dead.

"Does anyone else want to be a hero?" Hawknose was asking, punctuating the words with little jabbing motions of his smoking pistol.

"I'll give it a whirl," Lukas said from his concealment in the underbrush.

Hawknose and his people spun about, surprised, to catch Lukas's shots full on. The four men collapsed like sacks. The tall one's fedora rolled across the clearing on its brim, a grotesque cartwheel.

The silence was heavy. As he and Gretl emerged from their cover, Lukas asked, "What happened here?"

Otto cleared his throat. "Well," he managed, "they came at us from behind while we watched for you. The colonel made the mistake of going for his gun."

"What are we going to do now, Lukas?" Manfred asked. "You're Jamieson's second-in-command. What's our move now?"

Lukas gave this some thought. Then: "Klaus, you and Dieter bury the colonel. Make a note of the map coordinates for Graves Registration. Otto, you and the captain and Ludwig strip the clothes, wallets, IDs—everything—from the Gestapo people. Josef and Manfred and Franz, I want you to strip everything usable from the 232 and the truck. I mean everything we can carry in the two Gestapo cars. Select the things you consider absolutely basic to our operating on the run. Leave everything else."

Josef gave him a worried stare. "What's your plan?"

"This incident, the colonel's death, has knocked everything silly. It would be useless to attempt to carry on as before. Our only hope is to buy some time, to fool the Gestapo into thinking their people have wiped out a phony SS column and have moved on to some other job. Josef, Franz, Manfred and I will go on to Munich, using the IDs of these Gestapo people. The rest of you will hit the trail for the safe house in Memmingen."

"What about these vehicles?" Franz asked.

"The four of us will put on the Gestapo clothes. We'll dress the Gestapo people in ours. We'll put them in the truck and the 232, then Franz will shoot up and burn the lot. We want to make it appear to whoever might care, that the SS unit was wiped out and the Gestapo people have gone to other things."

Otto asked, "What about the VW you left in the village?"

"You SS types are going to retrieve it for your ride to Memmingen. Once you're under cover there, the safe house manager will dump it in a river or something." Lukas glanced at each man in turn. "Any other questions?"

"Yes," Gretl said. "What about me?"

Lukas considered her somberly. "You will stay here, of course. With the Ressels, as before."

"I can't stay with the Ressels. After all that's happened here, the Gestapo will turn Eckerdorf inside out. What do

58

you think they'll do when they come across me? I'm unpapered. I'm an automatic arrest. I've got a chance only if I get back to Munich, where a friend of my late husband can supply me with updated documents that will get me to my apartment in Kitzbühl. If I don't go back with you, I'm finished."

"This thing has turned very dangerous. And our work in Munich will be even more dangerous."

"What can be more dangerous than being on the wrong end of the Gestapo? Come on, Lukas. I'm one of you now."

Lukas glanced at Josef. "Can we fix her up with some papers?"

Josef shrugged. "Only travel stuff. A phony Kennkarte. Some bus tickets. A paid-up rental receipt for a bombed-out room, maybe. But nothing that will cover her for any length of time."

"That's good enough," Gretl said. "Give me those. And until I get better documents, we'll say I'm your mistress, Lukas." She paused. "And don't forget. I know Munich. And I can help you, whatever the hell you've got going."

He humphed. "Are you ready to get your ass shot off?"

"No. I'll work very hard to keep that from happening."

"Good. Any other answer wouldn't have done." He regarded the group. "Anything else?"

Nobody spoke, so he nodded and they went to work.

Gretl, Lukas noticed, continued to watch him. There was something in her expression that suggested amusement.

Entry in Personal Diary of C. G. Brandt
Dijon, France
26 April 1945

My office is not in the château. Privacy is my primary need, and the château is like a country club. There is simply too much noise: canned music, clattering dishes, humming vacuums, the ringing of phones, the slamming of doors. This facility serves as one of the three major OSS holding areas—the others are in Harrington, England, and Namur, Belgium—where secret agents receive their final grooming before they set off on their missions. The agents are babied here—no mere trade jargon, but a real process in which men and women who await planes for one-way rides into some Pentagon-selected hell can indulge literally any appetite. To the uninitiated, this is sheer profligacy; to an insider, it's common sense. Those who face midnight drops into a vast malevolence need all the signs of positive support they can find.

As an insider, I understand these things, but I have much work to do, and, since the psyches of somebody else's agents are not high among my priorities, I prefer to do my work where frat house highjinks are not part of my problem. So I have set up my own closed shop in a cottage beside the river (the chiefs know only that I'm working under some kind of top Washington priority that permits no questions). I'm equipped with an overseas scrambler; a branch phone; a TWX with London, SHAEF and Washington; and courier service. The Joan-Eleanor with which I communicate with Team Lukas is, of course, installed in the RAF Mosquito bomber that flies me out of Dijon airfield.

This evening, after my supper of steak, eggs, and Riesling, I sat by the window overlooking the still-wintry river and thought about the Lukas thing.

Line-crossings are not my favorite maneuver, even for single pedestrian agents on tourist missions. Casualty rates are unacceptably high, thanks to mine fields, machine-gun scissors fire, and tight defense matrixes overall. And even if the crossing is successful, the amount and quality of information returned are usually low due to the shallowness of the penetration. Compared with the usual, the Lukas caper is a freaking technicolor spectacular, what with its veritable squad of people, its convoy of vehicles and its Montgomery Ward inventory of documents and costumery, all shoved into Germany from a nerve end of the U.S. Seventh Army. That Team Lukas made it, and is now careening through Bavaria in a race against time and the Russians, is a feat comparable to Hannibal's crossing of the Alps on elephants.

My desk is a Jacobean table piled with messages, reference books, photos, maps, phones, inkwells, rubber bands, paper clips and seven tons of additional detritus of the Compleat Spy Handler. I was staring at it, unhappy, when the branch phone rang.

It was Perlman, at Reception. He told me that Mr. Rutan had arrived and was being brought to my office in the jeep.

As I waited, my mind created little visions of the city from which the bureaucrat had come—its glistening monuments, its teeming streets, its cabs and trolleys and buses, its stenographers, politicians, bobby-soxers, tourists, soldiers, whores, G-men, and God knows who else, cursing and promising and praying and lying and hoping in the business of being American. Lucky Strike Green Has Gone to War. I'll Be Seeing You in All the Old Familiar Places. Chattanooga Choo-Choo. Knock-Knock, Who's There? Goodman, Dorsey, Waller, Hines, Sinatra, Pidgeon, Garson, Stewart, Gable, Harlow. The Three Stooges. Chew Mail Pouch. Ipana, for the Smile of Beauty, Sal Hepatica for the Smile of Health.

As usual, I was aware of things. Tires crunching on gravel outside, and a jeep motor snorting, then falling to idle. Muffled voices, and the buzzer. I went to the door. A

61

swirl of winter air admitted Rutan, a tall man who wore a ski parka and carried a Madison Avenue briefcase.

Rutan placed his briefcase on the floor and gave me the government sincere look. "I appreciate your receiving me on such short notice, Mr. Brandt. You have enough to do without interruptions from Washington, I'm sure."

I allowed as how we were all tilling the same soil. I indicated the easy chairs beside the fireplace. "Sit down. How about some cognac to chip away the ice?"

"I'll be eternally grateful."

"After a liter or two, you'll be able to take off your parka."

We exchanged smiles. Rutan, I saw, was wary, in the manner of one who has entered strange and not necessarily friendly country. He looked like a man who had enjoyed the good life. Smooth skin; fashionable horn-rim spectacles; thick hair, white at the temples; large hands that looked as if they had done very little heavy work. My years in government have taught me the signs of officious bureaucracy. This man wore them all, which was not surprising since his visit had been initiated by the State Department.

"So, then. What can I do for you, Mr. Rutan?"

"First, I'd like to correct any impression that the State Department seeks to meddle in your affairs." He took a lingering sip of his cognac. "My visit was arranged at the request of the secretary, who hopes only to learn what is known about the apparent suicide of the Russian general, Chesnikov. We understand that you, while serving as press secretary to our ambassador in Moscow, were fairly close to the general and, in fact, witnessed his death."

I reminded him that I had sent several lengthy reports to that effect through channels. "They were complete in all respects. I can't imagine what else I could add that might help the secretary."

"He would like a follow-up. A kind of update on what you've been doing lately and a clarification of a few points." Rutan continued to study the cognac in his glass.

"Why didn't he write a letter to the OSS director? Why send you all the way over here to question somebody who's already told all he knows?"

Apparently this was one he was waiting for, but not with pleasure. While his answer was quick and smooth, it carried a touch of annoyance. "He tried to do just that. But the director says you're on detached duty and behind a very tall gate."

"That's right. I'm off-limits to everyone. Even the secretary of state." Knowing what I knew of Rutan and his background, it pleased me to say this.

The satisfaction was short-lived. Rutan pulled his brief-case to him, lifted it to his lap and flipped the catches. He withdrew a sealed envelope and handed it to me. My eyes focused on the White House letterhead.

"And that's why the secretary authorized me to check with the president," Rutan said easily. "I did, and Mr. Truman asked me to give you this."

I slit the seal and read the message, handwritten in black ink:

4/25/45

Mr. Brandt:
Please tell Mr. Rutan what he needs to know. Sorry to bother you with this.

Regards,
H.S.T.

I gave Rutan a thoughtful stare. "When you carry credentials you don't screw around, do you?"

He smiled in that way of his and said nothing.

At this point I decided the conversation should be

recorded. To cover me if the recording is destroyed or lost, I'm transcribing it here:

"What is it you'd like to know, Mr. Rutan?"

"The secretary understands that you are pursuing more info on General Chesnikov's claim that a well-positioned Soviet would be defecting to us. Since your findings could throw light on matters our department is looking into, they might be helpful."

"You want it from the top?"

"Of course."

"Bits and pieces is what it is. It began when I was serving at the embassy in Moscow. As public information attaché and, covertly, OSS resident manager, I had developed quite a daisy chain of intelligence sources. There is a layer of liberalism in the Soviet hierarchy, no matter what the prevailing Washington wisdom might tell you to the contrary—well-placed individuals who are loyal to their country and, in general, supportive of their government and its goals but who are nonetheless unconvinced that the USSR's best interests are served by ruthlessness and devious militancy. They favor compromise and cooperation over *Sturm und Drang*."

"They have plenty of counterparts in the United States."

"But unlike those in the United States, these guys have to hold their views pretty close to the chest. Love and kisses for outsiders is antithetical to peace of mind in the Soviet bureaucracy."

"General Chesnikov was among these, ah, deviationists?"

"Presumably. Chesnikov, like Stalin himself, had risen to the heights the hard way. I say 'presumably' because he'd never given me the slightest indication that he was anything but unbendably hard-core.

64

Friendly, amusing, smart as hell. But a very stiff-necked Bolshevik. And when he approached me at an air show outside Moscow last February, telling me he was about to betray his country, I almost, as the GI saying has it, pooped a brick."

"You think he meant 'betray' betray? Like in treason?"

"I don't know. I have no way of knowing. I know only that he felt very bad about talking to me—about what he was getting set to do. Then, when he saw the NKVD closing in, he chose suicide over arrest. So, from this, we can assume that, first, what he was about to do would benefit the United States to a considerable degree and, second, that the NKVD knew about it, saw it as outright treason, and was about to pop his bung."

"And with his suicide he left the NKVD still wondering how much he had managed to tell you."

"Mmm. Recognizing that, the department, in the form of your old friend Cathcart, was worried that the NKVD might take exceptional steps to cut me away and interrogate me. He flew me home and put me in charge of the effort to determine just who the defector might be and to find out precisely what he has on his mind."

"I'm going to make some notes, Mr. Brandt. Is that all right with you?"

"I don't see why not."

"I'm a note-taker. It's an ailment I contracted when I discovered that good notes got me through Botany Four-oh-one, two hours lecture, three hours lab, prerequisite to prelaw and general undergraduate serenity."

"Why in hell should a lawyer have to know about botany?"

"Green things. He has to know how to count green

65

things." (Rutan laughs, then continues.) "I don't mind telling you that the secretary's temperature is rising on all this. The Russians have begun to cheat like hell on their Yalta agreements, which, in itself, is enough to send him into a hot spiral. Specifics on an important defector could do much for the secretary's peace of mind, since he is meeting with the president and the military honchos the day after tomorrow. At noon. He'll need details on what you and your people are doing about all this."

"The day after tomorrow? You're going back to Washington that soon?"

"I leave in an hour."

"You won't even catch supper—"

"On the plane. C-rations, I understand."

"You sure as hell aren't like any Washington hotshot I've ever seen. The rule of thumb is to stretch every trip and live like a king on the way."

"I'm no Washington hotshot, Mr. Brandt. I'm a hard-working civil servant."

"I'm glad there is one."

"You've determined who the defector will be?"

"I had two choices: Georgi Lano, a key member of the Narkomvneshtorg, or Commissariat of Foreign Trade, who, it was said, was due to be purged for wavering political enthusiasm; or General Vladimir Zelinkov, a deputy director of Soviet military intelligence, who, having worked so hard to get information on the Americans, had decided the Americans, being political nincompoops, have a much better way of life. Our dossiers suggest, and a very reliable informant has confirmed, that Zelinkov is a hedonist who likes shiny cars and sleek women, both of which are in short supply in Russia these days. It turned out to be Zelinkov."

"How did you determine that?"

"Actually, it was confirmed almost at once by subsequent developments. For one thing, Lano fell, or was pushed, from a window of his sixth-floor office on February fifth."

"Do we have any idea why?"

"Not really. We have to assume that his political enthusiasm was wavering a mite too much. So to speak. But the main confirmation came from Zelinkov himself. He messaged me through a chain of embassy cutouts on February seventh that he wanted my help in arranging an incident that would cover his defection. He'd schedule an aerial reconnaissance of the Tyrol front on April fifteenth. He would be in his personal plane, flown by his longtime personal pilot, who also wished to defect. The pilot would radio that they were being attacked by German planes. They would crash-land in the Tyrol on the high meadows of the Kaisergebirge, near the Alpine town of Saint Johann. My job was in two parts: first, to initiate reports that Zelinkov and his pilot had been killed in the crash, and, second, to have agents on site—reliable men who could lead him and his pilot to a safe house, where they could await an eventual overrun by the American army. In return for this assistance, and for his subsequent lifelong protection—in the States and under a new identity—he would reveal the Soviets' most carefully guarded secrets."

"So what do we know about Zelinkov, Mr. Brandt?"

"He's one of the old boys. Drafted by the czarist army in 1916, went directly to the Red Army when it was formed in 1918, and rose steadily to the top as a cavalry officer, then as a specialist in tank warfare. Studied armored operations at Frunze Academy, did a turn in the Manchurian dustup with Japan in the thirties, and subsequently became one of the Kremlin's fairhairs when he discovered and rounded up a British spy ring in Leningrad during the Russian-Finnish war. He was transferred to intelligence work shortly thereafter, and he's smart, I'll tell you. He gave me and the other embassy people heavy nightmares now and then."

"So he should be in a very well informed position. Able to tell us very high-level things. Right?"

"There are few in the Kremlin who are better informed, Mr. Rutan."

"Continue, please."

"I reported all this immediately to OSS Washington and General Donovan himself authorized me to make the team selection. I chose Colonel William Jamieson, an experienced commando officer, as leader of a two-man team. As the second member I chose an army private named Lukas, who is fluent in German and Russian and could serve as team spokesman. I found him buried in a basic training regiment after a heavy search of Adjutant General files. Jamieson and Lukas hit it off well from the start."

"So what went wrong?"

"The date, the weather, and the Germans."

"Explain, please."

"Our plan was to paradrop Jamieson and Lukas so that they could be waiting for Zelinkov's crash-landing. The plan was that our people would lead the defectors north and west to Memmingen, Germany, where we have another safe house whose overrun by U.S. troops is virtually guaranteed. But on April first the news came: Zelinkov would be making his aerial recon on April tenth, by order of Marshal Zhukov. Since Zelinkov had no alternative—Zhukov's the law on everything over there these days—we scrambled to revise our own do. I rescheduled Jamieson and Lukas so that they would be dropped at the rendezvous two hours before the Russians got there. But on April tenth there was a localized blizzard over the rendezvous point. Our drop plane couldn't even find the drop zone and had to bring Jamieson and Lukas back here. Zelinkov and his pilot were forced down smack in the middle of a bivouac of German Alpine troops. The Russians were captured, of course, and turned over to the Gestapo for interrogation. Our last location for Zelinkov—code name Dingbat—is at a Gestapo interro facility in Obermensing, a suburb on the west side of Munich.

"I redesigned the mission. Munich is an intense-security zone; a drop was out of the question. So a line-crossing in force was indicated. Four days ago Jamieson, Lukas, and a small group of specialists from OSS penetrated the lines via a Danube bridgehead and were making their way to Munich."

"How will they rescue the Russians, Mr. Brandt?"

"The plan is to commandeer them. The team is disguised as an SS special-interrogations unit. It has forged documents that authorize it, in the name of SS National Security Chief Himmler himself, to take charge of the prisoners and move them to Berlin. But instead of to Berlin, they'll take them to a safe house being set up in Eckerdorf, a Bavarian village, where an anti-Nazi religionist has established a resistance movement. They'll wait there for an American over-run."

"Then there should be no real problems, eh?"

"There's a very real problem, Mr. Rutan. The Soviets have found out that Zelinkov is really a defector and they want him back. They're after him, too."

"Damn."

"You should have heard what *I* said."

"That means the Soviets are racing us to Obermensing?"

"That's right, Mr. Rutan."

"And even if our team gets Dingbat, the Soviets will keep trying to grab him back—here or Stateside. Right?"

"The Russians do not want us to have conversations with Zelinkov. They'll do anything to keep that from happening."

(An interval of silence here.)

"May I ask one more question, Mr. Brandt?"

"Sure."

"When in hell are you going to pour me another drink?"

The recording continues with some superficialities, and I turned off the machine when Rutan stood up and said his good-byes.

I am pleased to have the opportunity to shaft the son of a bitch.

I am not at all pleased that Lukas missed his J-E contact last night.

If he doesn't report in tonight, we've got trouble.

CHAPTER 8

**Munich, Germany
27 April 1945**

They arrived in the city at dawn, only to be stalled at a checkpoint at the east end of the Maximiliansbrücke.

Military activity west of Munich was intense, thanks to the Wehrmacht's preparations for the great horde of Americans pressing in from Augsburg and areas to the north. To avoid major checkpoints, Lukas directed his cars over a loop of back roads that led into the city from the southwest. After a nightmarish drive that took them past the Ammersee and through Starnberg, then north through Pullach, Harlaching and Haidhausen, they were virtually immobilized at the city's rim by a horror of wagons, carts, army

71

trucks, bicycles, charcoal-burning buses and a lava-flow of refugees.

Eventually their Gestapo credentials, combined with much threatening talk, enabled them to bypass the jam and cross the Isar, only to be stalled by traffic again. They left the cars to stand in a forlorn huddle, staring silently at one hundred and twenty square miles of broken concrete, splintered wood and shredded trees. Uprooted trolley rails twisted skyward; toilet bowls and bathtubs hung from palisades of laths and plaster; the streets were mere lanes coursing through canyons formed of smoldering bricks; and old women poked at the wilderness with sticks, weeping soundlessly under their shawls. The air was redolent of sewage and decay and gas leaks and char. Lukas and his people felt an insistent need to gag.

Manfred sighed and, with a hand, shaded his eyes like an Indian scout examining a sunny distance. But the others weren't fooled. There was no glaring sun, and they'd long known from his accent that Munich was his hometown. And so they said nothing, out of respect for his struggle to hide his crushing sense of loss.

It was a loss they all felt in different measure, Lukas suspected. He himself had never before been in Munich, yet details were poignantly familiar: a door of oak and beveled glass, like the one on the Hertel Avenue house; a woman's shoe, which could have come from his mother's closet; a 1936 Ford, holed and torn and charred; an empty Bayer aspirin bottle, unaccountably upright on a scarred gate-leg table. The city was drifting into death, and it was everybody's city, the whole world's city, and for anyone who breathed there was something here, some single sight or thing, that made the death a cause for personal mourning.

Lukas decided it was time to jettison their excess baggage. "Frau Keller, come here, please."

"What's up?" Her face was rosy in the morning light.

72

"I must ask you to leave us now. We have some heavy work to do, and I'm sure you're anxious to get home—"

"I'd like to stay with you as long as possible. The police are buzzing around like flies."

"That Kennkarte Josef gave you should carry you through. You'll make out fine."

"Please?"

"Sorry."

"If that cop sees me walking away from your group now he'll be very suspicious." She nodded toward the dust cloud rising beyond the stalled cars ahead, where laborers in striped fatigues struggled to clear a brickslide that had blocked the way. A member of the Hilfspolizei supervised importantly, rocking on his heels, hands clasped behind him.

"God, but Germans are insufferable." Josef, who had been watching the man, sniffed. "Put a trolley driver's uniform on one of them and he becomes Julius Caesar in Gaul."

"You are a German," Lukas reminded.

"So I've got a right to complain, right?"

Franz snickered.

Lukas, giving up on the woman for the moment, approached the auxiliary policeman and flashed the Gestapo credentials, a green folder with LUKAS, ALEX, typed across the marbled flyleaf, his photo glued neatly opposite, his signature scrawled below. "Berlin District, RSHA," he announced in the arrogant manner of a professional bully.

The man, an amateur bully, groveled in the presence of this superior force. "Good morning, sir. What might I do for you, sir?"

"A question. How do I find the Gestapo district office in all of this disgusting garbage?"

"I'm not at all sure, sir. I believe there's a temporary bureau near the Stiglmayer Platz. Across from where the Nymphenburgerlandstrasse begins. You can get firm directions from the SS checkpoint at the next intersection, which is around the corner behind that building there." He waved at a sagging tower of junk that could have been, at one time, an apartment house.

"How do I get to the Nymphenburgerlandstrasse from here?"

"Well, sir, it isn't easy. I suggest you turn left here and pick up Hildegardstrasse to the dead end at Herrnstrasse. Right there, then follow the rubble lane to Ludwigstrasse. Left on Briener to the Stiglmayer Platz, and there you are."

"How about petrol?"

"There's an SS Tankstelle near the first-aid station in the park, sir. They serve SS and War–Important Work vehicles upon presentation of certified trip tickets or travel orders. But they're out of gas today, according to their sign." The man smiled sympathetically, oily. His eyes were close together, and he smelled of ancient sweat and boiled cabbage.

"All right. Thanks." Lukas called to Manfred and Franz, who were returning to the Opel. "Follow us. Keep close."

As Lukas inched the Mercedes into the left turn, Josef asked, "What's all the interest in Gestapo headquarters?"

"That business at Eckerdorf put us badly off balance. We're out of sync with our J-E contacts. We've got to regroup and set up a new J-E schedule."

"At *Gestapo* headquarters?"

"If we're lucky."

Josef shook his head. "You are a very odd fellow."

"I'll say."

"He makes me nervous, too," Frau Keller said from the backseat.

Lukas ignored her. "By now these cars have been missed by some Gestapo motor pool and there's a search on for them and their people. We've got to find other wheels. Soon."

74

"I've been thinking about that," Josef said. "I think it's best we go back to our SS IDs, uniforms and all. We can dump the cars and steal a truck or something. Something big enough to carry the four of us and our radios and gear."

Lukas disagreed. "Not yet. A Gestapo guise gives us muscle. We'll steal some new tags for these two cars. It's a long shot, but the benefits are worth going for."

"And you plan to steal the tags at Gestapo headquarters?"

"If the situation allows. But the main reason we're visiting Gestapo headquarters is to use our wireless."

Josef groaned. "Have you popped your bung?"

"We have to get word to Brandt. We need to use the wireless, because he can pick us up on the J-E only if he knows where to circle the plane. We'll wireless some coordinates and set up a J-E conference for midnight, or early tomorrow morning. But to use the wireless we need a power source. A power source that's reliable and not likely to be monitored by the Gestapo. What reason would they have to monitor the current at one of their own headquarters buildings?"

Josef gave him a look that was part incredulity, part admiration. "You mean we'll walk into Gestapo headquarters, plug into an outlet, and radio Brandt at Dijon?"

"If we're lucky."

Josef made a face. "My aching, GI back."

During her teens, while still enrolled in Moscow's Korsakov International School of the Arts, there had been a student from Leningrad, name of Sergei Kobol, a flannel-shirt smart aleck whose father, an important Party functionary, thought Sergei might benefit from a year or two of study among the sons and daughters of the Soviet upper crust and Moscow's diplomatic corps. Sergei, it turned out, enjoyed an extraordinary talent: he could copulate so skillfully and so sneakily he managed, at four separate

75

Saturday afternoon socials and in a reception hall full of girls, their dance partners, and a pair of chaperones, to bring the greatest of all adventures to four of her more devil-may-care classmates. This was no mere giggling dormitory apocrypha; this was straight stuff. She had twice (on advance information from Mitzi van Ober, one of Sergei's beneficiaries) observed the phenomenon from a well-placed balcony. She had never availed herself of Sergei's services—he was too meaty and rustic for her tastes—but she had evermore marveled at his athletic audacity during Optional Ballroom Interlude with partners whose dresses buttoned down the front.

There was something of Sergei in Alex Lukas.

She'd thought otherwise at first, of course.

But now she was compelled to admit that she had been wrong. A warrior he was. Inventive. Capable. Audacious.

Like Sergei Kobol.

"Why are you laughing?" Lukas wanted to know.

"It's nothing. Keep your eyes on the road."

"What road?"

"That area ahead, where the brick piles are lower than the other brick piles." She laughed again.

They found the place eventually. It was a large house, with a pocked facade and mansard roof and tall windows whose shutters hung askew. There was a courtyard to one side, now serving as a parking area for three Mercedes, two VWs, a Horch and a very large Maybach. Two uniformed SS riflemen bracketed the front door. They looked cold and unhappy.

Lukas pulled the Mercedes alongside the Maybach, and Franz parked the Opel near the gate, facing the street.

Lukas said, "All right, Frau Keller, this is the absolute end of the line. I want you to get out of this car and walk down that street there and keep going until you get to your home."

"I—"

"You've had your free ride. We have work to do, and you're in the goddam way."

"No reason to get huffy about it."

He glared at her.

"I'm going, I'm going." She eased her splendid legs from the car, stood erect, pulled her coat about her, and strode off peevishly, her heels clicking on the cobblestones. She did not look back.

Lukas turned to the men. "I'll be going into the building with you, Manfred, and you, Josef. Manfred will carry the briefcase with the wireless, Josef will carry the musette bag with the grenades and extra ammunition for our three pistols. You, Franz, must switch plates on the cars. Take the ones from these other vehicles that fit best on the mounts—Mercedes for Mercedes, VW for our Opel. Then stand guard and cover this side door with the Schmeisser. Not too obvious, but not too skulky, either. We must keep things looking normal. Questions?"

Probably because he felt somewhat left out of things, Franz asked the obvious. "What happens inside?"

"We play it as it comes. I'll do the talking. The rest of you say as little as possible if somebody speaks to you. I would like to get as near the roof as the inside layout permits. I would like to develop a situation where we are under minimum observation by whoever is in there. But the main thing is for all of us to keep loose, adaptive, ready to exploit any advantage. When in doubt, take your cues from me. If it all looks hopeless—if nothing works right and there's obviously no way to get on the air, then we'll just walk out, get in our cars and drive off. Nothing fancy. Just leave. Okay?"

Franz says, "And if things don't go so well?"

"We're soldiers. We shoot our way clear. But only as a last resort. The mission is to get to Obermensing without attracting notice. To spring Dingbat and get him the hell back to SHAEF. But we can't do that with hot cars that are low on gas and no word to Brandt on where we are and why."

"If I plug in, what do I tell Brandt?" Manfred asked.

"To J-E us tonight at midnight from coordinates that place him between the eastern terminus of the Augsburg–Munich Autobahn and Obermensing. We'll try to have our set in defilade beside the Wurm River, halfway between Obermensing and Blutenburg. Got that?"

Manfred's pen made tiny notes on the palm of his left hand. "How about a KL signal?"

"No. The mission isn't blown yet. Just off course and in need of retailoring."

"Any questions for Brandt?"

"No. I'll save them for the J-E contact."

Franz settled into the Opel, his Schmeisser on the front seat beside him. Josef followed Lukas and Manfred around to the front door and up the steps. They nodded politely in answer to the rifle salutes delivered halfheartedly by the guards, then pushed through the boarded door into a reception hall at the foot of a large and badly scuffed staircase. A Rottenführer sat at a desk that supported a 1930's telephone switchboard. "Help you?" he murmured, indifferent.

Lukas showed his credentials. "Sturmbannführer Lukas, RSHA, Berlin. Where is the officer in charge?"

The corporal was no longer indifferent. "Oh, good morning, sir." He stood and straightened his tunic with two quick pulls at its tails. "Ah." He glanced vaguely over his shoulder toward a large room whose entrance off the vestibule was marked by partially closed French doors. "I believe that Obersturmführer Vogel is on the phone, sir. Ah—"

"The phones are working?"

"Only the field phones, Sturmbannführer. The municipal lines have been out since last night. We are trying to have them repaired."

"Are there any lines through to Berlin?"

The corporal tried hard to control what seemed to be a
78

mad desire to laugh. "Well, no, sir. We haven't had direct phone contact with Berlin for some days now. The city seems to be cut off from our trunks. Our conversations with RSHA are few and pretty much confined to the wireless."

"You have a wireless here?"

"Yes, sir. In the second-floor radio room."

"Excellent. I have a top-priority message I must send at once to Reichsführer SS Himmler. Show us the way."

The Rottenführer faltered, his eyes showing uncertainty. "Well, sir, I suggest you talk to Obersturmführer Vogel about that. All wireless traffic has to be cleared through the officer in charge."

"Very well. Vogel is in there?" He nodded toward the French doors.

"Yes, sir, but he's on the phone—"

Lukas ordered his people, "Come along."

They entered the large room, where a thin, balding man in a blue serge suit lolled behind a huge desk, resting in a swivel chair, his drooping eyes contemplating the city beyond his partially boarded-up window. Lukas saw that the desk phone was off its cradle, evidence that they had caught Lieutenant Vogel, red-handed, at woolgathering on Gestapo time.

"Wake up, Vogel. There's a war on, and I have a message that must reach the Reichsführer SS before noon. And stand up when a Sturmbannführer speaks to you."

The man blinked, then managed to rise to his feet without upsetting his chair. "Sorry, sir. May I ask who—"

"I am Sturmbannführer Lukas, Special Operations Section, Amt Four, RSHA, Berlin. I and my people are here in this godforsaken city as emissaries of Reichsführer Himmler. He is expecting a report from me and there are no phone lines open. I must therefore have my man here"—he jerked his head toward Manfred—"send a coded wireless message. Your receptionist says I can't do this without your approval. I do have your approval, don't I, Vogel?"

79

Vogel stammered. "I most certainly don't want to interfere with—I mean, I'll simply have to ask you for your ID and a copy of your orders. Not that I—"

"Stop whining, Vogel. Of course you must see my papers. I'd have you up on charges if you hadn't asked." He threw his Gestapo folder and orders packet on the man's desk.

Vogel read, his lips moving slightly, then handed back the documents. "Thank you, sir," he said apologetically. "Come with me, please. I'll lead you to the radio room."

They clattered up the scuffed stairway and were taken to a corner room packed with radio gear. A Sturmmann slouched at a set, earphones bulging. When he saw his CO, he threw his cigarette into an ashtray and rose quickly to attention.

"Out of the way, Pieck," Vogel said briskly, trying to salvage something of his dismal first impression on these important visitors. "The Sturmbannführer's man wants to signal Berlin."

"As ordered, sir." To Manfred the man said, "The set is on and ready. You might want to adjust the key—"

Manfred slid into the chair, and, as his hands moved expertly about the machinery, he said, "No matter. Berlin recognizes my fist." Glancing at Lukas, he asked, "Any final instructions, Sturmbannführer?"

"No. Just send the code phrases the Reichsführer has stipulated."

"Yes, sir."

In forty-two seconds, Manfred had messaged Brandt at Dijon and had received acknowledgment.

Gretl Keller knelt in the blue shadows of a ruined apothecary, feeling the cold in her bones and an uncharacteristic depression in her soul, or whatever it is in the chest that measures moods. She opened the musette bag, lifted the inner flap, and threw the key on her battery-operated
80

KK-3. Glancing about once more to confirm her aloneness, she tapped out her ID and sent in code:

BOLSHOI: MEET ME POINT A. AMIS ABOUT TO MAKE MOVE. OLGA.

CHAPTER 9

As they descended the stairs, Lukas observed that Obersturmführer Vogel was less than delighted with the way his morning was going. Which was understandable; assignment to a desk, with nothing to do but catnap between phone calls that never came from a hopelessly cutoff headquarters far to the north, was the heaven soldiers dream of, but to have a gaggle of hotshot visitors from that headquarters materialize in mid-daydream was the stuff of nightmares. When one had successfully eluded all that glorious fighting and dying out there, it was a dreadful turn when the Out-There marched in, waving bossy documents and demanding radio time.

"Tell me, Vogel: Don't you get bored sitting around this wretched place when there's adventure and excitement to be had only a few miles to the west?"

Vogel became even unhappier. How did one answer such a question? To say yes would be to invite a transfer to where adventure and excitement could be had; to say no was to admit that one was lacking enthusiasm for the war. To say either to a stiff-necked Nazi autocrat was sure to bring on a badly ruined day.

"One serves where one is posted," Vogel said glumly.

"Ah, yes. To be sure. But one can be posted to all kinds of pleasant places, depending how well one plays the game with one's superiors."

Vogel gave him a swift little glance. "I don't altogether understand the Sturmbannführer—"

"It's quite clear, I think. Help me, give me what I need and when I need it, and nice things can happen in your career. In polite society, it's called bettering one's self. In military patois, it's called covering one's ass."

At the door to his office, Vogel asked carefully, "What might I do to better myself, sir?"

"You have already bettered yourself considerably, Vogel, by facilitating my radio contact with Berlin. I won't forget that, I assure you. But I do need a few more things."

Vogel seemed vaguely relieved. "Name them, sir, and if I can provide them they're yours."

"Ah. Good." Lukas smiled primly. "But first: How many men do you have in the building right now?"

Vogel considered this. "Well, there are two men at the door, a man on the switchboard, three staff noncoms, a radioman, and three guards in the cellar. Ten, all told. Not counting the ten agents out on assignments, that is."

Lukas, pulling on his gloves, asked, "What are the guards guarding in the cellar?"

"Prisoners, sir. Our jail is in the cellar."

83

"I see. Which brings me to my next request. The radio message I just received from Berlin orders me to Obermensing, where I am to take custody of a prisoner currently under interrogation. But to get there I must have more fuel for my two cars. You have a supply here, I'm sure."

Vogel shrugged. "A very small supply, sir. And the octane is nothing to rave about. It's kept in a field tanker parked in the rear courtyard. You are welcome to fill up."

Lukas told Manfred, "Go see to it, then. You, Josef, stay with me."

"I have to find the latrine, Sturmbannführer."

"Well, take care of it and come right back."

"Yes, sir."

Vogel watched indifferently as Josef disappeared down the corridor.

"Tell me, Vogel: What do you know of the thing at Obermensing?"

Another quick glance, this one wary. "I'm afraid I don't know very much about it, sir. Only that it's a special interrogations center for special prisoners. And that the one time I asked questions about it I was told most bluntly to shut up and mind my own business."

"Do you have a phone connection with it?"

"Yes, sir."

"I want to call out there. I want to advise the commandant that I'm on the way to pick up the Russian general."

Vogel's eyes betrayed his surprise. "Russian general?"

"Yes. Zelinkov. The one they've been questioning. My orders are to pick him up."

"Well, sir, you'd be going considerably out of your way. The Russian isn't at Obermensing. He's downstairs. In our jail. He was brought here last evening."

It was Lukas's turn to show surprise. "Well, now, that's an interesting turn. Why was he brought here?"

"Safekeeping, the escort said. Obermensing is in the

84

direct path of the American Seventh Army. My orders are to hold General Zelinkov for pickup by an Oberst von Klieg of the Abwehr's Foreign Armies East."

Lukas, recovering, let his annoyance show. "Who gave you such an order?"

"I received a phone call from Bad Reichenhall. Oberst von Klieg himself. He said General Zelinkov was to be interrogated personally by the head of Foreign Armies East, General Gehlen."

"How did von Klieg know Zelinkov was in your jail?"

"Because he had also called Obermensing and ordered the commandant there to transfer the prisoner to my control."

Lukas snapped, "Do you always do what the Wehrmacht intelligence people tell you to do? By mere phone calls?"

"Sir, everything is so confused today. Nothing ever makes sense anymore. Orders, counterorders. Decisions, decisions altered or cancelled. Officer A in charge in the morning, Officer B replaces him in the afternoon. I simply take things at face value. I take things as they are and as they come. First things first. Anything else is madness."

Lukas sniffed. "Well, there is one thing you need not be confused about, Vogel. You can be quite sure that I am about to take custody of General Zelinkov."

"As you wish, Sturmbannführer." Vogel shrugged. "As I say, I take things as they come. You're here first, you get the Russki hotshot. It's nothing to me."

"Good thinking, Vogel. Now, would you be so kind as to have General Zelinkov brought to me? Along with his interrogation transcripts and other related documents."

Vogel called across the reception area to the man at the switchboard. "Ring up Schultz and tell him to bring me the Russian general and his papers. At once."

"As ordered, sir."

"Would you like to wait in my office, Sturmbannführer? I have some excellent brandy."

85

"That would be nice. But I really must get on the road as quickly as possible. Berlin might be entirely cut off soon, and Reichsführer SS wants to talk to the Russian as a possible armistice intermediary."

Vogel understood. "I see. Now it begins to make some sense. I was wondering why you'd go to all the trouble of getting a Russian general to Berlin, which is due to be taken by the Russians any day now."

Josef returned, his face pink from a scrubbing. "This place could use some hot water in the washroom," he said to no one in particular.

"This place could use a lot of other things," Vogel said, an edge in his voice.

Josef gave him a moment of thoughtful appraisal. Then: "Don't misunderstand me, Obersturmführer. I am very grateful for your hospitality. I am not complaining, I am commiserating with you and your people. I don't know how you keep your cool good nature with all the provocations you must endure around here."

Lukas was about to ask Vogel what was keeping his guards so long when they appeared at the far end of the corridor, two huge Bavarian bookends bracketing a reedy and thoroughly unhappy man wearing the remains of a Red Army uniform. As they approached, he could see that the Russian was more than unhappy—he was puff-eyed, lacerated and multihued with bruises and knuckle marks, and he wasn't walking, he was being dragged, boot toes scraping, by the beefy guards. His breathing was a pained wheezing.

Lukas glanced at Vogel. "I see you have been questioning him. Will he live?"

"Who's to say?" Vogel examined his fingernails. "But don't blame me for the condition of the merchandise, Sturmbannführer. That's the way he arrived from Obermensing."

86

Josef went to the ungainly trio and peered closely at the Russian's face. "This man is in very bad shape," he said. He looked at Lukas. "We'd better get him into the car right away. I'll do what I can with the first-aid kit."

Lukas, feeling slightly ill, pointed a finger at the Bavarian SS men. "You two get him outside and into my Mercedes at once. And carry him. Carefully. Or you will have first me, then Reichsführer SS Himmler to answer to."

They left the building in a loose huddle, the Russian and his carriers first, then Obersturmführer Vogel, followed by Lukas and Josef. Franz and Manfred waited beside the cars.

They placed General Zelinkov in the backseat of the Mercedes, where Josef sat, fussing with bandages. Lukas was climbing into the driver's seat when the firing began.

At first it sounded like the firecrackers at a Chinese parade—scattered poppings, pings and bangings. Then the glass beside Lukas's shoulder turned milky with holes and webs, and there was a terrible drubbing and crashing. He managed a look at the courtyard, and his mind registered vignettes: Franz swinging a Schmeisser like a garden hose, and three men in a Wehrmacht weapons-carrier tumbling to the ground in a welter of arms and legs and clattering weapons; Manfred lying on the cobblestones, his head a red smear; Vogel sprawled on the stone steps, mouth gushing blood; the two guards, running, being cut down by the flare of fire from a Horch sedan near the gate.

"Get down, Josef! And keep the general covered!"

"Get this fuggn car moving, Lukas," Josef snarled. "I'll give you covering fire!"

He slammed the Mercedes into gear and spun the wheel, and they fishtailed across the cobbled courtyard, sideswiping the Horch en route. The backseat filled with a rattling thunder as Josef emptied a Schmeisser clip into the sedan's flanks.

87

"I got two of the bastards!" Josef exulted.

"And they got Franz and Manfred."

"Who are they?"

"Russians, is my guess." He consulted the rearview mirror. "Hold on. They've broken clear and are coming fast. How's your ammo?"

"Two more clips. Three grenades."

They careened around a fountain in a square, then picked up the broad avenue of Nymphenburgerlandstrasse, heading west at a speed that had the Mercedes keening. Bomb damage was much lighter here, and the street was generally clear of rubble.

"I'm going to let them get a little closer, Josef. Then do what you can."

He used the mirror to watch the action.

The Horch closed quickly to within twenty yards. Josef, kneeling on the backseat, pulled the pin line on a potato-masher, waited a frightening few seconds, then almost gently tossed the grenade to the street. It detonated at the front and to one side of the pursuing sedan, and he saw whirling smoke and a confetti of fenders and wheel parts. The Horch became a sudden ball of fire that zigzagged, a drunken comet, across the avenue, through a fence and down an embankment to a conclusive explosion in a drainage ditch.

Lukas steered the car to the curb and braked to a halt.

"Are you all right, Josef?"

"I'm all right, but I think General Zelinkov has bought the farm."

"He's dead?"

"Not yet. But he has two bullets in the wrong places."

Lukas climbed out and went to the back door. He leaned in to examine the general, whose head lay in Josef's lap.

"He's saying something," Josef said softly. "In Russian, I think."

88

Lukas listened for a time, then pushed himself clear of the car and took a deep breath. "Well," he said in English, "that's just dandy, that is."

"What is?"

"'There's a fox among our poplar trees.' Whatever that means. And I think he said he's left a very important message at a roadside crucifix near Saint Josef in the Tyrol."

"The *Tyrol?* Kee-rist, that's—"

"At least fifty miles south of us. In the heart of the remaining German army."

The driver, a smelly man named Tokov, eased the car to a halt behind a gutted gas station. Through a gap in the ruins, Gretl Keller could see Lukas and Josef finishing the job of burying the dead Russian.

"I want you to do something, Tokov," she said.

"What is it, Comrade?"

"Shoot the shorter man. Then bring the other here. I want to interrogate him."

"As you wish, Comrade."

She watched as Tokov stole along the broken alley. When at last he moved into the clear, his gun made three popping noises, and Josef whirled madly and tumbled down a slope of rock and timber.

Lukas, she saw, was frozen, helpless, mute with shock and anger and loss.

She took position in the shadow of a rubble pile. Aiming carefully, she sent two bullets through Tokov's thick body, and he collapsed lumpily, like a gut-shot bear.

She went then to Lukas, who stood staring at the bodies, and handed him the pistol.

"What in hell are you doing here?" he managed.

"That man—he said he was a Kripo detective—arrested me for having faulty papers. He was driving me somewhere when he saw you being chased. He followed you here. When he left the car to get you I found that gun in the map pocket."

Lukas peered at her as if she had just arrived from the moon. "Why did he shoot Josef?"

"I—I don't know."

"You realize you've just killed a cop?"

"Yes," she said softly.

"You're in real trouble now, you know."

"I know."

"And you're now on your own. I have to go to Austria."

"Austria? That's my home. The Tyrol, remember? I'll help you. Besides, all your friends are gone. I'm the only friend you have left."

"I'm a soldier. I have a mission."

"Lukas. Please. You're all I've got left."

He sighed. "Well, then. Let's get these bodies under the rubble. Where's the cop's car?"

"Over there. Behind that gas station."

"The bastard didn't have to shoot Josef like that."

"War is cruel. Filled with unexplainable things."

"He just walked up and shot him. He didn't even say a word. Just walked up and shot Josef in the head."

"He would have shot you, too. I couldn't allow that."

"Why, for Christ's sake? Why couldn't you allow it?"

"I just couldn't. It's—well, unexplainable."

He waved his hands, exasperated. "All right, all right. Go get the goddam car. You do drive a car, don't you?"

"I'm a good driver."

"Then go get the goddam car."

"You won't regret this, Lukas."

"Bah."

CHAPTER 10

The Mercedes was useless. Holes were everywhere, in the radiator, the fenders, the roof. The tires were in shreds. The fuel tank had burst. Most of the glass was shattered, and there was a hissing, the dripping of oil.

The police car was a beauty—a large touring sedan, a lustrous black, accented with polished nickel fittings. It looked as if it could go a hundred miles an hour. But its motor turned over, ran briefly, then wheezed to silence. The gas gauge read stolidly, immutably empty.

Lukas shrugged. "So we will walk."

"To *Austria?*"

"It'll work to our advantage, actually. The alert is out for two men and

91

a woman in a Gestapo Mercedes. We'll have a better chance as two soldiers hitchhiking to a new assignment at the sappers' school at Murnau."

"How in hell will we manage that?"

"In the backseat of the Mercedes is my Sturmbannführer uniform. There's also Josef's Scharführer's uniform. That will do for you."

"What about my hair, my chest? I have a very impressive pair there, in case you haven't noticed."

"I've noticed."

"So?"

"So pile your hair under the steel helmet and wear that Wehrmacht raincoat that's in the car. That should hide your assorted feminine features. But bring along those clothes you're wearing. Carry them in that big musette bag of yours. It might be necessary to have you change sexes again."

She began to rummage through the gear in the backseat. "How about travel papers? Two soldiers without them won't make it through Munich, let alone to Murnau."

"Hand me a sheet of that 223d SS Panzerdivision letterhead. And the typewriter. I'll put us both under the same orders. The portable won't match the London typeface, but we'll just have to take the chance that nobody will see the discord, or give it any importance if they do see it. I have my officer's ID already, but I'll have to make up an entirely new paybook for you by altering Josef's Wehrmacht Soldbuch."

"How long will that take?"

"With Josef's documents kit, about twenty minutes."

"How can you get my photo where Josef's is?"

"I'm going to tear the cover, then rip your jacket to simulate a shrapnel graze. If anybody questions it, we were caught by strafing planes and narrowly escaped."

She sniffed. "Dear God, nobody'll believe that for a single second."

92

"If you've got any better ideas, let me hear them. If you don't, you've got two choices: start walking for the Ami lines or do what I say. And I say shut up and change your clothes."

Her temper flared, matching his. "I just don't want to get my ass shot off by some nervous little pimple-faced squid at some nowhere goddam checkpoint. If you think I'm looking forward to that, you're out of your frigging mind."

"Keep your voice down. And stop using that rotten language. It doesn't become a woman, talking like that."

"Don't lecture me, you self-satisfied bastard."

"Keep it up and so help me I'll shoot your ass off myself."

She refused to retreat. "You need me too much."

"I need you for nothing. In fact, it would be an excellent idea if you were to simply turn that way"—he waved an arm—"straight west and walk until you meet the Seventh Army. It's out there, and coming fast."

"Why should I do that? I'm a German."

"As a German with no papers you stand a better chance with the Ami enemy than you do with your German friends. And that's a fact, sister."

She spread her arms in extreme annoyance. "Look who's talking, for God's sake. How come you go on with all this, Lukas? Why don't *you* head straight west?"

"I haven't completed my assignment."

There was a silent interval in which they dealt with their preparations. He wondered why she infuriated him so. She was right, of course. He did need her. He needed all the help he could get.

But what was it about her that made him so uneasy—so quickly angry?

As they walked, he continued to fret. Eventually he simply had to ask. "Where did you learn to shoot like that, Frau Keller?"

"My husband taught me. He liked guns, hunting. He taught me."

"Pistols are close-up weapons. You hit that cop between the shoulders from a range that had to be fifteen, twenty meters."

"Nothing special for a nice girl like me."

They walked in silence for a time. Then: "You seem to be little affected by having shot a policeman, Frau Keller."

"I feel rotten, as a matter of fact. I puff and blow. Make like a woman of the world. But there's a lot of marshmallow inside there, somewhere."

He wondered why he didn't believe her.

They had managed to catch a ride with an NSKK postal truck driven by a sour-faced woman in her fifties who assured them that the Führer's V-weapons would lay England sufficiently flat to force the Allies to the peace table by midsummer. Meanwhile, she said, all the ruin in the Fatherland did nothing but stiffen the German spirit.

"Did you hear the news this noon?" she asked.

"No," Lukas said, partly to humor the woman, partly to satisfy his curiosity.

"The Health Ministry is launching an all-out attack on the epidemic of venereal disease among the female population. The Führer's very upset by the fact that there are so many housewives and mothers among those being hospitalized, then jailed, for promiscuous traffic with diseased transients. The Führer considers such women, who are unable to withstand temptation while their husbands are away fighting for the Reich, to be subject to the punishments for common treason against the State. Wives must remain true to their soldiers. It is appalling to learn that so many are not, and that so many of these traitors are paying the price in disfiguring, maddening and eventually fatal infections."

Lukas, vaguely irritated, said, "You sound like a newscast yourself. The way you talk."

94

"Well, that's what it said. I'm only telling you what the radio said."

"What else did it say?"

"Oberkommando der Wehrmacht is considering the postponement of leaves and furloughs for troops on all fronts due to the unavailability of transport. Rail lines and motor buses are currently hard-pressed to meet military operational needs. Soldiers with valid passes are not to attempt visits home by begging rides. It not only further crowds highways but also often gets the soldiers summarily shot when their authorized dates and travel times have expired." Her voice took on a special harshness. "Oberbayern and the Tyrol are on special alert for Anglo-American spies. Reichsführer SS Himmler has asked all of us—civilian and military alike—from Ulm, on the west, through the Ammersee and the Starnbergersee east to Bad Reichenhall, to be on the watch for parachutists. These areas, as well as the slopes and high meadows of the Kaisergebirge, south and east of Kufstein, have become highly favored in recent weeks as drop zones for enemy agents. Loyal Germans who are approached by strangers asking directions to military units or for other information of suspicious nature are ordered to contact the Gestapo at once. Or the Hilfspolizei. Or the nearest military headquarters. We're supposed to be especially alert for strangers who offer large sums of money and unimpeded passage to territories temporarily dominated by the Americans. The radio says this is a common technique of the infiltrators who have showered down in past weeks: They seduce people with promises of wealth and pleasant living for themselves and their loved ones if they agree to collaborate. But the Reichsführer SS promises that those who fail in their sacred duty to the Fatherland merely to wallow in American decadence will pay the price in blood." She shook her head in disbelief. "I can't imagine any true German being willing to abandon National Socialism, as bad

95

as things are, for mere money and Ami posh living, can you?"

"That's hard to believe, all right."

"I hate the idea of spies, traitors." She gave Lukas a severe glance. "That's why I insisted on seeing your papers before I let you ride with me."

"You can't be too careful, I suppose. Still, it seems a little silly for the radio to be nattering on about such things when the Reich is virtually overrun by Amis, Englishmen and Russians."

"Things haven't been going too well, to be sure. But you wait: The Führer still has plenty of tricks up his sleeve. You can count on that."

"I imagine he does." He decided to change the subject. "How far are you going today?"

"Bad Tölz is the end of my run. But the main office wants me to take this indirect route through Starnberg and Seeshaupt because the highway to Tölz is sure to be jammed with military junk. Ami airplanes are as thick as flies around a cow's rear. They've turned all the main traffic arteries—highways and railroads alike—into hellholes."

"You deliver mail in Starnberg, then?"

"That's right."

"I used to know some people in Starnberg. Bigshot UFA movie people."

"They're still there. A small colony of them outside of town, by the lake. Fellows named Taras, Michel, Von Diehl. And Richtermann, too. Hang out a lot together, it seems. Make propaganda, Wehrmacht training films. That kind of thing. They get a lot of mail. Or did, before everything started coming apart."

There was a lull as they rolled into Starnberg. Lukas considered leaving the truck here, but decided against it. It wouldn't look right for a pair under orders to Murnau to give up a ride going so far as Tölz. Still, he would have liked

96

to scout the UFA people. Communists or no, they could be helpful in a jam.

A few kilometers outside the village of Penzberg the road came to a dead end, and a signpost pointed east to Bichl and Bad Tölz. A mobile Kraft Durch-Freude canteen was parked there, and a small knot of soldiers—transients, from the appearance of their gear—was gathered around it, eating.

"I'm famished," Lukas said. "Stop here. I'll get us something to eat."

The woman was displeased. "Absolutely not. I'm carrying mail. I'm not a sight-seeing bus."

Lukas presented the matter to Frau Keller. "Are you hungry, Scharführer?"

She nodded.

"Doesn't say much, that one, does he," the driver said.

"Throat wound, taken in the Ardennes last winter," Lukas explained in the manner of one sharing a confidence.

"Oh. Too bad. But even so, you got a choice, me or the food. I haven't got time for both."

Gretl touched Lukas's sleeve and nodded toward the canteen.

"All right, then, food it is." To the driver he said, "You've been a great help. And you are a fine Nazi. The Führer would be proud of you."

The woman permitted herself a faint smile. "Sieg heil, Sturmbannführer. Have a happy life."

She drove off in thunder and blue smoke.

"God," Gretl exploded, "I couldn't stand that old hag's Nazi gabble another living minute."

"You have to give her one thing: When she listens to the news, she listens."

After a trio of Luftwaffe trucks passed, grinding and clattering, they crossed the road and elbowed their way to the counter.

97

"What's yours, sweetie?" The big woman in the dirty apron gave Lukas a weary smile.

"What do you have?"

"A rainbow sandwich. Black bread, red sausage, yellow cheese—all with green mold." She chuckled, a deep sound that shook her enormous bosom.

Lukas answered her joke with a good-natured grin. "I'll take two. If I have enough money and ration stamps, that is."

"Three marks twenty, dearie. And two stamps."

"Sold."

While they waited, Lukas glanced about. Most of the soldiers were from a mountain regiment, and most of them showed signs of recent hospitalization. Two of them still wore bandages on their heads, and one teetered on a crutch, gnawing on his rainbow. The others sat on the concrete railing of a bridge that spanned the tiny creek, a line of gray-green birds on a branch. Their conversation was spasmodic, subdued.

Lukas called to the man on the crutch. "Hey, Landser. What are you people waiting for?"

"A bus, sir. It's supposed to take us to Augsburg." He smiled. "Isn't that funny? Augsburg has been in Ami hands for days now. But our orders say we should report to the replacement center in Augsburg no later than tomorrow morning. Whose replacement center? Patton's?"

Lukas winked. "Well, you might get lucky and the bus won't show up at all. And you can spend the rest of the war right here, eating these moldy sandwiches."

"The rest of the war? The war's over, Sturmbannführer. Look around you. Look at the glorious Third Reich." The man turned and made his way to the bridge, his crutch making thudding sounds in the gravel.

They sat on the grassy embankment, chewing at their sandwiches and thoughtfully regarding the Alps, a stupen-
98

dous wall of variegated blues and grays and restless mists at the distant rim of the Bavarian plateau. The sun was warm, and there was a breeze that smelled of fresh clover and pine.

She finished her meal, then fell back in the grass, her head cradled by the steel helmet, her eyes closed, her face raised full to the noonday light. "I could sleep for a month. I am so tired of running, of being watchful, and worrying."

"All the same, we've got to be on our way soon."

"Just what are you trying to do, Lukas? I mean, I know it's something to do with that man you and Josef were burying when that cop—When I shot the cop—"

"Don't bother yourself with it. I can't tell you anything. So stop fretting about it."

"All this running around. Cars, cops, shooting—"

Lukas, staring off at the mountains, said slowly, "I remind you, Frau Keller, that you're on probation with me. You can be helpful, I think, and you do provide a kind of company, despite your, ah, peculiar ways. If you want to play the friendly tour guide, it's all right with me. But that's where the relationship ends. After that, you must mind your own business and stay out of mine. You are not allowed to ask me questions about my business. Clear?"

She held up a peacemaker's hand. "All right, all right. As you wish. I'm too tired to blather about all this."

They fell silent again, and he saw that she was drifting into sleep. Her eyes were closed, and her breathing was deep and even, and he realized that his own days of sleeplessness were at work: It was as if he were shutting down, circuit by circuit—as if someone, inside him somewhere, was flipping switches.

He studied her.

At rest, her face took on new characteristics. She was no longer the arrogant and profane woman of the world. A softness was there, a kind of vulnerability in the full lips, in the cheeks whose down glowed in the sunlight, in the long

99

lashes, dark, not matching her fairness. Her uniform, shapeless, soiled, booted, couldn't quite hide the ample breasts, the lazy curve of hips. She was a lot of female, and he had a moment in which to enjoy a secret, licentious examination of the things that certified that truth.

He had never had an easy time with women. He liked them, and they seemed generally to like him. But he had exited each of his few major amours with the sense that, having been invited to a banquet, he himself had been the pièce de résistance. He enjoyed a roll in the hay as much as anybody, but bitter experience had convinced him that women, even while proclaiming selfless love, were cunning, egocentric and cruelly manipulative, and so he had since gone warily when female sonar pinged on his hull.

She was heavily asleep now, and lying there, listening to her breathing, and drifting along the shore of his own unconsciousness, he took stock.

Zelinkov was dead and buried. But with their chase crews also dead and with the disappearance of the surviving Amis, the Russians could not be sure of that fact. In truth, they could be sure of nothing. So they had to assume the worst—that the general was alive and in American custody and talking—and they would have to act on that assumption. And even if they were to go to the other end of the scale of possibilities and assume that Zelinkov was in fact dead, they would need to determine how much he might have told the Amis before he shot the rapids. So the Russians' only option was to find Lukas and ask him exactly how things stood. They would follow wherever he went, whatever he did. Even if he opened a hot-dog stand in Cleveland, they would be calling on him sooner or later. And the conversation would be brisk, brief and unpleasant.

He tried to consider things from the Russian commander's point of view: Since the Germans had been interrogating Zelinkov with fists and rubber hoses, it was likely that he hadn't yet told them anything of practical value. Had
100

they learned of his attempt to defect to the Amis, of his willingness to share some secret plan of Stalin's, they'd have been very much more circumspect in their proceedings with the general. The war was lost for them, so they'd really gain nothing from further military intelligence. But if they thought they could crowbar themselves into a deal with the Americans, buying amnesty at best, leniency at worst, with Zelinkov's information, they would have played Zelinkov more carefully, more gently, more diplomatically —promoting him from punching bag to show dog. No (the Russian would most certainly decide), the Germans were out of it. Only the American, this Lukas fellow, would be suspect. He would have to be found and negated.

He dozed.

He had a dream about Josef. Holding a bottle of whiskey. Laughing and calling out something.

In and out of sleep, he recognized that Josef would not be drinking again. Ever.

He was aware of a terrible sadness.

He surfaced, feeling her scrutiny.

"You're still here." Her voice was husky.

"Where else?"

"Just now, as I woke up, I was afraid you had gone off without me."

"The idea had occurred to me."

"Why didn't you?"

"I'm not sure."

She rested on her elbows, looking down at him with eyes which now, because they were shaded by the helmet rim, seemed larger and a deeper blue. "Do you want to make love to me, Lukas?"

"No."

"I'm pretty hot stuff. Especially on grassy hillsides."

"I'm working."

101

"Ah. I knew it. The Puritan ethic. Thou shalt not enjoy thyself. Especially on company time."

There was an interval.

"I'm not asking you about your business, Lukas, but I am curious about something that rather involves me, too. Why were you so interested in what that mail-truck driver had to say about the UFA film colony communists? Do you think the communists might help us out of this jam we're in?"

"If they're truly communists, they are anti-Nazi. And if they're anti-Nazi, they're allies of my government. If they're allies, it could be that they'd be helpful. Simple logic."

She shook her head. "I'd go carefully there, if I were you. My husband, rest his soul, said those commies have one hell of a network. He said they are so organized you wouldn't believe it. They have groups—cells, they call them—all across Europe, and when they want to pass the word it goes like the wind. And they're great for telling outsiders one thing, then doing just the opposite. He said you can't trust them."

"Your husband was a Nazi. I'm supposed to trust *him?*"

"He wasn't a Nazi." She pouted. "I wouldn't marry a Nazi. I should think you'd know that."

"All the same, everything in life is a hazard, Frau Keller. You can't really trust anybody in this world."

"Is that why you're so puckered?"

"Puckered?"

"You know—Puritan. All tight lips, clenched jaws, narrow eyes. What makes you that way?"

"What the hell kind of question is that?"

She was about to answer, but there was a rumbling on the road, and he turned to find its source. He put his hand on her shoulder and forced her to lie facedown in the grass.

"Our friends have picked up our trail," he said, his voice low.

"Which friends?"

102

"There's a weapons carrier up there on the road. I recognize two of the people who were shooting at us in the Gestapo courtyard. One's driving, the other's looking hard at the transients on the bridge."

"What'll we do?"

"Nothing. If we move they'll see us."

They remained motionless, breath suspended.

"Damn," Lukas whispered eventually. "How could they have picked us up so quickly?"

"I told you they have a network."

Entry in Personal Diary of C. G. Brandt

Dijon, France
28 April 1945

We have lost Team Lukas.

I got an emergency wireless in which Lukas requested a J-E rendezvous just west of Munich for early today. But my plane circled the spot for an hour and a half before I gave up and directed the pilot to return me to Dijon. Ironically, the U.S. Seventh Army, sweeping in from the west, is at the very gates of Munich and probably was no more than a few miles away whenever what happened to Lukas, happened. We may never know. There's been no major battle for Munich, just a shoot-and-move pass-through by Patch's Seventh as it makes its way toward the Tyrol, and neither Army G-2 nor Ike's G-2 at SHAEF have received any word from agents—within the city or elsewhere—that might hint at the team's fate. I've reported this to the president via scrambler, of course, and he urged me to keep trying to reestablish contact, because he's anxious to get some idea as to what the Soviets are up to before he goes off to meet with them in Potsdam in July.

Truman continues to fascinate me, and I'm not sure why.

He's not a very compelling person, in the sense of striking appearance or commanding mien or what my late wife called "presence." In fact, if you can set aside the overwhelming vibrancy of the presidency itself and consider him as a mere mortal, there's something of the cliché civil servant about him—the plain, deliberate ways, the crisp, sometimes impatient speech, and an attitude suggesting that the federal government is an irritation to be endured, not a giant to be tamed. Also, several times in my talks with him, and in the TWXs he's sent, I've had the impression that he has taken over the war as his personal property and that the rest of us clods are to be granted admission only if we behave ourselves. It's a subtle thing. There's no overt arrogance, only that faint air of resentful toleration which the expert careerist often communicates when dealing with the Outside.

Still, he's the kind of man I'd want with me in a fight, I think. Aside from the aura of capability and determination that rather hangs about him, there's this suggestion of steadfastness, reliability—of that quality that treats friendship with great seriousness. But, then, maybe I'm wrong. Maybe he's just a slick actor. My whole career, at times my very goddam life, have hung on how well I judge people and their motives. But I've learned over the years that there's always somebody, lurking somewhere, whose ability to con is greater than my ability to see. Not often, by God. But it's happened. So who knows about Harry, eh?

He seems to be heavily preoccupied with the Potsdam thing. He told me his current thinking is that he will go by ship, sailing from Hampton Roads in Virginia to Brussels, and travel from there to Berlin by plane.

What gets me is the cool assurance that Berlin and nearby Potsdam will be available for a meeting in July. True, the Nazis are only a breath from collapse and, true, the Soviets are sure to command Germany's capital city by then. But who can foretell the German temper at that time?

104

Who can say that Berlin and its adjacencies won't be crawling with Nazi guerrillas who would delight in disrupting a summit conference of their enemies? It seems to me that everybody is preparing for the conference in the way kids get ready for summer. Good old Camp Scratchass will be right there where we left it last year, the lake will be just as clear and the sun just as bright and the forests just as green and cool. So who cares if the place is infested with angry brown bears? Who cares if all the buildings and tents are either burned down or pierced with holes? We're gonna meet there, by God, and we're gonna sing all the old favorites around the campfire, evenings. Yesiree.

The Pacific, though, is something else. My Washington sources tell me that Truman's staff conferences are producing all kinds of gloom and doom. The Joint Chiefs are presenting statistics that make the impending invasion of Japan a horror story to end all horror stories. They report that there were almost twenty-six thousand Marine casualties in taking Iwo Jima, a Japanese-held island measuring no more than some seven square miles. Almost fifty thousand Americans died or were wounded in the battle for Okinawa, another island on Japan's perimeter. The Chiefs are telling Harry they expect at least one million U.S. battle casualties in the assault on Kyushu and Honshu, two of the five Japanese home-islands.

A million, yet. And with three islands still to go. How did the world get itself into this horror?

Any president might be shaken by the implications of these staggering numbers. But if Harry is, he hides it well. This morning he came across as Mr. Serene, as if he has some special knowledge, some precognition of a divine intervention that promises to work on behalf of the United States and its affiliated white-hats.

He even philosophized again. On my recording he says, "There's the emperor. We mustn't discount his influence. I have a hunch that he's the one force that can keep those

105

hotheads on the Japanese general staff in line—can cool down the kamikaze fever. None of our hotshots seem to give him the time of day, dismiss him as a mere figurehead. Well, I'm not so sure. And I'm not so sure he isn't sick up to the eyes of a war that's destroying his nation's entire culture."

This was familiar. My sources tell me that some of Harry's advisers are appalled by what they see as his midwestern naïveté, his fecklessness. Others perceive him as the confident combat commander, unflappable in an unprecedented emergency. As for me, I place him somewhere between these extremes. It's my guess that, while he is deeply anxious over what could be American history's greatest and most lengthy bloodbath, he sees an alternative forming.

His single greatest need at this point, he says, is hard conversation with General Vladimir Zelinkov.

Lukas, where in hell are you?

CHAPTER 11

Saint Josef im Tirol, Austria
30 April 1945

The afternoon was chill and gray, and wet snow formed a haze among the lofty crags beyond the town. Dirty smoke eddied from the chimney pots, then was laid flat and hastened across the roof tiles by an insistent wind. Yet summer was in the wind. She could feel it. A smell of distant greening. A bird calling. A cowbell tinkling.

The area was a sea of German soldiers and their jetsam. They were a sad lot, ragtag and dirty, and they seemed to cluster, driven together by implacable external forces, like fallen leaves compacting in the swirl of a sewer drain. Wood-burning trucks, horse-drawn caissons, battered recons, motorcycles, an occasional half-track, silent and cold,

107

choked the highway outside the village. A gaggle of officers stood at the crossroads, arguing and waving their arms over maps. But the troops remained aloof, choosing to nap, or to sit on fences, or to huddle over smelly cookfires.

She thought of all the towns, all the arrivals during her brief lifetime. Large towns, small towns. Tall buildings and the gritty blare of traffic; dusty flatlands, with weathered boards and tumbleweeds in the sun; stately brick and ivy under rain-freshened elms; drab concrete facades and high windows, blank in the deep of a Eurasian winter. And here was yet another, an amalgam of medieval stucco and timber, with shutters and bargeboards painted colors without names. A town that had endured two thousand seasons, waiting now for the latest of mankind's wars to run its course.

How suddenly tired she was of arrivals. Of transience. Of war. Of killing and ruin. There had been a change in her—odd, inexplicable. Indescribable. The restless, adventurous traveler, the seeker of far horizons, had taken to thoughts of how good it would be to have arrived somewhere, to have settled, to be growing fat in some tranquil locality. To belong to some place. To somebody.

She glanced at Lukas, seated beside her. In the twilight there was a sadness about him, and she had a moment in which she could see him in the winter gloaming of some American place, a small town like one of those in her girlhood postcard collection, maybe, where naked trees arched over the streets and the lampposts were shaped like carriage lanterns and houses with cheery windows sent glows across the lavender snow. She had many times speculated on those fortunates who lived in such places. What kindly fate placed these particular persons in that particular town and allowed them to spend their lives along those cozy streets, private and serene behind the big white porches and the lamplit windows? Why had the God of Belonging condemned her to a lifetime of outsideness, roaming a malevolent world, alone and unfulfilled, like some kind of female Wandering Jew? Why could she not own a man like that one there—the angular, sad-faced, beautiful one who blew on his cold-numbed hands and managed to make her miss things she'd never had?

The Wehrmacht uniform itched and was heavy with sweat and mountain damp; the raincoat stank; the helmet's weight was unbearable. She sat low in the cycle's sidecar, hating the long-ago aberration that had led her to expect glamour and excitement from this line of work.

Lukas crouched in the saddle beside her, his compressed lips and slitted eyes showing the effort needed to control the monster. He had pulled his SS rank and confiscated the machine from a dispatch rider who, parked behind the mobile canteen, munched a rainbow sandwich and waited for somebody—anybody—to give him a dispatch to carry to anywhere. Lukas was not a motorcyclist; he was all over the road, and the engine wanted to stall. But once again he had demonstrated his soldierly perseverance and adaptability. And she found her increasing admiration for him awkward and disconcerting.

He maneuvered them into the clutter of a Gasthof courtyard and turned off the motor. The sudden silence brought relief akin to that which one feels when the dentist finishes with drilling. They had spent the time since dawn cruising the hardtop road between Kufstein, the Austrian border town, and Kitzbühl, a prewar ski mecca and tourist trap to the southeast. At each roadside crucifix, where wooden likenesses of Jesus awaited the whispered pleas of the lonely and anguished, Lukas had dismounted and searched the surroundings, kicking at the turf, kneeling and running his fingers through the dirt. He'd finally given up and followed her advice to come here for the night's R and R.

"So what now, Lukas?"

"I think I'll go into my Sturmbannführer act again.

Maybe I can persuade the local gendarmerie to share some information with a hotshot out of Berlin."

She sniffed. "I wish you luck. It's obvious that Berlin hotshots aren't very popular hereabouts these days. You've seen the looks we've been getting from the locals."

He shrugged.

"You're going to have to help me out of this sidecar, Lukas. I feel as if I've been welded in."

"I am not about to help you out of the sidecar. A Sturmbannführer would never help a Scharführer out of a sidecar—or out of anything, for that matter. Especially if the Scharführer has a pretty face. We'd be nailed as a couple of gay blades. We've been pressing our luck as it is, with me driving and you sitting on your rump, enjoying the scenery."

"You think I have a pretty face?"

"Damn it, get out of there and help me find the police station."

"I've got a better idea. You find the police station and I'll look for some food and a roof to crawl under. We'll meet here at the bike in a half hour."

"You might as well resign yourself to reality. Look at the crowds. We'll be spending the night under a shelter-half in some godforsaken meadow, like everybody else. Like we did last night."

"Tonight Gretl goes first-class."

He gave her a doubting glance, then busied himself with a chain, which he wove through the motorcycle's front wheel spokes and fastened to a hitching post with an NSKK vehicle padlock. She slung her musette bag defiantly and headed for the entrance to the Gasthof Ludwig.

Softly, he called after her. "Remember your throat wound. Whisper. Don't talk."

She held up her hand in a casual Nazi salute and gave him a wink.

110

The inn was a great jam of officers, most of them arguing with the proprietor, a fat old man in a barkeep's apron who had barricaded himself behind the reservations desk and was delivering the throng a blue-faced, apoplectic glare. She pressed unnoticed down the side corridor, glancing right and left, searching. At the rear of the place, near the door to the service yard and carriage barns, there was a utility room. She stepped into this and slid a broom handle through the iron door-hasp. The noise from the front of the hotel was still considerable, even back here, and for this she was grateful.

She removed the radio from its pocket behind the third panel board from the north corner and, with one of the new Zeus connectors, tapped the overhead light. The Zeus and its transformer, when coupled with a ZZK-3 radio, were viewed by radio surveillance teams as a curse, since the combination drew no more juice than a standard light bulb and was, therefore, virtually impossible to pick up at electric utility stations. The radio itself was a marvel—the size and shape of a cigar box—developed by the famed SS Communications Major Peter Siepen, with a range of a thousand miles and an accelerator that turned Morse into a sound like paper tearing. A German invention that had been seized and sophisticated by the Soviets. An agent radio surpassed only by the Amis' new Joan-Eleanor.

Checking the codebook, she tapped out Ressel's call letters, encyphered her message, pressed the accelerator actuator button, and listened to the rasping. While waiting, she rid herself of the uniform and long underwear, then pulled on fresh panties, bra, and the red party dress and pumps she had carried in the musette since departure from Field Nine. She held her pocket mirror to the light of a slit window and combed out her hair, pinched color into her cheeks, and reddened her lips with a touch of the rouge she carried in a matchbox. She needed a bath badly, but first

111

things first. Besides, everybody east of the Rhine was filthy, so who would know the difference?

Ressel acknowledged, and she sent: ON STATION, GASTHOF LUDWIG. OLGA.

The tiny receiver hummed: GO TO DESK. ASK FOR ROOM.

Sending: INN IS JAMMED. DOES IT MATTER?

Receiving: NO. YOUR CONTACT IS WAITING.

Sending: ANYTHING ELSE?

Receiving: RETURN HERE SOON AS POSSIBLE. CELL CHAIN ALERTED FOR IMMINENT ARRIVAL SEALED INSTRUCTIONS FROM MOSCOW.

Sending: TWO DAYS HERE SHOULD SUFFICE.

Receiving: AFFIRMATIVE. END TRANSMISSION.

After returning the radio to the wall and cramming the uniform into her bag, she eased the door open, peered warily down the corridor and, when all was clear, stepped out.

The clamor in the reception area became instant silence.

It seemed to her that at least eighty million eyes were directed unblinkingly at her, forty million mouths were wide with astonishment.

She made her way to the desk and smiled at the blue-faced man. "Good afternoon, Herr Innkeeper. I need accommodations for two. Can you help me, perhaps?"

"Two, Fräulein? I have no room for a gnat—"

"My brother and I—he's an SS Sturmbannführer on compassionate leave—are en route to Salzburg, where our aged mother is ailing and in great need. I—"

A stir went through the transfixed crowd. Someone said, with undisguised relief, "Ah. She is traveling with her *brother*."

Another added, pleased, "To see her poor, dear mother. Touching. Most touching."

She felt the current running her way. "We need only the one room, Herr Innkeeper. I realize it might offend your
112

sense of propriety, but I assure you it will be quite decent. My brother's habit is to drink himself unconscious every night so that he can sleep. He'll not even know I'm in the room. It will be as if I'm entirely alone."

"I'm sorry, Fräulein, but—"

"Hold on." The deep voice, calm, came from the card alcove beside the corner tile oven. "The young lady and her brother can share my room."

He was, of all things, a brigadier general. When the crowd realized this, there was a community sigh of disappointment.

She fluttered her eyelashes. "How kind of you, sir. But I wouldn't think of inconveniencing a high officer of the Wehrmacht. It's absolutely necessary for you to be rested sufficiently to make the decisions that will protect us all."

"Ah," someone murmured, "isn't she wonderful?"

"There are only six of us in our room," another man called. "You won't be inconveniencing us at all. And we aren't protecting anybody these days."

The general waved his hand impatiently. "It's done. There will be no further discussion. Innkeeper, see that the lady's bag is taken to my suite."

She crossed to the alcove and took the general's hand. "You are indeed a generous man, sir. Perhaps I can make it up to you somehow."

"Ah-h-h," the crowd said.

She turned to give the assembly a winning smile. "You naughty boys. That isn't at all what I meant—"

Laughter and applause.

They met at the motorcycle, as agreed. Lukas stared at her, eyes wide.

"What in hell are you doing in that rig?"

"Don't complain. It got us a room for the night. Of course, we have to share it with General Otto von Fetzer, newly appointed commandant of the Three-Twenty-Third Moun-

113

tain Regiment. But he's a pretty nice old coot, and he even has a bathtub. And I've promised him that you will drink yourself into stupefaction before ten o'clock tonight."

"Have you lost your mind? What are you talking about?"

"Trust me," she beamed. "Meanwhile, how did you make out with the cops?"

He shook his head, dubious. "Well," he managed, "I've got to go into the hills in the morning. There's more looking around to be done."

"Great."

He gave her another inspection. "Not you. Me."

"I'm going, too, and that's that."

"You wouldn't last a minute in that flimsy stuff. It's still winter in the high country."

"General von Fetzer also worries about that. He's afraid that I might catch cold as you, my dear brother, and I cycle our way to Salzburg, where we shall visit our sainted and ailing mama. So he has provided us with a heated staff car and fur-lined mountain troop coveralls. Isn't he a love?"

"You've been busy in the past half hour."

"Generals can work miracles if they think there's a piece of quality tail in it for them."

"You're disgusting."

She was about to answer when there was a sound—at first a distant keening, then an explosive thundering that seemed to congeal for a moment in a palpable cloud just above the rooftops. There was a mad racketing of machine guns, the crumping of bombs, the eruption of instant bonfires among the gables and chimneys. Shouting. Screams. The whinnying of horses.

She heard Lukas cry out, "Get down—"

Something hit her somewhere, and she felt herself rising in the air, turning.

How silly, she thought. *How very silly, to be killed by a passing American airplane.*

114

Entry in Personal Diary of C. G. Brandt

Dijon, France
30 April 1945

I have received a wireless report from Choo-choo, a U.S. agent working a black propaganda trick out of a Munich cellar. Choo-choo has observed the debacle in which Lukas and the remainder of his team were wiped out. A gaudy gunfight in the courtyard of a Gestapo headquarters building in Munich. Many dead and wounded. A man and a woman escaped in a black Mercedes, hotly pursued by a car full of gunmen. A gap, then other sources report the recovery of the chase car and the Mercedes, both riddled, their interiors burned to ashes. All occupants are presumed to have been incinerated.

It was natural, I guess, that the news brought back my first tour in Moscow, in the 1930s. Thanks to its tensions, its rinky-dink procedures, its spartan life-style, it had been a drab experience, filled with precious few rewards and pleasures. Despite the leavening of parenthood itself and the sobering understanding that coolness and stability were a necessity for a small family like ours, trying to exist in a culture that would always see us as unwelcome aliens, Gertrude had remained emotionally immature, a vulnerability that oppressed her, warped her child and tyrannized me. Of a morning, she could be merry, forward-looking, industrious—seeming still to feel a vestigial childhood excitement over life's newness and mystery; by evening, the household would be deep in the shadow of her unrequited love for a man who had married someone else. Gertrude had become my wife on the rebound, and her subsequent melancholy was chronic, overcome only on short term and most notably during embassy parties, when her beauty (and her American wardrobe) would mesmerize the pale moths that fluttered out of the dimness of Moscow's social wilderness.

She and the kid, victims of the violence that has characterized my life, are gone now, beyond retrieval or redemption. And I, myself, feel impossibly old. Believing in nothing and in no one. Planting one foot before the other on a lonely and indifferent march to God knows where.

Without a war there would be nothing. The war's madness is the only thing that has kept me sane.

Somewhere in all this, Perlman appeared in the doorway, polite, smiling in that dim way of his, to place the morning's intelligence summaries on the worktable.

He proposed some fresh orange juice. That and a ham sandwich, maybe. I told him no thanks. He suggested that I really ought to eat something, since I can't live long on coffee and cigarettes.

I asked him why anyone would want to live long.

After an awkward moment he changed the subject by reminding me of my meeting with the resident manager in his office at 1330 and my haircut appointment at 1600.

I was glad when Perlman left.

The G-2 intelligence summaries, issued daily to a select theater-wide list by SHAEF, are like house organs written by especially inept Journalism 101 students. Their tortured syntax, their bureaucratic puffery, their pseudoacademic tone, are the stuff of dark comedy. I thought briefly of the waggish summary writer—a gent who will remain anonymous, unfortunately, and who will therefore never be cheered where good soldiers gather for fun—who one day issued the Italian Mainland Summary under the heading WOP SECRETS: DESTROY BEFORE READING. Not one among the recipient top brass ever noticed. Of those lesser lights who did see the heading, none read it with more hilarity than did Giuseppi Minelli, chief of the Corsica-Sardinia-Sicily Desk at the time. Giuseppi wanted to send the writer

116

a bottle of Irish, and that's when it developed that nary a soul at SHAEF would admit to knowing who the man was—or to knowing anything else about the matter.

There was nothing amusing about these summaries, though.

I nearly always skim the parts on U.S. Domestic, Mediterranean, China-Burma, and Pacific situations, then give full attention to the large block of text devoted to "USSR and Satellite Political Entities."

Possibly as much if not more than any individual in American military intelligence, I respect the Soviet Union's capacity to make war. The nations of the West persist in seeing Russia as a nation of Slavic rubes, boorish, plodding, slow to make decisions and loath to take responsibility, when, in fact, it is a nation whose people possess great energies, who are dedicated to self-improvement and achievement, who are courageous and deeply patriotic. The Nazis have learned this the hard way: Their campaign against the Soviet Union was guaranteed to fail, from its very conception in Hitler's clouded brain, because Hitler and his generals failed to see—or to admit the existence of—Russia's immense capacity for resistance and counterattack. The Nazis, like many others among the world's political and military professionals, have a tunnel vision formed of racist snobbery and hatred that makes it impossible for them to see the Russians as anything but stumblebums and losers. Some icy objectivity and an abacus could have shown Adolf Hitler in 1941 that there was simply no way for Germany to win a conventional war against the Soviets. And today, in the spring of 1945, there are importantly placed Americans and Britons and Frenchmen who are blinded just as fatally by the same myopic arrogance vis-à-vis the USSR.

Just as bad, and worse, probably, is the Russian capacity for underestimating the West. The Soviets are afflicted by their own form of snobbery—a reflex contempt for Western

117

decadence, a serene conviction that their economic and political system is without fault, a hypocrisy that permits them to talk glibly and self-righteously out of both sides of their mouths—and it promises someday soon to bring out a disastrous Soviet misjudgment of those forces that simply don't want any part of communism's heaven-on-earth and will fight to the death in rejecting it.

The Soviets, according to today's summary, have fielded a total of 402 divisions, mostly armored infantry, and almost all of them pointing west. The United States has assembled ninety divisions, only sixty-one of which are in Europe, facing east. Together with units provided by the UK and France, the Allies have only eighty-one divisions in the entire European Theater, with many of these badly mauled and understrength.

The rough numbers: A U.S. division, with reinforcing battalions, numbers about seventeen thousand. A Soviet division can be expected to have an average of eight thousand men. So basic arithmetic shows that, in terms of trained ground units facing each other in Europe, Soviet manpower outnumbers the Americans about six-to-one and the entire Allied European ground force by some five-to-one. Which means that, even when allowing for the difference in the size of divisions and for the desperate mauling the Soviets themselves have taken, there is still a gross disparity between the conventional military capabilities of the East and West.

As of this very damn date.

And not counting the will to fight.

The Allies are already deciding how and when who should go home, now that the Nazis have been licked. Everybody on both sides of the Atlantic, in the military and out, is preparing an orgy of celebration. We've won, so let's tear down the goalpost in Berlin and go back to Des Moines and this year's pennant race, and let those poor yuks in the Pacific handle the Japs. Pass the hamburgers and Cokes.

Meanwhile, the Russians are planning, too. But with them, it's: Never Again. Those Who Are Not With Us Are Against Us. And Those Who Are Against Us Must Be Destroyed Before They Destroy Us. Never Again, No Matter What The Cost, Will Our Beloved Russia Be Faced With Extinction By Aliens Or Traitors. As Of This Very Damn Date.

That it has already begun is apparent.

There's the Soviets' insistence on occupying Berlin, and on owning the eastern half of Germany, all of Poland and Austria and the Baltic and the Adriatic. They're readying a bid for Japan, the Korean peninsula, the Southeast Pacific, Mongolia and even the Middle East.

There's the American willingness to shrug and say, "Why not? The Russians have had a bad time. What's wrong with their pushing out their fence lines? Just leave us alone with our barbecues and our World Series."

There's the mysterious Soviet radio traffic.

There's the subtle shifting and concurrent refitting of those hundreds of divisions—all but a handful of them still facing west.

And there's that double-damned, insistent, nagging thing Chesnikov said about the poplars. *A fox in our poplars.* What in God's name did he mean by that?

The next war is already forming up.
I wonder if I can last out the intermission.
My loneliness is intense.
Where is Gertrude now?
Where is the Kid?

CHAPTER 12

Near the Wildem Kaiser, Austrian Tirol 2 May 1945

The Kaiser range was an east-west arm of the Tyrolean Alps that terminated Germany's southern reach and served as a natural rampart along the northwestern rim of Austria. Its mountains suggested a line of snaggleteeth in the jawbone of some stupendous fossil; their scarps glowed redly in the morning light, as if vestiges of the creature's last meal had petrified with the rest. Its valleys and hemline plateaus were gentle, amiable, but in the upswept towers of granite there was a malevolence—an eternal and baleful warning against trespass.

In the approximate center of the range was the Wildem Kaiser, and at the foot of this were broad, elevated sweeps of meadowland, thick with

120

clover and dotted with black-green patches of firs. Central to it all was the village of Going, a cluster of chalets and farm buildings dominated by a tall yellow church with an onion-topped steeple. At the crossroads below the church, Lukas sat atop his muttering motorcycle and studied the heights through field glasses.

He had driven the motorcycle, because General von Fetzer's car would be restricted to surfaced roads, and the charts showed that where he was going there were only wagon lanes and shepherds' paths. The general, a thoroughgoing patsy for Gretl Keller's absurd playacting, had been very solicitous. A sensible officer—no matter how blinded by lust—would have sent a discreet inquiry to Salzburg, first to check on the truth of the tale and second, if there was indeed an ailing mother, to determine her current condition, thereby establishing thoughtful compassion for his quarry. But what the hell. How much could he expect of a general-grade reservist who had been given command of a decimated regiment of tatterdemalions?

He thought now of Frau Keller recuperating from shock, a possible concussion and three shrapnel dents, all guaranteed to leave no serious marks on her undeniably extraordinary derriere. It had been nearly impossible to keep her in the general's bed this morning; she'd insisted that she was well enough to continue on her trip to Mama's. But the regimental doctor—probably under bribe or threat from von Fetzer—had ordered her to remain abed for at least another day. Apparently attempting to mollify her, the physician, enthusiastically seconded by the general himself, suggested that Lukas might run ahead on a quick round trip to check on Mama's condition. Thus disarmed of further logical protest, Frau Keller had been trapped by her own fiction, a fact that now brought a dim smile to Lukas's face.

What a woman.

121

Comparing the actual terrain with his map, Lukas identified the eminence called the Regal Spitze and saw the pattern of lanes and paths that provided the most direct approach to the area. The wreck, according to the Saint Josef police chief, a fat little fellow dressed in lederhosen, lay there. Lukas's major problem could be snow. Great accumulations still covered the upper reaches, a fact attested to by the police chief and confirmed by the binoculars. The burgeoning spring was already at work; as he stared he noted an occasional shifting in the creamy sparkling beyond the shadows of woodland and crags, with crystalline mists rising above the subtle readjustments of winter's weights and forces.

He decided to worry about that when he got there.

He rode as far as the tree line, then, dismounting, he chained the bike to a pine. Map and compass oriented; Walther pistol loaded and on safe; field coat pockets full of bread, cheese and matches; canteen full of schnapps. The sky was clear and bright, promising a hike untroubled by storms.

He took his azimuth and pushed through the trees to a tableland of rock and shrubs. The land rose here, a gentle upward sloping toward the zigzag of evergreens that delineated the baseline of the great mountain wall. His boots made crisp sounds against the frosted stone, then squeaked in the still-brittle snow of the occasional surviving drift. He half walked, half climbed for two hours by his watch.

The wreck lay in the open, not far from the final tree line. It was a sprawl of junk, mostly, but the cockpit section, tilted on its side, seemed relatively intact. The propeller had torn free and stood in upright isolation some twenty meters away, its three blades forming a bent cross against the sky. The smell of oil came down the slope on the restless wind.

122

Lukas stood for a time, studying the scene, seeing in his mind the plane's last moments.

It must have descended in a shallow glide, touching down where the shrubs had been shredded. A high bounce, a return to earth for a disintegrating slide across that spread of rock and dirt, taking out those two scrub pines and eventually coming to rest against that granite outcropping.

He made his way to the ruin, stepping over a wing section emblazoned with the Soviet red star and pulling himself to a position from which he could peer into the tandem cockpits. They, too, were junk, all dangling straps and wires and broken things. The parachute seat packs were gone, and there was blood in the aluminum buckets in which they had nested. The map pockets were empty; the pilot's chart board had been stripped. All instrument sockets were mere holes, the machine-gun sights and triggers had been removed, and the bomb toggles were missing. Anything of possible utility had been scavenged by Zelinkov's German captors.

He sat on the wing section, feeling the spring sun, full of a sense of waste.

Weeks of training, days of peril, arbitrary slaughter, chases, gunfights, duplicity, role-playing, instantaneous decisions, with his life the lives of others—at risk. Grubbing about crucifixes, the supreme, epochal symbol of man's brutality and arrogance and ungodliness.

He had come all this way to look at just another of war's trash piles.

His loneliness was sudden, almost crushing.

A bird circled, sounding a thin, unhappy call. He watched it for a time.

His gaze, wandering, fell on the propeller, glinting dully in the noon sun.

A squat, leaning cross in the high meadow.

Cross?

Crucifix?

What had Zelinkov gasped in his final moments? Had he said crucifix?

Or cross?

Which?

Precise recollection eluded him.

But what difference did it make? Here was a cross. Right in front of him, yards away.

What difference, indeed?

A stir of excitement, tempered by an unwillingness to be disappointed once again, sent him to his feet. He half ran, half stumbled across the gentle slope, leaped a fissure, then sank to his knees in the propeller's shadow. His eyes searched, his hands stirred the thin layer of snow, his heart beat quickly.

Here.

Simply lying on the ground, like mere litter.

A cigarette box. Crumpled. Weather-stained.

Its legend told him it once contained Zenith cigarettes— long, flat, in the Russian style.

Now it contained nothing but a heavy-caliber machine-gun cartridge.

He thought about this. His mind showed him Zelinkov, hurt, struggling free of the wreckage, aware of German voices calling out in the distance. Placing a cartridge in the box as a weight against the wind. Placing a message in the box. Crawling to the propeller. Crawling back to the plane. Then lying in pain as he awaited the approaching mountain troops.

His fingers disassembled the packet, working slowly, with care.

It was behind the foil. A neatly folded message flimsy, torn from an airman's pad. The handwriting, small and neat, was hurried. The Russian was clear.

As he began to read, a shot—insanely clangorous— slammed into the propeller blade beside his head, then caromed in a diminishing whine.

124

He rolled, unthinking, to the side, then tumbled and slid down a face of rock into the defilade provided by the fissure. The shot had to have come from down-slope; it would not have struck the propeller at that angle unless the rifleman had been firing from—let's see—down there. About there, in that crook of woods.

He rose slightly, cradling on his elbows, and ventured a sweep with the binoculars. It was a mistake. Another shot tore the glasses from his hands, spraying his face with glass and metal shards, numbing his fingers with an electric stinging. He fell back into the fissure, lips pressed together against the shock and pain.

He was trapped.

If he moved out, he'd lose his cover. If he remained where he was, the rifleman could close in—could keep just beyond the range of a Walther pistol, easily within range for a military rifle.

And then, with Lukas dead, the rifleman would have what all the searching, following and shooting had been about.

Unless—

Lukas remembered.

The crook of woods lay at the base of a jagged crest. And atop the crest—

He dared another look over the lip of rock, and his memory was confirmed. It was as he remembered.

He rose on his haunches, then slowly pushed his service cap to the rim of the fissure. Almost at once another shot slammed into the rock within inches of his hand.

He moved the cap again, and again the rifle barked.

One of those shots would do it. One of them simply would have to do it. He'd have to risk another try. But the fear was almost debilitating—paralyzing. He shifted in his hiding place, seeking a more advantageous position. As he moved, he noticed an ancillary crack in the rock, through

125

which he could see the top of the crest. And as he watched, the crest began to move.

There was a shifting, a sliding, then a rushing of snow and rock. He heard a rumbling, which almost at once became a hissing roar and, daring a clearer view, he rose to a crouch. Transfixed, he saw that the crook of forest was disappearing in a gigantic leap and tumble of rock and splintered trees. Boiling clouds of snow, climbing into the sky like a hellish steam, echoed with a thunder that was an almost unbearable violence in his ears.

At last there was quiet. He stood, slowly.

The crest had been flattened by the avalanche. The patch of woods was gone. There was only a great, angry sprawl of dirty snow, boulders and shredded timber. And silence.

He sat down and read the message.
Jesus God.

THE
DEAL

CHAPTER 13

**Going, Austria
2 May 1945**

The day, earlier so sunny and promising, had dimmed with astonishing suddenness and now was slate colored and cold, a bitter wind coming down from the Alpine vastness to stir the snow and send a restlessness through the trees.

Lukas hurried, his descent aided by the sharp wind at his back. He was weary beyond endurance, and the acid taste lingered in a mouth made tacky by fear. There was a moment of panic when he failed to find the bike, but then he realized that the tree to which he had chained it was in a grove of birch, and a brief, further search brought him to it. It had not been disturbed.

He kicked the machine into life, and rode off, his boots skittering through the snow crust. He made it across the glacial rock, through the blue shadows of the fir forest, and down the lane to the log bridge that spanned a torrent whose thundering echoed in the lowering afternoon.

He saw them at once, but his speed was too great and the bike slid on the icy gravel, halting inches away from the weapons carrier, a dull green lump that filled almost the entire width of the bridge. There were four of them—one at the wheel, the others standing in the snow beside the truck, and their rifles were trained on him.

This was the tricky part. Here was where his gamble was to be resolved.

The tallest man stepped forward, waving a pistol and commanding in husky English, "You will from the machine dismount. The hands will be held in the air."

Lukas moved carefully, the way the man would want it.

"We will speak," the Russian said. "My English lacks. German goes better."

"German's all right with me."

"Very well, then. Climb onto the truck. And make no quick moves, please. Vassily, search him for weapons."

Vassily snarled in Russian. "Let me kill him. He killed Sergei today—"

The leader snapped back, his Russian smooth, educated. "Idiot. We've been trying for days to catch him, to force him to talk to us. We will first take him to Starnberg for a complete interrogation. You can kill him later."

The gamble had paid off. They obviously assumed he didn't speak Russian.

Lukas sighed. Something had to go right once in a while.

CHAPTER 14

Starnberg, Germany
2 May 1945

These Russians had done a lot of planning, Lukas saw.

West of Going, in a notch of alders beside a stream, they pulled to a halt and clambered out of the weapons carrier. From the corner where he huddled with wrists and ankles bound, Lukas watched as the leader, the tall one named Taras, carried a map case to the creek bank. The man knelt beside the water and dampened a sheet of paper, which, when he returned to the truck, proved to be a decal—a white star of the type the Allies used to identify their vehicles. This was large enough to cover the German cross on the engine hood. After Taras's subsequent trips to the stream, the smaller crosses on the door panels were similarly

131

masked. A neat touch was the Cross of Lorraine insignia applied to fenders and rear hatch, followed by bumper designations of the First French Army.

The final move was the crew's change into the uniforms and berets affected by Gaullist troops.

He discovered soon after the drive's resumption why Taras had gone to so much trouble. The road junction at the village of Soell was awash in olive drab.

Three recon jeeps were parked in tandem across the intersection. To one side was a pair of weapons carriers. On the other side was a half-track armed with a bracket of fifty-caliber machine guns. All the vehicles bore Seventh Army designations. All were overflowing with bedraggled, stubble-faced GIs who watched warily as the Frenchified truck ground to a halt, engine muttering.

One of the GIs spotted Lukas. "Looka there," he said in a low drawl. "One a them big-deal Nazzy SS fellers. Special delivery."

A man swung slowly from one of the jeeps and walked toward them, looking tired to the bone. Lukas could see second lieutenant's bars on the filthy field jacket.

"Who are you guys?" the lieutenant asked, seeming not really to care.

Taras gave a Gallic shrug. "Franch. We is Free Franch." He nodded toward Lukas. "Prisonaire. We haff ze prisonaire. Freiburg. We take to Freiburg."

The lieutenant squinted thoughtfully. "You're a hell of a piece out of your bailiwick, buddy." He jerked a thumb over his shoulder. "The French First is west of here by quite a few miles."

"We go incorrect in ze chase of zis Nazi. Zis Nazi, he iss by the General de Gaulle most badly seeked."

A sergeant had joined the lieutenant. "They look fishy as hell to me, sir. Want me to rummage them a bit?"

"Well," the lieutenant said softly, "the decals do look

132

awful fresh. And their story is about as impressive as a hiccup in a hurricane."

"Not only that, but what the hell they doin' in a Kraut weapons carrier?"

"No telling what the Free French are likely to be driving these days, Smitty. I've seen some of them tooling around in Model-A Fords, for crissake." The lieutenant yawned and stretched. "To hell with it. We got a timetable. The whole fuggn Seventh Army is down around the bend. Let somebody else worry about this bunch of oddballs."

Watching, listening to the easy Virginia inflections, Lukas felt a rush of homesickness and self-pity. A word, a gesture, a phrase of army slang, and he would be identified as one of them, would be instantly confirmed as a stockholder in the American dream. But the dirty-faced soldiers, a mere hand's reach away, were a universe removed from the comradeship he needed in this moment of lostness. They were there, squinting into the raw wind, smelling of tobacco and sweat, as real as the world around. But they were also an illusion, an unreality, for him as untouchable as thought itself.

It took everything he had to keep silent as the weapons carrier lurched on its way.

At Kufstein the highway was choked with American convoys, a great olive ribbon that stretched north and west as far as they could see. Taras ordered the driver to turn west on the Tegernsee road, and from there around the lake to Bad Wiessee and Gmund, then west to Bad Tölz. The Seventh Army traffic, while somewhat lighter on these back roads, was often nearly impassable, and they were bombarded by GI catcalls, most of them containing hooted suggestions that, if the goddam Frenchies would only learn to read a goddam road map, they wouldn't be so goddam far off their goddam reservation.

133

As the truck rattled through the Bavarian beauty between Koenigsdorf and Wolfratshausen, the Russians fell into an easy conversation, in the manner of young men on a holiday. But after a time the chatter segued into a bitching session, the kind soldiers have after a day's chores. Lukas concentrated on maintaining an expression conveying a total lack of comprehension. He sat rocking with the vehicle's motion, eyes dull and vacant.

Boris, the rifleman: "You have to agree, though, that this has been a rotten little assignment. Nothing's gone right from the start."

Nikki, the grenadier: "Pfah. It's been a dream duty, as far as I'm concerned. You'd say the same, Boris, if you'd done a tour on the Kiev front. Now there was a duty that qualifies for the word 'rotten,' I'll tell you."

"What the hell you talking about? I was at Stalingrad. Three months in the line, without break."

"My piles bleed for you."

Taras: "All right, that's enough. I've got too much on my mind to have it rattled by all your great heroics."

Boris: "When are we going home, Taras? I'm so tired of this war I don't think I can endure it another minute."

Taras: "Then think again. You'll endure it whether you like it or not. We have much work to do if we're to chop down the poplars before they begin to seed."

Nikki: "I have to relieve myself, Taras."

Taras: "Do it out the back of the truck."

Nikki: "For what I have in mind that would be somewhat hard to manage."

Laughter.

Taras: "Just hold it, Nikki. We'll be in Starnberg in a few minutes."

It was a large, wooden house, with many gables and chimneys, and a porchlike projection that provided a splendid view of Starnberger See. Due to the war, probably, it badly needed paint, and a section of roof was missing some shingles. As Boris pulled him from the truck bed and prodded him up the front steps, Lukas's mind went to the big house on the lakeshore, between Buffalo and Erie, where Dr. Doubet would stash his wife and kids in the summers before the war. Doubet was a dentist, with a very successful practice on Delaware Avenue in Kenmore, who hired Ma Lukas to do a heavy cleaning of his offices every Saturday. She used to take Lukas along sometimes, riding the trolley to the end of the line and walking the rest of the way, and he'd got to know the doctor and a couple of his kids, who would come to the office now and then when their old man did some weekend book work. Doubet and his wife, a very pretty brunette, had taken a fancy to Lukas and invited him to spend a week at their shore place, and although the Doubet kids tended to give him the snooty treatment because he was the cleaning lady's son, it was one of the best times he'd ever had, man or boy. The memory picked at him now, and he felt a deep, nameless pain.

He was locked in a back room and given some bread and cheese and a bowl of lukewarm tea. As he ate, he thought of the conversation in the truck.

"Poplars" again.

What had Taras meant by "chop down the poplars"?

Where were the poplars, and why were they important to the Russians?

The door opened and Taras entered, accompanied by a small round man with a bald head and heavy eyeglasses, who wore the classic Bavarian farmer's lederhosen and embroidered jacket.

"This is the American who has led us such a merry chase, Georgi," Taras said in German. "He says his name is Lukas. He says nothing else."

"Well," the short man said, "let's see if he can do better. Leave us, please."

Taras nodded deferentially and, stepping into the corridor, shut the door behind him.

Georgi sat in the chair across the table and gave Lukas a moment of thoughtful evaluation. The light from the barred window, reflecting in his spectacles, made it difficult to see his eyes.

"I assume you're a reasonable man, Herr Lukas. You are a most inventive and indefatigable fellow, and I admire the tenacity you show in pursuing your mission. But we are not at all clear on what your mission has been, and it's this matter I'd like to discuss with you now. And reason must certainly tell you that there's nothing to be lost by answering my few questions. After all, you are an American, and I am a Russian, and that makes us allies."

Lukas sniffed. "If we're allies, why have you been trying so hard to kill me and my people?"

"We have not been trying to kill you, Herr Lukas. We've been trying to get you to sit still for a conversation like this. We have reason to believe that you have acquired some information, which, if it falls into the wrong hands, can cause much difficulty for the Union of Soviet Socialist Republics. We want to know precisely how much information you have acquired and from whom you acquired it. If you cooperate, if you answer all questions to our satisfaction, you'll be given a clean suit of clothes and driven to the nearest American authorities for repatriation."

"I don't feel like answering questions."

Georgi smiled. "You will answer them. It simply would be much more comfortable for you and convenient for us if you were to do so willingly. We want to keep you whole and well, yet we also want to beat a certain deadline. Cooperation on your part could achieve both ends."

"So what do you want to know?"

"First, who are you?"

"Alex Lukas."

"Are you a member of the American military?"

"I'm a private first class, and my serial number is one-three-one-two-two-five-eight-two. Who are you?"

"Who I am is a matter of no importance at this time."

"I think you are a Nazi pretending to be a Russian."

Georgi chose to ignore this. "You can't expect me to believe you are a mere private first class. The leader of a commando team, charged with assaulting a Gestapo headquarters miles behind the enemy lines? Come now."

Lukas shrugged. "I don't care what you believe."

"What was your mission?"

"I don't know. Colonel Jamieson was in charge. He alone knew the details. The rest of us followed his instructions, and he gave those to us piecemeal."

Georgi pursed his lips and penciled a note on the little pad he had placed on the table. "Obviously his last command to you was to liberate a Red Army general being held in a Munich Gestapo headquarters. What was your interest in this officer?"

"I'd been told only that his name was Zelinkov, that he had been in a plane shot down by you Germans over Austria."

"I am not a German, Herr Lukas. I am a Russian."

"The Russian army is many miles east of here. The Amis are around us, everywhere. Which means that you Germans have a larger problem than I have."

Georgi adjusted his glasses, and Lukas could see his annoyance. "Let's get back to the subject. What—"

"I've got a better idea, Georgi. You and your people surrender to me, right now, and I'll see that you are taken to the best of our detention centers, where you will be guaranteed protection against prosecution as ranking Nazis."

"Herr Lukas, you don't understand. You are in no position to offer me anything, to bargain with me in any way. You are the one who is in trouble, not I."

"You have a very warped perception of things, Georgi. I

am surrounded by the American army. By my friends. You are surrounded by enemies who consider you to be a war criminal. Now tell me again who's in trouble."

Georgi's face was livid, and his fist pounded the table. "Enough of this nonsense, damn you. What did you learn from Zelinkov? Answer, or I'll shoot you where you sit."

"I learned nothing from Zelinkov."

"You were seen retrieving a message. You picked up and read something near the propeller of the crashed plane—"

"I don't know what you're talking about."

"Answer, damn you. What did you learn from Zelinkov?"

"Up your ass, you Nazi pig."

Georgi's face was crimson now. He leaned to one side, his right hand groping in a jacket pocket, and suddenly Lukas understood that he had pushed too hard.

He saw the blue metal of the automatic pistol.

He heard the clicking as the safety catch was released.

He stared into the muzzle, and a point of light there ballooned into a cloud of yellow-white that rushed toward him across the table.

The noise was so stupendous it was soundless.

He was enveloped by the light, and his head exploded, and there was a great nothing.

Entry in Personal Diary of C. G. Brandt

Dijon, France
8 May 1945

The war in Europe has ended.

The German government signed the official documents of unconditional surrender late yesterday and the cessation of hostilities took effect last midnight.

And today is Harry Truman's birthday. Some present, eh?

138

I admit it. I've been deeply moved by the news. I can't remember the last time I thought of such things as God and Country, especially in those terms and with anything approximating sentimentality, but I actually got all choked and patriotic when the announcement came over the radio, when Harry proclaimed May 8, 1945, to be Victory in Europe Day, or V-E Day, as the newsies are already calling it. The streets in all the cities have gone wild, it seems, with dancing, parading, singing, flags waving, car horns blaring, beer bottles splashing, youngsters in uniform swept up by crowds that seemed intent on smothering them in affection. It's truly what the commentators are calling it: an orgy of emotion and relief, with little evidence that anyone is thinking of the war still to be fought.

My exuberance, if it can be called that, has been alloyed by thoughts of James Madison and what he wrote in *The Federalist:* "Security against foreign danger is one of the primitive objects of civil society. It is an avowed and essential object of the American Union."

It's an avowed and essential need for the Soviets, too, and we're running head-on into a terrible collision. That's been on my mind all day.

To reassure myself, I've made silent little speeches: "We are the most powerful nation in the world today. The most powerful in history. The Soviets are tattered, disheveled, war-weary beyond imagination. Whether they like it or not, they'll have to treat us gingerly for some time to come."

But then a kind of rebuttal forms: "Don't bet the rent money on it. Their national will to prevail, to excel, is inflexible, fanatical—an unwavering, fundamentalist religion. Their Bible, the 1917 Manifesto, requires them to knock everybody's socks off. They have been working on it ever since."

And so it goes. I shrug. I worry. I shrug. But the worry remains. They don't understand the American people, the

139

American idea. They'll underestimate us some day—hit our hot button when they don't actually intend to.

But that's a two-way street. Americans have a pretty awful tendency to think that everybody else in the world thinks and feels the way they do. That everybody out there, if treated openly, fairly, if smiled at and shaken firmly by the hand, will return in kind. Americans don't understand that there are people out there who consider an offer to split 50-50 an admission of weakness, who view a smile as a sign of duplicity or aggression, who are repelled by the idea of touching a stranger's hand.

So, stir together the pride, the blindnesses and the idiosyncrasies of two huge nations and you've got a very volatile cocktail. That's what we're dealing with today.

I've learned that President Truman feels pretty much the same way.

He called me this evening on the special phone to see if there was follow-up on Team Lukas. The phone and its scrambler were installed for precisely that purpose—to give him direct and up-to-the-minute access—and we've talked on it frequently. But I still feel surprise when the damned thing rings. It rings, like any other goddam telephone anywhere, but when you pick it up the president of the United States asks you how you are and you want to sputter. So the damned thing rang tonight, and I didn't pick it up right away because I didn't want to sputter. But I did answer it finally, and told him right up front that the team was missing and presumed destroyed. As he so often does, he became quite pensive and went into one of his soliloquies. This time it was my impression that he was explaining himself—not to me, but to himself. Here's some of the recording:

"Joe Stalin worries me a bunch. My advisers in the striped-pants department keep telling me what a practical politician he is. But that can be a problem.

140

Most practical pols are slow to grasp important new ideas, to appreciate inventive departures from the old ways. They get so busy with the business of shelling peanuts and popping them in their mouths that they resist suggestions that peanuts might taste good smashed up and spread on bread with jelly. I mean, they rarely recognize social changes while they're going on—they merely exploit them after they've happened.

"Which makes me a rare bird, I guess. I'm a practical pol, but I've also read my history books and my philosophy books and I have a hell of an eye for what goes on in this sad old world. A lot of people don't know that about me. People want to put me in a box, to typecast me. The liberals make me a Fascist, the conservatives make me a pinko. And very damned few of the betweeners give a hoot what I am, because they just can't take their idea of me beyond the image of the Missouri ward heeler, the Prendergast gofer. I've been those things, sure enough. But what those people miss is my grasp of history, my sense of the future. My understanding of power. I know how power works and how it's acquired. I understand the art of compromise, the you-give-some-and-I-give-some-and-we-both-get-most-of-what-we-want school of politics. I have a very damn good idea of what everybody wants, what Churchill and de Gaulle and Hirohito want. I even have an idea of what that maniac Hitler was after.

"But what worries me most is what Stalin wants. What Stalin wants is an absolutely one-hundred-percent-safe environment for Mother Russia. And he really doesn't seem to see that under the natural scheme of things there are no guarantees of safety for anyone—only trade-offs that offer everybody a realistic chance to live and let live, unhassled. There's an unwritten law: the law of social stability. It says that

141

security comes from understanding what your enemies need of you and making compromises with what your friends demand of you—not from stiff-legged, self-serving tantrums. Joe ignores that law."

Brandt: "There's a heap of American understanding for the Russians today. Sympathy, even."

Truman: "And there are a heap of Americans who have stuck their heads up where the sun don't shine, too. Especially in our government. Russians and their communism have become chic among our elite—inside government and outside. And these limp-wristed faddists have sponsored all sorts of nifty little fictions. Hollywood moguls produce movies with big stars playing the brave, sacrificing Russian resistance fellows, showing Mother Russia to be the Promised Land, taking on the bad old Nazis single-handed. No suggestion anywhere among all these sob sisters that only a few years ago Communist Russia was murdering its own people by the millions, allying itself with the Nazis, gobbling up the little countries on its hemline. No mention anywhere in all of this that when the Nazis turned on them and they were on the verge of getting their asses knocked off, these same commies came running to us for hundreds of millions in money and supplies. No mention of the thousands of American lives risked and lost to get food and bullets and trucks to the Russians. Well, between you and me and the gatepost, the Russians are political hypocrites when they cozy up to Hitler and social ingrates when they deny the fact, the existence, of all that American help. They make me sick, I'll tell you."

Brandt: "Well, maybe they'll sweeten up, now that they've got a war to recover from."

Truman: "And maybe I'll sing soprano."

Brandt: "What's to do about it, Mr. President?"

142

Truman: "There's one thing I can do about it, I'll tell you. I can cut off their water. And that's exactly what I'm going to do. Right now."

Brandt: "Stop Lend-Lease?"

Truman: "The faucet's turning this very minute, pal."

Brandt: "There'll be a lot of hell raised—"

Truman: "Already is. And every la-de-da, pollyanna, Soviet-apologist complainer is going to get a Harry Trumanism stuffed right up his patrician kazoo."

(I really didn't know what to say to that, so I said nothing. He obviously caught the meaning of my silence.)

Truman: "You think I'm being inconsistent, don't you, Mr. Brandt."

Brandt: "Well, it does appear that just as you present a case for going carefully with the Soviets you hit them over the head with a Lend-Lease two-by-four."

Truman: "Nothing inconsistent at all. It's politics. Prendergast politics. When a pol does another pol a favor, and the favor's not returned, or there's no practical expression of gratitude, the Big Shaft comes out of its scabbard. And unless the offending pol makes amends, or pays his dues, he'll have to spend the rest of his life watching his own behind. Joe Stalin's a pol who has become too big for his britches, who has begun to believe his own publicity. Worse, he's trying to ignore another law—the Prendergast Law, which is a basic law of the political universe. And I'm going to remind him—one pol to another—of the price he has to pay for that kind of sin."

Brandt: "All respect, Mr. President, but you are a real doozy of a character."

Truman: "You ought to hear what Bess calls me."

(My laughter here is polite.)

Brandt: "Did you get my report on the visit from Rutan, Mr. President?"

Truman: "Speaking of Red-lovers. Yes, I got it. I'm glad you kept him at a distance. We can't afford to have his pack get into full cry. We can't afford a major domestic hassle at this delicate point in the scheme of things."

Brandt: "That's the way I saw it. Not because Rutan's a Red-lover but because we don't need a bigger mess than we've already got."

Truman: "Now that we've lost Team Lukas, we don't know anything more than we knew before. Now that Zelinkov has died before we could find out what was on his mind, we're back to square one. So what's next over there?"

Brandt: "We'll beef up our efforts to penetrate the communists' European structure—to tap the instructions flow from Moscow to the cells in the boonies. Meanwhile, I'll be taking steps to move my office to Germany. I have to get closer to the action there. I have to organize the machinery I need to operate in the postwar jungle."

Truman: "I hope you have more luck than I've been having on that score lately."

Brandt: "From where I sit, Mr. President, it looks as if you're doing just fine."

Truman: "I've been doing a lot of dumb-playing. I learn a lot by playing dumb sometimes. There are a hell of a lot of people who tell me more than they mean to or want to because they feel superior to this dummy from Missouri and they shoot off their mouths, thinking I won't really understand their game. Most of these pompous bastards are Red-lovers. That's why I like to talk to you. You're a realist when it comes to the Russians. You can take them or leave them alone, like

144

olives. Sometimes I think you are the only one west of Churchill who's willing even to listen to my concerns about the Russians."

Brandt: "As a matter of fact, I really like them. As people, they're smart, energetic, warm, intuitive. But as a nation, they're a pain in the behind, because their national security paranoia makes it impossible for me to mind my own damned business."

Truman: (He chuckles.) "That pretty well says it all." (A pause here.) "What do you think happened to Team Lukas, Mr. Brandt? What went wrong?"

Brandt: "There's no way to guess, sir. War's like that. You make your best plans, rehearse everything well, then get knocked out of the box by coincidence, by the fickle finger of fate. I once had a prime operation go down the chute because an agent had the runs. He was sitting on the pot when he was supposed to be catching a bus."

Truman: "You think something like that happened to the Lukas people?"

Brandt: "Maybe."

Truman: "Is it possible that somebody on the team was a Russian sympathizer?"

Brandt: "Possible. But unlikely. The team members were very thoroughly screened, politically speaking. And it would have been to the Russians' advantage to capture the Lukas team in good health, to interrogate its members, to find out what we're up to. But very reliable sources report that the team was destroyed in a shootout in Munich. So it appears that our people simply ran out of luck and were canceled by the Gestapo."

Truman: "Let me have their names in a memo, will you? I'd like to know who they were, where they came from. They must have been pretty special folks."

Brandt: "They always are, Mr. President."

145

(A pause here.)

Truman: "Is there anything you need, Mr. Brandt? Anything you're not getting I could help with?"

Brandt: "No, sir."

Truman: "Call me if there is."

I transcribe all this here for the usual reason.

I've just reread the intercept file on wireless traffic between Red Glare and Olga—as sparse as it is. The texts reveal a sad truth: Olga is a very audacious agent, and Red Glare, as Olga's control, can manage to be helpful only after the fact.

Olga is the personification of espionage and its techniques.

There are too few Olgas. Too many Red Glares.

On both sides.

Olga, I salute you. Whatever the hell you're up to.

Meanwhile, I'm going to hit the goddam sack.

CHAPTER 15

Eckerdorf, Bavaria
12 May 1945

Georgi, Gretl had learned, was a Guards colonel who had served as a division intelligence officer in the First Ukrainian Army and was now on special duty with the NKVD. He was also a supercilious snob, thanks to the fact that the various automobiles and refrigerators and wrist watches he had confiscated and subsequently black-marketed in his travels through Austria had made him a millionaire.

The Ressels didn't make him any easier to bear; they virtually fell over themselves in their efforts to please him—giving him the best room in the house, serving him the best cuts of meat and cheese, bowing and scraping with yes, comrade, this and no, comrade, that—all the time

147

mouthing a grotesque admixture of Party clichés about classless societies and pseudoChristian beatifications of suffering and poverty.

He was not so obtuse as to miss her resentment. "Ah, Comrade Gretl, you are not pleased with me," he said.

She was severe. "Indeed I am not, Comrade. You did not consult me before doing this to Lukas."

They both regarded the bed, where Lukas's long body lay stiffly, arms to his sides, battered boots thrusting out over the footboard.

"The interrogation was going nowhere, my dear Gretl. I remind you that—"

"Don't patronize me, Georgi. I am not some naïve little cadet. I am here as a special administrator, awaiting orders from the Kremlin itself. I am therefore in no way subject to your petty tyrannies. And, I assure you, I will not tolerate your taking drastic actions without first consulting with me. You and Taras, that wriggling pilot fish of yours, seriously jeopardize our government's plans by going off on tangents like this."

This was brave talk. She knew very well, and she suspected that he knew she knew, that his mission was twofold: He was indeed charged by the NKVD with discovering what the Americans might have learned from the treasonous Zelinkov; but he had also been sent out by his army-level political adviser to keep tabs on this woman who carried a letter of appointment—signed by no lesser light than Commissar Mikoyan—as district administrator for Oberbayern and the Tyrol. The question belaboring everyone, herself most of all, was, administrator of exactly what? Mikoyan, as head of the People's Commissariat of Foreign Trade, was a party boss of the first magnitude, of course. But his personal involvement in clandestine military operations in southern Germany and western Austria was a matter that stirred great curiosity among the cognoscenti. Now that the war had ended, many unusual

148

evolutions could be expected, to be sure, but the fact that one of the Soviet Union's most exalted luminaries was grubbing about in the garbage of a conquered enemy was extraordinary. Had new duties been assigned Mikoyan, the black-eyed Armenian superboss? Or was this mere subterfuge—high-level chicanery calculated to mislead unspecified enemies of the State?

Whatever, Comrade Gretl found her patience being tested as never before, simultaneously awaiting a mysterious message from Moscow that would order her to do hell-knows-what while fending off the nosy intrusions of lightweight Machiavellis like Georgi and his army chieftains.

Something very big was afoot, and every Party member from Moscow to Pimpleass-on-the-Rhine wanted to know what it was. And because she was part of it, present in Eckerdorf by virtue of an Olympian letterhead, she was the object of much interest and no little fear.

Lukas twitched.

"I'd better get out of here for now," she said. "See that he is attended to—something on that cut on his head, or whatever."

"You sound as if he has suffered the wound of the century, Comrade Gretl. It was only a knock on the head, timed to the blank cartridge. I've seen Taras give his lady friends harder taps than that."

"I've no doubt about that. He's a sadistic wretch."

"Prisoners often become quite talkative after they find they have not really been shot to death. Life—survival—takes on new meaning after the darkness, and all that."

"I suspect you won't get much talk out of Lukas no matter what you do. For an American, he's a tough bastard."

"Pfah. All Americans turn up sissies when you find the right button to press."

Lukas groaned and raised a hand to his head.

149

She slipped out the door and headed for the kitchen, where General von Fetzer, now dressed in faded lodens, sat at the table, sipping his schnapps and remembering past glories.

The pain was one of those throbbing, intense things that wandered beyond the wound itself. He lay quietly, willing himself to consciousness behind closed lids, exploring with his returning mind the individual achings that composed the dominant discomfort.

His awakening impression had been one of curiousity; he was dead, of course, and yet there was sensation—this awareness of his body, running with inner currents, resonating faintly to a beat. Hurting. What would come next, now that he had traveled intact to the other shore? Angelic choirs? Misty satraps, taking stock of his lifetime, issuing or denying visas? An interview with God? Why was he not more excited about this? Why did he keep remembering the minutiae of boyhood—climbing the apple tree, the smell of rain on autumn leaves, the clanging of streetcars, smoking cigarettes behind the garage, Ma's blue apron?

That light over there. It looked exactly like a window with a sunlit garden beyond. Footsteps nearby. The smell of pipe tobacco and sweat.

What kind of death was this?

Death in itself is nothing. We fear to be we know not what, we know not where. . . . Who the hell said that?

Smart-ass. The world is filled with smart-asses.

A voice.

Speaking American English.

"President Truman today announced an immediate halt in Lend-Lease shipments to the Soviet Union, saying that economic aid to the Russians is no longer needed now that the Germans have surrendered. Informed sources concede that the move was due in great measure to Truman's anger

150

over what he sees to be growing Soviet obstructionism. In a—"

Music.

The Dipsy Doodle?

The warble and hiss of a dial being searched, then another voice, this one using haughty German to introduce a Handelian interlude. (Who was the musician who said, when offered the opportunity to play the pipe organ once used by Handel, "Ah, what an honor; to handle the handles Handel handled"? Now there was a smart-ass for you. Eh?)

There followed another void, and when he was aware again it was night. Or at least dark beyond the window, which itself was lighted faintly by what seemed to be an oil lamp on the table beside it. And he knew he was not dead because he found himself considering means by which to get out of this here, whatever and wherever it was, and get back to the there in Dijon for a talk with—What was his name? Brandt.

A serious talk. About waste, and impulsiveness, and stupidity, and excess.

There was a bandage on his head, a slab of tightness over the deep pain. He tried to sit erect on the cot but was held fast. His imprecise gaze passed from the window and its lamp, to the whitewashed walls, to the ceiling beams, to the plank floor, to the ropes that lashed his wrists and ankles to the bedposts.

The fact of the ropes was more than he could deal with. He subsided, ready once again to be deeply asleep.

He struggled against the need.

"Wake up, Lukas." He heard his own voice, a croaking in the silence. "Turn your head. Look at von Fetzer. Look at the table beside you."

He answered himself. "Why should I? Von Fetzer is sleeping. The table is—"

"Don't argue. Look."

* * *

151

The message had arrived.

At last.

In a rather impressive coincidence.

It had arrived exactly when the tension and doubt had brought her to the rim of panic. The earlier exchange with Georgi, her own gathering sense of danger and incipient failure that built with each day that passed, the confusion over Lukas and what she should do about him—all had grown until her readiness to cut and run was at ultrapitch. But then came the rattle of a motorbike in the lane, the tapping on the door, the hushed conversation between Ressel and the rider, a man who wore a Wehrmacht overcoat dyed navy blue and who insisted on a password before he would speak another syllable.

"Windowpane."

Ressel's word, delivered from the shadows of the foyer, had produced a sound of relief and a muttered good-bye from the biker, a fading of the motor's burbling in the misty night, and a plastic-wrapped envelope, now resting heavily in her hands. She had gone to her room at once, Ressel and the others watching after her. Now by the light of her lamp she undid the packet. Her mind, in a kind of aberrant independence, called up the long-gone schooldays poem:

> From an old English parsonage,
> Down by the sea,
> There came in the twilight
> A message to me—

The barely remembered words, their cadence, the thought they left uncompleted, moved her in a subtle, physical way, actually hurting her breast with an inexplicable sadness and foreboding. It was still with her, this depression, and it evoked what amounted to relevant irrelevancies: the gloom of the Muscovite years and the family's teeterings between giddiness and despair; her

152

father's brave coping with his personal lostness; her simmering at having been cheated of what she could think of even then as a normal childhood in a normal household in some normal somewhere.

To hell with it. On with the job.

She read the contents of the packet. Then, with Fetzer guarding Lukas in the bedroom, she gathered the others—Georgi, Taras, the Ressels, Boris and Nikki—in the upstairs common room. They sat on the hard Bavarian benches and regarded her with undisguised curiosity. She took a seat at the oak desk, placing the packet of documents under the lamp, where she could refer to them as she went.

"The next phase of our campaign against the capitalists begins tomorrow morning, my friends." She kept her voice low, her tone even. "We have received our orders, and we all have our tasks. Mine, obviously, is to see that you and all the other comrades in the Bavarian and Tyrolean territories do your tasks well. For now I'll summarize, hit the highlights, as the saying has it. Detailed assignments will be given each of you later this evening." She paused in the interest of dramatic suspense, and the cuckoo clock's ticking was loud in the room.

"This past winter, at Yalta and elsewhere, the Western capitalists agreed to a partitioning of Germany. The Red Army is to occupy the eastern half of the nation, except for Berlin, where France, Britain, and the United States will be given token sectors to administer. Overtly, the USSR will go along with this general arrangement. But the orders we have just received set in motion a clandestine operation which, if all goes well, should, by the end of the year, place all of the German national territories under Soviet rule."

She paused again. There was tension in the air, almost as tangible as the tobacco smoke that drifted in the lamplight.

"The Red Army," she said quietly, "is regrouping. A
153

saturation occupation of the German national territories will be accomplished on or before year's end. Our forces are presently occupying areas along the Niesse River, thereby already overreaching the limit agreed upon at Yalta, which was the Oder River. Currently, fresh divisions are being formed around combat cadres drawn from the Leningrad–Finnish fronts, and these will be brought in to augment the forces needed to establish the new Soviet western frontier, the Rhine River itself."

The tension broke as she expected it would. There was a stirring, and Taras, predictably, called out, "My God, Comrade Gretl: This will put us in a shooting war with the Amis and the other capitalist swine. How can we fight a war that size at this time? Our forces are depleted, our—"

She held up a hand, partly to keep control of the meeting, partly to be a good sport by parodizing a priestly blessing. Tara's reference to God had provoked general amusement —it was considered droll in high Party circles these days to blaspheme—and she wanted to show that she, too, had a sense of humor in face of sobering crisis. She knew she had been successful when the tittering became laughter.

"Indeed they are, Comrade Taras. But the Americans are, curiously, in even worse shape. They have a huge army, an unsurpassed air force here on the Continent, to be sure. But these enormous military entities are, even at this moment, in rout—falling apart, disintegrating in face of the overriding fact that all American soldiers are wanted at home by their mamas."

"What the hell does that mean, Comrade?" Boris asked, chuckling, shaking his head.

"The Amis are demanding, now that the war against the Nazis is won, that the GIs in Germany be returned home at once. The American Congress, as you know, is extremely emotional and superficial in its thinking and, thanks to its need to be re-elected every two years, bends with every little shift in the political winds. Well, a gale is forming in
154

the American political skies today, comrades. And, since the members of Congress want to keep their jobs more than they want to keep Europe stable, the storm will return America's little boys to their mamas and deliver absolute control of all Germany to the Soviet Union. Without a shot being fired."

Georgi sneered. "No one is a stauncher communist than I am, Comrade Gretl, and no one can claim greater confidence in the sagacity and constructive daring of Generalissimo Stalin and our other leaders. But I find this—this extravaganza—to be ill-timed and ill-conceived. The Americans, for all their childishness, are still stupendously powerful and dangerous."

"You must hear me out, Comrade. The USSR will not attack Anglo-American-French forces in the west of Germany. There should be no need to. Comrade Stalin has shrewdly foreseen the precipitous demobilization resulting from the emotional demands of the Amis. He has decided, as I gather from this packet, that once the American rout is in full scramble, he can move Red Army troops directly through territories 'held' by disorganized dregs of Anglo-American forces without armed resistance from them. He has further decided that the American people won't stand for a new war against the Soviet Union when there's still a war against Japan to be won. They will see that they simply cannot—even if they wanted to—mount a continent-size war against us when they have no resolution in the Pacific."

"But I thought we were committed to entering the war against Japan. To helping the Americans—"

Gretl nodded. "So goes the lip service. So suggests our pretended regrouping of troops for such a campaign. But according to my papers here, we will declare war against Japan only when it suits us. That will be if and when a vacuum follows a military impasse between the Amis and the Japanese. Then, of course, we'll walk in and pick up the chips."

A silence followed as the epochal idea was digested.

"I still think the Amis will fight."

"Comrade Stalin cites a precedent that gives him confidence that they will not. In 1940, while the USSR was in accommodation with Hitler, Russian troops occupied the Baltic states on Nazi Germany's perimeter. Comrade Stalin assured Hitler that the USSR was merely putting an end to 'discords' caused by anti-Soviet interests there. Hitler was furious, of course, but he was preoccupied with his conquest of France, and he was compelled to accept the fait accompli. According to the summary in this packet, there is strong likelihood that a war-weary U.S. public—still persuaded that the USSR is an ally—will be indifferent to, perhaps even support, Stalin's friendly moves to counter incipient Nazi guerrilla activity swirling in the wake of homeward-bound American soldiers."

"Well—"

Gretl persisted. "And if the Amis do manage to mount some kind of military resistance to our sifting invasion, they will be defeated. And all this gabble would prove to be academic, because then we would then, in actual fact, control the world."

Another silence.

Frau Ressel, ever the worrier, asked, "So what are we to do in all this? We outland Party members?"

Gretl was ready for this. "Cells throughout Germany will prepare the way for Red Army troops. As they did in the Baltic area, and are continuing to do in Poland and the Balkans. There will be heavy propaganda campaigns. We must recruit disaffected members of the German military, infiltrate labor and management remnants, establish supply depots, form quasimilitary guerrilla units up to battalion strength, usurp elected political offices, staff bureaucracies with Party faithful, and so on. Those of us here tonight have been given great responsibilities. I shall serve as district administrator, as I've said. Each of you, as

156

a member of the leadership corps, will carry the plan to predetermined locations between Emden on the northwest and Bad Reichenhall on the southeast, where you will revive dormant Party cells, lead organizational efforts, and, subsequently, direct zonal guerrilla support for incoming Red Army troops."

Frau Ressel asked, "Can't my husband and I stay here? This is our home, our—"

"No, you cannot. The Party needs you elsewhere." Gretl consulted her papers. "As a matter of fact, your husband will be assigned to Frankfurt am Main, while you will be located in Hannover."

Frau Ressel looked unhappy. Herr Ressel seemed to be working hard to smother a smile.

An even longer silence ensued, broken by a sudden clattering on the stairway. Fetzer appeared out of the gloom, his eyes wide with concern. Shock.

"The American," he rasped. "He has escaped."

They all leaped to their feet.

"How? How did he get away?" Gretl's face was white with anger.

"I don't know—The ropes—they were cut, and—"

"Taras, you and Boris search the south end of the village. You, Ressel, look in the barns along the alley. You," she snapped at Frau Ressel, "guard the car, in case he makes a try for it. Georgi, you and I will search the town north to the highway."

"What do you want me to do?" Nikki asked, excited.

Gretl gave him a savage glance. "I want you," she said deliberately, "to take that old fool von Fetzer to the cellar and shoot him."

CHAPTER 16

**Frankfurt am Main, Germany
4 June 1945**

It was apocryphal, but the story was that, after his invasion of France, Eisenhower looked over pictures of buildings and locations that might make a nice headquarters for his postwar administration of Germany and chose the I. G. Farben Building in Frankfurt am Main. The word went out immediately to the U.S. Eighth Air Force in England: Bomb Frankfurt to splinters but don't damage the Farben Building. And from what Lukas could see, the order had been followed with mind-boggling precision. Umpteen thousand acres of city now lay devastated, with most of their offices and homes and factories standing no higher—and looking perhaps a little worse—than the Jersey City dump.

Yet in the middle of it all, pristine, lawns and trees greening in the benign spring, every window intact and every shingle in place, the six floors of Farben rose in regal hauteur above the squalor and death-stink at their hem.

Inside, Eisenhower and his deputy, Lucius Clay, the general who would serve as military governor for all the Katzenjammer Kids, were setting up shop. Along the layered arcs of its corridors, fanning out from Ike and Luke's centrality, were the legions of brasshats, clerks, secretaries, guards, communications technicians, mechanics, handymen, janitors, cooks, maids, and window washers who would implement the American national will and see to the secondary interests of the UK, France and all the other Allied powers—including, in one of history's most absurd absurdities, those of the Soviet Union.

Lukas did not enter the compound, which was guarded by magazine-ad U.S. soldiers with polished helmets and white scarves and boots so shiny they looked like candied apples. He drove past, heading east from the Palmengarten to Holzhausen Park, just beyond the Eschersheimerlandstrasse, and then doglegged to the old grammar school which served as his headquarters. He parked the jeep under the schoolyard trees, padlocked the steering wheel, then went inside and climbed the ancient stairs leading to a room under the eaves, where it was his lot to sit at a desk amidst blackboards and chalk dust and make like Superspy.

As expected, something had been added to the office in his lunchtime absence.

"Hullo, Lukas."

"How did you get in here, Frau Keller?"

"Some question to ask of a lady friend who's been through a war with you. You think I came in on my broom, maybe?"

"It's a natural question, you'll have to admit that." He

159

hung his cap on a wall hook while giving her a sidelong inspection. She was wearing what appeared to be a new dress, a summery thing, and it did great things for her, even sitting as she was in one of those godawful office chairs that mocked human contours and grace. Her eyes were bright and merry, and her skin—one of her best features—seemed to glow in the afternoon light.

"You look tired, Lukas."

"The last time I saw you, you were propped by the pillows of a German general's bed."

"And the last time I saw you, you were popping off on that silly motorcycle. What in hell happened to you?"

"I got captured by the Amis. It took me a while to explain the Sturmbannführer's uniform. But, then, here I am again, all properly American." He paused. "Seriously, how did you find me?"

"The war is over. Where do you start looking for a soldier when the war is over? At headquarters. The top headquarters. I begged rides to Frankfurt. I made friends with an Ami aviator stationed at Rhein/Main—a major who drinks a lot. I asked him for a headquarters phone book, the idea being I'd try to make friends with a drunken officer in Personnel, or something, who would be able to trace you for me. But, behold: As my finger ran down the columns it came upon Lukas, Alex, Special Projects, G-2, Schoolhouse Annex, Holzhausen Park, Phone 743. Then, summoning up my extraordinary ingenuity, I hopped one of the few trolleys running in this pigsty town and came to your office. Which I found unoccupied, unguarded and, I must say, extremely unbusy."

"Why, Frau Keller? Why go to all the trouble of looking me up?"

She tossed her head. "I had nothing better to do, actually."

"Come on. Be serious."

She shrugged. "I am being serious. There is nowhere to
160

go for me. There is nobody who cares about me, or I care about. You're the only person in the world who even remotely understands me or tolerates me."

"That doesn't make any sense. Where are all those men who lust after you? How about that general—What was his name? Von Fetzer?—who wanted nothing more than to take care of you?"

"He wanted to take care of me, all right. He kept trying to get into my pants."

"What's wrong with that? He was obviously crazy about you, and people who are crazy about each other—"

"I wasn't crazy about him, you dumbhead. I'm crazy about you."

"Hold on, Frau Keller. Just because we've been through a few adventures together—"

"A few *adventures?* My God, Lukas, we damned near got killed together. That tends to make people close."

"Well, I simply can't get all worked up over all that."

Her face reddened. "Well, I can. Besides, I need your help, damn it. I spent my last thirty marks on this dress, just so I'd look good to you. The least you can do, now that you've spurned my advances, is to give me a helping hand."

"I don't have a hell of a lot of money myself."

"I don't want your money. I want a job."

"A job? I'm not the goddam Personnel officer."

"You can hire me. To help you as I did before."

He gave her a look calculated to show he had enjoyed her little joke. "The war's over, Frau Keller. Swashbuckling's no longer chic."

"I can help you find Hitler."

"I'm not in that business. I am the boss of a one-man department. My job is to write a military history. Besides, Hitler's dead."

"You can't write. You can barely talk."

"Tell it to the U.S. Army." Lukas glanced at his watch.

Frau Keller recrossed her legs and sought vainly for

comfort on the rock-hard chair. Her gaze, dark blue, thoughtful, wandered to the window and the mellow day it framed. "I can't go back to the Tyrol, Lukas."

"Why not? It's your home."

"There's nothing back there for me. It's a place where women are always on the bottom, in bed and out. God, I've done and seen everything there ever was, and now I'm supposed to go back to a duplex in Kitzbühl and marry a shopkeeper and have babies and worry about the ironing and what's for supper? Can you imagine me sitting in the lace-doily parlor, chatting over chocolate with the pastor's wife? Just what am I going to say when Frau Pastor Strudelkopf asks me, all breathless, if Gertrud Flump's winning the crocheting award wasn't the most shocking thing I ever saw? What will Frau Pastor Strudelkopf say when I say, no, the most shocking thing I ever saw was seven Austrian housewives using a child's skipping rope to hang a Russian paratrooper from a barn rafter by his balls?" She sighed, and her hand made an impatient motion.

"You won't be the only person trying to adjust to peacetime, Frau Keller. There'll be a lot of us."

"That's wonderful. That cheers me considerably."

"Well, you want sympathy, go to Pastor Strudelkopf."

"Let's go out and get drunk, Lukas. For old times' sake. What do you say?"

"I say no. It's the middle of the workday."

"What kind of workday does a man have who's writing a history nobody'll ever read? I'll wager that Eisenhower himself is out on the golf course about now."

"Where's Eisenhower going to find a golf course in Frankfurt?"

"'Find'? Eisenhower says at breakfast, Dear me, I wish there was a golf course around here, and twenty thousand German prisoners pick up their shovels and he's teeing off by noon. So diligent Alex Lukas is going to stick to his duty

162

and parse all the sentences in Chapter Ten when he has a chance to get blotto with the sultry, the winsome, the salacious, Gretl Keller? Don't be ridiculous."

He sat back in his swivel chair and rubbed his eyes. "You wouldn't have any fun. I'm a burn-out. There just isn't anything that's fun anymore."

"That's absolute nonsense. I've watched you long enough to know that you're a warrior. You'd never burn out. You aren't the type."

He leaned forward and, with elbows on the desk, gave her a long, not-unfriendly stare. "I know why you're here, Frau Keller. You're not interested in me, you're interested in a job—any kind of a job. But I accept that. I don't hold that against you. So the reason I'm telling you to get out of here is not because you offend me. It's because you bore me. All people bore me. I'm so lonely I want to cry, but I can't stand people. What the hell am *I* going to say to the pastor's wife, Frau Keller?"

She considered him for a moment, her eyes unblinking. Then she stood up, straightened her dress, slung her bag, and said, "Come on, Lukas. We're going for a ride in that jeep of yours. We're going to a place I know in the Taunus hills, and I'm going to introduce you to the best damned bartender and cook in all of this Scheisshaus country—a little fellow named August Katz, who runs a Gasthof brimming with black market whiskey and red beef and bread that floats in the air." She nodded toward the door. "Come on, it's time we got reacquainted."

He shook his head. "Civilians aren't allowed to ride in U.S. Army vehicles. Not only that: Eisenhower has decreed that there will be no fraternization between U.S. personnel and German nationals."

"Lukas, for God's sake. You and I are all we've got. There's nothing else out there." She waved at the window.

He stared at his hands, saying nothing. Outside, beyond

163

the trees, a truck snorted into life and ground its gears. A man shouted something, and another replied with a good-natured obscenity. The truck drove off, blattering.

She went slowly to the door, then turned. "You're missing out on a good thing, Lukas."

"Run along, Frau Keller."

"I can't go back to the old life," she said, her voice low. Without looking at him, she said softly, "I'm special. I'm a very special person. And one thing I promise you: No matter what it costs—you, me, or anybody—I will not go back to being just some Hausfrau on some godforsaken side street in some godforsaken Tyrolean hamlet."

After another silence, she left.

Lukas pushed the button on the chalk tray and waited for the panel to slide full open. Then he stepped through to the inner room and, blinking in the dim light, regarded the man sitting at the table.

"I was right. She's here to find out how much I might have overheard at the Ressels' place that night," Lukas said. "God, what an actress that woman is! She's tricky, sneaky, dangerous, and I think you're out of your mind to lure her here to Frankfurt the way you did."

"Perhaps. But I think we should take her up on her offer to work with you," Brandt said. "After the Great Zelinkov Poop-Out, we need all the help we can get."

TOP SECRET

TWX   7 JUNE 45
TO: BRANDT, FRANKFURT/MAIN C/O SHAEF G-2
FROM: ABIE, HONOLULU
    RE UR TWX OF 6 JUNE 45: UPDATE PACIFIC SITUATION HEREWITH.
    WORD HERE SAYS FUJIMURA, FORMER JAP NAVAL ATTACHE IN BERLIN, HAS SUGGESTED TO OUR OSS RESIDENT CHIEF IN BERN THAT HE CAN INDUCE HIS

164

GOVERNMENT TO ACCEPT U.S. TERMS FOR PACIFIC CAPITULATION. SIMILAR OFFER SAID TO HAVE BEEN RECEIVED FROM MILITARY ATTACHE, GENERAL OKAMOTO, VIA INTERNATIONAL SETTLEMENTS BANK IN BASEL. URGE YOU CHECK BERN OSS FOR DETAILS.

DECODED CABLE TRAFFIC BETWEEN TOKYO AND ITS MOSCOW AMBASSADOR CARRIES FREQUENT REFERENCE TO EMPEROR'S INTEREST IN ESTABLISHING JAP-U.S. DIALOGUE VIA SOVIET CHANNELS. HE IS SAID TO WANT AN END TO THE WAR SO AS TO AVOID CATASTROPHIC BLOODBATH BOTH SIDES. SOVIETS ARE PLAYING COY, REFUSE TO SEE JAP EMISSARIES.

MEANWHILE, TOKYO IS SCENE OF MUCH PUSH AND PULL. KEY MILITARY CHIEFS ARE REPORTED TO BE ANGRY OVER EMPEROR'S STANCE AND HOLD TO THEIR BELIEF THAT LAST-DITCH FIGHT, SCORCHED EARTH POLICY, WILL BE SO COSTLY TO U.S. INVASION FORCES AN ARMISTICE WITH TERMS MORE FAVORABLE TO JAPAN WILL LOGICALLY EVENTUATE. RUMORS ARE THAT SUPREME COUNCIL FOR DIRECTION OF THE WAR (SCDW) IS SPLIT ON QUESTION, BUT MAJORITY LEANS TOWARD CONTINUING WAR. THIS LATTER NOT YET CONFIRMED BUT FURTHER WORD IS EXPECTED EARLY DATE.

DESPITE IMPERIAL PEACE AGITATION, PREVAILING OPINION ALONG DAISY CHAIN MY INFORMANTS IS THAT JAPAN WILL REFUSE TO SURRENDER AND MILITARY OPERATIONS WILL BE EXTREMELY COSTLY BOTH SIDES, PROBABLY ENDING IN STALEMATE WINTER OF 1946–47. IF RUSSIA DECLARES AGAINST JAPAN, IT'S ANYONE'S GUESS.

CLASSIFIED FILE LKJ/556M

SPEC. CC: HST

TOP SECRET

CHAPTER 17

Hauptbahnhof, Frankfurt am Main 8 June 1945

Gretl met Ressel in the shadow of the great railroad station, now not so great, thanks to the twisted steel of its high lattices, to its shattered glass and its crumbled masonry and its shrapnel-pocked facades. They sat on a tuft of sandbags left near the side entrance in some long-ago afterthought of some long-gone Luftschutz coordinator, and from here they had a commanding view of the square and its tributaries, where Ami vehicles, like outlandish, olive-hued insects, rumbled about in the business of disassembling the Third Reich. Inside, somewhere in the station's bowels, a train chuffed and squealed, and the smell of coal smoke and steam amalgamated with the ten thousand as-

166

sorted stinks drifting along with the ragtag itinerants who wandered the concourses with their sorry duffels and backpacks and cardboard suitcases filled with curled shoes and half-eaten wurst.

"Well," Ressel said in a fake-jolly way, "I see you're still at liberty."

"We were lucky. I was just about convinced Lukas had overheard our briefing session. Obviously he didn't."

"You took a hellish chance, walking in on him that way. He might have arrested you on the spot."

"That was the whole idea. If he didn't arrest me, we'd still be in business. If he did, Moscow would have to go into its alternate plan."

"Still, it was risky."

"It's our job to take risks."

There was a pause, stilted and with a certain tension.

"So what's so urgent?" Gretl asked without rancor.

Ressel's eyes avoided hers. "Something has come up. Another problem. It could be serious. Very serious. I thought you should know about it right away."

"That's no answer."

"Well, what I mean is, there's been this, ah, development, and it seemed to me it shouldn't wait until our regular scheduled meeting next week."

She saw that he'd have to tell it in his own way, so she stopped pressing him.

"As you no doubt know," he went on, "my wife has been, ah, shall we say, antagonistic toward you since your arrival in our cell, and—"

"She hates my guts, as a matter of fact."

"Well, that's rather strong, but Frau Ressel has always been suspicious of strangers—it's a trait that runs in her family—and your sudden appearance out of Russia has been somewhat difficult for her to handle." He held up a hand of hasty disclaimer. "Oh, I admit that Russia is a logical place for a communist to appear from, especially one

167

carrying impeccable credentials and a commission to lead. But my wife is not always logical. That is to say, she is quite intuitive and often emotional, if you know what I mean, and it is because of this idiosyncrasy of hers that we are having this conversation. Her, ah, uneasiness about you, Frau Keller, her rather single-minded, angry disapproval of you and your leadership methods, has inspired her to message Samovar. And not only that, but—"

She was compelled to break in here. "Samovar? What do you mean—Samovar? Why would she send a mutinous message to our Moscow supply agency? Is she crazy?"

"Not the agency. Belenko, Samovar's chief. He's a longtime friend of hers. He is very, ah, political—has many excellent contacts in very high places. She has asked him to talk to somebody about getting you transferred, or recalled. Or, failing that, to have the inspector general visit for an inquiry into your competency. Which, no matter how it turned out, would practically ruin your record—your career."

She thought about this incipient crisis. "When did she do this?"

"The night you opened the instruction packet. When she learned she would be assigned to Hannover and you refused to revise, she wrote the letter to Samovar and had Nikki take it to the Schwabing courier."

"Does Georgi know about this?"

"No. My wife pretends to like him—but she really doesn't like him or trust him at all."

"Anybody else?"

"No. Just my wife and I. And now you."

She stared at Ressel. "This is a most serious offense, you know. Going behind the back of her designated superior, sending unauthorized messages through emergency channels, attempting to subvert the lawful orders of Stalin

168

himself—Just one of these offenses could get her shot. Summarily. By me."

"I told her all that," Ressel said unhappily.

She stood up, a kind of reflex reaction to the danger she felt gathering around her. The day was warm, but she hugged herself against the Bahnhof's cavernlike chill. Jealousy, spite: two among the most lethal of the uncountable malignancies that eat away at the human soul. They had invaded the core of a Bavarian housewife, that deeply private center where the woman's perceptions and attitudes and sense of self are borne, and she'd become so riddled with emotional decay that social, political and, eventually, physical suicide seemed acceptable.

Frau Ressel had placed herself in the most precarious position a communist could be in—presenting herself, without careful political preparation among key peers, as superior to her boss. Yet an even larger problem confronted Gretl Keller: what to do by way of effective damage control. And she saw at once that the key to that was Ressel himself.

She fixed him with a stare. "The woman's your wife. By telling me this you could be pronouncing her doom. Why?"

His eyes, faded blue, didn't waver. "I hoped you would understand that she's sick. I hoped you would forgive her."

"You know better than that. She's broken every rule in the book. Unless she can give valid reasons, she faces almost certain punishment—perhaps execution."

Ressel spread his hands in a gesture of confusion.

"Answer my question. Why did you tell me?"

"There's no simple answer," he said, miserable.

"Then give me a complex one."

His shoulders rose and fell with a sigh, and he gazed off at the rubble mountains beyond the square. "I want to prove to you," he said softly, "that I am a loyal champion of the cause."

169

"You've already done that. What's the real reason?"

There was an interval in which he seemed to be assembling the resources needed for confession. True to form, he began far afield. "I was a convinced Nazi from the first. Even in his beer hall days, Hitler was saying all the things I felt—denouncing all the injustices and articulating all the craving for revenge that had consumed me since boyhood, when I'd seen my father come home from the trenches in 1918, haunted, lethargic with indifference and despair, betrayed by the warmongers and exploiters who had stayed home to become rich and powerful while he had fought, fallen twice, and then contracted the tuberculosis that finally killed him. 'We shall get even,' the Führer was saying, and I found myself screaming, 'Yes, yes, yes—Sieg heil!' And then it was my turn to go to France and fall for the Fatherland, and it was the same: 'Nice job, lad; sorry you lost your arm, but we're busy now, so go somewhere where we can't see you, where your difficulties won't give us more guilts and resentments than we have already.'

"Then I got into organized religion, but that proved to be a farce, too, because all I found was blind smugness hardened by centuries of hypocrisy and not even the slightest interest in the root question as to whether there is a God and, if there is, what his intent for us really is.

"My wife? An arrangement between two families and a man and a woman who didn't really like each other much, but who had the same basic angers in common. I discovered that she had been a communist for years, and we talked and talked about it, and it all began to make sense to me—communism and Christianity are not too far apart, except that Christianity asks you to change your ways, your basic personality, where there is no such demand from communism—it exalts you the way you are, glories in everybody's fundamental equality. And—"

She broke in, her impatience with all this specious
170

grandiloquence at an end. "All right, Ressel. So what does this have to do with me, with what your wife has done?"

He did not look at her. The traffic sounds resonated in the blackened hollows of the building behind them; the breeze, hot and dry, carried diesel fumes laced with faint reminders of ruptured sewers, plaster dust, and sweeps of pine in distant hills. She saw in him the personification of the German duality, an amalgam of Goethe and Himmler—one of those trick portraits in which the separate features become dominant, more apparent, depending on how it's turned to the light. And she glimpsed in her own lack of surprise at his answer a measure of her inurement to treachery and dissimulation.

"I cannot," he said hoarsely, falteringly, "get you out of my mind."

"What's that?"

"I—From the first—You are the most incredibly compelling woman I've ever known. Not just your looks. You."

"You mean you have the hots for me?"

"Well, I—I'm not very good at this kind of thing. My experience with women is, ah, limited. And my wife—"

"Is a crashing sexual bore, eh?"

"Understand, she's not a bad woman—"

"But she's a rotten lay. Is that what you mean?"

"Please don't make it sound so—grubby."

She found it difficult to keep a straight face. Here was this fatuous cowplop, reeking of murder and adulterous ambitions, who pleaded for fastidious language in discussions of his perfidy. As one who recognized and accepted her own warts, she had little patience for fools who indulged in euphemism and self-delusion. She was a soldier, and she had killed without compunction, because the victims had been trying to kill her—or would have readily killed her with proper opportunity. She had developed double-talk and flimflam to the level of a performing art; but

171

these skills were excluded from any dealings with herself, since deception, a noble obligation in the context of war, becomes self-destructive idiocy the moment it's allowed to cross the threshold of one's own house. Her mother's voice came back in that moment: "You can freely lie to me, you can freely lie to your father, you can, maybe, freely lie to God and his angels—but you can't lie to yourself without paying a rotten price somewhere down the line."

So a man who would kill simply to satisfy a craving for sexual adventure and then smother that truth in pretty words was not the kind of man Gretl could easily tolerate. But even in her contempt she perceived that Ressel's vulnerability provided her with a weapon against the threat represented by Frau Ressel and Belenko at Samovar.

She had killed as a patriotic duty. She had lied as a grand strategy. Now, as she had also done before, she would screw as a tactical maneuver.

"I'm not being grubby," she said. "I'm being frank, realistic. When two people have the hots for each other they should admit it. Name it for what it is. Submit to it. Get it out of their systems by direct, immediate action."

There was a suspended moment while he digested this. Then: "Two people?"

"You don't think you're the only one, do you?"

"You mean—"

"I mean I've wanted to tear your clothes off from the moment we met. Where's your place here?"

He stared at her, his expression part elation, part disbelief, part shock. "My place? I—I have a room in a damaged townhouse on Myliusstrasse. It's not bad—"

"Take me there at once."

"It's midafternoon. I mean, broad daylight—"

"It's the best time. We can see what we're doing."

"Well—"

172

"Would you rather be raped this instant? In sight of all these people?"

"My God—I'm speechless—"

"Come on. I will soon make you pants-less."

Lukas returned the binoculars to their case on the seat beside him, and waited while Frau Keller and Ressel crossed the Bahnhofsplatz to a blue Opel sedan parked in the shadow of a ruin. She entered the car. Ressel raised the hood with his good arm, took the distributor cap from his coat pocket, inserted it in the motor, then drove off.

Easing the Mercedes into gear, Lukas joined the traffic flow, keeping an unobtrusive fifty meters behind the blue car. He stayed with them until they braked to a halt in front of a riddled brownstone on Myliusstrasse, near the Palmengarten.

They were in a hurry.

He could tell, because Ressel didn't bother to remove the distributor cap before they scurried up the steps and disappeared behind the scarred brown door.

CHAPTER 18

"Gretl?"

"Mm."

"That's the most extraordinary experience I've ever had. You are unbelievable."

"You're pretty hot stuff yourself."

"You really think so?"

"Your wife doesn't know what she was missing."

"We've got to stay together. I mean, I simply have to have more and more and more of this—"

"You can have all you want. With one provision."

"Provision?"

"You've got it as long as you keep me completely informed on whatever falls out of your wife's letter to Belenko. I must know everything. Everything. If I find out you're hold-

174

ing back, or otherwise not keeping me informed, there'll be no more of this."

"Small price to pay."

"Now let's do it all again. I'll start, you finish."

"Oh, God—You are absolutely wonderful—"

Entry in Personal Diary of C. G. Brandt

Camp Ritchie, Maryland
12 June 1945

On Saturday afternoon I was still in Frankfurt, sipping cold ones in the Farben Casino with Roger Wagner and reminiscing about the old days in the Moscow embassy. Now here it is, Tuesday night, and I'm sitting on a GI bunk at the War Department Intelligence Training Center near Hagerstown, trying to write down the impressions of the intervening days. Well, hours, actually.

The order came in on the G-2 TWX just before dinner, and I had just an hour to pack and get to Rhein/Main and an Air Corps DC-6 that was already running up its engines for the flight to Anacostia. I slept most of the way to Gander, but after we were airborne again I got into a penny ante poker game with a couple of army nurses on TDY from the hospital at Wiesbaden who were en route to Walter Reed for additional training on burn therapy. They were nice kids, somewhat intimidated at first by my grizzled face and civies, but after I lost a few they got to calling me Pops and accepted me as one of the bunch. More or less. I know they were very curious about who I was and where I was going, but they showed the right stuff and didn't ask any questions.

Nor did the people at Harry's meeting.

The news that Stalin plans to steal Germany is still very much under wraps. The president is cool and deliberate

175

about the whole thing; having been suspicious of the Soviets for so long he is apparently less than surprised by this godawful turn of events. But he has spread the word sparsely and on a need-to-know basis, since his overriding concern is that word will get out and the American people (read Congress) will go into a hot tight spiral and demand either (1) a precipitous military action that has no hope of success or (2) meek acceptance of a Europe that has been split forever down the middle.

He frankly admitted at today's meeting that he cannot guess which way Congress would come down.

The meeting, which was not carried on the president's appointments schedule, began in the Oval Office at noon. He introduced me simply as "one of General Eisenhower's senior advisers on German affairs." The others present were the secretary of state, James Byrnes; the secretary of war, Henry Stimson; the chief of staff, General Marshall; Harry's military adviser, Admiral Leahy; and Charles Ross, White House press chief. There were sandwiches and coffee, but nobody ate much, what with all the high-powered conversation.

Harry sat at his big desk and the rest of us were spotted around on chairs and sofas. I'd heard about these people, and had read about them in the papers, and I tried very hard to be impressed. But it was as always before when I've met VIPs: I saw them as nothing more than guys with gray suits, ties slightly awry, freckles, thinning hair, and dots of bridgework here and there. They shifted in their seats like anybody else, scratched their noses, stifled yawns, crossed and recrossed their legs, and doodled on cheap yellow pads. They were ordinary people, made famous by the luck of the draw, by being in the right place at the right time when news reporters happened to be hanging around.

Harry seems to think they all know their stuff. He would listen with interest and care whenever one of these gents

176

got off on something, although I admit I had difficulty following some of the thoughts expressed.

There was a lot of talk about a big new bomb that's in the works. From what I gather, it's based on a new kind of explosive, very much more powerful than TNT, with one bomb able to do the work that usually requires several blockbusters. Stimson did most of the commenting here, going on about upcoming tests out west. Marshall expressed some concern over the unwieldiness of the weapon and its implications as a point of political contention. Stimson said that if we can get one of the damned things together to fit in a plane, it should have a decisive effect on how things go in the Pacific next year. Ross said the biggest political problem lurking in the device was its humongous cost. The price was up in the jillions by now, and if the thing proved to be a dud we'd all be looking for jobs come next election.

What burned me most was the leisurely way they all got around to the real problem: Stalin's plans for a filter invasion of Germany. That was the only reason for my being in the room, yet I had to wait until a quarter to one for Harry's invitation to explain what was going on over there.

I went over it all, from Chesnikov's suicide at the airfield last February, through the Lukas line-crossing that resulted in our pick-up on Keller's briefing of the Eckerdorf cell, to our current attempts to penetrate the German advance party for the Russian coup. Only Harry showed the slightest concern. The others continued with their doodling, their nose-scratching, their yawn-stifling. But then General Marshall took pains to explain the prevailing dilemma:

Demobilization fever is already consuming the armed forces, fed by hot winds from Capitol Hill; military units being transferred from Europe through the United States

177

to the Pacific are near open mutiny; public opinion polls are showing that more than 70 percent of the American people approve the point system by which soldiers are being returned Stateside for discharge; the consensus of mail received by congressmen and bureaucrats is that America has won half the war, so why shouldn't half the army be allowed to come home? The U.S. military capability in Europe, General Marshall said with detectable bitterness, is rapidly approaching impotence. Admiral Leahy (whom I disliked for some reason) was even more blunt: If Uncle Joe Stalin wants to take Germany he'll get it, because all we can do in Europe right now is bellyache.

To his credit, Harry broke in here: "Now listen here, you fellas, we're just not going to let things go by that easy—not while I have anything to say about it. I just won't hand over Germany to those goddam Russians, and that's all there is to it. Now I want you service fellas to get your heads together with Jimmy Byrnes and work out some plans. Mr. Brandt here will be available by TWX or radio if you have any questions. But be sure to carbon me in. And, if you value your skins, boys, you won't say a word about any of this to anybody—including your missus—because you'll have me to answer to if you do. I want something to take with me to the Potsdam meeting next month, and I don't want it all in the papers before I even get on the goddam ship."

So it's all a lousy mess. Lukas, my other deep-dish people, work their asses off to find out what the hell is going on, and what happens? The president of the United States has to lecture his trusted advisers on carbon copies and not shooting off their mouths and they scratch their damned noses and disappear into the Washington woodwork because all the damned moms have suddenly become expert military strategists and want half the army home because there's only half a war left to fight.

After the meeting I came back here to Camp Ritchie to

be with old friends and get the taste of Washington out of my mouth. But even that hasn't worked out. The army and navy intelligence structures are being cut to the core. The OSS is being disbanded and will be replaced by some kind of central clearing agency for intelligence matters. The CIC is being moved out of Chicago and will be stuck in a corner of Fort Holabird, a nothing post in Balti-goddam-more.

Here at Ritchie, all the good guys have already been demobbed, thanks to all the points they racked up over the years of war.

They have been replaced by a handful of fuzz-faced kids.

Only one in four I talked to at the officers club this evening can even read German.

None of them has ever heard Russian being spoken.

What do I tell people like Fred, Sam, Toni, Lukas—the others?

What do I tell myself?

CHAPTER 19

Frankfurt am Main, Germany
20 June 1945

Lukas sat by the lagoon between
the Farben Building and its dining
casino, watching a cluster of sparrows fighting over a potato chip
dropped earlier by a snacking fatty
in an UNRRA uniform. The birds
were hungry and angry, like almost
everybody else indigenous to this
godforsaken country. And, like almost everybody else, they didn't
seem to mind who they pooped on as
long as they got theirs.

His watch told him he still had
eleven minutes. The meeting with
Lieutenant Colonel J. M. Reevy, a
secondary honcho in the Theater-
level MI supply section attached to
Eisenhower's G-2, was essentially a
move, suggested by Brandt, to line
up some resources for what was now

being called Operation Termite. Reevy was a product of the college ROTC system, vintage 1936, who seemed never to have left the frat house. Thanks to years of whiffenpoofing down at some Mory's or other, both in the service and before, his face had become beefy, with reddish veins in his drinker's nose; he wore his black hair in a severe pompadour that glistened with Vitalis, and he was just so crazy about himself he could hardly stand it. Worst of all, the man was asserted to have "social connections" with Lucius Clay, the Big Honcho in the upcoming administration of the German West Zone. This, if true, was bad news; if Reevy had had "social connections" with Ike instead, there would have been less to worry about, since Eisenhower was due to return Stateside for—it was said—a run at the U.S. presidency, and Reevy's clout would dissipate quickly. The out-of-sight-out-of-mind rule applied in local army politics.

Reevy would have been endurable if he'd truly known something about intelligence work, but on the few occasions Lukas had watched him operate—mainly at G-2 Monday morning briefings—he'd shown himself to be a sycophantic horse's ass who should have been counting tent pegs at Fort Dix. All of which made the approaching meeting the source of considerable depression for Lukas, already depressed by the news that he was about to be pretty much on his own because Brandt would be spending most of his time in Washington from now on.

"All right," he snarled at the sparrows, "break it up, you noisy little bastards. And get back to your goddam barracks."

The birds spiraled upward in a beating of wings, and two WAC lieutenants, passing by, gave him a sidelong glance and began to giggle. He watched after them—their Ipana teeth glistening in the morning sunlight, their tidy bottoms rippling under their precisely fitted green skirts, their shoulders squared so as to display the noble boobies

181

beneath their blouses—and he saw the impassable abyss between him and the likes of them. Their Betty Coed world was forever closed to him by the bodies of Leutnant Griessmaier and Unteroffizier Mueller, the nameless men on the ridge outside Eckerdorf, the Russian buried under tons of snow above Going, and God knows who else he, personally and with no real malice and the most dubious of justifications, had sent to glory. Frau Keller had it right: There was no one or anything out there anymore.

Frau Gretl Keller.

Who was she, really? Where had she come from? A tiny sod hut on the rim of Siberia? A somber brownstone on a gray side street in Minsk, or Pinsk, or Assholograd-on-the-Volga? Where and how had she learned to be such an actress, such a glib and duplicitous and conniving goddam amazon?

How could he have been so readily taken in by her crap?

How could he possibly have felt a stir of excitement when she'd given him those speculating, salacious stares?

Shee-it.

Lukas stood in the Farben Building's Erdgeschoss lobby and waited for the Paternoster—the elevator that moved up and down and around on an endless chain—to bring him an unoccupied car. The thought of crowding into one of those coffinlike boxes with a gaggle of lardy, briefcase-toting colonels and cologne-reeking civil service dandies was more than he could deal with this early in the day. But traffic was heavy, so he took the stairway and scrutinized the third-floor office numbers until he found the right one. It had a desk commanded by a pruny WAC captain who looked as if she ought to be presiding over third grade at Gump Junction Public School No. 3. She eyed him as if he'd just thrown an eraser and said, "Yes, Colonel Reevy is waiting. Through that door there."
182

The office was bright from the morning glare coming through the tall windows, where Colonel Reevy stood, surveying the parklands outside, hands clasped behind him, rocking on his heels in the style affected by leathery brigadiers in the British Army of the Rhine. His uniform—officer pinks, dark green shirt and Ike jacket, tan tie, lustrous combat boots, brilliant brassware, good conduct ribbons all the way to his chin—was a wonder to behold. Lukas was abruptly aware of his own scuffed shoes and his lumpy ODs, whose sole claims to elegance were brass officer-type U.S. insignia pinned to the lapels.

"You're Lukas, right?"

"Yes, sir."

"You work with Brandt in the OSS, right?"

"That's right. Colonel."

"What's your rank?"

"I'm not at liberty to say, sir."

"You're too young to be anything over a first John."

"Does it matter, Colonel?"

Reevy's dark eyes came around to regard him with displeasure. "You're damned right it makes a difference, young fella. I don't like to talk with anybody who hides behind anonymity."

"I didn't make the rules."

"I don't like your tone, fella."

"I'm not so crazy about yours, either."

"Now listen here—"

Lukas sighed. "Come on, Colonel. Are we going to have a meeting? Or are we going to have a pissing contest? Let me know. The fly on these pants is blue hell to unbutton."

The phone purred, and Reevy picked it up. His clouded face showed an instant transformation. "Good morning, General," he said heartily. "It's good to hear your voice. I saw you and the Theater Commander walking in the park a moment ago. You're looking fit, as usual."

The phone sounded a faint *lagalagalaga.*

Reevy's eyes turned to focus on Lukas. "Yes, General. Yes, sir. He's here now. Just walked in."

Lagalagalaga.

"I see. Yes, sir."

Lagalagalaga.

"You bet, General. That I'll do."

The general must have hung up, because Reevy returned the phone to its cradle with no further comment. After a suspended moment Reevy regarded him from under lowered brows, and said, with a somewhat rueful tone, "That was General Clay."

"Oh?"

"He says I'm to give you every consideration. I am to be filled in on what you're up to, then give you every consideration."

"How about that."

"What does he mean, 'every consideration'?"

"Beats me, Colonel. I had no idea he knows I even exist."

"It's Brandt. I sense his hand in this."

"I wouldn't be surprised. He seems to have a lot of friends in high places."

Colonel Reevy considered this unhappily. "That's the trouble with you OSS and CIC types. It's impossible to keep you sorted out, to know who's who and doing what."

"That's the idea, I guess, Colonel. To keep enemy intelligence people from sorting us out."

"A lot of melodramatic nonsense."

"Ain't it, though."

"Well, you might as well take a seat, Lukas." Reevy nodded at an ornately gilded chair that looked as if it might have been looted from the Reichsmuseum. Sitting behind the desk, he asked neutrally, "So what have you been up to?"

Lukas pondered the question. How did you tell a clown like this about life under the rock? What words would

184

convey the sight, the smell, the feel of, say, arguing with a Wehrmacht Unteroffizier in the red twilight, of drawing a pistol and shooting the man dead as he stands there, scratching his behind? Even more important: Why in hell should he be told anything at all?

"I've been trying to get to the bottom of a rumor that says the Soviets are planning some kind of large-scale political move. I haven't had a hell of a lot of success, I might add."

The colonel snorted. "Everybody knows they are about to declare war on Japan. How large-scale a political move do you want, for God's sake?"

"This is something else. Last February we got wind of a defection—General Zelinkov, a hotshot Soviet intelligence type. He was supposed to crash-land his plane in the Tyrol, and we were supposed to pick him up. But the weather went bad, we couldn't make the jump, and Zelinkov was captured by the Germans. I and some others made a line-crossing and jerked him out of a Munich jail, but he was shot in the move and told us before he died that he'd left a message near the wreck of his plane. I recovered the message, but it was nothing more than a letter of farewell from Zelinkov to his family. He'd written it on a message flimsy and curled it into an empty shell casing. 'Love and kisses, from Dad.'"

"You mean you went to all that trouble just to get a dead Russian and a good-bye note?"

Lukas shrugged. "It happens a lot in our business. Work your ass off only to find it's a dry well."

"Dear God. A trick like that must've cost a fortune in confidential funds. All for nothing."

"Yeah, we spent a buck here and there. Lost some people, too."

"An unconscionable waste, money as tight as it is."

"Yeah."

"Where do you go from here?"

185

"In the Zelinkov caper we picked up some people who seem to have a line on what Moscow plans. I'm trying to exploit these sources. But it's going to take the usual—time, movement, and money. And that's where you come in, I guess."

Reevy made a face. "Do you have the slightest idea, Lukas, how bad things are in the Theater at this time? Do you have the foggiest notion how difficult it is for a man in my position to keep things going, sorted out, when the goddam U.S. Army is coming apart at the seams?"

"Must be rough, all right."

Reevy leaned forward, elbows on the desk, his eyes narrowed in righteous anger. "There are ten acres of six-by-sixes and jeeps, all with tires and radios and every other goddam thing, sitting near Kassel, waiting to be burned because it's cheaper to burn them than it is to send them back to the States. But I can't get authorization to supply the Munich CIC office three lousy vehicles to use in transporting war crimes suspects from Stadelheim jail to the frigging railroad station. Ike and Lucius Clay are under orders to 'sanitize the German political system and restore the German national economy'—but the Yanks who know how to do this are being sent home, and the Germans who know how to do this are being sent to jail, for crissake, and all we got left is a handful of low-points draftees from Punkin Corners, Indy-goddam-ana, who spend all their time trying to lay Fraw-leins without getting caught in violation of that asinine no-fraternization law Ike passed against his better judgment. How the hell do you restore a national economy with a bunch of pimple-faced squids who wouldn't know a bond issue if it hit them in the balls? How do you sanitize somebody else's political system when your own goddam political system is run by airheaded assholes who think only of being re-elected and couldn't care less about the country's greater need and long-term interest? How do you do it? Eh?"

186

Lukas stared out the window. "Makes a guy wonder, all right."

Reevy ran his hands over his shiny pompadour, managing to look like a very irritable Basil Rathbone. Then, fixing his dark eyes on Lukas, he grated, "So General Clay says I should give you every assistance. So what every assistance do you want?"

"A permanent trip ticket, authorizing me to drive any vehicle, U.S. or European, up to and including six-by trucks and recon half-tracks. Unlimited gas ration card. Same for tires, and motor maintenance at any motor pool in the U.S. Zone of Occupation. Authorization to carry any and all small arms, U.S. and European. Authorization to wear civilian clothes, on or off U.S. military installations. Authorization to transport German nationals in any of these vehicles and to permit their carrying of any small arms under conditions I deem appropriate and in the U.S. national interest. Unlimited access to G-2 confidential funds, including U.S. dollars and the currencies of other major nations, to be accounted for monthly with the G-2 Finance Officer or his designated representatives. Unlimited access to the dossiers held in G-2's Central Registry in this building, as well as a phone code that will give me access from distant points. And access to phone and cable links to a Washington, D.C., number yet to be established."

There was a pause, during which Reevy stared as if Lukas had suddenly sprouted a second nose. Then: "Is that all?"

"For now."

"Even Ike doesn't have half those privileges, those resources."

"Ike doesn't have my problems."

"There's no way I can provide such a—a—"

"So tell Luke Clay. He's the chief sanitizer."

"You—You're impossible, Lukas."

"I'll say."

"Where do I find you?"

"Vom Rath Strasse forty-eight. The compound." He stood up and crossed to the door. Over his shoulder he said, "Cheer up, Colonel. Another nice little war will be along soon."

He went into the curving corridor, rode the Paternoster to the ground floor, saluted the MPs at the exit, and crossed the compound to his apartment, where he poured himself a water glass of Johnny Walker Red.

He tried to get drunk, but it didn't work.

TO: CENTRAL REGISTRY, G-2 SHAEF   20 JUNE 45
CC: C.G. BRANDT
FROM: MESSAGE CENTER, COMMUNIX BRANCH
ADD RADIO INTERCEPT FILE, DOSSIER "OLGA"DATE OF
INTERCEPT AND DECODE: 8 JUNE 45. MEDIUM: CODED
MORSE, 2575 KILOHERTZ. TEXT AS FOLLOWS:
RED GLARE URGENT, RED GLARE URGENT. INFO RE-
CEIVED HERE INDICATES SAMOVAR'S BELENKO BEING
ASKED BY LOCAL DISSIDENT TO UNDERMINE MY AU-
THORITY. PLEASE FIX SOONEST. MOST URGENT. OLGA.
MSGCTR FILE NO. 23354

CHAPTER 20

Bad Schwalbach im Taunus, Germany 25 June 1945

It was lugubrious.

This dot of a town, one of the lesser spas located in the Taunus hills above Wiesbaden, had been chosen by Eisenhower's G-2 as the processing center for the debriefing, decompressing and delousing of U.S. intelligence types— from documents fakers to deep-dish parachute agents —who might otherwise have suffered psychological bends upon their return to the States. The entire Nassauer Hof, the main hotel, was occupied by these ragamuffins, and the town and its Kurpark teemed with gaunt and scruffy individuals who had devised and carried out the dirtiest deeds imaginable against Hitler's henchmen. And glaring down on them from the veranda of a

189

hillside hospital, lined up like immaculate and judgmental deities on the rim of some forested Olympia, were scores of scrubbed and starched SS Sturmtruppen convalescing from wounds received while carrying out the dirtiest deeds imaginable against the likes of those sad sacks wandering the dales below. This irony alone would have been enough to make Lukas smile, if he'd been the smiling kind, but compounding the comedy of absurd proximities was the fact that Bolko Dietrich had taken a room at a pension whose ground floor was the local CIC office. In Lukas's eyes, this was akin to one of Al Capone's guys renting digs in Elliot Ness's headquarters building.

Ah, well.

He had traced Dietrich through dossiers maintained by Central Registry on the Wehrmacht intelligence branch known as Foreign Armies East. Dietrich appeared frequently in German efforts to identify and counter Soviet espionage networks, and while Lukas was making a routine cross-reference with U.S. military government files on the disposition of German war prisoners, he had come upon a Fragebogen completed by Dietrich in Munich on June 2, two days before his release from a POW compound near Tegernsee. The Fragebogen—a kind of personal history and career résumé that MG required of all Germans subject to the de-Nazification laws—was pretty candid. Dietrich had made no bones about his service as an army intelligence officer, and so some MG satrap, probably bemused by such candor in a world of baldfaced lying (Adolf *Who?*), had appended to the Fragebogen a handwritten Permit to Return to Hometown, which allowed Dietrich to leave Bavaria and take up residence in Bad Schwalbach. The Fragebogen and the relocation authorization, taken together, had been all Lukas needed to pop into the jeep and drive the few miles from Frankfurt through the pleasant Taunus hills. It really shouldn't have been so simple, but thank God for little favors.

190

He found Dietrich warming a watery soup over a Wehrmacht trench stove placed in a corner of his attic room. The German was tall, spare, friar-bald and generous. "Will you join me, Herr Lukas? It isn't much, but—"

"No thanks. You go ahead. I simply want to ask you some questions."

Dietrich bobbed his head amiably. "About my years with General Gehlen in Foreign Armies East, no doubt. All you Ami intelligence types want to know about that."

"Well, I'm interested only in a particular aspect of it."

"Glad to tell you anything I can remember. I know you won't believe this, because we Germans today deny all knowledge of, or complicity in, the Nazi thing, but General Gehlen and most of his trusted aides were basically contemptuous of the Führer and his idiotic posturing. I, for one, am happy to be rid of the swine. Just look at what he's done to our country."

"You're right," Lukas said. "I don't believe you."

Dietrich smiled. "See? But I appreciate your sparing me the playacting I got so often from my interrogators after my surrender at Bad Reichenhall. They all tried to convince me that they saw me as the archetypal anti-Nazi. I wasn't, of course. I was mainly an opportunist. I could 'Heil Hitler' with the best of them so long as it kept me in promotions and comfort. But in my private corner, down in that part of the soul where dislike and disgust are born, I disliked the Nazis and was disgusted with what they were doing. And I really don't care if you believe me or not, because I've been freed by your military government and absolved by your war crimes investigators. I can, quite literally—not that I would, because I'm not a defiant and arrogant fellow—tell you to kiss my round, rosy buns." He pursed his lips and blew on a spoonful of his soup.

Lukas sat on the edge of the carefully made cot. "I'm a working man, not a political scientist or a philosopher. I

191

simply need some answers to a couple of workaday questions."

"Which are?"

"What do you know about a female Soviet agent named Gretl Keller?"

Dietrich gave him a quick glance. "Ah. Now there's a woman. One of the toughest, one of the best they have. If she's involved in one of your cases, Herr Lukas, God help you."

"Is that her real name?"

"So far as I know. She was born in Berlin, as I recall. Her father was an early Bolshevik and was killed in the Hitler purges, as was her mother. Gretl swore vengeance, and she gave us fits, I'll tell you, especially in the Ukraine. So our Abwehr people put a team on her. They learned damned little, I'm afraid, because it seems that even her Russian handlers were not too clear on her origins, her motivations, her responsibility scope. One of her control officers, a man named Schansky, was captured near Odessa and interrogated by the Gestapo, and either he was a consummate actor or he truly didn't know the identity of Keller's top boss, because he died claiming ignorance in these matters." Dietrich raised the bowl to his lips and drained the remaining soup. Making a face, he said, "What swill."

"What did she work on mostly?"

"Political resistance. When we invaded the Soviet Union, the general populace was quite supportive—happy to see us, ready to see us as liberators. General Gehlen and other influential staff officers urged the Führer to exploit this by various means calculated to enlist active civilian aid. Hitler vacillated, apparently torn between his ethnic snobbery and his practical needs. As you know, snobbery won out and he lost forever his greatest opportunity to nail down a victory over Stalin and the communist government. Keller was one of Stalin's most valuable tools in generating and focusing civilian outrage over German, ah, ineptitude."

192

"Ineptitude. What a lovely word for the systematic slaughter of a million farmers and their wives."

"It wasn't a million."

"Oh, excuse the exaggeration."

"Don't use your sarcasm on me, Herr Lukas. I was one of Gehlen's officers. I agreed with him on the question. It sickened me to see the atrocities Hitler ordered."

"Sure." Lukas gazed out the narrow dormer beside him. An overcast was forming, giving the slate rooftops a bluish tint. He changed the subject. "Do you have a line on German Red agents named Friedrich and Elsbet Ressel, or on the cell at Starnberg—some guys doing films for UFA?"

Dietrich shook his head. "Sorry. They would have been the concern of the domestic Gestapo, perhaps Foreign Armies West. Although I do recall that one of your people—a man called Brandt, something at your Moscow embassy—had been in communication with the UFA personalities at one time. We intercepted a few radio messages but were eventually cut out by a switch in code."

"You know Brandt?"

"By repute only. One of our Moscow people was always mentioning him in his reports. 'Das ami Arschloch,' he called him. That is, until Gehlen ordered him to stop using obscenities in official communications." Dietrich laughed softly.

"That's all?"

"Willi Grosser, one of our counterintelligence specialists, did a study on Brandt. I read it, but I don't remember a great deal about it. Brandt was a native of the Ukraine, as I recall. His parents emigrated to the United States in the twenties, before the lid went down. He got a good education somewhere—quite a linguist, too, I think—entered your State Department's foreign service branch and ended up in Moscow. He pretended to be some kind of press specialist, but everybody knew he was an intelligence operative. Quite successful, it seems. He had a very effective chain of

193

informants in high places and, I suppose, still does. Grosser tried to exploit Brandt's personal tragedy, but nothing came of it."

"What was Brandt's personal tragedy?"

Dietrich stood up and crossed to a table and, after pouring a pitcher of water into the basin there, rinsed his bowl and spoon, dabbed at his lips and dried his hands on a shred of toweling. "Brandt had taken his wife and kid to Moscow with him. She was a rather pretty woman, I gather. But she proved to be mentally ill—manic depressive, or something—and she died, and Brandt sent the child back to the States, but word was that the kid had died, too—traffic accident, or something—and Brandt went into a heavy depression. When war came, certain of our Abwehr people made an approach or two through a Moscow cutout, but by that time Brandt had emerged from his mourning and plunged into his work with new dedication. Something like that. I wasn't paying too much attention to Grosser's machinations; I was busy with our invasion plans."

"How come you remember Brandt at all? I mean, as busy as you must have been between 1941 and this past winter, why would Brandt, well, linger in your memories?"

Dietrich hunched a shoulder. "You tell me. Why do I remember the earrings Frau Irmgard Gittelmann was wearing when she took my virginity on my twelfth birthday? You'd think all that heaving, naked flesh would linger, as you put it, not a pair of fake pearls."

"I daresay."

"The fact is, though, Herr Lukas, that there was something particularly poignant about Brandt—for me, at least. I was an orphan, and my wife, the only person who had ever shown me any affection, had just run off with a wine salesman. I was very lonely, and I identified with Brandt, I guess. In any event, the human mind, the memory processes, defy explanation."

194

"Especially mine." Lukas stood up, adjusted his jacket and made for the door. "But maybe, along with the earrings, you can remember the names of some of the people who served as informants for Brandt when he was in Moscow."

"Not really. The summaries would come through quite bare sometimes. You know: 'All quiet on the Eastern Front.' That kind of thing. But Grosser put out a memo that was fairly comprehensive. I don't recall exactly when— around the time we were falling back from Kiev, I believe."

"Was Gretl Keller among them?"

Dietrich's eyes widened in astonished amusement. "Haven't you been listening? I said Keller was a Red amazon. She would tear the balls off any man who so much as flirted with treason against the USSR. In fact, Grosser reported last winter that she was the prime mover in the Chesnikov investigation."

"What was that?"

"Chesnikov was a general in the Red Army. He apparently tried to peddle information to Brandt, or one of you Ami types. Keller got wind of it and was said to have thrown all her energies into a probe of the Chesnikov affair."

"What did she do with Chesnikov?"

"He committed suicide when facing arrest. Last I heard from Grosser on the matter, there were other defections and she was trying to negate their effect via all kinds of intervention—in Russia and elsewhere."

"By elsewhere, you mean Germany?"

Dietrich shrugged. "One could assume so. As a matter of fact, I remember General Gehlen mentioning at a lunch in Bad Reichenhall that one of Chesnikov's peers, a General Zelinkov, had tried to defect to you Amis and Keller— herself, personally—was heading for Germany to get him back. I never heard how it turned out. Maybe if you find Gehlen he can tell you more."

"Maybe."

"Whatever you do, let me offer you some friendly advice: Treat Keller as if she's made of nitroglycerin. Because she is. Absolutely. One of Stalin's slickest, most dangerous weapons."

"Thanks."

"So then: anything else, Herr Lukas?"

Lukas opened the door and, from the hallway, said, "Only one thing."

"What might that be?"

"Have you ever heard the Russians use the term—maybe it's a code word—'The poplars?'"

Dietrich thought about this. Then: "No. No, I haven't."

"Have you ever heard *anybody* use it?"

"Only you."

Lukas nodded, swung the door shut, and ambled down the stairs and into the gray day.

He steered the jeep into the turn at the post office and, Wiesbaden-bound, began the long ascent into the hills.

His mind went to the recent night in which he had shared a bottle with Karl Thoma, an MI type waiting in Heidelberg for his points to take him home. The late hour, the booze, turned the talk to The Meaning of Things and Why People Do What They Do. Somewhere in all of it, Karl mentioned the Lion of the Post Office, who was already a legend in Hesse in general and in the Taunus in particular.

"Courage?" Karl said. "Audacity? Standing for principle in face of impossible odds? You find them in strange places. Even in an old coot like the Lion. Hell of a man."

The Lion, Karl said, was an ancient leatherworker named August Something-or-other. He'd been born in the Taunuses, grew up there, learned his trade there, left there to go to World War I, and was, at the close of World War II, doddering through old age there.

His home village, an insignificant dot, had survived the war virtually intact. Even so, the townspeople, mostly
196

grampas, grammas and orphans, had been dreading the American arrival, because their Nazi Gauleiter told them that Yankees made a sport of shooting old people and babies.

The populace agreed that if the Amis were sighted, everybody would stay off the streets and white sheets would be flown from all windows and nothing, absolutely nothing, would be done to annoy the enemy troops as they passed through.

August was the only dissenter. "You mean we're simply to hand over our village, our lives, to those foreigners? Without an argument?"

The mayor, according to Karl, said, "We've been arguing for five years. We've lost the argument. Now we shut up and try to stay alive."

Inevitably, an Ami tank column came down the road into town. As agreed, white sheets flew from every house—except August's. And just as the tanks and their lead jeep entered the town square, August appeared in his World War I infantry uniform, complete with jackboots, pointy helmet and Iron Cross, second class. He took a position in front of the town post office, and, raising a hundred-year-old fowling piece, fired a single round of grapeshot. It fell short of the Amis by a country mile.

The Yankee column halted, and every cannon, machine gun and rifle turned to bear on August. The townspeople, watching from behind closed shutters, were sure that the old boy was about to meet his Maker. Instead, the Ami commander alit from his jeep and, slowly, deliberately, took the shotgun from August's thin blue hands. He swung the gun against the cobblestones, smashing it to pieces. Then he marched August to his house, where, at the door, he shouted an order for the entire column to present arms. Every Ami in sight did so, and August returned the salute, fingers to rim of helmet. Then he sniffed and slammed the door behind him. The Yankees roared off,

197

never to be seen again, and from that time on August had been known as the Lion of the Post Office.

Lukas wondered if the story was true, and whether he—at any age—would have been able to stand in front of the Buffalo post office and fire a shotgun at an approaching German tank column.

The jeep let out a scream and went crazy.

He was aware of the right front dropping, of the car's careening, of sparks and dust erupting. Struggling, forcing his fear-frozen muscles to act, he managed to control the mad skidding and bring it to an end four feet from the rim of a fifty-foot cliff.

Later, when the GI wrecker came, the driver, a corporal wearing rumpled GI coveralls and an old-style flat-brim campaign hat, shifted his cold cigar to the other corner of his mouth and nodded at the jeep's right front. "You got somebody real mad at you, buddy?"

"What do you mean?"

"Lookit your front wheel. The bolts. They was unscrewed, loosed up. The wheel held till this here hard turn on this here nice downgrade, and you was all set for a nice header offa this nice cliff into that there nice valley." His hand traced a downward arc through the air. "Kava-voom."

Lukas turned and walked to the wrecker cab, climbing into the passenger seat to wait while the corporal hooked up the disabled jeep. He sat quietly, ignoring the rattling of chains and the clanking, relishing the soft breeze, the gentle tossing of the trees, and the cool of oncoming twilight.

He heard himself saying, "Stick your pointy helmet where the sun don't shine, August."

THE
BET

Entry in Personal Diary of C. G. Brandt

Washington, D.C.
3 July 1945

Harry has asked me to accompany him to Potsdam.
Well, it's not really that dramatic. Yesterday he mentioned the upcoming trip to me, and I suggested that
Potsdam might prove to be a bit dicey in view of what Stalin
planned for Germany. He gave me one of those owlish looks
and said I should pack a bag, because he might want to have
me on hand during the meeting. I haven't the foggiest idea
what he has in mind for me. Since I don't appear on any of
the State Department's lists of those who will sail on the
Augusta this Saturday, I'm assuming that he hasn't told
anybody yet. Either that, or he sees me as some kind of
swami and will have me stowed out of sight below decks, to
be called out for consultations during the dark of the moon,
or something.

At any rate, he's sent me a handwritten memo that is to
serve as a special ID and authorization. I'm to present it to
the *Augusta*'s skipper on Friday night. Also at hand is my
authority to use the *Augusta*'s communications facilities as
needed, so long as my business doesn't conflict with presi-

dential traffic. I'm permitted to mix with the crew but must keep my distance from the presidential party itself. When the ship docks at Antwerp, Harry and his gang will drive to Brussels and then fly to Berlin, where they'll take cars again for the ride to Babelsberg, a suburb of nearby Potsdam, where the Russians have set aside guest quarters for them.

Me?

I'll be flying straight from Antwerp to Berlin on a DC-6 carrying the luggage. The Russians, knowing me as well as they do, will assume that I'm using the Potsdam conference and my credentials as a White House security guard as cover for an intelligence mission. They'll be watching me very closely, of course. Which is okay, since I *will* be on an intelligence mission and I *do* want them to watch me closely.

I'll be wanting them to watch a lot of things closely.

If they don't, this little thing I'm stirring up will be one grand fizzle.

TOP SECRET

ADD TERMITE FILE

Telephone conversation, 1123 hours, 3 July 1945
Caller: C. G. Brandt, spec. asst. to President
Receiver: A. L. Rutan, Dept. of State

BEGIN TRANSCRIPT

Brandt: Hello, Mr. Rutan. This is Brandt, your fellow whiskey drinker from Dijon.

Rutan: Well, hi there. Welcome back to Washington. I heard you'd been transferred to the White House. Big improvement over that freezing hole in France, eh?

Brandt: Well, Dijon was cheaper to live in, believe me.

Rutan: I daresay. (Pause.) So then, what might I do for you, Brandt?

Brandt: Just a quick question. I've got to get a special shipment to our embassy in Moscow. A rather sizeable wooden crate. And I'm not sure of the drill—just how to go about getting it from here to there. I could've called your executive liaison people, but I called you because it gives me a chance to say hello.

Rutan: Glad you did. It was good to talk to you on that little hop, and I especially enjoyed your hooch. As for your question, no problem. Just truck your crate to State's service hangar at International under a White House work order and slug it 'Diplomatic Material.' Our people will put it on our regular courier plane.

Brandt: That wouldn't be so easy to do. This crate has to go direct from the Santa Fe area—most likely on a MATS cargo DC-6. That's the rub, you see. If it weren't so damned big, it could be sent diplomatic. But, well—I don't know exactly how you boys handle those things these days. Like, how would you send something big over there?

Rutan: Big? How big?

Brandt: I'm not sure, really. All I know is, the president wants to get what he calls a very large package from Santa Fe to Moscow via MATS. He didn't give me the details.

Rutan: (Pause.) Well, I—I'm not quite sure how we should

go about this one. Tell you what: I'll call around, talk to a couple of people, then buzz you back.

Brandt: Hate to trouble you.

Rutan: Nonsense. I'll be back to you before noon. 'Bye.

Brandt: So long. And thanks a bunch.

END TRANSCRIPT

TOP SECRET

CHAPTER 21

Frankfurt am Main, Germany
3 July 1945

The tap water was running, but it was cold, thanks to the failure of the little gas-operated heater in the side court. But the room was warm in the summer afternoon, and so she filled the wooden tub. Her bath proved to be quite refreshing. Ressel was in Nagelfeld for two days (Happy thought!) to make arrangements for next week's meeting, and it was good to have the privacy, especially after weeks of being closeted in this shrapnel-pocked garret with the world's dullest man. Fortunately, his lust far exceeded his capability, and so, except for two rape-like sessions on lazy Sunday mornings, he had been content merely to gaze at her pridefully, like an over-the-hill hunter admiring the deer head on his wall. She had kept busy scrounging for food, checking out the help wanted postings on the kiosks, and, at night, planning moves and countermoves that might be made if Frau Ressel's little gambit showed signs of taking hold. The worst scenario was a confrontation with the inspector general; to deal with this she needed Red Glare's timely intervention, and there was no assurance that this would come. Without it, therefore, she was in for a bad time—perhaps death. With it, the best scenario would deliver to her Moscow's unqualified support. As a pragmatist, she hoped for a play-out that would center between these extremes.

There was a tapping at the door.

She pulled the robe over her nakedness, glancing quickly around the room to be sure that no maps lay about, no communist tracts or guerrilla field manuals. No document-forgery equipment. No firearms.

"Who is it?"

A muffled voice came from the hallway.

"I can't hear you."

"I said it's Lukas. Open up."

She threw the chain lock and swung the door wide. "Well, now. An old and cherished face comes through the mists of time."

"What in hell does that mean?"

"It's from a poem I wrote when I was thirteen." He looked very nice in his uniform of dark green and pink and brown and shiny buckles. His cap, with its brass U.S. eagle device, was set at a jaunty angle, and his cheeks glistened from a recent shave. His smile, as usual, was barely discernible. But it was there.

"May I come in?"

"Please." She stepped back, waving at the tub, the trail of water, her bare feet. "As you see, I'm freshly bathed and as bare as a baby beneath this thing. How about a romp?"

"It's illegal for Americans to fraternize with Germans."

206

"We won't be fraternizing. We'll be screwing."

"Besides, your lover might object."

"Lover? What lover?"

"Your brother-in-law. Herr Friederich Ressel, former Wehrmacht, former cleric, former loyal husband. You're living with him here, according to Housing Registration reports."

"Pfah. Him? Sure, I'm living with him here. But not *with* him." She pointed. "That's his cot there, that's mine over there. Besides, he is an absolute, unredeemable, stifling bore."

"So why, then?"

"Come on, Lukas. Don't be an ass. Have you any idea how hard it is for a German national—especially a single woman—to find housing in this city? I'm staying in this miserable dump with Ressel because Ressel is the only one who'll let me in a door."

"So what does your sister have to say about this—arrangement?" He crossed the room and peered out the narrow window at the street below.

"She's in Hannover, living with some friends. She and Ressel don't get along any more." She rubbed her hair with the towel and gave him a glare. "And what's it to you? You're some kind of Ami morals patrol, maybe?"

He took off his cap and sat on the cot she has designated as hers. "I really don't care one way or the other how you choose to live, Frau Keller. It's no business of mine."

"Then just why in hell did you come here? If not to lay me, not to condemn me, why then?" She took the brush from the table and stroked her hair with angry vigor. Outside an Ami truck ground by, thundering and sending its exhaust stink aloft to the eaves, and somewhere in the near distance a concertina wailed mournfully. *Komm' zurück . . . ich warte auf dich . . . denn du bist für mich . . . all mein Glück; komm' zurück . . . ruft mein Herz immer zu . . . nun erfülle du . . . mein Geschick . . .*

207

Everything in Germany was mournful these days—the landscape, the faces, even the goddam music. Everything spoke of leaving, of farewells, of death and dying and lostness and solitude. A flash fire of anger moved through her: so much misery for so many people, guilty and innocent alike.

He turned the cap in his hands. "Do you still want a job, Frau Keller?"

She paused in her brushing, feeling the surprise. "You mean a job kind of job? A working job?"

"The last time I saw you, you were talking about continuing the, ah, relationship we had in the last days of the war. The derring-do, and so on."

"So?"

"Something's come up, and, if you'd like, we can make a deal. My headquarters has authorized me to hire an assistant. A person who speaks German fluently. A person of demonstrated intelligence and discretion." He added, "And courage."

She sat on the room's only chair, leaning forward, elbows on her knees. "German and intelligence and discretion I'm good at. It's that courage part that bothers me. Why would I need to be courageous?"

"I've seen you in tight spots. I've seen you think fast. I've seen you con a German general out of his hotel room. You are a very gutsy female. And that's what I need. A gutsy female."

She shook her head. "I don't think so, Lukas. The war's over, and my nerves have just begun to settle down. I don't think I'd enjoy tight spots anymore."

"That isn't the tune you were singing the last time we talked. 'I can't go back to some lousy Tyrolean village,' you said. 'I'm special,' you said."

"Well, I meant it at the time. But my spring has wound down. There's a big peace shaping up, and I feel peaceful."

"The job pays a thousand American dollars a month. It

208

provides all documents needed for complete freedom of movement in the U.S. Zone. It provides a furnished house, a full U.S. military officer's food ration. It provides a car, unlimited gasoline, and a new wardrobe."

She threw her hands above her head and laughed in unrestrained hilarity. "I've reconsidered. I'll take the job. I love tight spots. You bet your sweet behind, I do."

He gave her a wry look. "Agreed, then?"

"*Agreed?*" She was still laughing. "My God, Lukas: I'm rich! I'm liberated from this rotten hole! From that horse's anus, Ressel! What the hell do you mean, *agreed?*"

He pulled a sheaf of papers from his tunic pocket and, unfolding them, spread them on the table. He offered her a fountain pen. "Sign at the X."

Still chortling, she said, "I'll sign anything. But what is it?"

"The Ami army is fond of paperwork. This is the form our government uses when it hires foreign nationals. In it you release us of all claims if you get, ah, hurt on the job. You agree to no pension, other fringe benefits."

She happily scribbled her name. "When do I start?"

"Right now. Get dressed. Pack a bag."

"May I leave Ressel a note?"

"Why?"

"I don't want him to come looking for me. He would, you know. He's like that."

"All right. Tell him you've found a job and will be in touch with him later."

"Why not tell him good-bye forever?"

"Because I might need him someday. As I need you now."

Her face clouded. "You don't mean that I might have to go back to—this. Do you?"

"No. It's just that, in my business, I never know when I might need help. It isn't smart to cut off a source of possible help if I don't have to. Ressel isn't too bright, as you say,

209

and he's pompous and filled with wind, but he was available in Eckerdorf when things were thick. I can't sniff that away."

She considered this. She must keep the cell machinery in motion, and as long as possible; Red Glare was adamant on that point. The Stalin ploy must be carried to a denouement, and that was that. Given an even break on the Frau Ressel contretemps, given even so little as probationary approval from whatever inspector showed up, and Red Glare's order could be fulfilled. And now another opportunity was opening and she could, with the approval of both interests and with maximum convenience to herself, become part of the American machinery. Under these circumstances, Ressel was a liability that could, with luck and smart handling, become an asset.

"All right," she said. "Just don't ask me to share any more rooms with the clod. Agreed?"

"As I say, that's your business."

They drove west along the curve in the river, through the industrial litter of Hoechst, then on across the rolling plain and through the orchards and vineyards to Wiesbaden, once one of the world's most beautiful cities and now a melancholy nothing, with a scar of crumbled masonry and splintered trees directly through its middle, thanks to a stick of bombs jettisoned one unhappy night, almost as an afterthought, by a homeward-bound British bomber. The jeep's motor and gears whined the peculiar harmonies of a military vehicle at cruise speed, and the wind, warm and filled with summer smells, felt good against her face. The highway sloggers, with their dyed Wehrmacht jackets and peaked Wehrmacht caps and overloaded rucksacks, glowered at her, the angry question in their eyes: Who is this woman in the red dress, laughing and windblown, who dares to ride with an Ami? You can all go to hell, she
210

thought in answer, because I'm free now, and I have my favorite man beside me, and I'm going to my own house, where I'll have many things to eat and to wear, and even if it lasts no more than a week—if the bastards catch up with me and do me in—my last week on Earth will be one in which my belly is full, my skin and hair clean, and my bedding fresh and cool. I'm a soldier, and I've paid my soldier's dues, and I can die tomorrow knowing that I don't owe anybody a frigging thing. So to hell with your dirty looks, you Nazi Arschlocher. This goddam war was *your* idea.

"Lukas?"

"What is it?"

"What will I be doing for you?"

"Later. I'll tell you after we get to the house."

"Where is the house?"

"On a hilltop, off the road to Bad Schwalbach."

"Will I be there alone?"

"There's a gardener and a maid. An old man and his wife—and they live in the gatehouse. The rest is all yours."

"Good God. Maid? Gardener? Gatehouse? I've become royalty." She laughed.

"There's a price. You'll have to be available at all times. You'll have to be ready to jump when I say jump. No questions permitted, no excuses acceptable."

She laughed again. "What the hell. I don't have anything else to do with my days. Eh?"

They spoke no further for a time, and she lost herself in the pleasure of the drive—up the Taunus rises, through the majestic forests, along the curving ledges, above the misty valleys.

"Quite a drop there," she said, peering downward.

"I almost took a drop into a hole like that last week."

"How so?"

"I was visiting a fellow in Bad Schwalbach. As I headed

211

for home I found that somebody had removed the bolts from my right front wheel, the idea being that the wheel would hold until I got to one of these nice stressful curves."

"So that's why you walked around the car when we left my place. I wondered. You looked like a pilot before takeoff."

"A man can't be too careful these days."

"I suppose not."

So, she thinks. *That's* what that poophead Ressel was up to that day.

"I'm off to Bad Schwalbach," he'd said. "Just a little trip to visit a friend," he'd said.

Pfah.

Jealousy did the damnedest things to a man.

That Ressel: following Lukas, watching him, waiting for a chance to bugger his jeep. For a chance to eliminate a rival for the hand of that lovely, demure, winsome and self-effacing Jungfrau, Gretl the Blushing Flowergirl.

What an ass a man will make of himself over ass.

Bizarre.

CHAPTER 22

**Washington, D.C.
5 July 1945**

The plane turned, and Lukas gazed off the wingtip at the grandeur of Mount Vernon, its gentle white arcs and vast expanses of lawn wheeling majestically in the noonday haze. Ahead, rising on the tilted horizon like a chalky finger of admonition, the Washington Monument certified that, yes, this is the American capital city and if he has the slightest idea of being anything less than choke-throated with patriotism while he's here he'd better go back where he came from.

The engine rumble subsided, and the slowing propellers made flickering shadows against the mellow Virginia countryside that rose from below. Behind him, the Air Corps T-5 who served as steward advised

213

everybody politely that there'd be no smoking and seat belts should be fastened. There was indeed a slight turbulence, and the DC-6 danced and waggled as it flattened out above the Potomac and whispered into its landing.

The tires chirped, there was a mild lurching, and he was once again in his beloved homeland. Nothing, nowhere, he decided, looked half so great as the United States when you haven't been there awhile.

The plane unloaded at a MATS hangar, and, joining the olive drab flow that descended the aluminum stairway, Lukas caught sight of the dark Chevrolet parked in the building's blue shadows. He slung his B-bag and strode through the American sunlight, aware of his heartbeat.

Brandt, who stood beside the car looking oddly rumpled in his expensive gray suit, shook his hand with acceptable warmth. "Hello, Lukas. Have a nice flight?"

"Long. Tiring. But okay."

"I've made it quite a few times myself. Just as you've decided it'll never end and you're doomed to spend the rest of eternity in that narrow goddam seat, there it is: the big D.C. And you want to cry."

"Imagine what it was like for Lindbergh at Paris."

Brandt smiled dimly. "Now there's a guy for you. Must have a tush made of iron and a bladder as big as a Zeppelin."

They stowed his bag in the car's trunk and Brandt drove them through the airport complex, onto Memorial Drive and across the Fourth Street Bridge. Lukas struggled against appearing the visiting rube, but it was all he could do to keep from staring goggle-eyed at the teeming traffic, the great white buildings, the surging crowds.

"Where are we going, Brandt?"

"To my office in the White House."

"How long will you need me in Washington?"

"About an hour, I'd say."

"An *hour?* Why in hell didn't you use the teletype, or the
214

phone, for God's sake? That godawful ride, just for an hour in your office, then back to Frankfurt—"

Brandt corrected him. "You're not going back to Frankfurt. At least not right away."

"Where, then?"

"First, give me an update on things over there."

Everyone, everything looks so *clean*, Lukas thought. The women: their hair shone, their legs showed no traces of scurvy, their faces glowed with good food and excellent circulation and frequent scrubbing with real soap; they walked gracefully in fitted shoes, not bent and clumsy like the German women clomping around on wedge sandals made of wood. The civilian men wore light summer suits of linen or seersucker or Palm Beach weave; Panama hats, two-tone shoes, bright four-in-hands or bow ties, crisp white shirts, starched collars and cuffs. Snappy. No tattered army uniforms dyed dark blue here. Tenderhearted *Jesus*, didn't any of these people know what was going *on* over there? Didn't they know there were children fighting over garbage pails, women selling their asses for a dish of soup, men selling their souls for waterlogged, rat-infested corners of rubbled cellars in which to house their families? Who *were* these broads with the flashing teeth and bouncing boobs and swinging behinds? How had *they* managed to escape the death stink, the caked sweat, the bleeding gums, the hunger-swollen bellies? These Hotshot Charlies, with their straw skimmers and silky handkerchiefs peeking coyly from breast pockets: Why had *they* been spared the sobbing?

"Well, I've engaged the services of Gretl Keller. I think you had the right idea in the first place. I think I was wrong. She might turn into an asset after all. In any event, she's agreed to work with me."

Brandt gave him a lingering glance. "You think she might be suckering us?"

"Who can say? She's a slicker, all right, and I'll have to

215

watch her like a hawk, but I think with the proper control she can be a very useful tool for us."

"How's she doing on her job?"

"As far as I can tell from Frankfurt Special Team stakeouts and G-2 radio intercepts, plus the feeders I get daily from OSS alumni in France and the Low Countries, she's making good progress. The German cells are in bad shape, of course, having been compelled to hide from the Nazis for twelve years, but she and the Ressels, with the help of Georgi Lagolin, that darling of the Red Army brass, have managed to put them together in a daisy chain and have psyched them up for the coming push. The Ressels have had some kind of domestic falling-out—he's in Frankfurt, she's in Hannover—and Keller has been sharing digs with him in his dear Frau's absence. She claims they haven't been shacking up, but I rather think they were."

"So what?"

"Well, so nothing. I mentioned it only because there's a dynamic there, the tensions that come when poon is mixed with hard-case sedition and murder."

"You sound a bit, ah, irritated by this situation."

"I'm irritated only because it complicates things, not because I care about Keller's amours. I want to watch her as she organizes communists, not as she tosses and moans in somebody's sack."

Brandt made a right turn onto Pennsylvania Avenue. He sent a quick look at the rearview mirror, and Lukas had the feeling that he was pleased by what he'd seen there. "Well," Brandt said dryly, "that might be when she's doing her most important organizing. Eh?"

"Come on. You know what I mean."

"Don't be so touchy. It was only a little joke."

There was a moment in which they were separated by a kind of silent reappraisal. Then Brandt got back to business. "Speaking of commie organizing, there's a lot of it going on everywhere right now. In fact, the Communist party here in the States is undergoing a convulsion of change. It's dropping the so-called support it gave the U.S. war effort for a new policy of unqualified support for the Soviet Union's general aims worldwide. The whole world tree is trembling in the wind from Moscow, but the major restlessness is in Western Europe. The Communist party is one of the three major political parties in France today, for instance, and there's no doubt that the French Reds can make or break any government the Socialists or Popular Republicans come up with. We have a heavy eye on those characters, believe me, because they can fix our wagon but good."

"What's our wagon, Brandt? Just what wagon is it we don't want them to fix?" He felt his irritability burgeoning into an anger that stemmed partly from the business-as-usual he saw around him, partly from a vision of himself as hopelessly entombed, forever and ever, in the detritus of the war just ended.

"There's nothing very complicated about it. We and our pals want pretty much to restore the prewar power structure in Europe and elsewhere around the world, in effect ringing the Soviet Union with self-determining governments sensitive to the laws and ethos of a United Nations dominated by us good guys in the West. But the USSR says, 'Up yours, buddy; it ain't gonna happen.' To the Russians, practical politics is the seizure of power by any means, legal or sneaky, and they sneer at the idea of a United Nations they can't—or don't—dominate. They want to re-establish the frontiers they lost in World War One and surround themselves with governments that they control. They see us and our allies as Big Bad Guys, and they'll do anything they can to stick it to us. And Stalin's starting the process with a total takeover of Germany—or what's left of it. So what do you have? You have another war shaping up. And it's going to be a real gutbuster, this one. If we don't stop this maniacal rush to demobilize, if we don't stop screwing around with la-de-da at the so-called United Nations, if we don't stop trying to romance the Russians into loving us and trusting us, we're going to get our asses knocked all the way to Jupiter. That's our wagon, Lukas. And Stalin's getting set to put square wheels on it."

"All right, all right." Lukas shifted in his seat, hot, impatient. "You want me to preserve life as we know it? You want me to save the world? So wait'll I get into the phone booth and change into my red-and-blue underwear."

"My, we're testy today, aren't we."

"When in Christ's name are you going to stop all this insanity, Brandt? When are you bastards going to let me find some kind of home and let me stay in it without having to shoot somebody's balls off for the right to stay there? God almighty, Brandt: You—all of you—are lint-picking goddam crazy. When are you going to leave me *alone?*"

Brandt drove without comment for a time, his eyes consulting the rearview mirror with apparent interest. Only as they approached the White House did he break the silence. "Don't include me, Lukas. I'm one of you. I've lived twice as long as you have, and I've seen them, the political bastards on both sides, closer up than you ever will. And I guarantee you, all of them do indeed have a form of madness. It's a blend of egotism, egocentrism, childishness, paranoia, schoolyard bullying and he-man bullshit, all wrapped up in euphemistic catchwords—'Patriotism' and 'national honor' and 'the national security' and 'for the greater good.' The sons of bitches will tear the world to tatters just so one of them can end up saying sanctimoniously 'At last we have peace in which the brotherhood of man will prevail,' and all the time he—this final holder of the tatters—is thinking, 'Look at me: I'm the hottest shot who ever lived. I am a historic goddam figure, so kiss my
218

goddam boot, you clodhoppers, because nobody's smarter or tougher or more wonderful than I am. I had to destroy the world to prove it, but by God, I've proved it.'"

"You say that's what Stalin's up to?"

"No, goddam it! I say that's what they're *all* up to. Do you think for a minute that so-called public servants enter public service to be servants of the public? Like hell. They enter public service so they can have a crack at becoming historic figures. The only difference between a Stalin and your local councilman is a matter of breadth of turf and methodology. Stalin wants to be remembered as the first guy to boss the whole world, and he'll kill any son of a bitch that gets in his way; the councilman wants a plaque at city hall that says he was the father of modern Framusville, and he'll kiss any ass that's presented to him, make any deal that's necessary, to see that it happens. I've watched the process for most of my adult life, Lukas, and I know what they're like, and don't you ever—ever again— include me in their group."

"Come off it, Brandt. You and I are a hell of a lot worse than they are. We do what they tell us to do. We buy into their bullshit. We're their enablers. What kind of a Mafia don would be a threat—have any power—if every man in the world were to say, 'I don't *want* to be a gangster'? How many wars would we have if every man in the world said, 'No, I won't go'? But every man in the world dreams of some kind of conquest, some kind of fame or influence, some kind of wealth and, most of all, some kind of relief from the humdrum; and so he'll break legs for Mafia kingpin Benzino Gasolini in the hopes of becoming even bigger than the don someday, or he'll go marching off to shoot the pee out of all those slobs in Lower Intestinia, ostensibly to make the world safe for Democrats but really—underneath all the catchwords—to break the goddam time-clock monotony of his life and maybe get to be a famous hero in the bargain."

219

Brandt, pulling up to the entrance gate, gave him a sidelong glance. "Is that why you enlisted in the army? To break the monotony?"

"No. I enlisted for a chance to show all you native-born bastards I'm as good as you are. What a fool I was."

"Yes, you were a fool. The natives'll never think you are as good as they are—no matter what you do. I should know. I was born in the Ukraine, came over with my parents. As a kid."

Lukas shrugged. "Big deal."

"This country has its warts, Lukas. And it's overloaded with horse's asses. But it's the best place there is."

"You sound like my mother."

"Then your mother knows what I mean."

Brandt parked the car in a cul-de-sac next to the immaculate garden. As they stood on the macadam and felt the summer heat, he nodded toward a small door almost hidden by the shrubbery below the great portico. "Let's go."

"What happens in your office, Brandt?"

"You take a nap on the chaise, I get some paperwork done. Then we return to Washington National, where you board another plane for a little town out west. There you pick up a package, stow it on a cargo DC-6, and fly with it to Moscow, where you turn it over to the Marine Corps security people. That done, you take the same plane back to Frankfurt and await further orders from me."

Lukas stared, incredulous. "That's it? All of it?"

"That's it."

"Now I'm a *delivery* boy?"

"No. You're an enabler."

CHAPTER 23

Nagelfeld, Germany
9 July 1945

The town, despite its modest size and light industry, had received the attention of the Ami air force. Its business and residential areas were merely tacky, but the industrial sector was a wilderness of broken buildings, twisted railroad tracks and fallen bridges. On this rainy night, the whole suggested a surrealistic rendering of Hell itself.

They had come here as a compromise. Frau Ressel had, of course, suggested Hannover, hating as she did the slightest inconvenience. Her husband had been for meeting in Frankfurt, and for the same reason. Keller, as boss, had decided on Nagelfeld, ostensibly because it was a neutral middle ground but really because she couldn't stand the

Ressels and it went against her grain to play to either. She had reminded them that Nagelfeld, while solidly in the Ami Zone of Occupation, was only a few kilometers from the conjunction of the American, British and Russian zonal borders, and she wanted to look it over as a possible site for future meetings of guerrilla leaders from all three.

She refused to take Ressel's offered arm and leaned into the restless wind, squinting against the needle-sting of the lashing downpour. The weariness was heavy, almost a physical weight on the span of her shoulders. They had made the trip from Frankfurt in the fake UNRRA jeep, its bumper number doctored to agree with their fake travel orders and UNRRA uniforms. Ami checkpoints, such as they were, had posed no threat; the soldiers on duty were either clean teenage innocents, fresh from the States, or resentful, underpointed veterans who, reeking of wine and sweat, had shown more interest in her legs and chest than in the stolen military government stationery that authorized her and Ressel to travel "at will throughout the U.S. zone to determine the food needs of civil populations in the next winter." But the tension and the unrelieved dreariness of Ressel's company had combined to produce a fatigue that reached into her very marrow.

Her general discomfort was compounded by the fact that she hadn't seen Lukas for nearly a week.

He had taken her to the place in the Taunus, a house of great beauty built in the late thirties for a Nazi Party functionary and friend of Ernst Kaltenbrunner, the notorious chief of the SS Sicherheitsdienst. Lukas's instructions had been simple: Wait here until you hear from me. Then he and his jeep had disappeared down the long curve of driveway, leaving her with the problem of how to stand by for further orders from him while meeting her obligations as district chief of the communist reorganization effort, the most important being this Nagelfeld conference. The Party would give her no choice. Last night, four nights after his
222

departure, she had settled on a stopgap explanation—just airy enough to fit her new pose as the semiretired adventuress—to use if, whenever Lukas returned, he happened to catch her playing hooky (Sorry, but I didn't realize you meant for me to actually *stay* here, and I had a lot of shopping to do with all that wonderful advance expense money you gave me).

"Here we are, Comrade," Ressel said, his head cocked close to hers so that she could hear him over the storm.

"That door there? The ruined warehouse?"

"That's it."

"Couldn't you find a better place than this?"

"You know how things are, Comrade. We're lucky to have any place at all. And this one's made better by the fact that it's the property of Klaus Menzing, our man here. There won't be any questions asked."

They sat around a Wehrmacht camp table that had been covered with a sheet of burlap. There were seven of them: Glueck, from Emden; Alois, from Bonn; Rachmann, from Weimar; Ensminger, from Nuremberg; and, of course, Menzing from Nagelfeld, Ressel from Frankfurt and his Frau from Hannover.

The meeting had been tainted from the outset by Frau Ressel's hostility. She didn't like the meeting place; she hadn't had time to prepare; what did they have to talk about, really? All they had to do, if shooting started, was break out their sabotage kits and support the Red Army. The others sought to jolly her out of her acrimony, but she wouldn't play their game. Gretl was forced to intervene with a demand that Frau Ressel relinquish the floor so that new business could be introduced. Frau Ressel balked, so Gretl called a recess. It was during this hiatus that Georgi and Taras showed up, standing for a moment in the doorway, smugly flanking a white-haired, trenchcoated stranger who presented his NKVD credentials and identi-

223

fied himself as General Andrei Mikhail Mandonovich, personal emissary of Comrade Commissar Mikoyan, just arrived from Moscow via Prague.

So then, Gretl thought, this is how it ends. Frau Ressel's protest to Samovar had produced an inspector. There was a hotness in her face, and her stomach tautened.

Frau Ressel was looking her way, triumph in her eyes.

Friedrich Ressel was pale, watchful.

The others tried to contain their curiosity.

Mandonovich stood under the single oil lamp, and the light and hard shadows made a death's-head of his face. Even so, he was cool, amiable, and his German, while heavy with Muscovite harshness, was exceptionally fluent. "Let me assure you at once, comrades, that Commissar Mikoyan and the others who direct our government are most appreciative of the promptness with which you have responded to our call for assistance in the realization of the great plan initiated by Comrade Stalin. Without your help the task would be ever so much more difficult." His green eyes examined each of them in turn, fleetingly. Then he got down to business.

"I am here at the invitation of one of your group, who feels the need of some sort of clarification of aims and philosophies. My visit would have come eventually, of course, but it's been advanced because of this member's ah, uneasiness over matters of identifications and command authority. I feel we must deal with this before we get into the meat of our business—the organization and equipment of the network we'll need to support the advancing armies —because without an understanding here, all else would be academic." He cleared his throat in the manner of a teacher preparing to move on to Lesson Two.

"First is the matter of Comrade Keller's identity. I'm sure she would agree that her arrival in Bavaria last April was of such a nature that her validity as an agent of Moscow rested—of necessity, given the active war situation at the
224

time—entirely on the documents she presented to you. Since documents can be forged, it's natural that Frau Ressel, others, would seek early confirmation by other means, and thus this meeting." He gave Frau Ressel a condescending nod, and she responded with a pleased upturn of her thin lips.

"Yet such is the suspicion and mistrust in our poor world that you must question even your messenger. Am I indeed who and what my credentials claim me to be? Am I indeed Andrei Mikhail Mandonovich, major general of the Red Army and special emissary of our beloved comrade, Commissar Mikoyan? Party members, partisans such as yourselves, would be remiss if the questions were not asked. By way of answer, I turn to your trusted friend and compatriot, Lothar Rachmann." He glanced at the man in the corner. "Lothar, my dear friend, would you tell these comrades who I am?"

Rachmann stirred, shifted his meerschaum pipe to a more comfortable position in his mouth, and said around the stem, "You are a hero of the Soviet Socialist Republics, my dear Andrei Mikhail. You are the brave one who rescued me in Berlin in 1918, when my own countrymen were planning to execute me for my belief in the Bolshevist ideal. Who are you? You are my friend of nearly thirty years. You are my savior."

Mandonovich waved a hand in modest dismissal. "So then, I am who I say I am."

"And who is this—this Keller woman, Comrade?" Frau Ressel's voice was harsh, her impatience had burst through the flimsy dams of protocol and self-control.

The Russian considered her with rebuking eyes. "Our central file registry has produced an identification photo of Gretl Keller, one of the USSR's most trusted and aggressive foreign agents. The photo, along with a copy of Comrade Keller's current orders, issued and signed by Comrade Mikoyan himself, was handed to me in the

225

Red Army's Moscow headquarters by one of our premier counterintelligence officers. In the interest of amity and trust and efficiency within this group, which will carry the brunt of our great enterprise, I now hand the lot to you, Frau Ressel."

As she took the file and began to examine its pages, Frau Ressel's face registered shocked surprise and disappointment. She stared for a taut interval at the photo, then closed the file. To her credit, she handed it to Alois, sitting next to her. "Pass it around."

When the file came to Gretl, she saw that the picture was an old one, taken one day by Trina Tibault during a break at the Moscow School of Performing Arts. She discovered that she was able to make a little joke. "This makes me look like somebody's bratty grandchild. Doesn't headquarters have something better?"

There was a round of genuine laughter, and even Frau Ressel seemed to relax.

"As a matter of fact," Mandonovich chuckled, "there was a selection of the usual passport-type pictures, two of which are affixed to the inside back cover of that packet. But this one was so much prettier I thought you'd appreciate my showing it rather than the others." Riding the moment of general good humor, he added, "As you see, Comrade Keller's mission had two parts. First, she was to intercept and cancel a Gaullist agent known to be parachuting into Bavaria under orders to determine what plans our German cells have for linking up with the French Resistance. I'm happy to report that she made a successful intercept, and the de Gaulle people have been left blind to our intentions." He gave Gretl a smile and a wink. "Secondly, and much more importantly, her orders require her to join your group and take command of planning its support for The Day We Steal Germany."

They heard the capital letters, and the Russian's emphasis triggered more laughter.

226

Frau Ressel pushed, taking advantage of the air of good fellowship that filled the room. "Comrade General Mandonovich, what of something called 'The Poplars?' It is spoken of frequently, and with a kind of secrecy, by our Red Army soldier friends. Are you at liberty to share its meaning with us at this time?"

There was a moment of embarrassed silence. This represented the grossest kind of faux pas, and the group, Gretl noted, appeared to take sudden interest in the floor and the ceiling. They had all wondered precisely that, of course—Georgi and Taras sometimes used the term as if it were an old joke—but to ask openly about it was much like breaking wind at a meeting of the Presidium.

The Russian, obviously, wanted to maintain his posture as a benign messenger. He handed this hot potato to Georgi. "Colonel Lagolin, would you answer that question, please?"

Georgi drew himself up, like a staff officer chastening a subordinate. "The question may not be answered, Frau Ressel. To have asked it is presumptuousness of the worst kind. The term is the code word for a military secret. I emphasize 'military.' Its meaning is known only to a very short list of very high-ranking and strategically placed officers and technicians. No, we are *not* at liberty to share it with you at this time."

Frau Ressel's face reddened, but she said nothing. This had not been the best of days for her.

For an interval everyone seemed to listen to the wind and rain that rattled the tin roof above them. The Russian general cleared his throat again. "Let's move on to operational planning. Would you like to give us your views on the subject, Frau Keller?"

This, Gretl realized, was her time to resume command. Mandonovich had given her control of the meeting, a tacit acknowledgment that the Ressel mutiny had been resolved. Now she must convince the general and Georgi and Taras

227

that she and the group were indeed to be trusted as collaborators.

"Thank you, General," she said briskly. "Since the plan is to take over political control of all territory east of the Rhine without resort to overt attack, I see our job to be quasimilitary, in that we will play a dual role as civilians and as soldiers. As Red Army units move across the German national territory, presenting themselves as a police force that has been invited by the German populace to forestall anarchism caused by American abandonment and derelictions, we will, in our role as soldiers, provide covert flank protection—sabotaging any military efforts the Amis might try to mount." She gave Mandonovich a direct stare. "To do this effectively, General, you should begin—as soon as possible—sending us arms, ammunition, explosives, radios, tires and fuel in amounts sufficient to supply at least a thousand men and women who will derail Ami trains, disable Ami vehicles and planes, destroy Ami motor pools and airfields, cut Ami communications lines, burn Ami barracks and warehousing, and assassinate Ami leaders. We need maps, blankets, compasses, field rations, tenting, water purifiers, generators, hammers, nails, twine—all those myriad things any army needs in the field. We—"

The Russian waved a warning finger. "Hold on, Comrade Keller. Your enthusiasm is admirable, but in a practical sense your eyes are larger than your stomach. Not only is it difficult logistically to provide such items in the amounts you're talking about, but it's also very hard to hide them once they've been delivered. You can't just plop a thousand rifles, a thousand pounds of explosives, into somebody's rear garden—even in the best of times. Now, in a Germany about seventy-five percent ruined, it's next to impossible. Your covertness will become overtness in very short order."

She smiled. "Not if it's all carefully packaged and labeled

'Property of the U.S. Army,' stored in open fields, and guarded by our people dressed as Ami troops. With the American army already so disorganized it can't find its trousers, with thousands of tons of Ami supplies being burned daily to save the expense of returning them to the States, who will be wondering about our little depots? All due respect, General, but in something like this you must cease thinking like a Russian. The Amis are wastrels in any event. So it's most unlikely that they will be interested in what is already acknowledged by their own government to be waste."

They all considered this for a time. Then the Russian asked, "How will this be coordinated? Are you suggesting that command of the guerrilla units will rest with you and the other district chiefs?"

"Not at all. I'm suggesting that the guerrilla units be under the direct control of Red Army officers assigned the task on an exclusive basis. We will need professional orchestration; we should be told where the Amis are to be hit, if they are to be hit, how they should be hit, and under what rationale and guise. The decisions should rest with the Red Army. The execution should rest with us. The Red Army is the benign peacemaker. We are the hell-raisers."

Frau Ressel broke in. "Who are all these hell-raisers you mention? There are hardly more than a thousand dedicated Party people in all of Germany."

"Yes," said the Russian. "Who will make up your quasimilitarists?"

"The Party people, of course. But there are thousands of former German soldiers who would be only too happy to join a resistance movement aimed at abbreviating foreign occupation of German soil. The trick will be to make them think it's a domestic group—a guerrilla organization of, by, and for the Germans. The Soviet presence must be obscured."

The general frowned. "How can that be done? If the

229

guerrillas are asked to attack only the Amis, the British, and the French, and told to ignore all those Soviet troops moving in everywhere, they will see through the plot at once.

"We will stage attacks on Soviet installations as well. I stress the word 'stage.' The attacks will be carefully arranged by the Red Army itself, with our units providing much noise and smoke, but no real damage, no real injuries. Such playacting will cease as soon as the Red Army has occupied and secured the country."

Frau Ressel spoke again. "Back to basics: Where, and from whom, will this so-called invitation to the Red Army be made? I mean, just how can what you call 'the German populace' issue an invitation of that kind? It's hard today to get two Germans to agree to share a room. How can we get all of them to agree to invite the Red Army to come in and save them from anarchy? Most Germans hate Russians more than they hate Jews. I mean, well, really—"

"This is where we play the role of civilians. As civilians, some of our people will visit every Bürgermeister, every major opinion leader, every cleric in every major city and town. With blackmail and terrorism we compel each of these Germans to cry out for help against the plundering and rape and general hell-raising that others of our group will be providing in those very same cities."

Frau Ressel was unconvinced. "I can't believe the Amis will be doing nothing about all this—"

"They'll be doing something. They'll be wringing their hands, moralizing, protesting, worrying that if they make the Soviets too angry the Soviets will launch an attack and gobble up all of Europe and imprison all the remaining Ami troops, making it impossible for them to return home. The Amis will begin demanding that the United Nations do something. And the United Nations *will* do something. Come autumn, the USSR will be a member of the United Nations. It will be no trick at all to get the United Nations
230

to ask one of its powerful members to 'step in and do something about that awful German situation.' The USSR, as such a member, will be only too happy to oblige. The European continent will stabilize, the Amis will get home safely, and peace will reign."

The general slapped the table and smiled. "Prima! You will indeed make an excellent leader, my dear Gretl Keller."

There was a murmur of approval in the room.

Below the table where they sat, under the burlap cloth there, she felt Friedrich Ressel's hand slide along her leg and pinch her knee.

She heard herself saying, "Thank you, Comrade General."

She felt Frau Ressel's angry stare.

Mandonovich pushed back from the table and stood, grimacing. "It has been a long day, a long journey. Airplane, motor car, bumpy skies, abominable roads. More of the same tomorrow, since Moscow, like time, waits for no man. But it's been a good meeting, albeit brief, and I think we have settled things for now."

They all stood, courteous. The general pulled his coat over his shoulders and gave Gretl a weary smile. "One more thing, Comrade Guerrilla Leader. Comrade Commissar Mikoyan has been reading your reports. Personally. And he is quite impressed. He is, however, much concerned over one aspect of your situation and he'd like you to take corrective steps."

"Of course, Comrade General."

"He is particularly impressed with the initiative and cleverness you've shown by developing a relationship with the American intelligence officer, Lukas. He feels as you do—that Lukas, given the proper handling, exploited in an audacious manner, could turn into a very significant source of information on the Americans."

"I am happy that he is pleased, Comrade General."

Mandonovich sighed. "But he is not pleased, Comrade."

"Oh?"

"He's concerned. He worries over Lukas's demonstrated skill as an agent. He is too dangerous to be trusted in our vicinity. He might sniff what we're up to."

"But I've tested him, Comrade General. He thinks I am no more than a silly, promiscuous Austrian widow whom he can use as a foil in his intelligence escapades. In fact, I am at this very moment supposed to be at a house in the Taunus mountains, awaiting an assignment from him. There's no way he can know what I am really up to."

"Even so, the commissar is worried."

"What would he have me do?"

"Commissars rarely say what we lesser mortals must do, or how we must do it. They simply let us know the problem and leave the rest to us."

"He wants me to kill Lukas?"

"He didn't say."

"He wants me to kill Lukas."

The general nodded at the meeting and touched the brim of his fedora with a fingertip. "Good-night, Comrades. And good luck."

TO: CENTRAL REGISTRY, G-2, SHAEF 9 JULY 45
CC: C.G. BRANDT
FROM: MESSAGE CENTER, COMMUNIX BRANCH
      ADD RADIO INTERCEPT FILE, DOSSIER "OLGA"
      DATE OF INTERCEPT AND DECODE: 9 JULY 45
      MEDIUM: CODED MORSE, 2575 KILOHERTZ
      TEXT AS FOLLOWS:
      RED GLARE URGENT, RED GLARE URGENT.
      MANDONOVICH HAS ORDERED GRETL KELLER
      TO EXECUTE
      OSS AGENT LUKAS. PLEASE ADVISE ABSOLUTE
      SOONEST. OLGA.
MSGCTR FILE NO. 47756

```
TO:   CENTRAL REGISTRY, G-2, USFET (SHAEF)
CC: C.G. BRANDT
FROM:  MESSAGE CENTER, COMMUNIX BRANCH
       ADD RADIO INTERCEPT FILE, DOSSIER "OLGA"
       DATE OF INTERCEPT AND DECODE: 9 JULY 45
       MEDIUM: CODED MORSE, 2575 KILOHERTZ
       TEXT AS FOLLOWS:
       OLGA URGENT, OLGA URGENT.
       OUR MISSION TAKES PRECEDENCE OVER ALL
       OTHERS.
       NKVD SUSPICIONS RE MANDONOVICH ARE NOT
       YET RESOLVED. TO AVOID COMPLICATIONS IN
       OUR INVESTIGATION AND TO KEEP MANDON-
       OVICH UNAWARE AND FUNCTIONING NORMAL-
       LY IN THE INTERIM WE MUST NOT PERMIT HIM
       TO BE CONTRADICTED OR COMPROMISED IN
       ANY WAY. THUS HIS ORDERS TO KELLER OR TO
       ANYONE ELSE MUST BE OBEYED. RED GLARE.
MSGCTR FILE NO. 47762
```

Entry in Personal Diary of C. G. Brandt
At sea, aboard the USS *Augusta*

12 July 1945

The ocean has always frightened me. At this moment, for
instance, the idea of seven miles of water—straight down—
threatens to paralyze me with visions of cold and restless
deeps, of crawling things, darting things, of horrors
feeding in the gloom. I am separated from this alien world
by no more than a few inches of steel and the engineering
notions of fallible men, and I struggle to keep my awareness of this truth from racing into panic.

The uneasiness is heightened by the claustrophobia of shipboard life, the inability to get off, to go somewhere else, to walk beyond boundaries made inflexible by the conjunction of metal and sea. I go on deck as little as possible so as to avoid the sensation of being confined, which is much stronger out there in the wind and spray than it is in the cubicle that comprises my living space. Thus restricted, I've managed to get much work done.

Most of it is by radio, of course.

My stateroom is only a few feet away from the communications area. The president has told the captain that, while I am not a member of his official party, I am on a sensitive assignment and should be given every consideration, including priority access to the ship's radio and ship-to-shore phones. I mystify the crew by appearing in their world only to deal with outgoing and incoming coded gobbledegook. They have begun to call me "The Phantom"—I overheard a conversation between my steward and a sailor shining brass, or whatever it is that sailors do when they bustle around, wiping things.

The ship teems with specialists, from the captain on the flag bridge and his crew to the platoon of bureaucrats and gofers who dish up position papers and run the errands it takes to get a chief of state from here to there. But for all of these yo-ho-hos and satraps, there are only a few who can be described as the president's traveling companions—the inner circle. This includes Secretary of State Byrnes; White House press chief Ross; Admiral Leahy, presidential military adviser; Brigadier General Harry Vaughn, one of the president's World War I pals and a kind of aw-shucks adviser; Matt Connelly and Jim Vardaman, old pols; and Fred Canfil, a Secret Service agent with roots in the president's Missouri political career. My steward, who is their steward as well, confides that, the way it seems to

234

him, these guys are along mainly because they brighten the president's days with good news and jokes, his nights with lazy-dazy, tobacco-fuzzy poker games. I understand that once or twice a day Harry gets together in a closed-door confab with Byrnes and Leahy, presumably to go over plans for what's to be said at the meeting with Stalin and Churchill et al; but mostly there's deck-walking, kidding, movie-watching and card-shuffling.

I was therefore somewhat surprised tonight when, answering a tap at my door, I found the president standing in the corridor, asking if he could come in for a chat. I pushed aside some papers and offered him my chair, but he said he'd been sitting most of the evening, watching Bing Crosby in *The Bells of St. Mary's*, and he'd rather stand. Besides, he said, he would be staying only a minute or two.

He wanted an update on my traffic with USFET G-2 regarding Operation Termite, our penetration of the communist German apparatus. Since there's no short way to go over that, Harry eventually sat down. But I abbreviated as best I could, telling him about Lukas's formulation of a surveillance team and describing the progress we'd made in exploiting Gretl Keller.

Harry showed a good bit of interest in this and was highly amused—well, let's say intrigued—by the idea of Keller's people thinking that she is using Lukas as a route into our intelligence system, while in truth we're using her as a route into theirs. I cautioned that such a game can be very tricky and, more often than not, unrewarding. You discover a dangling thread in your adversary's sweater; the more you tug at it the more the fabric unravels, and you end up, not with his sweater, but with a useless pile of string. He laughed, shook his head, and said, "My God, it sounds like a day in the U.S. Senate."

Knowing he likes poker, I compared the Lukas case with

235

a game of draw. Lukas was dealt a hand, the line-crossing, and as the game progressed he kept his hand hidden, working toward a specific showdown and pot—the rescue of General Zelinkov. Enemy counterplay, combined with whims of fate, forced him to discard and adopt new strategies based on his subsequent draw. Then in the middle of everything the game changed to stud, with five cards wild, and there were deals and redeals, and with each the dealer would specify a new game variant and new wild cards. Lukas, adaptable and gutsy, has coolly managed to become dealer and is now, via Operation Termite, naming some game variants of his own. It was a rather ragged simile, but Harry seemed to get the point, and, hell, that's all that counts.

In fact, he rather got in the spirit by confiding that he saw poker as a game that rewards the cool and smartsy guy better than any card game you can name. The player, he said, can decide whether to stay in the game or not, and he makes his decision on two considerations. First, what's the likelihood that his hand is better than anybody else's? And second, are the odds against his drawing the best hand lower than those offered by the pot? He can minimize his losses, even when playing with jerks, by dropping bad hands, something he can't do when caught up in a rotten little game of bridge, say.

I asked him outright: "Is that what you're doing in Potsdam, Mr. President? Sitting in on a poker game?"

He laughed, then observed that we had plenty left to do in the Pacific. I asked him if he'd been reading the traffic from Abie in Honolulu, and he said he'd been very busy with backgrounding on Stalin and had let other things slide. All of which sounded like a man who wanted to be updated if it could be managed without his being made to look too much the dull thud.

"Just today," I said, trying to sound as if the reason he hadn't heard was because it had happened only moments ago, "the emperor has flat-out told his staffers to initiate specific diplomatic moves toward an armistice. He's got the fire-eaters to agree to using the Soviets as intermediary, and Ambassador Sato will make the appropriate moves in Moscow. Abie emphasizes that certain cable chatter shows Japan admits defeat but hopes, with Russia's help, to turn unconditional surrender into a negotiated cease-fire."

Harry said that he'd be very happy if the Russians were to forward such a proposal to us—"But it isn't about to happen. The Russians will sit on any such proposal for two reasons: Not only are they committed by the Yalta agreement to enter the war against Japan, but they're also in no mood to end this or any other war before they get a crack at reparations."

"I think, Mr. President, that if you hold out the right carrot and let the Japs save some kind of face, you won't need that big firecracker we're making in New Mexico. You can tell the Russkies to kiss off. You won't even need those troops we're sending to the Pacific. Abie's convinced that you can get the Japs to sign right now if you persuade your own hotheads to let Japan keep its emperor."

He simply stared at me for a time, then rose from his chair and went to the door, muttering that he needed some shut-eye and he'd see me around.

It was with relief that I let him out.

All through our little chat I'd been afraid that he might ask me what Lukas is doing right now, and I'd have had to make up some little story.

In intelligence work, there are some things that simply must be kept from the politicians.

Especially from the president of the United States.

What the president doesn't know, he doesn't have to lie about.

THE
BLUFF

CHAPTER 24

**Near Santa Fe, New Mexico
12 July 1945**

A man introducing himself as Elliot Parker met Lukas at the Albuquerque airport. There was little conversation while they recovered Lukas's bags from the luggage truck and stuffed them into the trunk of the GI Buick. But once on the seemingly endless road to Santa Fe, Parker became absolutely loquacious. As tired as he was, Lukas was in no mood for cocktail party chitchat, but he decided that the more Parker talked the less he would himself be expected to say, and so he settled into the cushions, lowered the brim of his fedora, and grunted occasionally to show Parker he was still alive.

It was one of those nights, peculiar to western deserts, that seem darker

241

than usual. A hot, gritty wind was blowing, and it made a kind of seething sound against the windows. The road was a nothing, leading vaguely northeast through a vast nothing, and Lukas said as much in one of his communicative moments.

Parker snorted. "Wait'll you see Los Alamos if you're talking nothing. It sits on the Pajarito plateau, a chunk of boonie in the Jemez range. The whole damn place belonged to the Indians, which is exactly who it should be given back to, you ask me. The town isn't a town, mind, you—just a bunch of wood-and-cardboard buildings tacked onto the log damn cabins of what used to be—get this—a school for boys. I've been out here since forty-two, when somebody got the idea it would be a good place to do secret experimental work and began to build what's here now. I was on security patrol then, too, but the only thing to guard against in those days was coyotes and sunburn."

Lukas stared, unseeing, at the headlights' chalky glare ahead. "Is that where you're taking me, Parker?"

"Sure. Didn't Brandt tell you?"

"Brandt tells me very little. In this case, he said only that I was to fly to Albuquerque, where you would meet me and take me where I'm supposed to go."

"How long have you known him?"

"Couple months."

"Odd duck. Worked with him for a time at the Moscow embassy. Back then he was the life of the party. A real Jolly Roger type. But when his wife died and his kid went back to the States it did something to him. He got kind of quiet and—sour."

"People handle grief different ways."

"This was more than grief. Grief goes away finally. Brandt's personality changed—and stayed that way."

"Well," Lukas said, tiring of this, "things are rough all over."

242

"Yeah."

They watched the featureless night, saying nothing. Then Lukas asked: "Where's the crate I'm supposed to pick up? Los Alamos?"

"Yep. It was loaded on a flatbed truck this afternoon. You and the truck will take it to a special airstrip ten miles south of Santa Fe. Plane's waiting there."

"Why didn't the truck bring it to Albuquerque? Why do I have to come all the way up here to take custody?"

"Paperwork, my boy. Paperwork. General Groves—he's the project's honcho—is real chickenshit about procedures. He has all these wild-eyed eggheads to administer, and the only way he can keep them from using all those expensive labs to reinvent peanut butter is to keep his tape very tight and very red. He's a hard-ass spider, and you've just brushed against his web, that's all."

"All those people? All those labs? I thought you said the place was a nothing."

"That was at first. Today, it's still just shacks. But we're up to our kiesters with people. Wives, kids. Pets. Pipe-chewing mad scientists in lab coats, stumbling around in the wind, squinting at you through glasses that look like the bottoms of Coke bottles. Potbellied military types with gray hair and swollen egos. Mechanics, electricians, plumbers, carpenters—you name it. Ten pounds of people all squizzed into a five-pound sack. You put all that together with the heat and the wind and the dry that comes from no rain for God knows how many weeks and you don't need no bomb, buddy, because you already got one that's going to explode all over them goddam bureaucrats in Washington."

"This is where they're making that big bomb, then?"

"Search me, pal. The closer you get to the center of things, the less General Groves allows you to know. He's a great fan of compartmentalization. Everybody talks openly about something called Project Y, but whatever the hell

243

that is, exactly, nobody says—even privately, because nobody wants to get General Groves all over him—and so everybody has his own scuttlebutt, the main part of which is that the Slide-Rule Sammies in the long white coats have come up with a bomb that'll blow the ass off a rhino from a mile away. Leastwise that's the rumor, but I don't think anybody really knows."

Lukas's depression, a vague presence since his departure from Washington that afternoon, deepened, and he found himself hating the world anew, this time for its preoccupation with the absurd equation, bigger equals better. Where was the advantage in a superlarge bomb that would, if dropped from a plane, kill X number of people, when several smaller bombs that required no more space in the same kind of airplane could kill a like number? Where is the achievement? Is it in the creation of a single bang that's louder than several standard bangs? If so, who among those in the position to know best would be left alive to listen and compare and be impressed?

Lukas stirred in his seat and asked, "Have you noticed that those headlights have been behind us ever since we left Albuquerque?"

Parker's eyes considered the rearview mirror briefly. "They've been there, all right. But it doesn't necessarily mean anything. Thing about drivers out here: Nighttimes, they settle in behind a fast-moving car ahead so that the taillights give them plenty of notice of what's coming up, road-and-traffic-wise. Takes some of the labor out of making time at night."

"I still say that guy's following us."

Parker gave him an amused, sidelong glance. "You been in the trenches too long, buddy. Why don't you relax?"

"Because I'm still in the trenches. And I know a tail when I see one."

* * *

They went up a long, dark hill and came to the first layer of MP security checks, where there was much ado over Lukas's alien status. Then some light colonel showed up, waving some papers and announcing that Lukas was under White House orders and should be given the VIP treatment, toot sweet. In the next moment Lukas and Parker had been shoved into a jeep that voomed further up the hill to the mesa on which the tarpaper shacks and the clapboard barracks buildings and lab sheds stood forlorn in the insistent wind. After an hour of answering questions and signing forms and showing his AGO card and White House pass, Lukas was at last driven down the hill and eventually delivered to a large tin warehouse outside Santa Fe.

This time a bird colonel, all grim and starchy, brandished a clipboard outside the warehouse. "Sign here, Mr. Lukas."

"Why?"

"You're taking custody as of this point. The truck and its cargo are yours."

"Who's going to drive it?"

"Sergeant Finkel. You and Mr. Parker will be in a sedan directly behind the truck. Lieutenant Ramsdell will be in your MP pilot jeep, and Warrant Officer Tully's jeep will bring up the rear."

"An escort? This must be a hell of a package."

"Mr. Brandt specifically ordered it, Mr. Lukas."

"Brandt told me he wants to keep as low a profile as possible. How can I do that when I'm up to my ass in jeeps, cars, tractor-trailers, shiny brass buckles and tommy guns?"

"I don't know, sir. But those are my orders: to assure maximum security for you and your materiel while in this jurisdiction."

"What's *in* the crate?"

"I don't know, sir."

"Well, who does?"

"The people who packed it, sir. But I don't know who they are. There's a very tight lid on all of this."

"I'm supposed to fly halfway around the world with a big box that nobody knows what's in it?"

"That's something else I don't know, sir—where you're going with this thing. Nobody has told me that, and I don't need or want to know."

A Chevrolet staff car came around the corner of the warehouse, its lights dimmed. It squeaked to a halt, the rear door opened, and a man stepped out, pulling a large satchel after him. He came through the gloom and presented some papers, which the colonel examined under the beam of a penlight.

"So, then," the colonel said finally, "we've been expecting you, Mr. Coulter. Mr. Lukas, this is Mr. Coulter, whose orders say he will be accompanying you."

Lukas shook the man's hand. "Nice to meet you. What brings you into this little drama, Coulter?"

"Beats the hell out of me. As the colonel says, I've just been told to meet you here. That I'll be under your orders and I will go where you tell me to go. You want to know anything else, you'll have to write Walter Winchell."

"What's your line of work?"

Coulter held up the satchel. "I'm a very rich and famous explosives stylist. I make designer bombs, which I feature in my Fifth Avenue salon."

"I see." Lukas glanced at the colonel. "Anything else?"

"No, sir."

Parker coughed dryly and said, "Okay, then. Let's go."

The truck set a fast pace, and the jeeps and cars buzzed busily ahead and behind. A pinkness appeared in the sky to the left, and the countryside materialized slowly, a study of grays on gray, revealing low hills and vast sweeps of sandy stubble. Lukas dozed in the car's front passenger seat, rocking from side to side with the car's motion, half-aware.

246

Parker drove determinedly, silent at last, and Coulter, hugging the satchel on his lap, snored intermittently.

In the strange ways of semiconsciousness, Lukas's mind showed him, of all people, Gretl Keller. He saw her again, lying on the grassy hillside in her Nazi uniform, helmet low over her closed eyes, sleeping the sleep of the just. The association of such a hellcat with the idea of justice made him want to laugh, and he must have, because he sensed Parker's amused stare and heard the words, far off, "What the hell's so funny?" He tried to answer but instead slipped into sleep, and Keller appeared again, this time in a robe and bare feet, enticing him to join her in a canopied bed. They were there then, deep in silky sheets and clutching and gasping in their naked combat.

There was a squealing of brakes, and he lurched forward.

Parker shouted, "What the hell!"

"What is it?" he heard himself demanding.

"Hold on. There's a wreck or something up ahead. A car turned over in the road."

"Keep going. We can't stop for anything."

"The goddam lead jeep has already stopped. They're getting out and running to help."

"Don't let the truck stop. Pull alongside and tell the driver to keep moving. We'll take the lead."

Memory suddenly showed him the Rhineland road, awash in red twilight, Leutnant Griessmaier dropping like a rag doll and Unteroffizier Mueller rolling into a ditch. He was trying to deal with this bizarre replay when the dawnlight was dotted with nasty yellow flashes and the windshield exploded in a gush of shards and glass dust.

"Jesus and Mary!" Parker shouted.

"Keep going! Don't stop!"

But Parker couldn't keep going, because in the next millisecond his hat spun and his face came apart and his body fell wildly against Lukas, a warm wetness everywhere. Lukas shoved and pulled himself clear, slamming a

247

foot on the brake pedal and steering the careening car to a halt. The gunfire persisted, an irregular chattering and knocking from all sides.

"Coulter! Are you all right?"

"I'm all right. Just let me get out of this backseat. Give a hand with the satchel. Hurry, before those creeps shoot my buns off."

The truck, Lukas saw, was halted partly on the road, partly on the shoulder. Its engine was idling, but the driver hung out the door, arms limp, his back a red tangle.

"Follow me, Coulter! Keep low and run for the truck!"

They rolled free of the car, skittering along the mild defilade formed by the berm and its adjoining drainage. Bullets ruptured the air about them with loud snappings. One of the shots tore away the handle on Coulter's satchel, and he faltered, scooping up the bag and cradling it in his arms and yelling at Lukas, "If you don't get out of my way, I'll run right up your back!"

They reached the truck finally, and Lukas pulled away the driver's body and swung behind the wheel. Coulter tossed his bag through the opposite side window and leaped in to crouch flat on the seat beside him. Lukas threw in the gear, and the truck lurched onto the highway, its trailer bouncing. There was a final hurricane of gunfire and they were in the clear and drumming down the highway, tires singing.

"Where'd you learn to drive these frigging things, Lukas?"

"The OSS School for Wayward Boys."

"I knew you were bad news soon as I saw you."

CHAPTER 25

**Himmelschau im Taunus,
Germany 14 July 1945**

She sat at the desk by the large window and gazed west toward the Rhine, where towering cumulus, underlit by the setting sun, drifted in golden majesty above hills already lost in twilight mists. She decided it had to have been this kind of evening, with its soft hues and mountain quiet, that inspired Heine's immortal poignancy: *Ich weiss nicht, was soll es bedeuten, dass ich so traurig bin . . . ein Märchen aus alten Zeiten, das kommt mir nicht aus dem Sinn. Die Luft ist kühl und es dunkelt und ruhig fliesst der Rhein . . . der Gipfel des Berges funkelt im Abendsonnenschein . . .* The words echoed in her mind, insistent, as the little fable must have in Heine's, and her fingers tapped the rhythm on the polished mahogany.

Despite her determination not to, she thought again of Lukas. Well, not again—"still" was a better word because he had been in her thoughts almost continually since the meeting in Nagelfeld.

General Mandonovich had proved to be a combined blessing and curse. His certification of her as Moscow's district-leader-designate had brought her unprecedented respect from her colleagues. Where before they treated her as a somewhat onerous intruder, they now came close to groveling at her feet. Georgi had taken her fully into his confidence; Taras never addressed her without the polite "Comrade"; the others fawned. Except for the Ressels, of course. Friedrich acted as if he had been elevated to the Presidium now that his now-and-then playmate carried the imprimatur of the Kremlin itself. Frau Ressel was furious—a fact that she camouflaged with priggishness and a politeness so patently false it was lugubrious. Gretl reminded herself once again that something would have to be done about Frau Ressel, but how and when were matters she hadn't worked out.

Nor did she know yet how to handle Mandonovich's tacit order to kill Lukas. Technically, logistically, and psychologically the act of killing is no simple matter, even for a combat soldier under sworn obligation to slay as many as he can find of his government's armed enemies. But the problem is even more complex if, as now, civilian concepts of law and propriety are ascendant. In open warfare, killing had been a duty to be carried out in reflex, a deed to be remembered without guilt. In this quasipeace, it was once again murder, once again a capital crime, and to accomplish it successfully one had to take an inordinate amount of trouble and face distracting legal and emotional risks.

Further complicating matters was the fact that Lukas had put her up in this commandeered splendor, had seen to

250

her needs and wants, and then disappeared. Red Glare reported that Lukas had been sent to the States on a special mission, and Lukas's spoor had been picked up by Georgi's network in the States. According to the message flimsy on the desk before her, the American collaborator, Rutan, had reported White House plans to ship a large crate to the U.S. embassy in Moscow, and Lukas was said to be "somewhere in the West," preparing to escort the package. Georgi's postscript noted that steps were being taken both in the States and here in Western Europe to determine precisely what the package contained and if the Amis planned to ship it under diplomatic immunity. Either way, with or without immunity, Georgi said, an appropriate counterplan would be developed.

She was privately puzzled. Why would a shipping crate need an escort? Granted that it did, why send all the way to Germany for an experienced OSS agent to do the job? Certainly there were a few capable people remaining in America's domestic armed forces.

Ah, well.

Maybe Lukas would become deeply involved in other things, and she wouldn't have the need to kill him. Which would be a splendid break, to put it mildly.

Ressel came in from the library, where he had been exploring the Nazi's collection of erotic books.

"You wouldn't believe the pictures and things that man had in his library," Ressel said, beaming. "It's fantastic. And it's made me as hot as a furnace."

"Congratulations."

"I mean it. Come on, open your gate and let me in."

"Are you crazy? Your wife is downstairs in the kitchen. And Georgi's due any minute. In fact, I think that's his car in the drive right now."

Ressel listened, then sighed elaborately. "Damn. What a waste of a spectacular, ah, readiness."

She waved him toward the door. "I've got a meeting.

Show the pictures to your wife. Maybe they'll make her hot, too, for a change."

"Nothing makes her hot."

"I wouldn't underestimate her, if I were you."

"What's that mean?"

"Nothing. Now go on—Get out."

At the door he looked back. "Later, maybe?"

She riffled through her papers, ignoring him, and he disappeared, to be replaced by Georgi, who bustled in like a Wall Street exploiter, togged out in a pin-striped suit, white shirt and patterned tie, glistening black shoes and briefcase to match. She sensed that he expected her to enthuse over his finery—new clothes were as rare as ostriches in Germany—but she wasn't up to playacting.

"Hullo, Georgi. Do you want to start, or should I?"

He caught her mood at once and became all business. Settling into the big leather chair by the fireplace, he nodded toward the papers on the desk. "Proceed, Comrade."

"We have made progress on plans for the disposition of partisan black-propaganda groups in the event the Amis do manage to mount armed resistance to Soviet westward movement. Fritz in Hamburg, Willi in Lübeck, Elsbet in Leipzig, and Nikki in Mannheim have already established clandestine facilities that will originate fake or misleading radio broadcasts and print and distribute leaflets, news bulletins, counterfeit currency, ID and ration cards, driver's licenses, passes, permits, and American stationery and military documents. These activities, as well as the rumor-starters in all major cities, will be coordinated by an office set up in Augsburg by Ludwig Donner, who will work directly under your army group political commissar. This is so that we partisans can issue black propaganda that best meets ongoing Soviet military and political needs and dovetails with the international disinformation devised and issued by Moscow."

252

Georgi crossed his legs, folded his hands, and looked pleased. "Excellent. I'd like to go over all of this in detail with you, but I'm scheduled for two more meetings this evening and there isn't enough time. Let me have copies of all your key papers. Even though these forces may never be needed on a large scale, it's vital that Moscow has a record of all of it."

"What makes you so sure they won't be needed?"

"Well, I'm not sure, of course. But the likelihood is remote. The Putzi Affair taught us how quickly the Amis back down any time there's the slightest hope for peace and quiet. They backed down then, and they'll do it again. Mark my words."

He was truly a pain when he assumed this supercilious attitude, this here's-how-we-did-it-in-the-old-days school-teacher pose—an unspoken reminder that, compared with his length of service in the international intrigue arena, she was a rank newcomer. As much as he annoyed her, she asked anyhow. "What was the Putzi Affair?"

"The Kremlin-level code name for Eisenhower's attempt to negotiate the early surrender of German troops in Italy. Soviet Intelligence picked up evidence in 1944 that there was a serious schism between the Hitler-SS military faction and the old-line German army regulars, and we learned that a certain element of the Old Guard was making overtures to the Amis through Bern and other Swiss information drop points. We began to take this very seriously this past February, when the SS itself, in the person of SS General Karl Wolff, approached the Amis through an Italian industrialist with strong Swiss connections. Wolff was ready to surrender the German forces in Italy, presumably in return for personal amnesty under the Allied war crimes edict, and, much to Generalissimo Stalin's dismay, Eisenhower and his Allied counterparts were listening—even sending OSS agents to Bern for further talks. Generalissimo Stalin, knowing as he did that Presi-

253

dent Roosevelt believed that an amiable personal relationship between the two of them would assure the tranquility of the postwar world, decided to exploit Roosevelt's vulnerability. He sent some very angry—even insulting—messages to Roosevelt, in which he denounced the secret negotiations with Wolff as a hypocritical abandonment of Roosevelt's professed friendship for the Soviet people and their leader. He really brutalized old FDR, and FDR folded like a cheap accordion. One of the last things he did before he died was to issue direct personal orders forbidding any further talks with the Germans in general and with Wolff in particular."

Gretl made a small sound of skepticism. "That was then. Harry Truman is president now. And he's already shown a strong anti-Soviet stance, what with cutting off Lend-Lease."

Georgi smiled smugly. "True. But the Soviet sympathizers in the U.S. government who fed Roosevelt's personal-diplomacy fixation are still at work in Washington, some of them in astonishingly influential posts."

"Like Rutan, you mean?"

"Steven Rutan is one of our best friends in America, qualitatively speaking. He was most helpful in persuading Roosevelt to cancel the Wolff negotiations. And, as you know, he's still in a very powerful spot in the U.S. State Department. There's no reason to believe that he won't try to influence Truman as well."

"But will Truman listen?"

"Truman is a peasant. The worst kind of petty politician. If he thinks there's a vote to be had, he'll listen to Mephistopheles himself. He talks big, but he's a light-weight nothing."

"Still—"

Georgi's brows lowered in mock severity. "You're being very negative today, Comrade."

She shrugged. "I suppose I sound that way. I don't feel very well. Maybe I'm catching a cold or something."

"I hope not. Summer colds are miserable."

"Yes."

A pause followed, during which Georgi's gaze altered subtly. "Have you heard anything from Lukas?"

Georgi's tone put her on alert. She had come to know him well enough to hear potential trouble in his question. It was a touch too casual, which meant Georgi suspected—or had begun to suspect—that she had an emotional attachment to Lukas. Georgi was beginning to wonder if she had what it took to carry out Mandonovich's order. Putting on her steely executive's face, she said, "Not directly. And that bothers me a little. I've read your reports on his sojourn in the American West, of course, but I've heard nothing from him personally. Which is puzzling, since he set me up in this palace and told me to wait his further instructions as if he expected to be gone no more than ten minutes."

Georgi smiled primly. "Well, I have news. Word came in just as I left for this meeting. Lukas is, as of this very moment, en route to Frankfurt. He's aboard a MATS transport somewhere over Newfoundland. His ETA, after a London stopover, is ten-thirty hours tomorrow."

"Ah. Is he flying diplomatic?"

"No. He's aboard a freight plane that's on orders to deliver office equipment to the Ami embassy in Moscow. Which is odd. I would suppose such routine shipments would be moving by way of Tehran. This one, though, has been cleared through our Washington people for a direct route, Frankfurt-Brest-Minsk-Moscow."

"That's strange, all right. Why would our people authorize such a flight? Especially now that Lend-Lease has been canceled?"

"You want my very private guess, Comrade?"

"Of course."

"I smell the Mandonovich touch in this. I think he's moving Lukas through Frankfurt so that you can get your hands on him. I don't think our people expect Lukas—or his office equipment—ever to leave Germany. Eh? Ha-ha."

She began to see why Georgi had requested this meeting. He needed to know about the black propaganda machinations the way he needed to know about the recipe for borscht. He was really initiating another test. He was wondering about her sensitivities in the Lukas matter; he was watching the speed with which she rose to this opportunity to take care of an Ami itch. He had probably been listening to Frau Ressel. What was the old saying? Suspicion breeds suspicion? Frau Ressel had enough suspicion to breed an epidemic. Georgi had been infected.

It was now her turn to exploit a few vulnerabilities.

"Very good. You say you're off to another meeting, Comrade Georgi?"

"Well, yes—"

"Fine. Then you won't think me rude if I run off to Frankfurt. I have some arrangements to make."

"Oh. Well. Yes. By all means." He rose from his chair, collected the papers she handed him, and stuffed them into his shiny new briefcase.

As she ushered him to the door, inspiration flickered like heat lightning. A jump-circuit of memory showed her Marianne Lewis, the daughter of the American engineer on assignment with the Soviet ministry of rivers and dams, sitting on the school piazza. It was then—long ago—when Marianne had used, then explained, the classic American unanswerable question, "Have you stopped beating your wife?" Now she saw how to put Georgi and his judgmental hauteur into a box for good.

"While I have the chance, Georgi: Do you think it's a good idea for you and Taras to share the same house?"

He faltered in midstride, giving her a startled glance. "What makes you ask that?"

256

"Well," she improvised, "there's a lot of talk among the cells about your, ah, closeness. You know, and I know, that you and Taras are longtime army comrades. But you might want to put out some of the smoldering gossip by taking up separate residences. It's simply—"

Georgi was livid. "Are you implying that I—Taras—that we are more than good friends?"

"You didn't hear me. I'm inferring no such thing. I'm simply alerting you to some vapid gossip that could cause you unnecessary problems. After all, the hierarchy is quite harsh in such matters, and if you aren't lovers, you'd better make it unmistakably clear. In fact, it's even more urgent that you do so if you *are* lovers."

"This is the most outlandish thing I've ever heard—"

"Isn't it, though. I'm telling you about it because as your friend I'd hate to see you hurt by such slander."

She clattered down the stairs, leaving him agape on the landing.

Frau Ressel was being domestic. She was flour up to the elbows, and the smell of cinnamon and apples was strong in the kitchen.

"Well," Gretl said, feigning waggishness. "Living high on the Ami's larder, eh?"

Frau Ressel reddened. "The food is here. It should be used before it spoils."

"Of course. Where's your husband?"

"In the library, I think."

"He and I will be going to Frankfurt tonight. I want you or Hermann to spell off Bolko on the radio. We must keep it open through the night. I'll want any reports that might come in regarding Lukas."

"Can't I come with you instead, Comrade? I'm so bored."

"I'm sorry I've had to put you through this, Frau Ressel—this waiting for a meeting that never seems to come off. You'd be far more useful back in Hannover, I

257

admit, but Georgi is certain that General Mandonovich plans another visit, and I want the key district people here—together—when he arrives."

"My husband can stay here tonight. Let me go with you."

"Sorry. We'll be in a situation in which the cover calls for a man and his wife. Hotel rooms, and all that."

Frau Ressel's blush deepened. "Well—Why not take—well, Taras, or Hermann, or somebody—"

"Easy there. I don't have to explain myself to you, Comrade. Now, clean up and get to the radio."

CHAPTER 26

**Rhein/Main Air Base
15 July 1945**

"Sorry, Lukas," the lieutenant colonel said, "but we don't have any recourse. You're just going to have to sit pat until the Russkies lift the hold, and that's that."

Lukas struggled to appear cool. "Just what do you mean by 'hold'?"

"You were cleared through to Moscow, and now you aren't. That's the short of it. The Russkies have withdrawn their flight clearance. You aren't diplomatic, so you sit tight until the Russkies say you can go on." The colonel, whose name was Anderson, Assistant Operations Officer, according to the nameplate on his desk, adjusted his tie with thumb and forefinger and, gazing out the window, pretended to see something

259

important on the downfield hangar line. The man was, Lukas decided, an itinerant storm door salesman who had found a home in the army.

"I've been flying in that bucket of bolts outside for umpteen hours over umpteen thousand miles, wearing my ass flat on those godawful sidesaddle seats—from Santa Fe to Gander to London to wherever the hell we are now in this tarpaper heaven—and I'm not about to tolerate some flat-faced Russian telling me I can't continue to carry out my errand for the White House. I'm traveling under the highest authority. You've seen my papers, signed personally by C. G. Brandt, special assistant to Harry S Truman. You've seen the flight manifest. The cargo on that bucket of bolts is top priority."

"Sure. But in the territory east of us, buddy, when the Russkies say poop, you drop your pants. The White House and its priorities don't mean anything to those guys. So forget it. You ain't going nowhere until they give you the okay."

Lukas's exasperation was brimming. "Just what guys are we talking about, Colonel Anderson?"

"Who can say exactly?" Anderson selected a cigarette from a pack of Camels and rolled it in his fingers. "All I know is, some joadie in the State Department, name of Rutan, wired General Clay, saying the Soviet Mission in Frankfurt is sending all kinds of hell-raising cables to Washington about stuff destined for our embassy in Moscow going MATS instead of courier. And General Clay is raising hell about the Soviet Mission people going over his head to Washington, and Washington is raising hell over everybody raising hell. And what's all the fuss about? We want to fly a box of typewriters to our Scheisshaus Moscow embassy. Which is sure the height of hypocrisy, if you ask me, seeing how the Russkies fly anything and everything in and out of this here Zone of Occupation, any old time that suits them, and we just watch them and grin and say be our guest. Just why the hell we kiss the Russkies' asses so much beats the hell out of me. My God, every time they look at us cross-eyed we grovel around and wring our hands and say jeez, tovarich, excuse us all to hell for breathing. More'n likely, those sons of bitches would all be in Nazi prison camps now if it wasn't for us busting in and giving them guns and planes and ships and ammo and everything and taking on half the goddam Nazi armies in the bargain. And when we want to send rubber bands and paper clips to our frigging office help they say upski yourski. Shee-it-oh-dear."

"I take it you don't like the Russians."

"I like the Russians a very great bunch, 'deed I do. But I don't like a goddam bit the way they get their goddam way all over the rest of the goddam world. You hold out your hand in friendship to them, and they won't shake it, because they know their goddam government is going to pee on it. What the hell they thinking of, for crissake, putting up with a government like that?"

"They don't have a lot to say about it, it seems."

"That's plain crap. People get precisely the kind of government they ask for. A jillion Russians wouldn't put up with a couple thousand horses' asses running their lives if they didn't think it was a good idea."

"Well, I suppose they look at us and wonder the same. Why do we Americans let a couple thousand horses' asses run *our* lives?"

"Damn good question. Why do we?"

Lukas couldn't help it. He laughed. Colonel Anderson laughed, too. They stood there, looking at each other and laughing.

"Some world, eh, Lukas?"

"Some world indeed."

"Want a drink?"

"What you got?"

"Not yet. I'm on duty for another twelve minutes. Then

we'll go to the officers club and peer into a dish or two of Seagram's."

Lukas made for the door. "I'll meet you there. Meanwhile, where do I find a phone? I want to call SHAEF to see what can be done to get me on the way to Moscow."

"You're too late. SHAEF was dissolved as of the end of business yesterday. It's now officially USFET, and Lucius Clay and the U.S. State Department are beginning to return the government of the U.S. Zone to—get this—the same Germans we just spent the past four frigging years knocking the asses off. And while Luke Clay is reinstalling the Nazis, good ol' Ike Eisenhower is being demoted from supreme CO to candidate for U.S. president."

"You believe that? That Ike wants to be president?"

"What else can he do for an encore? Hell man, you run the armies and navies and air-e-o-plane fellas of half the world, you ain't going back to raising petunias and playing shuffleboard, that's for dang sure."

Lukas checked the wall clock. "The phone?"

"Down the hall two doors. It's marked 'Communix.'" A teletype in the corner dinged and began to clatter, and Anderson turned to read its unfolding message.

As he left, Lukas thought of Operation Termite and of the Soviet intention to occupy all of Germany. Even Eisenhower wasn't in on this little caper, and if it blew into a full gale, good ol' Ike would find himself running, not for president but for the nearest concrete bunker.

They were in the fake UNRRA jeep, parked on the shoulder of the highway that skirted the airfield. Ressel was behind the wheel, looking a bit silly in his olive-colored uniform, puttees, and beret. Gretl, no fashion exemplar herself in her lumpy UNRRA jacket and skirt, swept the view with her Zeiss glasses, a smooth motion that suggested the panning of a camera.

She was surveying a great plain marking the confluence

of the Main and the Rhine, dotted with trees and cottages and, centrally, the nondescript buildings that served the planes that hummed and throbbed in the summer haze. The smoky stretch that was Hoechst over there; the distant spires of Frankfurt there. Wiesbaden there.

Ressel stirred, seeking more comfort on the jeep's cruel seat. "What are you looking for?"

"The MATS terminal. I think we'll have to get closer."

"Why the MATS terminal?"

"It's where Lukas is."

"Well, why don't we just drive in the main gate and ask for it? We've got letters, trip tickets—"

"Because for what I have in mind we won't need the main gate. If the perimeter security is as loose as it appears to be, that is."

"What do you have in mind?"

"Later. I'll tell you later. Meanwhile, take me back to the Myliusstrasse apartment."

"We're going to spend the night in *that* hole? When we can go to the best hotels in Frankfurt or Wiesbaden as Herr und Frau UNRRA? Come on—"

"It's the only place we can have a meeting in relative safety."

"Meeting of whom?"

"While I'm taking a bath and catching a nap, I want you to round up your wife and Taras. Get Taras to visit Lothar in Bad Homburg and borrow at least three of his firearms specialists. Get your wife to pick up a box of those grenades we stashed in Offenbach and bring them to the apartment. The six of us will meet at twenty-two-hundred hours, when I will tell you what's on my mind. All right?"

Ressel leaned forward and started the jeep. "Suits me."

As they rattled and shook along the Frankfurt-Wiesbaden thoroughfare, a cobblestone artery clogged with GI traffic, she asked, "Does the Frankfurt cell still have that flatbed truck in the garage on Diemerstrasse?"

263

"Sure."

"Tell Taras to be sure it's fueled and standing by. And tell him to arrange for a moving van. A large one. Say, a Mercedes or a Maybach."

His glance was heavy with doubt. "My God, Gretl. You might as well be asking for the *Queen Elizabeth*. Where in hell are we going to find a big moving van on this kind of short notice?"

She ignored the question. "Also tell Georgi to contact the flight coordinator at the Soviet Mission in Frankfurt. Tell him to pull his rank and flash a few of those fancy Kremlin authorizations Mandonovich gave us. Tell the flight coordinator to have the C-47 cargo-courier standing by at the Tjindecken airstrip, serviced and ready for a long, fast flight."

"Flight? Flight to where?"

"Moscow, my lad. Moscow."

Entry in Personal Diary of C. G. Brandt
Potsdam, Germany

17 July 1945

The new weapon has been tested.

Harry has met with Generalissimo Stalin.

The Japanese have firmed up their offer to end the war if we allow them to keep their emperor and help them to save some measure of "face."

The conjunction of these three events within a 24-hour period makes my work all the more urgent.

The atomic bomb, as it is being called here among the very tight circle of Americans and Britons who know about it, is, of course, epochal in its ramifications. It was tested at 5:30 A.M. yesterday (New Mexico time) at a place called Alamogordo, and from reports Harry has permitted me to

264

see it was cataclysmic—so blindingly brilliant, so hugely explosive, it suggested the birth of a sun. The blast incincrated everything, literally everything, within a half mile, and its heat even turned the desert sand into glass. The concussion raced across the barren terrain in great, unrelenting rings, a man-made seismic event which eventually broke windows in buildings more than two hundred miles away.

It's not just a bomb. It's the fundamental force of the universe, and we've tapped it.

God help us all.

(Later.)

Harry seems to be entirely unmoved by the currents that swirl about him. The Russians have put him up in a lakeside villa in Babelsberg, a suburb of Potsdam. Neighboring houses are given to the use of support personnel, and nearby in the parklike adjacency is a similar compound occupied by Winston Churchill and his retinue. Here the atmosphere is clubby. Further on, where the Russian compound broods among the trees, armed guards and barricades discourage the kind of spontaneous visiting and cocktailing the Yanks and Brits are so fond of.

Stalin came calling on Harry. He arrived at noon, all gaudied up in his new generalissimo's uniform and accompanied by his foreign secretary, Molotov, and an interpreter. I was sitting in a car with Skip Foley, an old pal from the Secret Service who was in charge of one aspect of the complex security measures, and I tried to derive some sense of drama and excitement from the event, but it was no go. They were a clutch of Kiwanians and a comic opera basso meeting for lunch, and instead of drama I felt a dreary meaninglessness.

Two weeks to go. Two weeks of con and countercon.

Skip and I had supper at my place, and it was good to small-talk with an old friend who wasn't trying to impress me or to pry something out of me. We reminisced and told

265

jokes and packed in a lot of genuine Wienerschnitzel. When he left, I realized it was the first time in weeks that I have thought about anything but the job.

I've been assigned a small house of my own—another sign of my isolation from the mainstream. It's fine with me, though, because I find that I'm no longer able to play the little games fancied by diplomatic personnel. Once—only a few months ago, actually—their kind made up my world, but today they are no more than representatives of a dimly remembered species—forms and faces seen at a twenty-fifth class reunion—and I have nothing but a résumé entry in common with them. I find it difficult to believe that, in the so-called national interest, I once drank and wenched and gambled and played bawdy piano for the likes of these geopolitical dilettantes. Today, merely to nibble canapés and exchange inanities with them would be a burden too heavy for my altered social metabolism.

What happened to me? Why did I change?

All I know is, the world's wobbling out of control, thanks to the limp-wristed daydreamers in the West and the savage paranoids in the East, and as a man who has come to his senses I must do what I can to restore it to some kind of stability before we all go down the chute.

Harry wants the same thing, the way I see it. So does Churchill, and so does Stalin, I suspect. But for motives and goals different from mine. Each of those bozos is out first, and in the true spirit of egotism, to make his mark on history. Second, each wants to gain personal power and influence. Third, each wants to gain power and influence for his nation. And, last, each wants a world order based on his own definition of stability. Truman wants a world in the image of Thomas Jefferson and the Bill of Rights; Churchill wants a new British Em-pah, built with American re-sources and protected by the American suckers; and Stalin wants a Moscow protected by twenty-five thousand miles of well-armed, unthinking toadies. To achieve his aim, each

266

needs a world that remains basically out of balance. And so all of the sweet talk that surrounds this conference, all of the high-flown rhetoric attending the United Nations and its charter, is so much baloney. Discounting Churchill, who is really no more than a partisan onlooker, we're left with two short-tempered river boat gamblers who are screwing around with the future of humanity itself—rolling dice to see who's going to decide how the rest of us live. A fistfight is inevitable. The main trick now is to keep the brawl from throwing Earth out of orbit.

So that's where I come in.

It's my job to slip Harry some loaded dice.

You wonder why I don't sing and dance and put lamp shades on my head at parties anymore?

(Still later.)

I have been reading cable traffic.

A message to Secretary Stimson says that a second atomic bomb is being readied and promises to be as impressive as the one just exploded at Alamogordo. It's coded to read like a cutsey note about kids—a "little boy" being "as husky as his big brother"—and it makes me ill.

Another from Abie in Honolulu emphasizes the need to close out the Pacific war before the Russians are in a position to declare war against Japan. Agents in the Far East, he says, report heightened Russian military activity and there is wide agreement that Stalin will enter the Pacific war whether we want him to or not. Therefore, Abie insists, if we are to keep Stalin's mitts off Japan's main islands, and his nose out of our administration of whatever government evolves there, we've got to make a quick and separate deal with Tokyo. Abie, too, for all his capability, tends to be a jerk sometimes. He keeps sending this same message over and over again, as if all of us here are a bunch of blind idiots. Of course we've got to keep Stalin out of Japan. Of course we've got to move fast. Of course we've got

267

to listen to what Tokyo is saying about the emperor. What the hell does Abie think we're doing, for God's sake— sitting on our adorable asses?

There's a stack of stuff from Frankfurt, too.

Among the clutter of G-2 summaries and Russian order of battle analyses is a message recently added to the Red Glare–Olga File:

TO: CENTRAL REGISTRY, G-2, USFET
CC: C.G. BRANDT
FROM: MESSAGE CENTER, COMMUNIX BRANCH
ADD RADIO INTERCEPT FILE, DOSSIER "OLGA"
DATE OF INTERCEPT AND DECODE: 15 JULY 45
MEDIUM: CODED MORSE, 2575 KILOHERTZ
TEXT AS FOLLOWS:
RED GLARE URGENT, RED GLARE URGENT.
LUKAS STALLED AT FRANKFURT AS PLANNED. I AM
LAUNCHING NEXT PHASE OF OUR OPERATION.
WILL KEEP YOU ADVISED. OLGA.

I reread this several times, my mind's eye creating images of the stealthy comings and goings in back-alley intrigue. It's a lonely, gritty, deadly business that no normal person would consider for a moment. But Olga, wherever she is, whatever she's up to at this moment, is one of those who thrive on it.

For some reason my mind goes to Gertrude.

What an ordinary name for an extraordinary woman.

I miss her terribly.

CHAPTER 27

Rhein/Main Air Base
18 July 1945

L ukas and Coulter, the explosives
technician, were in the DC-6's cargo hold, sitting on packing mats beside the big box. Coulter called it
the Santa Fe Treasure Chest. They
were playing an inventive and des-
ultory game of two-man straight
while waiting for Major Guilford,
the pilot, to make still another
attempt to phone the assistant air
attaché at the Soviet Mission In
Frankfurt, a drinking buddy from
the old days of Lend-Lease layovers
in Tehran, to see if he could use his
influence to break the freeze on their
flight plan. The others—Captain
Ramsey, copilot; Lieutenant Julio,
navigator; Master Sergeant Fitz,
crew chief; and Sergeant Ballew,
radioman—were outside, sprawled
269

under the wing, arguing softly over football. The day was sultry, with a sky that couldn't seem to decide what it wanted to be.

"Come on. Ante up, Lukas."

"That's my dime right there. Minted in the good old U.S. of A. and fresh from Albuquerque."

"I didn't see it, it's so puny." Coulter dealt the cards and, pursing his lips, considered his hand. "You in?"

"I'm in. And here's another dime that says I got the winning hand."

"This here shiny quarter says OSS brave speaks with forked tongue."

"Raise you a quarter."

"You're bluffing, damn it."

"So are you calling?"

"I call."

"Two pairs, aces and jacks."

"I want proof. Showdown, please."

"There you are," Lukas said, picking up the coins. "The cards speak for themselves, as the old saying has it."

"As another old saying has it, I've had enough of this crap." Coulter gathered in the cards and returned them to his jacket pocket.

"Hey, I was on a winning streak."

"So go play with Truman. He's a cardsharp, I hear."

"I don't want to go anywhere near that guy. I'm under his orders to get this—this whatever the hell it is—to Moscow, and I can't even get it off this concrete slab."

"What do you think's in the box, Lukas?"

"Lead pencils, condoms, and Spam."

"Come on."

Lukas stared out the open hatch, his eyes following a climbing B-24. "I've been giving that some thought. It's my guess that it's an explosive security device of some kind. The Moscow embassy is the most sensitive and vulnerable we've got. Document shredders may not be thorough or fast enough. This thing's new, and they need you to install it."

Coulter wasn't convinced. "If it's all that important, why are there no guards on this plane? Why are we sitting out here in a clover patch, all by our lonesome?"

"You tell me."

"And another thing: Why all the razzle-dazzle? Why the secrecy crap?"

"It's obvious you've never dealt with the Russians. When you deal with the Russians, *everything* is secret, pal."

"Then why didn't they ship this thing diplomatic? Why ship it in a way that the Ivans are practically guaranteed to get hard-nosed about?"

Lukas gave him a long, somber gaze. "That is the question that's been giving me the fits, my friend. You've just asked the big one."

They said nothing more for a time. Then out of the airfield's ever-present humming and clatter came the sound of a car approaching. Lukas went to the hatch and saw Guilford climbing out of the Ops Office jeep.

"So how did you make out, Captain?"

Guilford looked up, squinting in the summer glare. "I came up with zilch, that's how I made out. I couldn't even get past the mission switchboard."

"I'm not surprised. But thanks for trying anyhow."

"The Ops Office had a message for you, by the way."

"Oh? What kind of message? And who from?"

"Here." Guilford handed up an envelope. "They asked me to bring it out to you."

Lukas tore the seal and turned so as to get better light. He read:

TWX, CO RHEIN/MAIN AIR BASE   18 JULY 45
ATTENTION: BASE OPERATIONS
PLS FWD WHITE HOUSE ATTACHE ALEX LUKAS, NOW IN
HOLDING, YOUR STATION. TEXT FOLLOWS:

271

HAVE BEEN ADVISED OF SOVIET FREEZE OF YOUR
FLIGHT PLAN. WORK ON THE PROBLEM HAS BEGUN.
STAND FAST UNTIL FURTHER WORD ABOUT THE FOX IN
OUR POPLARS.
SIGNED:
LITTLE WHITE HOUSE, POTSDAM

Lukas folded the paper carefully and placed it in the breast pocket of his jacket.

"Something about us?" Coulter asked.

"Yeah."

"Who's it from?"

"My boss, I think."

"What's it say?"

"I'm not sure."

"Mind if I read it?"

"Go ahead."

"What's this mean? This stuff about foxes and poplars?"

"Beats the hell out of me."

"You are in a very, very weird business, Mr. Lukas."

"You should see it from here."

"So what do we do now?"

"We stand by. Like the boss says."

"He's not my boss, damn it."

"That's right. He isn't. I'm your boss," Lukas said.

"I'll go over your head. Right to the top."

"The president is about as top as you can get. There isn't anybody topper."

"Oh, yeah? How about Mrs. Truman?"

"Get out the cards. I want to win some more of your money."

"Up yours."

"Come on, Coulter. The cards."

There was the ticka-tacka rumble of a diesel motor, and from the hatch they saw a large flatbed truck pull along-
272

side. The cab doors opened and three men wearing olive drab coveralls and army fatigue caps leaped to the concrete. Two of them confronted the men lying in the wing's shadow and covered them with Wehrmacht-issue Schmeisser machine pistols while the third vaulted up the ladder and pressed the muzzle of his pistol loosely, casually, against Lukas's belt buckle.

"Ah, Herr Lukas. The man of the hour."

"Still up to your Wild West tricks, I see."

Coulter snarled. "Who is this bastard, Lukas? And what's he saying?"

"His name is Taras. The two men out there are called Nikki and Boris. They're Soviet agents. And Taras has just used his faulty German to pronounce me man of the hour."

"Soviet *agents?* You mean like in spy novels?"

Taras swung the pistol barrel fast, hard, and the side of Coulter's head ran with blood.

"Ow, what did you do that for, you sumbish?"

"Lukas, tell your friend to keep his mouth shut. Tell him to be silent and do as we say or he will be shot."

Lukas asked, "Are you all right, Coulter?"

"Of course I'm not all right, you ass. I'm bleeding like a stuck pig, and you ask am I all right."

"You're not hurt bad. But this gent says you will be if you don't shut up and do as he says."

"How the hell am I supposed to know what he says? I don't speak Russian."

"He's speaking German."

"All the same to me. But you can tell him that he owes me one. And I'm going to collect. Somewhere, somehow."

Taras snapped, "Silence!" He called out the hatch, "Nikki, get those people into the airplane. Boris, back the truck around so that its tailgate is below the hatch here."

The aircrew came aboard, obviously shaken. Guilford muttered, "What the hell's going on, Lukas?"

273

"I think your cargo is about to be stolen."

Taras swung his pistol again, and Lukas staggered, his head ringing, his right temple sticky.

"I told you to be quiet. The next time you speak, it will be when I ask you to. And the next time you will use German. Or the next time I use the gun in the way it is supposed to be used."

"No you won't, you pimplehead. The last thing you can afford right now is to have all the Amis in this neighborhood hear gunfire."

Nikki drew a boot knife and waved it in mean little arcs. "Let me finish him now, Taras."

"Later. We need his muscle for the moment." Turning to the others, Taras said, in heavily tainted English, "We have no dangerous against you mans. Do my orders and you are living. Do not my orders and you are deading. Okay?"

Guilford, hands still raised, said, "All right. What do you want us to do?"

"Make loose the large box and move it from flying plane to autotruck. Quick."

"Gee, I dunno. That's a very big job."

The pistol barrel tracked from Lukas to Guilford. "Do as I have spoken."

"Tell him to stick it, Guilford," Lukas grated. "He's going to kill all of us as soon as he has us clear of this base. Don't do anything and he's had it. He doesn't have enough muscle to move the box and he doesn't dare to shoot us if he wants to get out himself. We've got a nice little impasse shaping here."

Guilford shook his head. "I can't afford to be a hero, Lukas. I got too much going for me at home."

"Me, too," Fitz put in. "I'm going to take a chance and do what the Russki says." His fellow crewmen, picking up on this, nodded agreement.

"You're soldiers, damn it. You're supposed to fight."

"Uh-uh. War's over. And we ain't mad at anybody."

274

Despite his injunction against further talk and for all the lousiness of his English, Taras had been listening to this with gathering amusement. "Ah. You see, Lukas? Your countrymen are reasonable, and you are shown to be the fool."

There was a taut, quiet moment in which the Americans were trading silent looks. Coulter sighed, then drawled, "Well, I guess Lukas isn't the only fool aboard."

Everyone stared, disbelieving, as Coulter snatched a flare pistol from its wall rack beside the emergency exit, pulled the trigger and sent an arcing ball of incandescence into the airplane's forward area. The Americans watched, immobilized by incredulity and fascination, as the cockpit area became a seething bonfire. And it seemed entirely logical when the hilt of Nikki's boot knife appeared magically in the center of Coulter's chest and the rich and famous explosives designer folded in on himself, dead before he hit the floor.

Taras broke the spell by leaping to the hatch opening, waving his pistol and shouting, "Lukas, tell those people to get that crate onto the truck. At once. If they don't, they are dead."

The aircrew needed no translation. They were throwing off the crate's lashings and sliding it toward the hatch before Lukas could utter a syllable.

"Hurry," Guilford yelled, "before this whole frigging airplane goes up! Hurry, goddam it!"

Down the field, beyond the transient aircraft parking area, where the hangars shimmered in the summer heat, a Klaxon horn bleated, raucous even at this distance. It was joined in a moment by the howling of fire engines and crash trucks, and there was the insistent clanging of a bell somewhere. The day had darkened under the spreading column of smoke that boiled upward from the DC-6's nose section.

"Tell your people that one word to the fire crews and you

all die." Taras underscored it by jabbing the air with his Schmeisser.

Guilford understood. "All right, you guys: Heave! Heave, goddam it!"

The crate was shifted to the truck and lashed down. The vehicle had moved to a safe distance by the time the emergency wagons arrived and a jeep, driven by a big man who sweltered in a yellow fire chief's slicker, skidded to a halt where Taras and Lukas and the aircrew stood.

"Anybody on that thing?" He waved at the burning plane.

"One man," Guilford said. "But he was killed in the explosion. He was—"

His lies were obscured by a crashing sound, harsh, as if a huge door had slammed, and the DC-6 dissolved in a balloon of flame and oily smoke. The wreckage sagged, then collapsed in its final throes as the firefighters' streams of foam poured into the pyre. There was great clamor and much running back and forth, and no one seemed to notice when the flatbed truck and its new cargo blattered off toward the east gate.

Lukas, crammed between Taras and Boris in the truck, felt a sadness so deep, so onerous, he wanted only to lie down and close his eyes and fall unconscious.

Nikki sat behind them on the jump seat and held the muzzle of his machine pistol against Lukas's nape. He laughed softly. "Your compatriots, the airplane drivers, are truly brave heroes, eh, Lukas?"

There were no words that would form any kind of answer.

The MP on the gate, all fancy in his white helmet and snappy white gloves, waved them through without glancing at the phony pass Taras held out the window for his inspection.

As the truck rattled down the highway toward Frank-
276

furt, Taras chuckled. "Brave airmen and vigilant sentries. Stars and Stripes Forever. Semper fidelis. Oh, say can you see Mom's apple pie?" His amusement became open laughter.

CHAPTER 28

Near Tjindecken, Germany
18 July 1945

Lukas was having a very bad time with his anger.

Or was it remorse? There was shame in it, to be sure. Something else, too.

Grief, perhaps?

Whatever, its base was rage. First, rage at the kind of almost casual dying done by men such as Coulter—breathing, blinking, wisecracking one moment and, in the next, collapsing with nothing more to say, ever. Men like Josef, the skilled alcoholic forger who, all those thousands of years ago, had died in midcomment as he stood on a rubbled street corner in Munich. Where was the sense, the relevance of such an irrevocable happening?

Then rage at the selfishness, the

278

sickening me-first state of mind of men like Guilford and his crew. Fear, Lukas understood. Likewise loneliness, anxiety, the deep weariness that came from protracted living with the knowledge that other men, anonymous and alien, were doing their utmost to kill you. But how could men like Guilford rationalize an uncomplaining cooperation with creeps like Taras? How could Guilford in good conscience equate his itinerant's homesickness, his readiness to cut and run when things became inconvenient or difficult, with the kind of mortal terror sublimated by the frontline doughfoot, month in, month out? How, for Christ's sake, could he have been so ready to bow and scrape after watching Coulter do what he did?

Coulter. What combination of genes and circumstance had enabled him to die with such offhandedness? Could a slam on the head with a pistol barrel have been the activating mechanism for some preordained mission to commit a socially useful suicide? But where was the usefulness in a self-destruction whose end result was no more than to assure the delivery of a shipping crate to a squad of smelly Russians—who were already nine-tenths in possession of it?

Why *had* the Russians gone to so much trouble to steal the shipping crate when its announced destination had been Moscow all along? Why couldn't they simply have waited until it arrived in Moscow and then stolen it—there, on their home turf?

Obvious: Taras and his bosses didn't want the crate to go to Moscow. They wanted to take it elsewhere, for reasons of their own.

A place closer to Frankfurt than to Moscow.

But that implied that the Russians knew what was in the crate.

How could they know that, when he didn't know himself— he, one of the good guys?

But, hell, that wasn't all he didn't know. He didn't even

279

know if there was a God—something so many people of so many persuasions in so many places in the world were so smugly certain of. He didn't even know why, if there was a God, God let people like Coulter get killed so casually. He didn't even know why or how God let him, Alexei Lukas of Buffalo, New York, get into this melancholy, sickening, inexplicable, crazy business. And, after all this time in this crazy business, he had just discovered that he didn't even know what his own boss was talking about. Foxes? Poplars? Certainly all the Russians knew what the term meant. And now, presumably, Brandt and maybe everybody else in the world knew. But not Alexei Lukas. Nosiree.

One thing for damned sure.

Alexei Lukas was not about to die casually. When Alexei Lukas died it would be a Technicolor extravaganza with an all-star cast, including the Rockettes, coming to you directly from that Big Radio City Music Hall in the Sky.

That was for damned sure.

They had skirted the west side of metropolitan Frankfurt, heading north on the narrow blacktops that led through Hoechst and Bad Soden, then northeast to Oberursel, that infamous town where so many enemies of the Third Reich had suffered their final interrogations and where now, in the cabins among the trees, muckamucks of the selfsame Third Reich were undergoing interrogations preliminary to the war crimes trials in Nuremberg.

Beyond Bad Homburg they turned full east on a pitted little road that ended in a large meadow outside a village whose sign said it was Tjindecken. A tin hangar huddled in a corner of the expanse of stubble, and the wind sock on its roof hung limp against the brassy evening sky. Two men in baggy Russian uniforms stood guard at a makeshift gate in a truly impressive fence made of what seemed to be miles of concertina wire. There was a sign here, too, and it announced in German, English and French that this was the property of the Military Mission of the Union of Soviet Socialist Republics to Headquarters, United States Forces, Europe, and trespassers would be dealt with most severely.

A C-47 bearing the red star insignia sat in the grass, lonely and tacky. Its wide cargo door was open, and three men in mechanics' coveralls puttered about the starboard engine.

Boris steered the truck across the ruts, its motor snorting and grating, its springs twanging, and brought it to a shuddering halt close by the airplane's cargo hatch. Taras elbowed Lukas. "Out. And stand where I can see you while I'm getting things together."

"I can't get out. These handcuffs keep—"

Taras swung out of the truck and, grabbing Lukas's jacket, pulled him through the truck door to a heavy landing in the grass. He kicked Lukas in the ribs. "On your feet. Or the next kick goes lower."

Nikki growled, "Why do we fool with this cowplop? Why don't we just get rid of him?"

"Because we have orders to bring him here, you idiot."

"But—"

"There are no 'buts' when it comes to orders, damn your eyes." Taras pointed an angry finger at Nikki. "You are in very deep trouble already, Comrade. We were under orders to bring in the other Ami, too, but you just had to use that sticker of yours, didn't you? Let me assure you of one thing: When the district leader asks for an explanation you are on your own. Don't expect any support from me."

"The man had just set fire to the airplane. He was calling the Ami troops for help."

"Bah! You saw what a terrifying result came from that. The Ami troops are so drunk or so bored they wouldn't know a threat if it hit them in the balls. The aircrew didn't chirp a note when we were surrounded and outnumbered

281

by ten to one. They didn't even call ahead to warn the gate sentry, they were so afraid of us."

Nikki, red-faced and angry, was about to answer but seemed to be deciding against it when a jeep, its gears whining, came off the road and jounced across the stubble. It was an UNRRA vehicle. Ressel was at the wheel, and beside him, recruiting-poster cute in her perky cap and tailored uniform, Gretl Keller looked pleased with herself.

"Ah, Lukas," she said amiably as the jeep came to a stop, "we catch up with each other at last. Surprised?"

"Oh, my goodness, yes. I'm simply speechless."

She glanced at Ressel. "Pretty cool fellow, this one. He discovers his lady friend is a Soviet agent and he hardly blinks an eye."

Lukas shrugged. "Hang around a chameleon long enough, you get used to color changes."

Ressel was elaborately patronizing. "You are a rather accomplished troublemaker, Lukas, and I'll be very glad to be rid of you."

"Say it isn't so."

Frau Keller looked about. "Where is the moving van?"

"We didn't need it. The Amis were so confused they not only didn't chase us, we never saw one cop or MP the whole way here."

"Good. But where is the other American? The explosives expert."

Taras assumed an expression of pious concern, then seemed to take great pleasure in recounting Nikki's transgressions.

She listened, then stared aloft at the sunset clouds. Her tone mild, she asked, "You mean you killed him, Nikki? Despite my explicit orders to bring him to me for questioning?"

"Well, yes, Comrade. As Taras says, he was trying to alert the Ami troops—"

"Ressel, punish this idiot."

"Of course, Comrade Gretl." Ressel pulled a Walther automatic from his UNRRA Ike jacket and pointed it, almost casually, at Nikki's chest. The three shots sounded flat in the quiet evening air, like the clapping of gloved hands.

Nikki gave Ressel a lingering stare, his face somber. "You didn't have to do that," he said, softly accusing, as if criticizing a child. Then he sat in the grass, seeming to give the distant hills thoughtful study, and died.

Frau Keller, calling to the soldiers at the gate, waved a hand at the body. "Get rid of this." To Lukas she said, "We'll just have to make do with you."

"Long live the Revolution."

"We're going to fly you and your big box to Russia."

Lukas, struggling with the shock—the sick-in-the-belly shock that always accompanies violent death—pretended indifference. "Funny thing: that's what I was trying to do."

"But you were going to the American embassy. We're going elsewhere."

"How come?"

She waggled a forefinger. "Lukas, Lukas. Always working. Always questioning and striving. Why aren't more men like you?"

"One Lukas per planet. Anything more would be an overdose."

"I'm mad about you, you know."

"To know me is to love me."

"I'm serious."

"I'll bet."

She left it at that. Turning to the others, she said, "Very well. Let's get that thing aboard the plane. We have a lot of traveling to do tonight."

THE
RAISE

Entry in Personal Diary of C. G. Brandt
Potsdam, Germany
18 July 1945

Today's opening plenary session of the so-called Big Three—Truman, Churchill and Stalin and their retinues—gave substance to my suspicion that this whole Potsdam thing is nothing more than a trio of alley fighters met to divide up the loot taken from a fallen bully. Transcripts were provided me by Charles Bohlen, a silver-spoon Ivy Leaguer who did a stint in the Moscow embassy while I was there and who, thanks to his experience as a presidential consultant at Roosevelt's wartime summit conferences, is now serving as Harry's Russian interpreter. Bohlen's a pretty good fellow, yet I get the impression that his close association with FDR is working to his disadvantage these days; he's in on the roundtable formalities, thanks to his language proficiency, but put on the shelf when the meetings are over. He's my obverse, I suppose, since I'm hidden under the rug days and expected to be Mr. Russia nights.

From Bohlen's notes it's pretty clear that, right in front of God and everybody, the boys are splitting Europe down the middle—the eastern sphere of influence to the Soviets and the western to the United States and Britain. Soviet troops occupy Poland and Polish communists are already forming the government, and no matter which alternatives Truman and Churchill proposed today, Stalin made no bones about it: There just ain't gonna be any busting out of that particular sand trap. Even so, as is usual in this kind of showcase travesty, everything is moonlight and roses on the surface. The talk is sometimes stiff, sometimes cordial, always polite—and meticulously tailored so as to snow both today's publics and tomorrow's historians. If it weren't so serious and potentially tragic it would be comical to read today's discussions of just how "Germany" should be defined. Churchill brought up the question: Do we mean Germany as Germany was before the war, or as it is now? Stalin was blunt, proclaiming Germany to be "what she has become after the war." Harry, in effect, said baloney—we're talking about a country as it was before all this crap began. Churchill, who started the argument, didn't seem to care one way or the other. From there on the meeting was all downhill.

Nowhere in the transcript is there, of course, the slightest hint as to what's really going on.

Stalin, contested only by Hitler as the world's most ruthless and circumspect exponent of the doctrine of egoism, murmurs altruistically, even referring to the Big Three as "we, the leaders of democratic Europe"—giving not the tiniest clue of his intention to overrun and tyrannize everything east of the Rhine before the summer ends. Truman speaks glibly of future peace conferences, when all the while he knows of Stalin's plans and is doing his behind-the-scenes utmost to slow demobilization so as to make remobilization easier in case he has to fight the son of a bitch. And Churchill, steeped in booze, pills, and memories of grander times, pontificates on the need to avoid interference in the internal affairs of other nations, when
288

the British Em-pah—what remains of it—is rooted in precisely that kind of interference.

It's all very dreary, ostensibly an attempt to assure world peace when in reality it does nothing but line up the reasons for the next war.

Jesus. When are politicians ever going to learn that we're not all as dumb as they think we are? And when are we going to learn that the politicians we get are the politicians we deserve?

My primary personal concern at the moment is, naturally, Lukas and his shipping crate.

It's altogether possible that I overreached on this one. Gretl Keller is very much onto it and, thanks to her urgent messages to Red Glare and her radioed advisories to General Mandonovich, her recently acquired champion in Moscow, the whole daisy chain of civilian cells and ancillaries between Calais and Prague have heard of the impasse at Rhein/Main. They are enchanted, since the stand-off is deemed to be a tidy paraphrase of the developing confrontation between Mother Russia and the capitalist world. In fact, the Communist party chief in Paris has (according to Bebe, our resident mole there) drafted what amounts to an invitation to Moscow to place elements of the Red Army in France as "a sensible measure aimed at sustaining the public order in face of the growing American impotence and basic indifference to Europe's need for tranquility." The implications of such a draft are enormous, especially if the unprecedented popularity of the Party in Western Europe parlays into seats in national legislatures.

The phone is ringing. More later.

A storm is brewing in the State Department. All very discreet as yet, but growing in heat and power. At the core, as I understand it via my call of this evening to Billy Gordon, former OSS station chief, now working for the

Senate Foreign Relations Committee, are four highly placed, very vocal Soviet sympathizers (at least four of them, including that asshead Rutan) who fear that State is turning hard right under Truman. One of them (probably Rutan) is said to have learned of the Japanese peace feelers and is ready to go public with a demand that, in the interest of saving lives, the president immediately sign an armistice and invite the still-neutral Soviet Union to serve as go-between. Obviously the pinko bastard hasn't got the word that the last thing under the sun Stalin wants right now is an end to the Pacific war.

Nevertheless, in the hope I can get Rutan out of the way for good—or at least keep him off balance and quiet during this critical period—I have just sent him a sealed-delivery, your-eyes-only cable to his Georgetown apartment:

I HAVE PIX OF YOU KNOW WHAT.

(SIGNED) BRANDT

There are no such pictures, of course. But every man has something, past or present, he'd hate to have his boss or his dear ones learn about, much less witness.

Let's see how Rutan handles this.

If I hear from him at all, I've got him.

I own Rutan forever.

I heard from him by return TWX in exactly forty-one minutes. "Ur meaning unclear," the wire said. "But let's lunch ur return Stateside."

On a hunch, I patched in my special phone to a source in Chevy Chase who owes me a fat favor—a gilt-edged madam who knows I can prove she caters to government brasshats. I asked if she knew what kind of bones hang in Rutan's closet.

She laughed. "Mr. Rutan? He has very expensive tastes. He likes junior high school bobby-soxers. And they must be blond and blue-eyed. Pays a premium for freckles."

CHAPTER 29

**Frankfurt am Main, Germany
18 July 1945**

"Good evening, Frau Ressel. Come in. Sit down. What might I do for you?"

"I regret having to bother you at this late hour, Comrade Georgi, but something is troubling me deeply. I need the advice—the friendly counsel—of someone who demonstrates a keen understanding of human nature. Someone like you."

"Well, my dear Comrade, you flatter me, of course. I try very hard to exercise good sense in my dealings with others, but I had no idea I've been demonstrating a keen understanding of human nature, as you put it."

"No, dear Comrade Colonel, it's not in my nature to use flattery. I speak the unadorned truth. I personally have witnessed your capabilities as a psychologist, and it's for this reason I've intruded on your time."

"So, then: what is troubling you?"

"It's a rather delicate matter, and I've struggled for days now trying to find a way to discuss it without being presumptuous, or offensive. I—"

"Come, come, Comrade. There's very little—probably nothing—in the way of human behavior that might still surprise or offend me. Mankind tends naturally to be gross, and I am no longer upset by that melancholy truth. Tell me what's on your mind."

"It's—well, it's Frau Keller. Comrade Gretl."

"So?"

"She's not fit to be our leader."

"Please, Frau Ressel, we've been through all this before. We even summoned an inspector general to our conclave at Nagelfeld, and he, Comrade General Mandonovich, pronounced her fit in all respects. And—"

"I regret bringing this up again, of course. Not only does it demean me—make me look like a vindictive nag, as a matter of fact—but it also saddens me that our cause stands to lose in some inevitable way because she is what she is. Because she is so, well, vulnerable."

"Vulnerable? You must be more precise, Comrade Ressel. I don't understand what you're getting at with all this."

"Frau Keller has a problem. A sexual problem."

"Don't wo all, Frau Ressel. Don't we all. Ha-ha."

"Please, Comrade Colonel, this is difficult enough, and your joking about it only—"

"Of course, dear Comrade. I'm truly sorry. In view of the manifold problems and tensions with which we've all been living in recent months, the idea that any of us—Frau Keller included—might have a problem with sex seems to me to be a droll understatement."

293

"I don't mean she's having a problem with sex as such. She's having a problem with the manner in which she practices it."

"Well. I agree that she tends to be somewhat casual in her liaisons. She's even had a fling or two with your husband, I hear. But—"

"Promiscuous is the word. She's not casual, she's plain promiscuous."

"Dear Comrade Ressel, there is no law against that. There is no Party or national regulation that names frequency of copulation as an actionable transgression."

"I'm not concerned about the law, Comrade Colonel. I'm concerned about the effect her practices could have on the morale and efficiency of the movement she leads."

"Please, Comrade Ressel. *Which* practices?"

"Frau Keller has—Well, ah—She has made advances. Frau Keller is, I'm afraid, terribly infatuated with me and is consistently attempting to seduce me."

"Frau Keller is a—You're saying she—"

"Please, Comrade Colonel, there's hardly a need for you to laugh so—so boisterously—"

"I find this to be hilarious. I really do."

"I fail to see why. I think for one woman to be sexually interested in another is prima facie evidence of a fundamental character defect that could cause critical damage to the morale of our movement."

"Oh, come now, Frau Ressel. Don't be such a prudish old nit. Ha-ha."

"Why *are* you so amused?"

"Because, dear Comrade, Gretl Keller has advised me of her deep concern over my own widely discussed homosexuality. She dares to call the kettle black. Ha-ha."

"I—I'm awfully confused, Comrade Colonel. I had no idea that you—"

"Oh, come off it, Frau Ressel. I'm no homosexual. But Frau Keller tells me there's a lot of gossip that says I am

294

having an affair with Taras. Can you imagine? Me, having the hots for that ugly ball of hair? Spare me, please. Ha-ha."

"I've heard no such gossip."

"You haven't?"

"Not a word."

"That would suggest, then, that Frau Keller is not only a lesbian, she's also a liar."

"It would seem so, Comrade Colonel."

"You swear she's made overtures to you?"

"Many times. She's even crawled into my bed."

"Ha-ha."

"Is that all you're going to do, Comrade Colonel? Laugh?"

"The question is, dear Frau Ressel: What is there to do? What do *you* wish to do about it?"

"Frankly, I'd like to see her purged from the Party."

"I wager you'd like to kill her, too. Wouldn't you?"

"Well, in a sense. I find her most repugnant. It's bad enough when she tries to steal my husband, but when she tries to include me in her sordid adventures, well, I'm revolted."

"I am, too. Ha-ha. I am absolutely torn up by it."

"So?"

"So I have an idea, Comrade Ressel."

"Which is?"

"Since we've both been victimized by her lies and licentiousness, let's the two of us arrange her punishment."

"How?"

"She and your husband have commandeered Lukas and his mysterious packing crate, right?"

"Yes."

"And they are presently flying it to the First Experimental Factory at Podberez'e Ivankovo north of Moscow for examination. Right?"

"So I understand."

"What would you expect to be the consequences if Frau Keller and your husband failed to deliver the suspect crate to Engineering-Technical Service, as ordered by C-in-C VVS?"

"There would be an almighty uproar, an investigation. . . ."

"A court-martial? Purging?"

"Even, ah, execution . . ."

"And, moreover, what would be the predictable result if you and I were to, say, recover the package, snatch it back, say, from a foreign agent—a notorious foreign agent like, say, Lukas?"

"Honors . . . medals . . . promotions, perhaps. . . . But I'm not seeking glory or honors, Comrade Georgi. I—"

"You are interested only in vengeance. Right? You want only to repay Frau Keller and your husband for their little treasons against you. Right?"

"I—I don't know what to say—"

"No need to say anything, Frau Ressel. I understand your hurt, your outrage. I have suffered similarly from Frau Keller's little wiles. And so your secret is safe with me. Just hand me the telephone, if you will, please."

CHAPTER 30

In Flight, Near Yurtsevo, Byelorussia 19 July 1945

This particular C-47, Gretl Keller decided, must have flown for the czar in 1917. It rattled and shook and grunted and wheezed, and cold wind hissed through its ragged seams and imperfect seals. The left engine showed an alarming readiness to backfire, even under a throttle and mixture control set for cruising. The pilot, a small, ratlike man named Fedor, seemed afraid to fly too high, as if by skimming the treetops he was keeping a foot on the ground, thus protecting himself against disaster. The copilot, who doubled as navigator, was Petrovich, a round man with sleepy eyes who gnawed on an enormous chunk of black bread and was given to incomprehensible mutterings in his radio mask between bites.

She rode in the jump seat behind these two. Ressel, sprawled on a sidebench, kept an eye on things in the cargo hold, where the big wooden crate was lashed down in shadowy solitude. Lukas was there, too, handcuffs attaching his left wrist to a bulkhead. He looked cold and wretched.

Below, suffering Russia was an indigo nothingness where occasional lights blinked dimly. The old lessons—learned in the bleak Moscow school beside the miniscule park with its gaggle of tired birches, each ringed with its little wrought iron fence—came back in this, the least likely of times. Byelorussia: a vast, rolling plain, half again as large as Britain, the buckle on the belt of the Soviet Union's European territory. The shining target that had enticed legions of foreign murderers over the centuries, Huns and Goths and God-knows-who-else-since plunging in from the west, Mongols and Turkics thundering in from the east and south—all of them hacking down children and their mothers, burning huts, and enslaving the surviving men. And now the Nazis, doing a reprise with more than two million Byelorussians killed, another half million forcibly moved to Germany. No wonder the lights were few in the rushing darkness below. No wonder Russia wanted its frontiers to be on the Rhine and the Pacific and the blue Mediterranean. No wonder she was sitting in this bucket of bolts, shivering in July and feeling lonelier than ever before, remembering little wrought-iron fences and a father she adored, a mother she never really knew.

She glanced at Lukas and understood that he was simultaneously the best and the worst to have happened to her. Best, because she had always known that in her somewhere, stifled, denied, locked in the inner ice, lay the ingredients of the classic wife and mother. Lukas had served unwittingly to begin the thaw, to break the jam and set the currents to running. Yet this was the very thing

298

that made him the worst. War, as the most universal of religions, was as essential to human life as the sun and oxygen and heartbeats, because it purged each generation of the spiritual necrosis produced by sublimated hatreds and envies. And she had become a priestess in war's temple, and someday, when she was too old and slow and afraid to celebrate whatever war might be raging at the time, she would retire into non-war, a purgatory in which she would have nothing but time to remember Lukas and how he had lit her fuse and how she had been unable—perhaps unwilling—to do anything about it.

She caught herself up here. Who was being fooled by such nonsense? Priestess indeed. Too old? Retire? Her chances of growing old enough to retire were as remote as Venus. In fact, her chances of surviving the oncoming day were not really worth guessing.

Fedor turned his rat's face to her and piped, "Smolensk coming up. We need fuel. I'm going to try for some at the fighter station there."

"Do we really have to? You gassed up at Minsk."

"We've got another three hundred and ninety kilometers to Moscow, and this old clunk's fuel gauges aren't all they should be. That, plus this rotten wind coming in from the south, which could turn into a headwind any time now, tells me I don't want to take a chance. Lots of ground fog reported ahead, too, and we might have to do some circling. I'd rather have full tanks, if you don't mind, Comrade."

Petrovich brushed some crumbs from his flight jacket, fussy little flickings of his pudgy fingers, and said, "We are also being invited to land. The radio is telling me that the commandant at the fighter station wants us to put down for consultations."

Gretl stared at him. "Consultations? I have no reason to consult with him. Or anybody else at Smolensk."

"He seems to be most insistent, Comrade."

"Tell him this is a special flight. A most urgent mission conducted by the NKVD."

"I have already done so, Comrade. The radio says the fighter station commandant is acting upon orders from the highest level."

Fedor tried to ease things. "Well, since we need gas anyhow, Comrade, there's no harm in dropping in as the commandant requests. A few words with him while we top our tanks, and everybody's happy."

Gretl was not taken in by this dissimulation. She knew the pilot had to have heard the radio traffic, and she deduced that he was using low fuel as a practical excuse to make a landing. She shook her head. "Shut down the radio."

The two airmen gave her an incredulous appraisal. "Surely you can't be serious, Comrade," Petrovich said. "I need the radio for navigation. I need it for—"

"Turn it off and keep flying."

"I can't do that," Fedor protested. "I—"

"You can do that, Comrade Fedor, because if you don't do that you will be in immediate and extremely uncomfortable difficulties with my headquarters. Would you rather press your luck with fuel gauges and a dead radio or with a highly irritated NKVD?"

The pilot shrugged, turned off the radio, and turned to his work. The copilot became absorbed in his map board.

The dawn had arrived, and they flew toward the rosiness. Below, the great plain emerged from shadow and she was aware of the occasional snaking road, the clumps of trees, a clutch of ruins, the tiny lakes mirroring the sunrise. The smudge that was Smolensk passed off to the left, and for a time they skimmed the mighty Dnieper until it made its swing north at Izdeshkovo. The left engine was sounding more raucous, and she saw Fedor glancing at the fuel gauges with worried eyes.

300

"We've got company," Petrovich announced, nodding his helmeted head to the right. Her eyes followed the motion, and she saw that just off the starboard wing a bullet-nosed Ilyushin 2m3 ground-attack two-seater flew beside them, rising and falling on the air currents.

"There's another one on our left," Fedor said uneasily. "The pilot is signaling us to land."

"Ignore him," Gretl said coolly.

"*Ignore* him? My God, woman: They'll blow our asses off if we ignore him! Don't you know that?"

She jabbed Petrovich's shoulder. "Get them on the radio. Remind them we are on an affair of state. We are officials of the NKVD. If we are delayed on our mission, they will be subject to the most severe punishment."

Petrovich mumbled into his facepiece. He listened for a moment, then reported. "The man says his orders come straight from the Kremlin. We are ordered to land for consultations."

"With whom and about what?"

The copilot relayed first the question, then its answer. "The man says he doesn't know. All he knows is that he's supposed to bring us back to his base or, failing that, to force us down and confiscate our cargo."

She considered all this, her mind rapidly sifting the possibilities. Intuition, her most reliable ally, told her that Frau Ressel's hand was in this somewhere. General Mandonovich had authorized this flight to Moscow, the certifying telegram specifically stating that the box and its contents were to be brought to his research center headquarters at Podberez'e Ivankovo "for examination and evaluation." To muster the kind of countermand represented by the two *Shturmoviks* outside their windows someone—yes, it had to be Frau Ressel, possibly in concert with that idiot Georgi—would have had to go either to someone of higher rank or to a source of equal or lower

301

Kremlin rank who was unaware of the importance given to this flight. The latter was more likely, and she was willing to wager that the source was Belenko at Samovar, the nincompoop who seemed always ready to do Frau Ressel's bidding in affairs of petty vengeance.

"Turn off the radio and keep going."

"My aching ass, woman—"

"Drop the plane as low as you can. Hug the terrain. Change your speed often. But keep going. The strip at Butova is where we're headed."

"You're crazy. You'll get us all killed."

"This cargo must get to its destination. At the earliest possible moment and at any cost. It's of fundamental importance to the national security."

Ressel came forward from the cargo hold, blinking in the morning light. "What's going on?"

"This woman wants to kill us," Fedor whined. "Those fellows out there want us to land, and if we don't they'll shoot our asses off."

"So land, then. What—"

Tired of all this, and frightened and angry, Gretl produced her automatic pistol and held its muzzle against the back of Fedor's head. "Ressel, get the hell back where you belong. You, pilot, fly this goddam machine to Butova."

"Butova? I don't get it. What's the idea? We're cleared for Ivankovo—"

"If I hear another complaint out of you there'll be no need for you to worry about any of this, because I'll have blown your ratty brains all over the windshield."

Ressel, plainly lost and upset, said, "I hope you know what you're doing, Comrade."

"I'm trying to get this secret Yankee weapon to Butova, that's what I'm doing."

"*Weapon?* Secret? What—"

"Shut up and go back to your post, damn it!"

302

There was a wild drumming along the airplane's flanks, and the machine tilted to port, trembling violently, and wind screamed in the holes, and dust and broken things flew about the cabin. Her startled glance through the side window showed her the starboard *Shturmovik* crabbing in on a sidling course, the man in the rear cockpit crouching, his machine gun aglow with tiny darts of flame. Then a vicious snapping sounded from the opposite quarter, and Fedor jumped in his seat, gave a sharp, despairing yelp, and sagged forward against the wheel. She pulled him away from the controls, shouting to Petrovich to take over.

"I've been hit, too," Petrovich gasped.

"Where?"

"In the legs somewhere."

"Can you move them?"

"Yes. It hurts like hell, but—yes."

"Can you fly the plane?"

"As long as I'm awake, I can."

"That fog bank to the left: Do you think you can hold out until we fly into it?"

"I won't know until I get there. But we're on our way."

"As soon as you're into the fog, set us down. Anywhere you can. The other planes won't be able to get a fix on where we settle. It'll give us a chance to hide."

"Why are they trying to kill us?"

"I don't know."

"God, what a world . . ."

She hurried to the rear, where Kessel crouched low, staring anxiously out the starboard windows. "What are those maniacs trying to do?" he screeched at her, his eyes wide and glassy. She ignored him, hurried to Lukas.

"Are you all right?" she asked in German.

"I might have wet my pants. I've had to go since Minsk."

"You're not hit or anything?"

"No."

"How about the box?"

"Two bullets right through the side. The goddam thing hummed."

"Hummed?"

"That's what I said. It made a humming sound. Loud."

"Oh, God."

"What's in it? Do you know?"

"All I know is, it shouldn't be humming."

"If you're trying to scare me, you're doing a fine job."

"We're going in—maybe for a bad landing. I'll take off those cuffs. Promise you won't do anything heroic? Anything to get us into more trouble than we're in already?"

"Woman, in a plane with a dead pilot, a wounded copilot, one engine out and the other on fire, with the Russian air force outside, trying to kill us, and a secret cargo that hums, we're already in as much trouble as anybody can be in."

She removed the cuffs, and there was a moment in which their bodies were close, their gazes meeting.

"I've never known a woman like you."

"There are no women like me."

"I wish we could've been friends."

"You would never have had a better one."

"You're a rotten little communist."

"And you're a filthy capitalist pig."

"Sit down here. Put your back against the bulkhead. Hang on to me."

Ressel was standing, groping for balance and a handhold. His face was white. "No," he called out. "She's mine. She belongs with me."

"Sit down, Ressel, you damned fool. We're—"

The airplane's belly slammed hard against something, and the fuselage slewed sideways with a terrible tearing sound.

This meeting of the titans seems to be interminable. They gather days at the Cecilienhof, a pseudoTudor palace in the woods on the rim of the Holy Lake, for hours of mumbo jumbo about councils and reparations and the establishment of borders that will take away land and livelihoods and give them arbitrarily to those who managed to survive the shooting and come out on the political topside. Then they retire nights to their lairs, where they scheme up the angles they will shoot the next day when they are again in their highback chairs around the big table. They did this nine times between the opener on July seventeenth and July twenty-fifth, when they took a two-day break to let the British people kick Winston Churchill out of the office of prime minister and elect a rather colorless fellow named Clement Attlee, the kind who always looks surprised when the sun comes up. Which amuses the hell out of me. The Brits, from their Foreign Office hotshots to their civil servant chambermaids at Babelsberg, have been insufferably superior and, despite Churchill's boozy charm and his obvious fondness of the president, have been condescending when it comes to Harry Truman. Now they've got a Man of the Peepul of their own representing them at this, the Con Game of All Time, and it does my heart good to hear their rationalizations of Attlee's ill-fitting suits and run-over heels and crooked neckties. Anyhow, Attlee and his foreign minister, a guy named Bevin, who looks and talks like a dockwalloper, showed up yesterday for what look to be at least four more days of plenary platitudes and night time nattering, and the shoe is on the other foot now, with Truman being barely polite to the Cockneys.

Before Winnie left for England and his humiliating rejection by the voters, he and Harry got together a paper

305

they called "The Potsdam Proclamation by the Heads of Government, United States, China and the United Kingdom." It was formally issued last Thursday and—with the radioed approval of Chiang Kai-shek—it spells out just what the hell they expect of Japan. Since Russia is still a neutral in the Asiatic war, and since Harry is very reluctant to invite them in, the paper simply states that Japan, if it goddam well knows what's good for it, will cut the crap and stop shooting. If this happens, then the U.S. and British will get around to letting the Japs live a little longer. All references to the emperor—the major preoccupation of the Japanese face-savers—have been omitted in the document and any hopes that the Japanese government will accept its demands are about as likely as banana splits in hell.

It is, I think, about the dumbest goddam piece of horse manure I've seen in my years of shoveling the stuff. It absolutely guarantees that the Japs will fight to the last man in the last ditch, and I hate to think of the number of Americans who will be lying in the ditch with him.

But even this kind of stupidity can be turned to an advantage by a cool head. I'm beginning to wonder if Harry's head is all that cool. He certainly seems to be going out of his way to exacerbate what's already a raggedy-ass situation worldwide, knowing what he does about Stalin's intentions. Worse, Stalin, for all his Good-Ole-Unca-Joe act in his cream-colored drum-major's uniform, has shown several times what a horse's ass he is. His meanness and his slickster's guile have shown through and, while Harry deserves credit for snarling back at him, Good Ole Unca Joe is still getting ready to occupy what ain't his and Harry shows no inclination to call Stalin into the street about it. Which worries me a lot.

I guess I wouldn't be so pessimistic about all this if things had worked out better with Lukas and the packing crate caper. It's been ten days now since he disappeared, and all
306

of my inquiries notwithstanding, not a whisper has been heard along the intelligence jungle trail. It must be assumed that he's dead, the box's secret either lost with him or exposed by the Soviets, and the entire ploy a bust.

I am, as they say in those Victorian novels, sick at heart.

Those Victorian writers knew what the hell they were talking about.

Sick is the word.

CHAPTER 31

**Near Telginovo, Russian
Federation 29 July 1945**

One afternoon in his twelfth year,
Lukas had visited Bud Durkin,
a schoolmate who lived in Kenmore. They got into playing "Tarzan
of the Apes" in an old apple tree,
swinging from branch to branch,
little Johnny Weissmullers yodeling
and pursuing an invisible Maureen
O'Sullivan. A branch broke, and
Lukas's fall seemed to be in slow
motion as the leaves and unripened
apples and gnarled trunk spun
together and rose away from him toward a misty blue sky. At last there
was the impact, and Lukas had
lain in the dirt, on his side, trying insanely to make his lungs work again,
aware that no air was flowing into him
and that he was about to suffocate. As he agonized, his dimming
308

sight took in a woman who, with her kid, stood on a sidewalk nearby, watching his struggle for life, and she pointed at him lying there and said to the kid, "There, you see, Roscoe? That's what happens when you act smarty." No attempt to help him; no expression of concern. Just a mean little lecture to her runny-nosed brat. He had hated her—along with the entire human race—and his hatred had, presumably, served to prime his pan-caked lungs, because his breathing had resumed and he'd eventually made it home, hurting all the way to his soul.

It had been much the same after the crash.

The C-47, its engines gone, its propellers windmilling, its wings holed and sagging, had gone down through cotton-batting fog to belly into the marsh. It had skipped like a flung stone, eventually settling on a stretch of reeded sand that defined an island just off the riverbank. The wild sluing action had torn away the tail section, leaving the cargo hold exposed, like a section of badly used sewer pipe. Lukas's crate had held fast, lashed as it was to the floor plates and fuselage spacers, but he and Frau Keller had been thrown violently against the cockpit bulkhead, then across the hold and into the cabin wall.

They had been crumpled together, Raggedy Ann and Andy in the corner of a toy box. She was unconscious, her breath a loud raling, and he lay against her in the fog among wet grasses and torn aluminum and oil smells, mouth working like a fish's, desperate for air that refused to come into him. What kind of world would put him into this kind of stinking situation, would uproot a man from his homeland and hurtle him into a pile of wet sand, where he could suffocate against the cold and heaving body of an alien woman who herself could be dying. Shortly after, he began to breathe again and, aching everywhere, bleeding here and there, he made it to his feet for an assessment of the disaster.

309

Fedor and Petrovich were dead, of course, the pilot of his bullet wounds, his partner of a neck broken in the crash. Ressel had been thrown clear and, landing in a dune, had suffered nothing but sand abrasions on his hands and face. Gretl Keller came to; she had a large knob on her head and a bad cut on her left forearm. As for himself, he had escaped with no more than a set of badly aching ribs and a blue welt on his chest.

The three of them huddled under the fog-shrouded scrub trees and listened to the *Shturmoviks* prowling above, fruitlessly searching for their spoor. The waiting had continued through the night, then the next day and night. The search planes had been replaced by ground parties, soldiers who shouted back and forth in the persisting fog and nipped vodka and entirely failed to see the C-47's wreckage, thanks to the fact that the area—whatever it might be—had been fought over thoroughly, leaving a system of rubbled trenches and strongpoints along the riverbank and a scattering of burnt-out half-tracks, disemboweled tanks and, miracle of miracles, two other aircraft wrecks. The soldiers inspected these latter quite carefully on the fourth day, but again they failed to spot the C-47 and its survivors in their nest of reeds and marshbrush.

They had plenty to eat and too much to drink. The wreck revealed an unscathed stash of U.S. Army C-rations, three gallons of drinking water, and a wooden box containing a dozen liters of vodka, each packed in excelsior. The problem was not how to return to physical capability—it was how in the long term to stay alive in a land where every man, woman and child represented a threat.

They had been in hiding for almost ten days. But now, with their physical recovery complete, with the sound of distant voices, the rumble of planes, the splashing of slow-moving boats no longer to be heard, they could concentrate on escape.

Lukas had dealt with the interlude as though it were a
310

peculiar paradox, partly a large-scale, three-dimensional puzzle requiring heavy study and mechanical audacity, partly a furlough—a period, oddly free of war's emotional litter, in which he had plodded barefoot and bare-chested across warm sands and through whispering reeds, listening to the slow-moving river and the creatures to which it meant life. The others, Gretl and Ressel, had been there, fussing, arguing, but they'd represented mere background noise; he knew what he must do, and whatever they must do bore only tangentially on his larger need.

His larger need. What was that?

To survive? To get the crate to the embassy in Moscow?

He asked these questions of himself, tacitly, cynically. Yet, for all his resentment, he understood—accepted—the fact that the yes-answer to each was an absolute, inescapable. He had no real choice. His very genes insisted that he must do his duty.

Complicating the problem was his need of Keller and Ressel. He was alone, deep in the heart of a nation whose government—and, therefore, whose citizens—considered him to be a dangerous enemy. He must use the two specific enemies here to provide him with protection against, and passage through, all the unspecific, amorphous enemies out there. . . .

Gretl Keller, while rarely one to tolerate self-pity, in herself or others, was nonetheless presently on a martyrdom spree. She felt put upon, abused, and she let the feeling run freely because it helped to smother a larger, more onerous emotion.

Yesterday, today, tomorrow; the sameness in each, the unending requirement to spend herself on the current crisis, to throw her energies and soul processes at the problem of now, to place every interest before her own. She recognized this as maudlin poor-me stuff, all dressed up as

311

the noble, long-suffering selflessness of the patriot. But even though she could see it for what it was, she had hopes that it might anesthetize her passion for Lukas.

Passion wasn't really the word. Her preoccupation with him had all the urgency of the schoolgirl crush, to be sure, and it had heavy-duty, adult-type sexual overtones as well. Yet there was this other thing, too—an understanding that something very special had happened, that she wasn't the woman she once was, and that this amounted to a vulnerability that could quite possibly prove fatal.

She applied to this sore spot the first aid of intense activity.

On the evening of the third day, armed with her NKVD credentials, she had left the wreck and waded to the high ground, ready to improvise a way out of her awkward entrapment.

She had wandered for a time through the rubbled fields, great flat sweeps of pockmarked plain, black with long-ago burnings. When she'd come upon the hub of a cooperative farm it was difficult to recognize it for what it was. There was one street—a lane of ruts in the vast panorama of mud. Small wooden houses with thatched roofs on both sides and, behind each, a rectangle that suggested a private attempt to grow things. A battered church, which had once served as a community center, sagged in the Y formed by a parting of the ruts. No more. Nothing to relieve the ugliness, the stark loneliness, the forlorn silence of the place.

She had stood there, stricken by the melancholy thought that here was the end of the world, when an old woman, her thin body wrapped in rags, her breathing heavy with exertion, had come out of a house and picked her way through the puddles to a pile of trash, where she paused, as if lost in thought.

"Ho, Mother, may I have a word with you?"

Too many summers, too many wars to permit astonish-

312

ment in the faded blue eyes. Only a kind of amiable curiosity. But it had been enough eventually to carry Gretl through to the village political chief, who, for his part, hadn't seen too many summers and wars to be unimpressed by her NKVD papers. He'd been behind a plank desk in the ruined church, and his squint had revealed that he was a fawner. Suspicious to a point, of course, as are all politicians, but a groveler at heart.

"What brings you here, Comrade Keller?" he'd asked.

"I am on a most secret and urgent mission for the NKVD. Certain traitors in Moscow have arranged to have my plane shot down, and I have been hiding nearby, waiting for the chance to escape to Moscow with an extremely important cargo carried in our plane. I guarantee you, Comrade Kurlov, that you will be elevated to hero's status if you help me to elude the treasonous ones and carry out my obligations to Generalissimo Stalin."

"But how," Kurlov had asked slyly, "can I be sure you are not the traitor, Comrade Keller?"

"By gambling on this, your single greatest opportunity to gain national recognition and a medal honoring your cool judgment and dedication to Mother Russia."

"I'm to gamble, then."

"In a sense. But at minimum risk and for very pleasant stakes."

"Very well. So how can I help?"

"Is that river down the way navigable?"

"Yes, for small boats and flat-bottomed scows. It's a minor tributary of the Moskva. It winds through a lot of marsh country. We use its main channel to carry crops to the market dock near Borodino. Why?"

"I want your people to help me get the cargo onto a raft, or a scow. I'll need a generator, a power winch, some cable and hooks, shovels, and as many men as you can round up."

Kurlov smiled. "Men? Our men are in the army, or have

313

been killed or stolen by the Nazis. We have only a few small boys here, Comrade. I can provide a squad of women, though."

"Women will be fine."

So it had gone. And now, on the tenth day, they were ready.

If only she were not encumbered by Lukas, and by Ressel. But she needed them both.

Ressel for his blind obedience, his oxlike muscle. Lukas for his perseverance and courage, for his role as fulcrum in the resolution of her mission.

And for this impossible feeling he had generated in her—whatever it was.

* * *

Gretl and her remarkable band of farm women had come up with a tractor whose motor and gear train had been modified to accommodate a power winch cannibalized from a wrecked Nazi tank. Ressel, with the help of the women, had built a flotation raft which now nestled against the gaping end of the C-47's cargo hold. He and the women would slide the wooden crate onto the raft, and the tractor-winch combination would then pull on the cables, which in turn would drag the raft across the sandspit and into deep water. The weak link, of course, was the cabling itself; a considerable length had been needed to reach from the tractor, parked on the riverbank, to the makeshift pulley system at the wreck on the island, and he feared that the chain would break when so much weight was bullied across so much sand and muck.

Ressel had welcomed the sweaty labor, the hours of push and pull and improvisation, because they helped to mitigate the raging guilts in him. It was as if he had been relegated to some special hell reserved for self-indulgent weaklings who give way to the allure of sexual adventure. Memories of Gretl tossing and gasping on the steamy bed in the Myliusstrasse place still set him afire, while simultaneous-

314

ly, in that gross paradox belaboring errant men since the beginning of sex, recollections of the long-ago good times with his stony but legal spouse froze his heart dead.

That his fixation on Gretl Keller had cost him terribly, he now admitted to himself. For her he had given up wife and home, his childhood religion and his self-respect, and that was that. But even in the depth of his remorse he was angry—a sense of having been made vulnerable to sin by his wife's indifference, her preoccupation with politics and its machinations, the infrequent and stereotyped sex she had brought to their marriage from its outset.

He wouldn't have been so hot for Gretl if his bedroom hadn't been so cold, damn it.

Nor would it be so bad now if he didn't have to be so close to Gretl. She needed only to walk past him, and he needed only to catch her scent, and his body would swell and the blindness would descend.

If only she weren't here. If only Lukas weren't here. He knew he could then handle all this so much better. He could live with himself so much better.

Yet as soon as the thought took form, the larger awareness—the larger truth—replaced it.

He needed them both.

He needed Lukas to hate for having taken Gretl away; hatred was a palliative, more powerful than guilt and more pleasant to endure. And he needed Gretl Keller to explain to himself just how it was he could have wandered so far from what he once was and from what he'd always wanted to be.

Forgive me, God. I am an unholy mess.

CHAPTER 32

**MOSCOW
30 July 1945**

'll have to be getting up soon.
Georgi and I are to meet General
Trifonov for breakfast at eight
sharp."

"A lot of good Trifonov has turned
out to be."

"Well, he's tried very hard to help
us. It's not his fault that the C-47
hasn't been found yet."

"He's like all the other bureaucrats
in this godforsaken city: all mouth
and no performance. That plane is
out there somewhere. Along with
that whore, Keller, and that salacious goat of a husband of mine. How
can a plane and its cargo and passen-
gers simply disappear on the Russian
plains? It's there, and they're there,
and Trifonov and his people just
haven't looked hard enough."

"You're a very impatient woman, Comrade Elsbet."

"And you're not impatient enough, Comrade General."

Vladimir Belenko, chief of Samovar, wearer of the Lenin Medal and countless other awards, and fornicator first-class, said, "In the Soviet Union, haste is made slowly."

"Except when it comes to double-talk like that."

"My, you *are* in a snit this morning, aren't you. I should think that after a champagne supper and three or four of those rather spectacular orgasms of yours you'd be all pink and dewy this morning."

"I'm not the pink and dewy type."

"Ah, but you *are* a spectacular bed partner. I really can't imagine why a husband would find the need to wander when his wife is capable of such, ah, shall we say, volcanic eruptions? Ha-ha."

"My husband never took the time to discover what I'm capable of."

"That makes him even more of an ass than I thought him to be."

"He's a stupid, profligate wretch, that's what he is."

"Then why are you so impatient to find him?"

"That's really none of your business, Vladimir."

"By the way, are you and Georgi lovers?"

"Don't be ridiculous. You're my only lover."

"Let's keep it that way, eh? Meanwhile, I'd better get dressed. Big day ahead. Trifonov says the search is narrowing. A massive effort's under way, despite your skepticism. Rivers or railroads. That's where your old man and his girl are likely to be found. If they're still alive, that is."

"There's the phone."

"Hullo. General Belenko here. . . . Oh, yes, sir. . . . Ah, I see. . . . Very good. . . . Right away. I was just about to leave. . . . Yes, sir. I'll round up Colonel Lagolin. . . . Yes, sir. Very good, sir. . . . Good-bye."

"I take it that was Trifonov."

"He says they've received a message—a very interesting message—from the political adviser to a collective farm in the Borodino area. A solid lead to the whereabouts of our errant little group."

"I want to be in on the arrest, you know. I insist on that. I've not come all this way to miss the arrest."

"Relax, my dear. You're invited to the party, too."

"Call me after your breakfast."

"All right. So then: up and away."

"Wait. Not quite yet."

"Ah. You are ready again?"

"I'm always ready."

Entry in Personal Diary of C. G. Brandt
Potsdam, Germany
31 July 1945

It's late, and I have just seen Harry Truman to the door of his lakeside villa after his surprise visit to my digs. The Secret Service guys, if they were present, were certainly invisible. I had the distinct impression throughout the extraordinary incident that Harry had sneaked out, like a high school kid dropping from the back porch roof for a midnight tryst. I did not ask him about it, as curious as I was, because there was no way to keep the question from sounding presumptuous. And after thinking about it, my impression had to be wrong, because there's no way the president of the United States can manage to stroll around in the darkness of an alien land without his security people picking up on it. He said his visit was to be considered supersecret, a matter between us only, but we both know it's really between us and a squad of very discreet shootists in dark blue suits.

318

Harry's primary concern tonight (last night, now) was what to do about the Japanese, because what he does about the Japanese will have a direct bearing on what he does about Unca Joe Stalin's projected caper. He didn't put it so baldly, of course, but that's the way it shakes out.

I was much relieved by this, because, as I've noted in this journal, the Potsdam Declaration issued the other day by him and Churchill and Chiang, by denying the Japs a chance to save face via the emperor, is absolutely guaranteed to keep the war going for the next two hundred years. And what I read to be his lack of concern over Stalin's plans wasn't that at all—it was (and will remain, he assures me) his effort to maintain a poker face. I'm glad Harry Truman is concerned, because he should be. The world's about to go to hell in a handbasket, believe me Agnes.

Today's plenary session was once again devoted heavily to the reparations question—a matter given incredible emphasis by the Soviets. Harry confirmed, in effect, that the agreements made in the session split Germany down the geographical middle and establish two political halves that could, before the decade is out, serve as the vehicle for an avant-garde civil war, if not a general European war. The language of the agreements is careful not to say so, being full of references to the unification of Germany and all, but the implication is there.

Yet the stickiest complication is Japan's surrender overtures. Harry thinks a surrender now is a lousy idea, because if Japan gives up before the big bomb is demonstrated, the Russians will never believe that (1) the weapon is really all that special and (2) that the United States, being so humanitarian and all, would use the frigging thing. Putting real hair on this supposition is the fact that a group of American and British scientists who have worked

319

on the device are trying to petition the government in general and Harry in particular not to use it under any circumstances because it will mark the beginning of the end of the world.

From my notes:

Brandt: "I'm sure you're aware, Mr. President, that if you use such an outlandish device on the Japs when they're running around showing the white flag there will be those who will accuse you of wanton murder."

Truman: "Who's saying anything about using it on the Japs? I'm talking about a *demonstration*. I'm talking about popping off one of the damned things in a barren wasteland someplace and inviting the Russians to come and watch the explosion. Of taking movies and dropping them off over the emperor's palace. I may be a lot of things, Mr. Brandt, but a murderer I'm not."

Brandt: "No offense intended, sir."

Truman: "I know that. But I want you to understand how strongly I feel about this. We must precipitate the Japanese surrender, but at the right time. Unguessable numbers of American lives will be lost if we are compelled to invade the Japanese home islands, and Russia will have plenty of time to enter the war and get lined up for huge reparations claims against the Japs. We actually could lose our controlling influence in the Pacific and Asia by bleeding ourselves to death on the Jap beaches and letting the Russkies pick up the pieces. So I absolutely must demonstrate the bomb early enough to make it clear that it forced the Japs to surrender—and therefore leaves the Russians with no excuse to minimize the clout it gives us."

320

(It was here when I decided that I must let the president in on the state of affairs behind the atomic scene. It was obvious that he hadn't the slightest clue as to what is really going on there. I felt that I had to feed him enough information to keep us all out of foreign military trouble, but not so much information that he might someday have to lie about what he knew to keep us out of domestic political trouble. The way I see it, when you protect the president from trouble you're protecting the country itself from trouble. Simplistic, perhaps, but pragmatic, too!)

Brandt: "I'm afraid, Mr. President, that the Soviets are already quite well informed on the atomic bomb and its development."

Truman: "What do you mean by that?"

Brandt: "They've been maintaining a spy at Los Alamos for some time now."

Truman: "Oh, God. A *spy?* At Los *Alamos?*

Brandt: "Last February, as you recall, when I was assigned to the embassy in Moscow, I was approached by General Chesnikov and warned that we had 'a fox in our poplars.' For some time this had no meaning to me—it stumped all of our people—until just the other day I tumbled to its significance. Chesnikov was speaking Russian. 'Los Alamos' is Spanish for 'the poplars.' But what did he mean by 'a fox'? That was a real poser until I again tumbled to the simplicity. He was translating there, too. Only he was translating German here. 'Fox,' in German, is 'Fuchs.' I got hold of a Los Alamos phone directory and guess what I found. A listing for a Klaus Fuchs, a British national, a scientist of some considerable repute. I did some fast checking around. Fuchs is the son of a German Protestant minister, a Christian Socialist himself, and a naturalized British citizen who, as a highly skilled atomic scientist, was among the contingent of British atomic specialists arriving for work at Los Alamos in December, last year. He is an ultraliberal in political philosophy, and thanks to this he decided, after seeing how far we'd progressed toward making a bomb, to do what he could to prevent another war by tipping off the Russians. In February, and again just last month, he passed along everything he knew about the bomb to Harry Gold, a Soviet agent."

Truman: "How do you know this?"

Brandt: "I had our people question Gold. He is now a Soviet spy who is working for us. Through him we expect to pick up a major Soviet apparatus in the States and Canada."

Truman: "Why haven't I been told about this?"

Brandt: "You haven't been speaking to me lately."

Truman: "You could've sent me a note."

Brandt: "All respect, Mr. President, but I see my duty as including the responsibility of keeping you out of hot water—of helping you avoid gaffes that might endanger you politically and the nation militarily, and, not only that—"

At this point Harry broke in, his face as red as a beet and his magnified eyes looking like burning silver dollars. I mean, the man was instantly and incandescently angry. I was so taken aback I failed to keep on with my shorthand, so all I can do is paraphrase. He told me that I was never again to take the powers and responsibilities of the president into my hands—that he was the elected commander in chief of the armed forces and as such was under orders from his bosses, the American people, to make the ultimate judgments as to military matters, especially in time of war. Where did I get off, he wanted to know, thinking I could decide what and whether something might hurt the presi-
322

dent? Who did I think I was, deciding what the president ought to know and ought not to know? He wound up by telling me flat-out that if I ever pulled such a grossly presumptuous caper again I would be given a nice long vacation—in Leavenworth, if he could make it stick.

God.

I'm certainly glad I never told him about Lukas and the ill-fated Los Alamos shipping crate caper.

What a lousy goddam business I'm in, eh?

Damned if you do, and damned if you don't. . . .

CHAPTER 33

**Near Moscow
1 August 1945**

The women had been magnificent, Lukas thought. Old, not so old, young, not so young—they had waded through muck up to their ragtag hips, sweated under the summer sun, pushed and pulled and hammered and strained. The winch had helped not at all; a cable snapped at the first engagement of the gears. But the women took over, using their backs to heave the crate onto a makeshift raft, then to shove the whole through the reeds and into the channel. They had even stood along the bank, waving and calling out good-luck wishes as he and Frau Keller and Ressel—now looking no better than any of them in their peasant clothes, borrowed to replace those torn and bloodied in the crash—
324

poled downstream for the produce dock near the village of Rogovo.

"Why do you think they helped us like that?" Ressel asked nobody in particular.

Gretl Keller, leaning into her pole, kept the raft clear of a sandbar to the starboard. "We represent their government. They are patriots. It's as simple as that."

"No," Lukas drawled, "they were crazy about me. Especially that one with the stainless steel teeth. She pinched my bottom at every opportunity."

"Trina? She's old enough to be your grandmother."

"Cute, though. And how many fellows my age have grandmothers who pinch their bottoms? Not many, I'd wager."

Ressel shook his head, annoyed. "You two are really exasperating. This is no time to be making jokes—Russians all around us, searching for us."

"Relax," Lukas said. "They've searched this area very thoroughly. I think they're concentrating on the territory to the north now. Our plane was turning into a northerly heading when it entered the fog."

Ressel sneered. "Herr Smart Aleck speaks. How do you know what our heading was when we flew into the fog?"

"I'm paid vast sums by the United States government to keep track of things like that."

Ressel snapped, "I'm asking you how you knew, chained to a bulkhead, no compass—"

"I had a window. We were flying east, parallel to the river. As the fog came on, the plane was turning left and the river was falling behind us. It doesn't take a genius."

"Then how come we *didn't* crash to the north of the river, Herr Smart Aleck?"

Gretl made an impatient sound. "Because the turn became a spiral, damn it. What's the matter with you, anyhow—making such a fuss over nothing?"

"I just can't understand how you can be so, so—cozy—with this capitalist swine."

Lukas sighed. "Because, you communist asshole, we need each other. If we're to get out of this fix before your fellow Heroes of the Red Revolution kill us dead, we've got to get along together. I suggest you put the Marxist dialectics on a siding until we see how all this comes out."

They continued their poling in silence for a time. Then Gretl groaned. "If only we had a motor on this thing."

Lukas said, "You remind me of that old chestnut about the Wright brothers."

"How so?"

"The Wright brothers' business manager, getting his first look at their plane, says, 'Well, I don't know, fellows: People won't want to fly all the way to the Coast lying on that wing, holding on to those struts. . . .'"

Gretl laughed softly.

Ressel stared stonily ahead.

Another haze formed over the river system, and they moved through a kind of green opacity for most of the afternoon. But as they made a kind of turn around a kind of bend in this suggestion of a river, there was the Rogovo produce dock, as promised by the women at the collective farm. It was a dreary place, as were all the man-made features of this sad, abused country. Its larger houses—there were three—were gloomy wooden things with high gables and carved, ornate bargeboards in the Scandinavian mode. The rest were no more than huts, also of wood, and aligned on the single mud street that came out of the vastness to the north and ended abruptly at the dock itself. But there was a railroad track. A battered little locomotive with four drive wheels and a funnel-shaped smokestack sat there, panting and snuffling to itself like an old man enduring a head cold. Behind it was a string of four-wheel

326

boxcars and then three flatbeds, the last one mounting a brace of badly neglected antiaircraft machine guns.

"It's there, as Trina said it would be." Lukas felt a sudden excitement. Here was his way into the city.

Apparently Gretl had picked up the same vibrations. Her face showed new animation, a special heat. "Those guns have no crew."

"The war's over. They don't have to have a crew."

"Then why are the guns on the train?" Ressel asked.

"Who knows?" Lukas said. "Ballast, maybe."

"The women said the train carries vegetables to the city," Ressel persisted. "Why would it be armed?"

"That's the point," Gretl said. "It isn't. No soldiers."

"So we have a good chance of talking ourselves aboard."

Gretl nodded. "My thoughts exactly."

"There'll be a train crew. They'll raise a fuss," Ressel grumped.

"Leave them to me," Gretl said.

Ressel bristled. "What are you going to do to influence them, Comrade? Screw them all?"

"Watch your mouth," she snapped. "I'm tired of your whining. I don't need your dirty mouth as well."

Ressel, Lukas saw, was suffering from a case of unrequited passion. He was eaten by resentments, jealousy, rejection, guilts. He was a man who looked as if he would soon break into tears. And this was a happy development for Lukas, who saw it as a possible aid to his plan to wrest the crate from the other two and rush it to the U.S. embassy. Yet the sorry truth was that he had developed no plan at all. Nor did he have the vaguest clue as to where the embassy was located in the enormous city.

Even so, he was bothered most by the question as to just why Alex Lukas was being brought along on this junket. Why was Gretl Keller tolerating his presence, now that the crate had been returned to some kind of mobility? She had

327

Ressel, and, his bleeding lover's heart and missing arm notwithstanding, Ressel's help was all she needed.

As a possible answer, he had even considered her professions of love. Almost at once he dismissed the thought. The idea that a hardcase agent provocateur and casual killer would keep him alive in the interest of amorous fulfillment was absurd.

Still, she needed him for something, sure as hell.

But *what?*

It was easier than Lukas thought it would be. Gretl Keller had approached the train chief, a dour and rangy man, presenting herself as a representative of the Narkomvneshtorg returning with her team from Germany, where they had confiscated an important piece of farm equipment for study in Moscow. Their truck had broken down between Gzhatsk and Borodino, and with the help of a troop of soldiers, they'd been able to fashion this miserable raft. Would he please be so kind as to permit them to load the device onto that flatbed car there, just ahead of the machine-guns? The man had asked to see her papers, of course, and, apparently satisfied, he had ordered some women dockwallopers to on-load the crate.

"Why does the damned thing hum?" the train chief was asking now.

"Hum?"

"Just now, as the women placed it on the floor, it hummed. I distinctly heard it."

Gretl glanced at Lukas. "Can you explain it, Comrade? You are the technical expert."

Lukas was ready with a Russian adaptation of American doubletalk. "Certainly. The frezamus inside the coregitor recharges when the ambient temperature alters by a degree of centigrade. It is warmer on the railroad car than on the barge; therefore a recharging."

328

"I see," the trainman said, somber. "Very well. See to the lashings. We'll be getting under way in four minutes."

"How long to Moscow?" Lukas asked.

"If things go well, and if that infernal locomotive holds together, we should be in the westside marshaling yards in two hours. About dusk, I'd guess."

Watching the women anchoring the crate to the flatcar, Gretl muttered, "The ammunition cans beside the gun mount: Are they loaded?"

Lukas nodded. "They're full of ammo, all right. But the guns themselves are sinners beyond salvation. I don't think they've been cleaned since Caesar's Gallic Wars."

"No matter. I suggest you load them anyway. You never can tell when they might come in handy."

"Take my word: The only use for those wrecks is to maybe scare somebody to death. To shoot them is to get one's face blown off."

"You a real worrier, aren't you."

"I'll say."

Huddled together in the crate's lee, the three of them watched the passing barrenness. Ahead, the locomotive clanked along, *toonk*-cha-cha-cha, *toonk*-cha-cha-cha, leaving a spoor of steam and damp soot, and the boxcars, rattling and swaying, trailed the smell of cabbages and cucumbers. After a time the buildings, pocked by bomb hits and shrapnel, became larger and more numerous, and there were power lines and telephone poles and, here and there, a paved street coursing through neatly piled rubble. Legions of women toiled at the stacking of bricks and mortar slabs; knots of soldiers stood about, seeming to wait for something—anything—to happen. Several long trains had rumbled past them on the westbound tracks, each packed to the eaves with silent, vacantly staring infantrymen.

The faces of Stalin's ambition.

329

Lukas's depression deepened.

The city gathered, seeming to stretch for limitless miles, and the engine's rhythms eventually fell away to hisses and clankings as the train pulled into a freight station that loomed dark and malevolent in the twilight. The facility was obviously a satellite in the railroad scheme of things; it was small, shabby and, set among forlorn huts and featureless warehouses, remote from anything that suggested major industry.

Once the train had squealed to a halt, Lukas stirred and regarded the other two. "So, then. We are in Moscow. Is this where our fight begins?"

Gretl yawned and stretched. "Fight?"

"I am going to commandeer that truck parked there by the warehouse dock. And I'm going to get this thing— whatever the hell it is—to the American embassy. If you have other ideas, there will be a fight."

Ressel, suddenly tense, said softly, "There will be a fight, I'm afraid. But not amongst ourselves. Look there."

Gretl looked.

Arrayed on the platform, almost like bureaucrats awaiting a visiting dignitary, were eight soldiers, faces bored, rifles ready.

Standing at their center—straight, alert, and positively aglow with self-congratulation—were Frau Elsbet Ressel, Colonel Georgi Lagolin, and General Vladimir Belenko, chief of Samovar and Frau Ressel's very good friend.

In a parade-ground voice, General Belenko issued a command to the soldiers.

"Seize the traitors!"

CHAPTER 34

Moscow
1 August 1945

Again, as if his psyche automatically downshifted in moments of crisis, Lukas saw and felt everything in slower time and motion. His thoughts were instantaneous, the ghostly flickerings of heat lightning, but his moves seemed to come heavily, long after the thought, as if his body had been immersed in engine oil.

Ressel, his arm aloft in the manner of a priest giving a blessing, stepped forward, his German rising above the locomotive's soft chuffing, even and clear and filled with sorrow. "Elsbet. I'm so glad to see you. I've wronged you. I love you. I want to come home."

There was no forgiveness in Frau

Ressel. "You are," she snarled, "a rotten, lecherous, adulterous swine."

She drew a Walther automatic pistol from the folds of her skirt and, raising her arm in a parody of the Hitler salute, she fired a single shot. Her husband reeled backward, slamming against the machine-gun mount, then he sank to his knees like a sinner before an altar.

"Elsbet—I'm so sorry—"

She fired again, and Ressel rolled slowly to his back and sighed. "Elsbet—"

Frau Ressel regarded Lukas full on, but her shrill words were addressed to Gretl Keller. "You have been ordered by the Kremlin itself to liquidate this capitalist wretch. And yet you have failed to do so. It will be my distinct pleasure to take care of that little detail for you."

Lukas became aware of Frau Ressel's pistol coming around to level on him. With no alternative, he bobbed to one side, reaching for the machine-gun handles, knowing as he did that he was already too late. But then Gretl Keller's shout rang in his head, and he sensed her leap, and then her body was against his, her arms around him in a savage embrace.

The shot sounded, and Gretl sagged, and then, in a welter of lights and darks and speed and lethargy, Lukas was free and swinging the machine guns and groping in a mad blindness for the safety lock and triggers.

The first burst lifted Frau Ressel from her feet, and she spun from the platform, a doll hurled by an angry child, onto the adjoining tracks. Georgi and Belenko followed like collapsing scarecrows, their green uniforms erupting with red. Then, because the soldiers were moving fast and focusing their rifles, Lukas swept them with a long and angry fire, and they melted away into inert, silent lumps.

A gaggle of bedraggled cargo handlers stood in the shadows of the platform overhang, their eyes goggling, their bodies frozen with shock. Lukas leveled the guns on

332

them and barked, "You people there: Get over here and prepare to unload this crate." To the truck driver, sitting stunned at the steering wheel, he commanded, "You: Back your truck around so that its tailgate is next to the flatcar."

"Yes, sir," the man called back. "Right away."

There was a moment in which Lukas knelt and, tenderly, turned Gretl Keller into a position that revealed her wound, an ugly red-black circle in the fabric of her peasant's smock, just below the right shoulder blade. She was semiconscious, her eyes vague and distracted, her skin clammy, her breathing labored and uneven.

"Gretl—Can you hear me?"

Her lips moved, but there was no sound.

"I want you to lie flat on your back. Can you do that?"

There was no response. He pulled off his jacket and wrapped her upper body in it, then placed her feet on one of the ammunition cans. One of the cargo handlers was at his side then, and she carefully spread a layer of potato sacks over Gretl's legs. "You must keep her warm, and her head down," she said in a low voice.

"Is there a doctor around?"

"No. Only an attendant at the first-aid station next to the dispatcher's office. I'll fetch him. If he's still there after all the shooting, that is."

"It could get you in trouble, you know."

"My husband died in a gulag. Anyone who shoots the monsters is my friend." She left in an ungainly trot.

There followed a suspended time, in which the cargo handlers inched the crate onto the truck and lifted Gretl onto a door, removed from a trackside toolshed, which would serve as a stretcher. The truck driver, a grizzled fellow too old for the army, watched all this with much interest.

"You're in a lot of trouble, young man. Shooting all those servants of the State the way you did."

"Do as I say, unless you want some of the same."

"Oh, I'm no problem to you. But I'd certainly appreciate it if, when they catch you, you make it clear to them that I was forced to cooperate with you."

"Just get me to the American embassy. You do that—as fast as possible—and everything else will be all right."

"The American embassy, eh? You are an American?"

"I'm an American."

"Capitalist swine, eh?"

"I'll say. Now get that truck turned around and pointed toward the embassy—wherever it is. Or I'll have this pistol give you a whole new set of belly buttons."

"As I say: You have no problem with me. I saw how handy you are with those things."

The woman returned alone, but she was carrying a first-aid satchel. "Just as I thought," she said, panting. "The gutless dummy ran at the first shot. But I'll take over."

"You?"

"I'm a nurse. A politically unpopular nurse, as you can see." She bent to her work, her gnarled hands moving gently and swiftly over the gasping Gretl. "She's a brave woman. She took the shot meant for you."

"She is the damnedest woman there ever was, and that's a fact."

"Where are we going?"

"We?"

"This young woman can't be horsed around in a truck without somebody taking care of her. And unless I miss my guess, you're going to be very busy with other things."

"I'm very grateful to you—"

"I asked you: Where are we going?"

"To the American embassy, wherever that is."

"Between that old coot at the wheel and me, we'll get you there. But we'd better get moving, because the man on duty in the signal tower has seen what's gone on here and,
334

knowing him for the rabid Party man he is, I'd guess the police will be here in a few minutes."

"Let's see what we can do to keep him from telling them which way we've gone." Lukas clambered back to the gun mount and, estimating the range at about one hundred yards, fired a sustained burst at the signal tower. The windows dissolved in clouds of glass and splintered wood, and there were subsidiary electrical flashes where a cluster of external cables fell to the ground.

The truck driver called, "There are phones in the dispatcher's office and the first-aid room. Down there at the end of the platform. Behind the green doors."

The guns rattled again, and the green doors collapsed in showers of dust.

"All right," Lukas said then, "let's go. Drive fast, but not so fast as to catch attention."

"I'll go the back streets. It'll take longer, but it should buy you some time. Even so, young man, you haven't got the chance of a bitch in heat."

"Shut up and drive."

Moscow appeared to have developed haphazardly over centuries, except that the important streets suggested spokes in a great wheel. Between the spokes were acres of buildings, many of them holed or gutted by German air raids, that ranged from large institutional buildings of stone to miserable peasant huts of scrap wood, the two extremes often cheek by jowl. Everywhere was drabness, the kind of sad, empty look Lukas once associated with Buffalo's Main Street on a Sunday morning. It was nightfall, and the streets were virtually empty, and those windowpanes that remained reflected the melancholy light of the setting sun. If an alarm had been sent out about the rail terminal shooting, there was no sign of reaction. They ground through the streets unimpeded, and once, at an intersection, a solitary traffic policeman seemed almost glad to see them, waving them through the emptiness with a broad and imperious sweep of his hand.

"How is she doing?" Lukas asked the woman.

"She will need a physician soon. I've seen worse wounds in my time, but she could very well die if she doesn't get some blood. The shock could kill her, too. She's very cold and sweaty."

The truck driver called out the window. "There are two cars behind us, coming fast. What do you want me to do?"

"Keep going. Speed if you have to. But don't let them stop us. I've got to get this woman to a doctor at the embassy."

"I thought the crate had priority," the man taunted.

"The woman has priority, goddam it. Remember: I have a pistol that says you can get me to the embassy at all costs."

"But those are police cars—" He gave them a name that sounded like "Zeese."

"Take your choice: my bullet or their questions."

The truck, badly in need of paint but otherwise in good shape, picked up speed and, when a fork loomed ahead, veered into the right branch, a narrow canyon between cliffs of rubble and shattered buildings. One of the pursuing Zeeses swerved too quickly and spun wildly, caroming off the canyon wall, flipping and overturning three times in a cascade of bricks, fenders and wheels.

"One down and one to go!" the driver shouted.

"There will be others. Keep going."

"I've already got it to the floor. This is the best this old bucket will do."

"How far do we have to go?"

"If we stay on this route, five minutes. If I dogleg to the boulevard, two minutes."

"Then dogleg. We've got some heavier bleeding back here."

336

"The cops will be as thick as flies around a cow's ass on the boulevard."

"We don't have a choice. Do it."

The driver was right. With their entrance to the boulevard, a broad, bleak avenue of brick divided by an esplanade and trolley tracks, three more black cars appeared. Two of them fell directly behind, Klaxon horns racketing, lights flashing, while the third, having been traveling in the opposite direction, attempted a U-turn that launched a bouncing roll ending with a wheels-in-the-air slide into a patch of bushes.

Lukas thought he heard shots, but in all the engine and tire racket he couldn't be sure.

"U.S. Embassy straight ahead!" the driver called.

"Faster!"

"You don't mind if I take you to the service entrance?"

"Anywhere! But get us there!"

"Holy Saint Peter! The gates are closed!"

"Who cares? Keep going!"

"Through the *gates?*"

"Go!" To the nurse, Lukas shouted, "Down! Stay down!"

He threw his body across Gretl's and shut his eyes, vaguely aware that he was shouting curses. The impact was surprisingly mild, a sharp thump, a screech of metal on metal, the impression of large dark things flying through the air. But the truck remained upright, despite its crazy yawing and sliding, even when it slammed sideways into the foundation wall of the large gray building that established the inner courtyard. In the shocked momentary silence that followed, he glanced about, partly in panic, still in shock. He shouted in English: "Medic! Get me a medic!"

"Easy, buddy. Easy. You'll be all right. The embassy doctor is coming down the steps right now." The voice came from a very large man wearing the blue and red of the U.S. Marine Corps.

"The woman has been shot."

"Okay. We'll take care of it. Just you calm down."

"I'm an American citizen—an army officer—"

"I know who you are, pal. We've been expecting you for days now. Your picture's all over the goddam building."

"The others—"

"They're all fine. The little round woman in the overalls has a dent here and there, but she's okay. And the driver is walking around trying to bum a cigarette."

"The Russian police—"

"Already gone. They buzzed a U at the gates you ruined, and took off. Couldn't see 'em for tire smoke."

Another man approached. This one wore a gray flannel suit and a twenty-dollar necktie. "Lukas? I'm Brenner, chief of embassy security."

"Good. I've just made a very important delivery, and I suggest you get it inside or something—"

"That's what I want to talk to you about. Would you step over here a minute?"

They went to the truck, which lay bent and atilt against the embassy wall, still emitting little hissing sounds.

Brenner stood there and pointed to the crate, which had ruptured its lashings and, having slid into the gray stone facade, was badly splintered at one corner.

"What's in it? I mean, *is* there something in it?"

"Beats me," Lukas said. "Why?"

"Why all the goddam urgency for that thing?"

Lukas peered through the crate's splintered side. In the dim light of evening he saw a slab of black, highly lacquered wood, on which there was a legend in gilt letters:

STEINWAY

Entry in Personal Diary of C. G. Brandt
Potsdam, Germany
0215, 2 August 1945

I have just returned from a very brief but altogether extraordinary meeting. I'd been trying to set it up for months, but as of last night I'd resigned myself to the idea that it would never happen. Most astonishing, of course, is the fact that I was actually invited to it.

It's imperative that I get it down at once—translate my shorthand while the flavor of the thing remains fresh, while I still recall the expressions and attitudes and gestures that are as much a part of the dialogue as the words themselves.

This morning's wee-hours supersecret session resolves matters once and for all. The pretense that the Brits make a difference has been dropped and at last it's acknowledged that there are now only two real contenders for world power—two men with the unlikely names of Harry and Joe—and that this thing is between them. Say all you want about the larger issues, I've seen with my own eyes that it's down to two hard-talking hardcases who hate each other's guts and are ready for a punch-out.

There were two plenary sessions yesterday—one at 3:30 P.M., the final one at ten last night. Truman, Stalin and Attlee sat for the obligatory photos and went through the predictable motions at each session, but each was a kind of rehash, a formal grinding to a halt of the fortnight's push-shove-bicker-and-bitch gavotte. The second meeting broke up at about 12:30 this morning, and I was going over the rough transcripts from Bohlen when the phone rang.

It was the Message Center, and I had just hung up, struggling with astonishment, when the phone rang again. This time it was the president. Stalin, he said, was on his way to the Little White House and he was, quite obviously, madder than a hornet. He had asked specifically in his

339

phone call to Harry that I—C. G. Brandt—be on hand, and Harry was giving me three minutes to get my ass over there.

I had met Stalin on several formal occasions during my Moscow embassy tour, of course, but as far as I knew I was to him just another American face, and until now I had no reason to believe that he remembered me from daisy dung. So his calling me into his secret personal meeting with Harry was astonishment atop my astonishment, and I felt the beating of my jaded heart for the first time in years.

Could Lukas have actually got that damned thing to Moscow? *Jesus.*

We gathered in a kind of enclosed porch, where the furniture was Teutonic and ugly and the lamps were turned low, which was de rigueur in the ongoing struggle against the Holy Lake's voracious mosquitos. The president was in a smoking jacket, casual slacks and black pull-ons; Stalin wore his cream-colored musical comedy tunic. His hair was slicked back and his eyes were hot and unfriendly. He was accompanied only by his interpreter, a man named Pavlov, and I was to translate for Harry.

As the four of us stood there, the atmosphere electric, Stalin ordered me to keep no record of remarks made here. I told the president this and the president said that for now this was his house and he was going to do what he goddam well wanted to in it and that included my keeping notes, and if the generalissimo didn't like that condition he could go pee up a drainpipe. For reasons of his own—perhaps because he's a worrier, too—Pavlov, his lips stiff and pale, put Harry's answer into a politer form, and after a taut moment, Stalin shrugged and sat down on a sofa. Harry took a straight-back chair across the coffee table from him and they traded icy stares.

Stalin fired up his pipe, and, eyes slitted, said in that soft, ominous voice of his, "I have asked for this very secret, very personal meeting, Mr. President, because I want you to know from my own lips just how very much the Soviet people resent what you did last night."

(I'm referring to my shorthand now, and what I write here is based mostly on those notes with a little bit of memory thrown in.)

Harry didn't even blink. "Oh? And what might that be, Generalissimo?"

"It will help things not at all, Mr. President, if you pretend ignorance of this matter."

"I'm ignorant about a lot of things. Which ignorance are we talking about here?"

"I'm referring to your flagrant violation of the rules of diplomatic immunity. Your arrogant invasion of Soviet territory by spies and agents provocateurs. Your causing death, destruction and injury within the territorial limits of the Soviet Union."

Harry said nothing, his expression stony.

Stalin took two irritable puffs at his pipe, then pointed the stem directly at me. "I am talking specifically, *Mr.* Harry Truman, about this man here, this Brandt, and his sly maneuverings, his Machiavellian enterprises—all of which have been calculated to embarrass and endanger the citizens of the USSR. All of which have been personally and secretly authorized by you as head of the capitalist empire. All of which I will no longer tolerate in any form or under any guise. You will have this man cease his activities, or I will personally see to it that you both are brought to an ultimate accounting on the things you are."

Harry listened to my translation, which I gave in its absolute sense, that is, with no shading or interpretation, and again he kept his poker player's face, his eyes never leaving Stalin's.

The Generalissimo went on, angry, and my translation resounded with the earth tones of Stalin's descent from a poverty-crushed shoemaker and his washerwoman wife:

341

"I'm giving you a direct order, you Missouri fop: Stop poking your pecker into my Motherland or I'll chop it off."

Harry, I could see, was struggling to arrange and study the cards as they came across the table. His expression changed not at all as he watched and waited.

The silence seemed to provoke the Russian into further heat. "This man—this Brandt—operating on your explicit orders, sent an agent named Lukas to your research center at The Poplars in New Mexico. I can give you the date: the night of July twelfth. There this so-called Lukas took charge of a large crate containing some kind of explosive device and transported it to Moscow under the pretense that it was supplies for your embassy there. He made his delivery to the embassy last night, after having, en route over an extended period, caused losses of Soviet life, limb and property in amounts so large they are still to be reckoned."

Harry said nothing.

"Your dissemblance, your postured silence, your silly playacting, will not serve you. The fact is, you authorized Lukas to transport an explosive device to your embassy. A device our counterintelligence people call 'The Hummer.'"

I could almost see Harry's intuition swing into action. For the first time at the meeting he looked at me through those thick glasses. "Mr. Brandt, will you please tell me what the hell happened in Moscow last night?"

It was my turn. I had this crazy, fleeting vision of myself on a huge stage-in-the-round in the Shakespearean mode, and all around me, stretching into infinity, were millions of people—the people of the world—and they were all tensely silent, waiting, breath suspended, for me to take a wild-ass guess as to just what had gone on in Moscow last night. I didn't know whether to laugh or to wet my pants.

"Mr. Lukas is one of our most audacious and tenacious agents, Mr. President." Gathering the lie about me, I went for broke. "But he has never visited Moscow. To give him a

342

familiarization trip, I instructed him to escort a piano that was scheduled for delivery to our Moscow embassy from a government storage facility in Santa Fe. The piano's movement was, of course, to be kept most confidential, at the request of the Secret Service. And—"

Harry broke in. "Confidential? Why?"

"Well, sir, the fact that you are quite an accomplished pianist is well known. But the fact that you plan a goodwill visit to the loyal and tireless staff members of our Moscow embassy is not well known. And the fact that pianos in the USSR—especially the one in the embassy—are in sad repair was also not so well known. To provide a piano for your enjoyment during your visit required the shipment of a new one from Stateside. But to foreshadow your visit in such a way would be to invite security difficulties. Therefore the Secret Service insisted that the piano be disguised as a routine shipment of office supplies. And—"

Stalin shook his massive head and made a sneering noise. "Do you people take me for an imbecile? That shipping crate originated in The Poplars. It was escorted not only by this—this Lukas—but also by a man widely recognized as an explosives scientist. Grand pianos are not made at The Poplars; explosive devices are made at The Poplars. And you people have, in a very clumsy way, violated the rules of diplomacy by transporting an explosive device from your laboratories at The Poplars to a location of diplomatic immunity in the capital city of the USSR. And I insist that it be removed at once. This very morning. Or you will have the fury of the Soviet peoples to face."

Harry cleared his throat. "Why was the NKVD so upset about the piano, Mr. Brandt?"

"Well, as you know, Mr. President, the generalissimo has placed a spy in our Los Alamos operation—a British scientist named Klaus Fuchs—and Fuchs obviously alerted the NKVD to the fact that we were sending a confidential shipment from Santa Fe to Moscow via MATS transport.

343

The Soviets, assuming the shipment was an explosives device, attempted to intercept Lukas and pirate his cargo. Lukas, innocent and outraged over what he must have considered unwarranted and inexplicable attacks, was, of course, compelled to defend himself. The results, it appears from the generalissimo's claims, were violent and expensive."

Harry regarded Stalin with somber eyes.

I could see that Stalin was now dealing with an almost unmanageable mixture of surprise and rage deriving from the twin revelations that we not only have identified his atomic spy but had also used that spy to hand him what amounted to a paranoid's nightmare. The anger erupted, then subsided within the moment, an incandescence that returned quickly to its core, like a solar flare. My translation: "I say you are bluffing. Our own scientists assure me that your atomic device is too cumbersome to be moved without cranes and other heavy equipment."

Harry said nothing.

"We can raid your embassy, neutralize the device." As soon as the irrational words had been spoken, Stalin seemed to realize that he had approached a loss of control. The low flatness returned to his voice almost at once, and his murky eyes watched me as I translated: "But I don't think that will be necessary, for two reasons. First, I am told that your atomic device cannot be exploded except from a high tower, which itself must be linked to many scientific instruments and control apparatus. But even assuming you could erect such a tower in your embassy compound without detection and interference from our military security forces, there is the second, more believable reason, which is that terrorist blackmail of this type is contrary to the American character. More especially, it is contrary to your personal character, Mr. President. I am told that you are a very moral man, for all your eccentricities. You are not a wanton killer. It is not in you."

344

Harry struck, a lightning blow from ambush. "But it is in me to warn you, Generalissimo, that for all their war-weariness, the American people simply will not tolerate a Soviet takeover of Germany. Germany is integral to Western Europe. Our roots as a nation lie in Western Europe. Our military security and our economic well-being are inseparable from those of Western Europe. Take Germany, and you will have all-out war on your hands."

Stalin froze. It was a momentary thing, a suggestion of the children's game in which the players pretend to be statues at the call of a word. But almost at once his brows lowered in a quizzical frown. "A takeover of Germany? What is this nonsense?"

Harry's voice was low and even. "We are aware of your plans to cross the Niesse and occupy Germany all the way to the Rhine."

Stalin's eyes appeared actually to dim. It was the only indication that behind his peasant's face there might be a striving for control. He stared off at the lake, puffing gently at his pipe, seeming to listen to the faint call of a night bird. When he spoke it was once again in that soft hoarseness. "There's not very much you can do to interfere with those plans, Harry Truman. Your European armies are in full rout. They are wanted at home by their mamas."

"You're overreaching, Joe. Remember what overreaching has done for Hitler."

Stalin frowned, slit-eyed, and delivered what he obviously considered to be a surprise of his own. I translated: "The Rhine? You amuse me, Harry Truman. Soviet troops will not stop at the Rhine. They will move on, mostly at the invitation of friendly governments deeply concerned by the political anarchy left in the wake of your departure. And then what will you do? Atom bomb us as we sip aperitifs in Paris? As we sunbathe in Cannes? As we go whoring in Copenhagen? You make big bangs at The Poplars in New Mexico, Mr. Harry Truman, but bombs you can't yet make

345

or deliver. And so to the seacoasts I go. Before the snow falls, I shall go."

"You cross the Niesse, Generalissimo, and I'll blow your ass off."

Stalin jabbed the air with his pipe stem, and Pavlov's voice raced. "You are bluffing, damn you. Even if you could make a bomb before I move, you will not use that thing against cities—our cities or anybody's cities. It's common knowledge that you are even unable to decide whether to use it against Japan—a nation that still makes war on you."

My translation echoed Harry's cool tone: "I will give you until August sixteenth—two weeks from today—to stand down your armies. If you do this, you have nothing to fear from us and our bomb—in Moscow or anywhere else. Conversely, if you haven't by midnight of that day canceled your plans for European conquest, the Soviet Union will enter a state of continuing mortal danger."

Stalin: "You can't make it work. You don't have enough time."

Truman: "I guess that's your gamble, isn't it, Joe? You're betting you can splash your feet in the English Channel before we can get rid of our tower."

Stalin: "There's no bet, you Missouri cowplop. It's a foregone conclusion you haven't the balls to use that thing—with or without a tower."

The president pushed back his chair and stood up. "Mr. Brandt, will you show this borscht-pot son of a bitch the door, please? I'm tired and I'm going to bed."

Standing on the porch in the sultry night, gazing after the two Russians as they disappeared down the dark, insect-humming lane, I took a deep, unhappy breath.

And so begins World War Three.

When I returned for my notebook, Harry was at the cellarette, clinking glasses and ice. He handed me a bourbon and considered me with large, sad eyes. "You've put me in a hell of a spot. You know that, don't you, Brandt?"

"Yes, sir."

"Stalin's right. There's still a lot of doubt. We can probably fit that thing onto a plane, but dropping it at precisely the right time and having it go off at precisely the right altitude are tricks nobody's sure we can pull off. If we can't make it work, Stalin's got us by the balls."

"Yes, sir."

"We are in fact planning to drop one of those babies on Japan from a B-29 this Sunday morning, our time. I'm told our boys have fitted the test device into a bomb casing. The casing and its timing medium will, they assure me, adapt to the B-29's drop mechanism."

He waited for me to digest this. Then he added, sounding as if he meant it, "I'm sorry that Japanese innocents might have to pay the price of keeping Joe in his cage. But they're already paying the price of their own warlords' ambitions, and they'll be paying for a long time to come."

"Well, as you say, it might not go off."

"We'd better pray that it does. Or a whole big bunch of Americans are going to die. In the Pacific. And in Europe."

Another of those peculiar periods of silence followed.

Harry, staring into his glass, sighed. "Was it Lukas who put us onto Stalin's plan to occupy Europe?"

"Partly. But most of the information came from a very deep-dish agent who had penetrated a Soviet guerrilla force. Do you want the agent's name, sir?"

"Names I don't know won't hurt me. Or them."

"The agent's findings were subsequently confirmed by a much-trusted Kremlin mole. Which was no mean trick, by the way. The mole—a general officer who's been the subject of a recent NKVD probe, thanks to his dalliance with an English diplomat's wife—had been excluded from the planning for Stalin's Operation Seacoasts and he needed

347

to call in every marker he had to find out what was going on."

Harry swirled his drink in its glass, and the ice made a friendly sound. "That agent deserves a medal. The mole, too."

"Yes, sir."

"Did Lukas really take a piano to Moscow?"

"You needed a trump—a wild card. He gave you one."

"But what if the Soviets had intercepted the package?"

"They'd have acquired a new piano. And looked very foolish indeed."

He gave me another of those magnified looks. "Playing president again, eh?"

"No, sir. Playing on the Russians' paranoia."

"What if Stalin hadn't insisted that you attend the meeting we just had? I didn't know any of this crap—"

"And I most respectfully suggest, sir, that you don't know anything about it now, either. The game isn't over yet, and there'll be hell to pay if the newshawks get wind of it."

"I asked you a question, Brandt."

I put a fresh piece of ice in my glass. "I didn't have to be here. You're a poker player, Mr. President. I was betting that if you found yourself in a game featuring a threatened Russian invasion and a Russian dictator irate over an unidentified U.S. something in Moscow, you'd figure some way to take the pot."

For a moment I thought Harry might smile. But it didn't happen. His stare was lingering, pensive.

"I can't make up my mind, Brandt," he said finally.

"About what, Mr. President?"

"Whether or not to put you in jail."

He could see I didn't know what to say to that, so he told me to finish my drink and get the hell out and let him get some sleep. He was, after all, supposed to leave for a long boat ride today.

As I reached the door he asked, "Where's Lukas now?"

"Approaching Rhein/Main Air Base, I'd guess. According to a call I got from the Message Center a while ago, his girlfriend's being flown to the Med Corps hospital in Wiesbaden. I gather she was hurt while giving him a hand in Moscow."

"*Girlfriend?* He had time in all that flapdoodle to find a *girlfriend?*"

I shrugged. "It's not the kind of thing we encourage."

"She must be pretty hot stuff to catch a fella's eye in the middle of all that hullaballoo."

"I hear she's that, all right."

"They were returned on the embassy's medical plane?"

"Amid horrendous Soviet protests, I'm told."

"I'll give them a call."

"That would be nice, Mr. President. But the newspeople might hear about it. They'd start prying. I'm flying down to Wiesbaden this morning. Glad to carry a note for you."

"Will you, for God's sweet sake, stop playing *president?* You're a real pain in the ass, Brandt."

"I've known that for a long time, sir."

THE
SHOWDOWN

8/6
VIA WIRELESS
TO: PRESIDENT TRUMAN, ABOARD USS AUGUSTA
BIG BOMB DROPPED ON HIROSHIMA AUGUST 5 AT 7:15 P.M.
WASHINGTON TIME. FIRST REPORTS INDICATE COMPLETE
SUCCESS WHICH WAS EVEN MORE CONSPICUOUS THAN EAR-
LIER TEST.
STIMSON
SECY WAR

7 AUGUST 1945
VIA WIRELESS
TO.   KAWABE, DEPUTY CHIEF GENERAL STAFF, TOKYO
      ENTIRE CITY OF HIROSHIMA DESTROYED INSTANTLY
      BY A SINGLE BOMB
      KKF, CIVIL SUPERVISOR
      DISTRICT OF CHUGOKU

BY COURIER
TO: L. BERIA
FROM: J.V. STALIN

7 AUGUST 1945

YOU ARE HEREBY DIRECTED TO ASSEMBLE THE BEST OF OUR SOVIET SCIENTISTS WHO SPECIALIZE IN NUCLEAR PHYSICS AND SET THEM TO WORK ON THE DEVELOPMENT OF AN ATOMIC BOMB. THEY WILL BE ASSIGNED NO OTHER DUTIES FOR THE DURATION OF THE PROJECT, FOR WHICH THERE WILL BE NO—REPEAT NO—LIMIT ON FUNDS OR OTHER RESOURCES.

MOST SECRET

F-L-A-S-H
BULLETIN   BULLETIN   BULLETIN
LEAD
WASHINGTON, AUG. 9—(AP)—THE SOVIET UNION TODAY DECLARED WAR ON JAPAN.
APW
STH

F-L-A-S-H
BULLETIN   BULLETIN   BULLETIN
LEAD
WASHINGTON, AUG. 9—(AP)—NAGASAKI TODAY BECAME THE SECOND JAPANESE CITY TO BE OBLITERATED BY A U.S. ATOMIC BOMB.
APW
JJE

MOST SECRET

BY COURIER
TO: ALL MEMBERS, MILITARY GENERAL STAFF
FROM: J.V. STALIN

12 AUGUST 1945

PREPARATIONS FOR OPERATION SEACOASTS ARE HEREBY CANCELLED. YOU WILL INSTRUCT ALL COMMANDS TO INITIATE A GENERAL STANDDOWN. REPEAT: THERE WILL BE NO FURTHER EFFORT TO EXTEND MILITARY OPERATIONS WEST OF THE ODER-NIESSE LINE. THIS DIRECTIVE APPLIES INDEFINITELY.

ADM/7745/FGH/45

MOST SECRET

F-L-A-S-H

BULLETIN   BULLETIN   BULLETIN

WASHINGTON, AUG. 14—(AP)—JAPAN HAS SURRENDERED UNCONDITIONALLY.

WORLD WAR TWO IS AT LAST AT AN END.

APW

LST

CHAPTER 35

Buffalo, New York
October 31, 1945

D ear Brandt:
    The streets in this part of town
aren't exactly ideal for soul-
searching, what with the traffic and
power poles and billboards, the exhaust stink and the stares of the
raggedy-ass merchants behind the
dirty plate glass. But since your letter arrived I've been walking them a
lot, deciding once and for all who I
am and what I am and where I might
be going with the rest of my life.

I might as well tell you up front: I
appreciate your job offer, but I won't
be taking you up on it.

For all the roll we were on, for all
the success of our deep-dish penetration of the other people's apparatus
—even that shell-game ride through
Russia with a goddam baby grand,

which came off, by the way, only because it shouldn't have come off in a million years—my string was running out. I think you knew it, too. And whatever work you give me now would have to be administrative—out of the cold—because I've committed the worst sin anybody in the trade can be guilty of: I've become famous. Notorious, rather. So my usefulness to you would be very limited at best.

But that's not the real reason for turning you down. The real reason is that after a couple of months of really hard-nosed self-analysis I have finally admitted to myself what's been going on: I've been having a tantrum, and it's lasted long enough.

Very few soldiers in wartime do the things they like to do; most of them are in roles they despise or are otherwise unsuited for, of course. But in my case the war had very little to do with the way I was doing things. My only aim was to show you, to show all those rotten snobs who had sneered at the foreign-ness of my family, and to show myself, that I was something special. I wasn't just a soldier acting out of some vague idea of patriotism and doing what had to be done to stay alive in the process—I had to be Superspy, the archetypal warrior, the killing machine, the razzle-dazzle artist supreme, just to be able to say, "Hey, look at me, you dummies. Selling me short, weren't you?"

Well, it's about time I cut out the grandstanding and get about the business of doing something constructive with my life.

I know how awkward you are about these things. You never really did know how to deal with me, and there's no likelihood that you ever will. But I'm going to remind you anyhow, as I used to as a kid all those years ago in Moscow: I love you.

At any rate, my dear "Red Glare," take care of yourself and let me hear from you now and then. Forgive my inability to take you up on your offer, and try to understand the sense of rebirth and freedom I feel when I say:

357

This is "Gretl Keller" and "Olga"—signing out. For good.

Your loving and devoted daughter,

Toni

P.S. Thanks for setting up the medals for Lukas and me, and for the nice phone call from President Truman. My wound is practically healed now. Lukas is fine, too, although he's still ticked off about not being told I was an American agent. (He doesn't want to hear my explanations re "believability" and "authenticity of his reactions," etc., etc. He'd rather pout.) We finish our visit with his folks tomorrow. He's en route to an interview for a newspaper job in L.A. and is letting me tag along. He isn't saying yet whether he'll include me as a permanent fixture in his future. But we'll see. Meanwhile, I'll keep you posted.

X X X

T.